K. B. PELLEGRINO

KILLING THE VENERABLE

IT'S THEIR TIME!

©2020

Livres-Ici
PUBLISHING™

Copyright © K.B. Pellegrino

Killing the Venerable Drawing by Joseth Broussard and Matthew Dubord
Atwater Studios, Springfield, MA
Technical and Artistic Coordination: Alchemy Marketing, Sutton, Quebec, Canada

All rights reserved. No part of this book may be used or reproduced
by any means, graphic, electronic, or mechanical which included
Photocopying, recording, taping or by any information storage retrieval
System without the written permission of the author except in the
Case of brief quotations embodied in critical articles and reviews.

This is a work of fiction. All of the characters, names, incidents,
Organizations, and dialogue in this novel are either the products
Of the author's imagination or are used fictitiously.

Livres-Ici Publishing is a registered trademark of WMASS OPM, LLC.

Livres-Ici Publishing books may be ordered through booksellers.

Livres-Ici Publishing™ of WMASS OPM, LLC
265 State Street
Springfield, MA 01103
1-413-788-0652

Because of the dynamic nature of the Internet, any web addresses or
Links contained in this book may have changes since publication and
May no longer be valid.

The views expressed in this work are solely those of the author and do
Not necessarily reflect the views of the publisher, and the publisher
Hereby disclaims any responsibility for them.

ISBN: 978-1-951012-04-5
ISBN: 978-1-951012-07-6
ISBN: 978-1-951012-08-3

Library of Congress Control Number: 2020921997

MAIN CHARACTERS

<u>West Side Major Crimes Unit Detectives</u>

Captain Rudy Beauregard

Lieutenant Mason Smith

Lieutenant Petra Aylewood-Locke

Sergeant Ashton Lent

Sergeant Ted Torrington

Sergeant Lilly Tagliano

Sergeant Juan Flores

Sergeant Bill Border

Sergeant Bobby Barr

<u>Other Recurring Characters</u>

Chief Coyne

Attorney Norberto Cull

Sheri Cull

Mona Beauregard

Mayor Fischler

Jim Locke

Luis Vargas

Roland and Lizette Beauregard

Monique Smith

Charlotte Torrington

Martina McKay

Lavender James

Quote from: The Beauty of Death – (Part Two – The Ascending);

…And I can hear naught but the music of eternity in exact harmony with the spirit's desires.

I am cloaked in full whiteness;

I am in comfort;

I am in peace.   **By Khalil Gibran**

VENERABLE: reputable, esteemed, honored, respected, worthy.

CONTENTS

1

Jerry and Herschel

Sergeant Lilly Tagliano was tearful as was Sergeant Juan Flores. Huddled together at her computer screen, they read the obituary of their friend, retired Palmer Police Lieutenant Buck Gagnon. Lilly raged, "Another senseless hit and run accident; not an accident, just another bum in a stolen car doing damage to good people. What the hell; Buck was the best of the best."

"Lilly, he was a good guy," Juan said. "We worked with him for the kids' athletic leagues. He coached. The kids loved him. He was just a fair guy, and an athlete himself with much to offer. They'll catch the bastard. News says it was a stolen car, a 2010 blue Honda Civic which they found a mile from the accident. Cameras caught a view of the car along North Main Street, but could not get any view of the driver and maybe a passenger, because the driver wore a hoodie and only a sliver of a picture caught sight of him. The video will help pin the time down, because no one discovered Buck until the next morning. He was found by or on the curb pushed into a snow bank. Retired, just lost his wife about a year ago, and then his son three years ago. He was desolate at his losses."

Turning to Sergeant Ashton Lent, Juan asked, "Ash, you saw him recently when he received an award by some Quaboag group for his contributions. Didn't matter who needed help; he helped the elderly, kids, and volunteered at several nursing homes, one in Palmer and the other two in Wilbraham. He also volunteered at the library and was a member of about every club in the city or town; whatever Palmer is. Am I right? Wasn't he volunteer of the year? You played in the band that night for the celebration, didn't you?"

Ash, who was waiting for appointment as a lieutenant and had enjoyed another career as a professional and classical violinist, agreed with Juan. "I heard nothing but good things about him. No one was talking behind the scenes negatively the night of the award, which is unusual when no one disses an awardee. He gave the greatest speech. He was funny and the audience included half the city. He did not look depressed that night. His daughter, her husband, and his granddaughter were all there. He was pleased with the award. A couple of guys who drove for the senior center spoke. The center there is named the Council on Aging, I think. Buck would substitute as a driver when the center could not cover picking members up in the van. What a loss to the community. He was a very young seventy-nine-year-old and moved faster than half our beat cops."

Lilly responded, "Don't let the cops hear your comparison, Ash; they'll not forget it. Buck works hard, retires, is involved, loses his wife, and then dies needlessly. Hate this. No sense to it."

"You gonna spring for coffee today, Jerry? It's only a buck for us seniors."

With a wise-ass smile on his face Jerry LaFollet scolded Herschel Levine with, "Did it yesterday, Herschel, not today. Good try though. I have to hand it to you, you do this about once every ten days. Besides, I have to leave to play pool at the Senior Center. George and the guys will be there. Did you see the news about that poor old guy who got killed in Palmer? Hit by a drunk driver. I'm not sure about this, but the reports say along a dark stretch of Route 20. I think Route 20 coincides with Route 32 for a while in Palmer. It may be along North Main Street. They've got a picture of the car, but it was reported stolen. They'll never get the driver unless police find fingerprints or something."

"Who was the guy; anyone we've heard of?"

"Just a guy who was a widower and apparently has some juice because there was a long story in the paper about his volunteering and getting awards. He was in his late seventies, I think; at least he had some good years."

Herschel asked, "You going to stay for the lunch program at the Center?"

"I forgot to put my name in. The new program manager wants to know who's coming a day before so they don't have surplus food. I questioned the change in policy and the wimp asked me if I thought it was a restaurant or something. I was going to tell him if it was a regular restaurant it'd be out of business in no time with his attitude, but you know, he'd talk about the 'price point' and I'd lose that battle then.

"I've got a date today with my seventeen-year-old grandson, Ethan. The best of the best in my family. My son and daughter-in-law have none of the kid's push. I was lucky to get Sid out of Community College and Ethan is top of his class. He's already got a full boat to Providence College. We're Jewish, but today none of that matters. I think that's where he's going. It'll be nice to have some family back here in the East. He's turning eighteen today. We all joined in on a used car for him; only a couple of years old, a 2016 Hyundai. He'll be thrilled."

Jerry said, "Lucky kid; lucky grandpa. I have five grandkids and my children can buy and sell me. I tend to give tickets to games for the boys and credit cards to the girls' favorite stores; cheaper than a third of a car."

"Alice meeting you tonight for supper, Jerry?"

"She does most every night. Sometimes we eat at her house. She's a good cook as long as I don't expect it. Her ex-husband was a demanding bastard leaving her totally resistant to any effort to direct her. She won't move in with me and we can't get married; it would screw up our money issues. This works, and she likes me. Can't ask any more of life than that. My dear wife, God bless her soul, was not an easy woman in herself. So, every day was not a good day. She wanted to be happy, but the slightest thing would set her off. Life is much easier with Alice; and she likes me. I said that already, didn't I? But being liked makes life wonderful. Enjoy your evening tonight, Herschel; I know your son and his family are leaving for home. Arizona's a long way for them to come back just to see the likes of your old hide."

"With friends like you, Jerry, I don't need enemies; but you're right. When they leave, I feel so lonesome for a couple of weeks. He's my only child. No family life for me when he goes back to his home. I can't go there to live. He and his wife want me. What would I do? I'm too old to start a new life. I like family life; though I haven't been part of one recently."

"How long has Marion been gone, Herschel?"

"Two long years and I miss her every day. She had such patience and was a wonderful cook. We traveled everywhere together. It's tough to go it alone. It gets me down sometimes; but then I push through and enjoy things. You have to keep pushing, Jerry. You just have to."

"Herschel, you do so much. I'm not blowin' kisses at you; I mean it. Between tutoring kids for nothing for that ed program and your work with the Shriners, you're busy thirty hours a week. You're eighty years old and contribute more to society than most thirty-year-olds. Be happy in yourself, friend."

"I keep getting up in the morning. I do push myself to get up. Marion used to tell me it was our duty. We were gifted with life. We should appreciate the gift. So, in her memory, I get up every morning one more time, Jerry. It's okay as long as I remember I must get up again. Not to worry about me, you hear?"

———

Captain Rudy Beauregard of West Side Police Department's MCU and his wife Mona joined neighbors for a fundraiser for the West Mass Senior Center in town. The fundraising theme was a chili cookoff with thirty-six local chefs and wannabe chef entrants. Two entrants shared each table consisting of hot pots of chili, rice, and assorted condiments. Mona said, "I never thought there could be that many versions. Look, Rudy, two tables have placards showing devils and fire. Must be the hot chili. One table on the left has a sign saying 'for wimps.' I think that's my table."

Members of the center provided guidance and advice to its patrons, cleaned off tables to allow turnover, and read from a pamphlet at each table with the history of each entry. Naturally, the pros had a following who packed their tables. Rudy noticed there was only one pro entrant at any table. He questioned that wisdom. Would the amateurs feel inferior next to the professional? He had his answer in an instant. One dabbler had a line longer than all the others. He himself was a senior. In fact, Rudy and Mona both knew him.

Given that Stan Korsecki was a most gregarious guy, they figured his personality was the reason for the long line in front of his table.

They quickly learned they were wrong. Defense Attorney Norbie Cull's wife Sheri insisted Stan's chili was the best non-vegetarian one to eat, saying, "He is awesome. I've known him for a very long time. After his retirement from the fire department, he volunteered with any agency who would have him. Often, he'd cook for fundraisers. Try the chili, Mona. It's to die for. Stan won't share the recipe. I've begged for it for years. I'm supposed to be a gourmet cook. You'd think I could pick out what's in it, but I've tried without success."

Mona agreed Stan was awesome but her reasoning had nothing to do with cooking. She sided with Sheri, and detailed some of the support Stan had given to volunteer home care for seniors group and the council of churches support for homes in crisis.

Sheri asked, "Homes in crisis, what's that, Mona? I've not heard of the group."

"I'm a board member," said Mona. "We serve support for marginal cases in a financial crisis, who are not on public assistance. Families whose main support has been lost through death, loss of a job, or illness. We can't do anything long-term with the exception of directing those in trouble to other agencies. What we can do is use our budget to cover utilities for up to three months and we'll buy groceries. The families must be truthful and we do investigations, but it is important work. Stan did much of the grunt work. He would go to Mildred's Community Pantry, pick food based on need, box it, and deliver it. Lately he's been eager to do too much. We've had to slow him down. I think he's depressed."

Sheri asked, "Why, Mona, it's been years since his wife passed?"

Mona answered, "He had a lady friend and they were very happy together. She died six months ago from a massive stroke. He's alone now; and Stan is a man who needs people."

Sheri volunteered to have Norbie invite him to some of the men's functions at the country club. The two thought it was an excellent idea. Stan would very likely enjoy playing cards, because in his off time at the senior center he would play with staff and seniors there.

Attorney Norberto Cull joined his wife Sheri, and Mona and Rudy. After kissing the cheeks of the ladies and giving a nod to Rudy he walked over to Chef Stan and said, "Stan, you can't show up Lance, the Pro next to you. He has to stay in business and your line is longer."

Lance, proprietor of the 'Living Healthy Café' overheard Norbie's remarks stating, "Not to worry, Norbie, Stan's dish is more inclusive. He's serving cornbread with wheat in it and all kinds of cheese with who knows what's in it. I'm here for the purists. Stan's clientele focuses on immediate taste and they pop a gas pill after eating. My clientele chooses every morsel to ingest based on its purity."

They laughed. Stan asked Norbie if he could help him for just a half hour until his volunteer assistants joined him. He explained he never expected so many people; but had thankfully made three extra-large crockpots of chili, which hopefully would allow him to stay the course. Agreeing to work, Norbie called Rudy over to also assist. The two men worked diligently with Stan until the two regular volunteers checked in. Stan greeted the man and woman and introduced Marcy Pollard and Orvie Thibideau, friends from the senior center in town. Rudy noticed the younger age of the two and asked what they were doing at the senior center. "Is the center open to any age? You folks are younger than me."

Marcy laughed and responded, "I hope so, Captain. No, we're volunteers. We drive for the center. We volunteer everywhere; or at least I do. You do too, Orvie, right?"

After some brief conversing, Rudy and Norbie joined their spouses who had bought several chilis to sample in addition to Stan's. Sheri noted on a sheet of paper each's favorite chili in order, by agreeable taste. From the results, Norbie and surprisingly, Mona, went for the hotter chilis, Rudy for the sweetest, and Sheri for the vegetarian. Sheri concluded, "I am the future. Rudy will eventually have diabetes, and my darling husband and Mona are looking for trouble."

When they reviewed their five samples of chili, Stan Korsecki's was number three on all their lists, leading Mona to conclude, "It's why you said he had the best chili. Most folks will eat

his. Maybe I liked the spicy one best today, but I already feel heartburn coming on."

Not able to prevent himself from responding, Rudy Beauregard replied, "About time Mona gets indigestion and not me."

2

Nina Jones

There was a traffic jam on State Street, Springfield on a Tuesday morning causing Nina Jones to swear softly under her breath. The Holy Spirit Church of God van she was driving contained food for families. Unfortunately, the van was missing its refrigerated unit. It was out for repairs. She thought, *every day something connected to this van is being repaired. I put ice in bags to protect the food, but I stopped for gas. I hope the meat will be okay. It's mostly sides of ham; it should stay well. That nervy nellie, Laycrima Timmons, never gases up this van. She is one lazy-assed volunteer. Why she's on the van detail, I don't know. I think they caught on to her habits in the office where she was previously assigned and stuck her with us. I don't know how much longer the Church will keep me on as a driver. I've had two fender benders in the last three months. I do need this job. It may not pay much, but I get to go to all the church suppers and brunches on Sundays and get first pick on the clothing donations; all for free. I'm one foot away from being on the street.*

A horn blasted and a suit in a Mercedes cut in front of her bringing blasphemous words to her mouth she'd forgotten she knew. Gaining control, she headed toward the women's shelter.

The delivery today was easy for Nina. There were helpers to unload the van. Sometimes she had no help. On those days, she would pretend she was fine, but moving the heavy boxes of groceries onto the wheelie without dropping them was stressful for her new knee. It was her second total knee replacement, known to all in her age bracket as a TKR. It was not the same surgery runners had. They just got ACIs or other knee repairs. The TKR was in her mind truly a horrible surgery. It wasn't the surgery so much because they loaded you with pain killers; it was the endless rehabbing required for recovery. Nina was certain rehab was the devil letting her know God would not save her. She did not listen to the devil and went at rehab with a vengeance.

Nina was pleased when she finished her route earlier today and quickly returned to The Holy Spirit of God Church (HSG) in time for the Wednesday night supper. She knew it would be pulled pork tonight. She said softly but aloud, "I love Wednesday's menu. No problem with hump day's menu. They'll give me seconds cause I'm so skinny. I just need to eat a lot to keep these old bones going. Stomach's not the problem, I got the joint problem. That orthopedic man told me my right shoulder was next to be done. It doesn't hurt that bad yet. Maybe he just wants to operate. Pastor says, 'You must be careful about what a surgeon says. He may be looking for new business.'"

At the church's center there was a full house of fifty-five folks; all were churchgoers who contributed to the food program. Most however did not have a surplus of anything in their lives. Wednesday nights' congregations included good people who worked for the church or who were active in fundraising and proselytizing. It was the best night of the week. Volunteer van drivers with their own vans were invited as a reward for their service. Most did service for the senior centers around and were do-gooders. Some actually had real jobs; but most were retired early or had lots of free time and needed people. They were also a good source of info about what was going on at the senior and health-care centers.

Pastor Aldrych kept his ear to the ground looking for new opportunities for the church. He often drained visitors' brains seeking possibilities for new programming. Pastor was a resourceful man and his wife Althea was the musical director. Nina believed Sister Althea must have been on stage once, thinking, *she sure has presence; what a great voice.*

Nina joined Sister Althea and Jerry LaFollet, a Wilbraham van driver. They ate at the main table and joined the hooting and hollering at a church member, Little JP, famous for his comedic impressions of local figures. Little JP was doing a number on some Springfield City Council members, but clearly left the Mayor of Springfield out of his repertoire. He had Sister Althea on edge. She knew JP would sometimes go too far and hoped he would not mimic the councilors who were so supportive of the church. She finally stood and ended the performance with a song. The members agreed she was second only to Elvis in singing, 'How Great Thou Art.'

As the table members finished their tiramisu, Jerry asked Nina, "Did you hear about the guy from Palmer, Buck Gagnon, being run over by a drunk driver?"

Nina shivered before she answered, "I'm so upset. I knew Buck a long time ago. He helped me when I was still drinking. He was my mentor; and Jerry, there were no white on black mentors at that time. Maybe there were in AA, but I wasn't in AA; I was in a church group for single mothers with problems. He sought me out. Buck was born to help; what my daughter who has a degree in psychology says, is an 'empath.' I don't really know what it exactly means but I think it's someone who knows about you without asking questions. He saved my life. The driver's not been found, right?"

"Probably won't be from what I hear from the police in Palmer.

Stolen car recovered with no prints and cleaned up with Clorox wipes inside. I don't want to end up as road kill, I can tell you that. Of all people, Buck didn't deserve dying like he was nothing."

"Jerry, I lived a hard life before I let go and turned to the Almighty for help. I know I've survived because some sort of angel was sitting on my shoulder, but where the hell was Buck's angel? Was he careless walking across the road?"

Jerry shook his head in denial. "Nope, no one complained about his age, and they would've if he'd been at fault; him being old and such. The car went up on the sidewalk, hit him, and then his body was dragged onto the snow bank and I heard that story from the state's engineering analyst who's a guy I knew way back. If he had any enemies, it would be murder. I still think it is murder because the driver was obviously drunk and in a stolen car. They'll never find him."

Nina said, "Do you know how many times I drove drunk when I was drinking, Jerry? I drove my kids to school when I could barely see the yellow line in the road. I could have killed someone. That angel protected me. Why protect me and not Buck? He volunteered to drive for every agency who would have him. I need the money and get paid for driving. I don't get it; I just don't get it."

Sister Althea motioned to Nina who left the table and joined her. She whispered, "Nina, the clothing donations came in. Don't say anything, but I pulled a warm and good-looking jacket in a size small for you. Come in the clothing storage room and take it before that fashion diva Justina Smith grabs it. She's on call in the morning to distribute and she doesn't need any new clothes."

In the back room, the new donations were piled up in a large crate. Sister Althea must have gone through it quickly because the clothes were not in any semblance of order. She pulled a purply-maroon long quilted jacket with a fur hood attached and happily modeled for Nina. They were the same size. She said, "Do you like it, Nina? You can see why I thought of you. It's a good designer item. The label says 'Eddie Bauer' and you know they make warm clothes. You need this; your cloth jacket is worn and I know you won't find anything as nice. I don't know why it ended up in this bin. It has no wear; the tag is still on it. Your angel is taking care of you again."

A tear climbed over Nina's lower eyelid as she tried, but could not coherently speak. Sister Althea pulled her into an embrace saying, "Be happy, Nina. I know you've been depressed about money lately. How else may I help? You are a godsend to us here at the church."

Nina huskily explained her vision problem. "I got cataracts in both eyes. I have Mass Health so it will get paid for, but they're going to make me wait about three weeks between surgeries and the doctor told me not to drive until two weeks after the last surgery. That's five weeks in total, Sister Althea. Who's going to drive the van. I can't lose this job. And eventually, the surgeon says I'll be up for a shoulder job."

Nina then sat on a nearby chair attempting to stop what she thought of as self-pity, saying, "I know I look like a blubbering idiot, but this job pays my rent. I work at the Dollar Store on weekends for the rest. I can't lose this job."

Sister Althea pulled a chair next to her, saying, "Nina, you've never once complained about money. I only noticed recently your coat looked worn. I can raise your hourly rate a bit when you come back and I'll talk to Pastor Aldrych. Maybe you can qualify for 'a hardship grant,' which will tide you over for five weeks. We certainly can directly pay your rent. You're in subsidized housing, aren't you?"

Nina had stopped crying. She took a moment before she said, "Sister Althea, I never asked nobody for anything. I thought you would take my job away if I was out sick. Who's going to drive for you? Can you get someone who won't want my job when I come back?"

"Nina, I'm going to ask the good guys who come here for dinner. Jerry's here tonight. He'll be happy to cover for you. Maybe he can get his friend Herschel. There's also a good guy in West Side. He'll help. He's so lonely; he loves to fill in for us. We'll cover for you. Now if you need rides to and from the doctor for surgery, we'll do it. Your family isn't here; consider us your family, Nina."

Nina looked stricken, causing Sister Althea to say, "What is wrong? Did I miss something? What else is a problem?"

Nina, not known for displays of emotion, hugged her good angel. She detailed her history which was unknown to Sister Althea or anyone else in the church.

"My daddy left the farm near Charleston, South Carolina in a rage in 1951. We lived in a shack with no running water and just a stove for heat. I was happy. What did I know? I was about eight then. His cousin had been in the service and when he got out he married a girl from Springfield. He said there was opportunity up here. People treated negroes differently then. They called us negroes then. Didn't bother me; probably would today. We had good food there; mostly we raised our own food. I was never hungry but I went to a segregated school with no whites. I didn't know any better about race. I delivered vegetables to a company store who sold them to whites. That's when I met some uppity white people and some nice ones. I didn't want to leave, but my daddy spoke and my mammy went with his ideas. Obeying your husband was the way and the practice didn't change for a long time. Now I think it's gone the other way; no better from my perspective.

"We moved to a third-floor apartment on Byers Street, Springfield. Lots of whites in that building. We couldn't grow our food; we had to buy it all. There were four of us kids. My brothers were older and got into trouble pretty quickly. We didn't know the rules. We didn't know how to socialize up here, so we were often silent. My brothers still don't do well expressing their thoughts. Anyway, they ended up in court as delinquents; nothing really bad, but they were taken away for a while. My daddy said it did them no good and I believe him. My brothers were tough when they got home, but in the end they did well in construction. My older sister ran away and got pregnant. He was an okay guy in the end, but my daddy never liked him. He thought he had no manners. Northern manners were just different. My daddy never took to Northern manners. He was not an easy man when he was drinking. Mammy said he drank when money was low, explaining, 'Nina Mary,' that's my full name, 'men are that way." He would treat Mammy badly. I'd cry and he'd stop. Mammy said he didn't mean it. It's what all wives say when they are hurt by their men.

"Later, my husband Homie did the same only he didn't drink. He just got mean. So, I became the drinker; givin' him a reason to be mean. I drank after my kids left the house; when only me and Homie were there together. That's when I got it. He was going to hit me no matter what; it wasn't the kids causing stress. He just got mean when life didn't go his way or when his friends didn't call him or when his lottery tickets didn't pay off. I was about to divorce him when he got killed in an accident on the turnpike by a drunk driver. Never caught that guy. It was just like what happened in Palmer. You're lucky if you drive and survive.

"I drank and drank and wouldn't listen to the kids when they visited.

I'd keep it all quiet but my girl, the psychologist, saw right through me. She brought me to a church that held something like AA meetings, and I met Jerry. I like life, Sister Althea, and I feel at home here in church."

Nina cried again and was consoled by Sister Althea. In a bit, Nina was asked, "How come I don't hear the Southern in you; maybe rarely, but I wouldn't have known you were from a Southern farm, girl."

"My daddy told us to get the language right. He helped us. He'd worked side by side on the farm with a white man who'd been in jail. His name was Possum. Possum told my daddy, 'If your kids don't talk and write right, get those articles proper, they'll be lost in the North.' My daddy made us pronounce by reading books aloud. They were easy books 'cause Daddy was uneducated. The books had to have words in them he knew, but it did the job. One man here asked if I'd gone to Community College, and why didn't I have an office job. I didn't tell him I hadn't gone to college, but did say I used to have an office job before I was married."

"Well, I think maybe you're in the wrong position here, Nina Mary. When you get back, would you like to be my administrative assistant; not for typing letters but for coordinating the restaurant and clothing projects. I'm doing it now and I'm just tired. Too much to do with all the civic duties and letters. What do you think?"

Nina Mary dissolved into tears again; only this time she mouthed a prayer aloud, "Dear Jesus, You listen to my prayers. I should not give up hope. I almost did this time. Those two fender benders were the hints for me to face this surgery. And I didn't listen to them; the almost accident today brought me to my senses. You gave me Sister Althea. Thank You, Jesus. I don't know why He bothered to save me; I didn't help save myself for a long time."

3

Howie's Dead

MCU Detective Sergeant Ashton Lent opened the letter. Petra noticed he did not do it cautiously. She thought, how different we all are. I'm even faster than Ash on my feet. We both jump out quickly to face scary situations. Lilly also does. The others in MCU approach situations more slowly with the Captain the slowest of all. Yet, unlike me, Ash faces life without any reservation. That letter is from the Chief's office. It's either a yea or a nay on the new lieutenant's position. They're nuts if they don't give it to him. If he gets it, he'll be reassigned. Everything changes. Lilly's going hot and heavy with Juan. One will have to leave MCU if they get married. Just like with Jim and me, but Jim had a profession outside of the department and he's happy. Where will they assign Ash? I truly hate starts and finishes. I'm all for going on as always. I'll be the most reluctant mother when my baby Carlotta goes away to college or gets married. Jim will be the one to help me face life. I don't like freakin change.

Ash smiled and for the faces watching him, all his fellow detectives, he said, "I got it. I'm to speak with the Chief today about my future. The Captain must know, right? He didn't tell me."

Juan said, "He wouldn't, Ash. He's one guy who will let the Chief get the credit, but you can be sure he had something to do with it. Passing the lieutenant's exam is one thing; getting a lieutenant's position is another. We all knew there was a budget opening, but wherever you'll be assigned, it won't be here. You know that. Good thing you were highest in passing; the next highest, Lilly's friend in sex crimes, has political pull with the mayor."

Ash said, "I don't want to be reassigned. I could have waited for the next position."

Ted laughed and said, "Ash, by the time the next position becomes available, your exam may be out of date. We don't have lieutenants made every day in West Side. We're not Springfield. Our department is much smaller. You know that."

Captain Beauregard heard some of the talk as he entered the Pit for the scheduled morning meeting. He smiled at Ash, congratulated him, and said, "Sergeant, now Lieutenant, see me after you've met with Chief Coyne."

The agenda for the day was to review files on several home invasions. Generally, because these assaults were drug related, the first on the scene was not MCU. When a shooting was connected, it became MCU's bailiwick. After a few moments, Sergeant Ted Torrington asked if anyone had seen the hit and run death in Russell, a few towns over. He was disturbed because the man who died had served with his dad in the same army unit in Vietnam. He disclosed, "My dad insists Howie Blanchard was a decent guy; a hill town guy through and through. Howie was active in the Russell Community Church and was in some Vietnam group down nearer us. My dad really feels his loss. They got together a couple of times a year as they got older; used to be more often, but Howie's wife is gone and he doesn't do the couples thing anymore. If I were to congratulate this younger generation for anything, it would be their inclusion of singles when they go out. Certainly, my dad's group of suburbanites still living in their own homes do not; maybe if they're in a nursing home it's different."

Juan said, "I went up to the Mennonite store in Russell called 'Cream of the Crop', I think. My Mamita wanted grass fed beef. She's become health conscious for my papa. Yaa, yaa, it was expensive, but get this; you paid for it by leaving your money and collecting change from the box below. I couldn't believe it. I looked for cameras to see if someone was watching, but couldn't see any. Imagine in this day and age, just twenty-five minutes from Springfield and you can leave thirty bucks in a box and take out your twenty cents change and no one's ripping them off. Couldn't believe it. Gives me hope."

The Captain said, "There are always good folks out there. We just see the worst, but never forget the good folks. The Mennonite Community members in Russell are great carpenters and farmers. They live in an area where the culture has kept some of our traditional New England ways. Change has come to them recently and more will come. The Russell police chief is probably answering many questions about who was the drunk driver in this Howie Blanchard case. We tend to surmise when there's a hit and run that a drunk driver is involved. That community doesn't see many incidents like this; first because it's so small with a little more than two thousand residents. Secondly, the violent crimes rate is less than fifty percent of the national average. Russell is a great place to live. It's not far from cities. I love visiting; it has a rural feel to it. Air smells great."

Ash said he played an outdoor event up there once, saying, "Lots of individualists living up there. Any one of them get an idea who the drunk who killed Howie is, he'll be dust. Sounds like Howie was a good old guy by their standards. Ted, does your dad know if Howie used to play a wicked banjo? The Howie from Russell I knew played all over western Mass and Vermont for all types of musical groups. He could play any kind of music and blend the banjo in. The banjo has a distinctive sound but Howie could soften the sound. I'm sorry if it is him and about the way he left us. How did it happen? Catching the drunk will be difficult. There're no cameras up that way. They'll have to hit the auto repairers; problem is a perp could hide the car in a barn up there for six months."

Sergeant Bill Border commented, "I used to go up to a lake in Otis, not far from Russell and spent some time in Russell when there were trout in Russell Pond aka Woronoake Lake. I liked the area. Did the accident killing Howie happen at night? It's damn dark on the roads up there at night."

Ted said, "Yeah, Bill, it was about eleven at night. Howie lived on a house on a hill near Jeb, his farmer friend. He was walking on the road after playing cards with Jeb, headed back to his house. He lived in an old converted small farmhouse near the edge of the road. The home no longer had a great amount of land attached. The road was really dark. Jeb heard the car crash. He said he immediately knew from the sound, along with the fact that Howie had recently left, that Howie may have been hit. He ran out and saw a small dark colored vehicle about one hundred yards past his house racing away. Howie was dead on the side of the road. What Jeb thought was strange was Howie's body was really off the road in an area where Jeb would sometimes park some equipment. He thought the driver would have had to be drunk to be that far off the road."

———

Chad tried so diligently to do what mother wanted, but mother was not happy tonight. The Olds were fussing in their beds. He had wiped their noses, given and removed bedpans, cleaned their hineys as mother taught and jacked off two of the old men to quiet their low pitch but exhausting screaming. He only had to rub some of the ladies and not that often. The old men, just two out of the four, were relentless in wanting relief. Mother said it was an urge and to shut them up, you had to do what you had to do. Today the Olds were restless and he was tired. Mother said he could not have double portions of dessert; he could eat what the Olds ate. Chad was in tears; he'd tried his very best to make the Olds happy. Chad couldn't help it if they were crying when Mother came home. She put him up against a wall and said, "If you've touched them and left a mark, I'll lose my patience. They pay for everything. My job at the nursing home pays peanuts."

Chad thought how he was already laughed at for being the skinniest most scraggly kid in class and he was hungry to boot. It seemed to him, he was always hungry. The doctor who came around to check on the Olds, also gave him a check-up each year at no cost. Mother said the doctor was obligated because she paid him money for the Olds' exams. Doctor Selden told him to eat more saying, "Listen, kid, you're seventeen going on eighteen. You look like a scarecrow; enough to frighten people. Do you ever go outside; you're pale. I can't do blood work on you. Your mom won't pay. How do you do in school? Do you have any friends? I never see anyone here but you and the patients."

No, I don't have friends. How could I? Bring them home here? No way! Nobody wants me around. I heard one girl say I smell like antiseptic. She's right, I do. I rub it on me to get that old people smell off me. Am I a good student you ask, Doctor Selden? What else can I do? My teachers think I'm brilliant. I'm not. I've learned so much from the Olds. They give me experience other kids don't have. I'll have to do better for Mother. The state will be inspecting this week. I'll have to make everyone happy. I'll tell mother the Olds look too skinny. She'll have to feed them more than oatmeal with an egg and a spot of applesauce for supper. Lunch is a 'love sandwich.' We kids say it's two pieces of bread so much in love with each other, they don't let nothing come between them. Breakfast is toast, a piece of ham, and fruit slices. This diet keeps them alive, but just barely; for me it's not enough.

His mother interrupted his studying that night saying, "Don't think for a minute even if you get a scholarship you're going to leave me. Your father was a nut case and I was glad to see him go. You are mine, and I need you to help me with the Olds. Chad, how will I survive without you? You owe me."

"Ma, I can go to community college. It takes less time away from here than high school. I need an education.'

"You know you can't call me, 'Ma.' Where's the refinement I taught. I came from mountain people, but you're from the city. Don't let me hear that word again. I'll think about community college but it better be in some program with a job ensured afterwards. You'd make a good physical therapist or nurse; something with a license. I could use it to help me get better paying clients. Private clients would be the best. Right now, I only have two of them and that's because the families can't deal with these two. All the rest are paid for by the state, and the state is always inspecting. You'd better clean those rooms better for the inspection. There's a new guy coming I've never met."

Chad appeared buoyed by his conversation thinking, nursing would be okay with me. If my mother were different, I would go to law school or take philosophy or even religion. The other kids in school are applying to big name schools for computer science and engineering. I wouldn't mind criminal justice. Cops, today, are really social workers except when a hood shoots them. How do you go from helping people to drawing your gun and arresting a bad guy? It must be hard to make those switches all day long. I'd be a good cop for the social working side; but I wouldn't like to be in danger. I'd be afraid. Social work or nursing is a good choice for me. Mother would never let me go into social work. She thinks our patients' social workers are complete jerks. I told her once they were licensed and she swore at my stupidity saying "licensed for what; to talk and do nothing." No, nursing will work.

***

Sergeant, soon to be Lieutenant Ashton Lent sat in Chief Coyne's office awaiting his swearing in as lieutenant. Mayor Fitshler had insisted on a press conference. There'd been some grumblings about increasing the police budget and the Mayor thought Chief Coyne could take this opportunity to explore the importance of keeping talent. Since the new Lieutenant came from the MCU, it was thought he could discuss all the murder cases solved by this unit and its Captain, etc. and according to the new Lieutenant use this bullshit to let the public know all their dollars were well spent.

Local press attended the swearing in. The Mayor hoped Chief Coyne would have Captain Beauregard speak on Ashton Lent's worthiness for promotion. The Captain was known to dislike politics and to stay in the background, but Fitshler knew the press loved him. One reporter was heard to say that Beauregard never spoke unless he had something worthwhile to say.

Chief Coyne had organized an exaggerated ceremony for a promotion to lieutenant. There were no other promotions at this time. Six months ago, a few other police officers were promoted: one to sergeant; one to lieutenant; and one to captain. There was less hype then. The Chief spoke about the department's excellent record and mentioned the MCU as the epitome of a unit meeting police standards as well as community standards. He then called on Captain Beauregard to speak about the new lieutenant's contribution to the department. Dressed in uniform, Beauregard oozed prestige and authority. Then he spoke. "… Detective Ashton Lent, as you know, almost gave his life for our work as did Sergeant Ted Torrington; both members of the West Side Major Crimes Unit. Their suffering journey is over but we should remember the events for what they always are; an ongoing threat to police from aggressive criminality! MCU's work hits every aspect of our society. We are called in to investigate whenever there is a death or assault. Now, how do these events occur? Let me list some of them for you: Domestic violence, auto deaths, criminal thefts and home invasions, drug and alcohol induced events, and so many other happenings spilling over in violence. Investigations are tedious with not many 'A Hah' moments. They are costly. Rarely are they easy to close. Our investigators must know the law, the culture they work within, have insight into many groups, know the elements of forensic science, and be able to understand mental health issues. Lieutenant Lent deserves this promotion. Our detectives all respect our community and deserve respect also. I sincerely hope our unit will have more promotions in the future. There is a personal cost to each promotion. Normally the promoted officer moves in keeping with the higher rank to a later shift in another unit. For MCU, the cost of Lieutenant Lent leaving us is a hardship; but again, he deserves promotion. Thank you."

The press was all over it asking the Mayor and Chief why Lieutenant Lent would not be able to stay in MCU. Chief Coyne covered for

Beauregard explaining the department had certain protocols. The Mayor switched the conversation when he was asked about potholes on Westfield Street.

Coyne grabbed Beauregard saying, "Quite a stunt you pulled. Rudy, you know I simply can't keep Lent in MCU; there'd be an uproar. You don't even have a big case load of serious crimes now."

Beauregard smiled and said, "Wait, Chief. They'll come. I wish you were right, but you're not. They'll come. Each time murders happen, they're not like before. Murder always requires our rethinking motives, opportunities, and our judgments of men and women. I do have five open home invasions with assaults and one death. I'm still trying to get enough evidence on the punk who planned it but stayed in the car. The doers are too afraid to name him. It'll take some hunting to get more evidence on him. Today we found the car used in the invasion and there are prints all over it. We think we know who he is and he is in the system. I hope we find his prints in the car. Chief, I can't operate with less detectives than I have."

"Rudy, I'm not adverse to moving a new sergeant to be an MCU detective over from another unit. I'll move Lent for six months and maybe I can bring him back to you then. Meanwhile, you can do some training on another sergeant I have in Traffic who's blowing up Traffic with his scrupulous detailing. Good guy, but not too flexible with our citizens. He is so rigid in reminding offenders about their civic duties that I've had a hundred complaints. I can't do anything about him because he is non-emotional and always polite. I solve your problem. You solve mine. Six months is not a long time, Rudy."

The two agreed. As Captain Beauregard walked away, he smiled.

4

A Party in Wilbraham

Half of West Side's MCU force had been invited to a party in Wilbraham at Dr. Jason Holbrook's home. Dr. Holbrook worked with MCU detectives, serving at times as an expert witness for the state. At other times, in insurance cases, he could be seen on the other side of the legal aisle. An invitation to his parties was always welcome. For Captain Beauregard and his wife Mona, it presented an opportunity to socialize with two people they both liked; Jason and his wife Denise. Jim and Petra Locke were also good friends stemming from Jim's work as a psychologist when he and Jason would tag team as expert witnesses in insurance cases. They often found themselves sitting next to each other on a bench awaiting the call by the court officer.

Also attending from West Side MCU were Ted and Charlotte Torrington and Mason and Jerusha Smith. Charlotte and Jerusha both were friends of Denise. They had history with each other when they served as counselors for the Division of Youth Services years before. The friendship held. And all were pleased to be at this gala with over one hundred-fifty guests flowing from the three-season porch through some sort of a pergola and spilling out into a green space with several water features. Winter was now a cold spring. The bar, located at the other end of the fenced-in yard, presented guests with a goal if they wished a drink. Mona told Rudy, "What a smart idea. I'll bet Denise thought it up; probably thought if they want a drink badly enough, they have to be able to travail the large yard which may require them to be sober."

Rudy answered sarcastically, "Mona, what would prevent them from just standing at the bar all afternoon and drinking; falling in a stupor on the grass?'

Petra had overheard the two. She said, "Captain, even those here with a drinking problem would keep up a front. This is a high-class party with police, lawyers, and important community citizens, all of which would be an impediment for misbehavior."

Jim Locke laughed at her, saying, "Honey, human nature doesn't work like that. A party with a little alcohol to loosen the tongue is an absolute stimulus for lack of personal control."

The crowd started to mix and lo and behold, noted Defense Attorney Norbie Cull and his wife Sheri joined the scene. Before long, Rudy headed over to Norbie who was surrounded by a group of folks including Norbie's uncle who was a retired federal prosecutor. Rudy did not know the others in the group. After some acknowledgements and introductions, most names Rudy knew he would not remember later, the previous conversation resumed. Norbie's Uncle Ed was talking aside to another retiree named Smitty asking him why his friend Jerry wasn't here, saying, "Didn't Jason invite him? He was at the last party. Great guy who spouts lots of philosophy."

"Of course, he was invited, Ed. He had a conflict, but will try to get over here before the food's all gone. He'll have to pick up his lady friend Alice. He goes nowhere without her. Right now, he's in Springfield covering the van for Nina. She's the driver for that inner-city church we sometimes cover when they're out drivers. She's having surgery and he thinks highly of her; says she's a go through gal who's had a tough life. I've met Nina. She'd do anything for anyone. I'm covering for her tomorrow because Jerry has to attend a funeral. A good friend has died, no one I know. Jerry is devastated. He said the guy was one of us; you know, decent and together with a few other drivers, they covered all the van driving in this area for organizations. At our age, things happen. We have to take care of each other. You know, Ed, most folks ignore us old geezers."

"You are not old. You have more energy than most guys I know at the gym. How'd Jerry's friend die, Smitty; was it cancer?"

"No, he was hit by a car out here near Mr. B's Billiards. Jerry says they'll never find the driver. It's dark out there at nine at night and no cameras in the area."

Norbie responded before his uncle, saying, "There is always hope the state police accident investigation team will find some debris on the body or nearby to help identify the car. Auto body repair garages could maybe connect a repair to the vehicle. They're really good processing connections."

"Norbie, you have more faith in them than I do. If it was a sixteen-year-old kid hit, they'd be all over it, but a guy, close in age for meeting his Maker, is not so important. It's bad enough many of us are shoved into nursing homes by family members who can't face assisting us a little bit. Think about it, most of those in a nursing home could stay at home if family arranged transportation to an adult day health center, visited occasionally, and sent over a couple of meals a week. I don't eat a third of what I used to eat at a meal. When any of us go to a restaurant for dinner, our take home feeds us for two additional luncheons or dinners. We sometimes go to Bernie's Railroad Car Restaurant in Chicopee and get takeout from our dinner equal to four meals. We don't need much; so why do families try to shove us into nursing homes? We were there for them. Jerry's friend lived a good life and he gets killed and there's not much of a reaction, like he's not important. He *was* important. I'm ranting, aren't I, Norbie?"

"No! No! I think the elderly seem to be ignored by many of their families, but Smitty, often their families are in another section of the country. Remember, families are smaller than one hundred years ago. Often in the past the wives were the caretakers because they were stay at home moms. Now everybody works and it seems to me many have lives too full for healthy living. I'm not disagreeing with your assessment, Smitty, I just think there's need for more diversity of services for our families. My mom and dad have each other. They are older, but so far are in good health. Do I visit them as often as I should? No, I don't but I hear from my mom on a regular basis; she finds it easier to connect with both me and my wife Sheri. My dad calls only when he's interested in a golf game. I have siblings too. Before nursing home transition may be necessary, Sheri and I want our parents to live with us. But guess what, they all said they want to be in their own homes until their bodies are so degraded, they will need twenty-four-hour care. It will take a small war to get them to give up their lifestyle."

Rudy interrupted, saying, "My folks still think they're supposed to be taking care of me and my family. They're French Canadians and Mom sends over Pea Soup once a month, tortiere meat pie for holidays and some other concoction once a week. Mona shops for her with her. My dad comes over the house and tells me what I'm doing wrong in carpentry and electric and corrects it. We're still the children in this situation. I think my mom's a realist and would come live with us, but

Dad likes his own space. This stuff is not easy, Smitty, even when the kids are willing to take over the job."

Smitty's answer oozed with sarcasm. "Like the whole world is like you two. Get real, some kids want nothing to do with their parents. Parents have nothing more to offer them when they get old. Not much loyalty out there today. If there's money, then they'll pretend to take charge, but in most cases it's to get the money. Their decisions will be based on how to keep the estate intact for themselves as heirs. You should see what happened when my friend and his wife got a reverse mortgage to enable them to live a little larger. When the kids found out, visiting their parents decreased by eighty percent. Maybe not all, but a lot of kids today just don't feel the love."

Norbie said, "You should be in law enforcement, Smitty, with your cynical view on life."

Jerry had arrived and joined the group. In tow was, as he called her, his lady friend, Alice. The conversation drifted back to Jerry's friend, Herschel Levine. The group could see Alice holding tears back, while Jerry explained how Herschel's family had just been there visiting not long before Herschel died. The funeral had been at Ascher's funeral home in Springfield. Jerry and Alice had not before attended a Jewish funeral. They expressed their interest in the service and especially the eulogy which they both thought captured Herschel's essence and his love for his late wife. Alice insisted vehemently, "Herschel was a very healthy man for his age and I think he would have had some really good years left. Granted, he would regularly bitch about being lonely, but he filled his life with people, and on a daily basis was happy. He was most lonely in the evenings when there wasn't an event to attend and see people. He did not like to go home to an empty apartment. As to his bitching, friends who have known him for years insist he was just a chronic complainer. They used the word, kvetch, which supposedly is Yiddish for someone who's never satisfied. I don't think it's the right word for Herschel. I think he just liked to complain so no one would think everything was wonderful. He liked a little attention, but he was fun to be with and had such a wit."

Smitty realized he had not introduced Jerry and Alice to the group. After the introductions, Jerry asked if Rudy was the detective who solved all those serial murders in West Side. An embarrassed Rudy acknowledged with a nod of his head and a mumbled answer asserting it takes a whole team to solve serial murders and the murders were not all serial murders. Norbie helped with a discussion of some of the cases and the differences between a series of murders and serial murders. Jerry asked, "Why in hell do people just pick people to murder? I just don't get it. I drive vans, when I don't have to, just to help folks out who are either too old to drive or too infirmed."

Rudy did not miss this opportunity to expound on the difference between a situational murder, murder for passion, murder goaded by a group, and murder by a sociopath. The discussion was lively; so much so that the hostess came over to suggest the group join the others at the plank table loaded with goodies and share with others their obviously interesting conversation.

While walking over to the table, Mona and Sheri had their own conversation. Sheri said, "Remember the chili contest, Mona. We have no clue to the size of the elderly population needing our help. While my kids were pre-school, I had little time to offer and when I did have time, it was in support of school functions and kids activities. If Norbie and I did not have such healthy parents still living their own lives, we may be more in tune with older folks' needs."

"I'm kind of with you, Sheri, but I have noticed Rudy's dad having some problems. His mom does most of the driving now. He has some vision problems you don't notice at first, and as Rudy stated he wants independence. He wants to help Rudy and me and not the other way around. It's funny but he'll let the grandchildren help him. That's okay. He enjoys when Rudy talks about his cases. He knows Rudy will say nothing when it's an open case, but once it's gone to court, then Roland's all over him; so much so Lizette tries to hold him back. Like you, Sheri, I'm with kids most of the day. I'm back teaching at the high school. Everything is fast in my everyday life. Living for my parents and in-laws is at a slower pace. Rudy's parents have about ten years on my parents because they weren't able to adopt a baby until they were much older and were successful in adopting Rudy because nobody wanted an older child then."

Sheri invited Mona into a conversation. "What do you think, Mona, I can give some time to help the 'before generation' as my mother calls herself? Maybe we can start with our folks with a light dinner at five o'clock one night a week. You cook one week; I'll cook the next. They'll get to know each other. We'll be able to see how good they are doing with their peers and not continue to expect them to run around like us."

Mona, always willing to help in any situation, thought the idea was wonderful. She expanded on the thought saying, "I still have two of my boys with me at home. I'll bring them into this little plot. It will just look like two families and maybe more later. The boys will create some diversion for conversation and will disappear when I tell them. They're crazy over their grandparents who also will come just to see the kids."

Sheri thought Mona was well into the spirit of the plan and she explained that her daughter Sidney would help. She and her brothers were all good cooks and would enjoy this.

It was the second week for the elder appreciation dinner night. This one was held at the Beauregard's. Mona and Sheri found planning the menu, implementing it, getting the kids to help was easy in comparison with getting the parents to attend. Apparently, between church, bingo, clubs, etc., unexpected movement in the evening appeared stressful to all the parents. Sheri had wondered whether her mother could easily mix. She lived in a condo purchased by Norbie. Sheri's mom had hired a professional decorator to ensure her new home would be special; it won an award for interior design in the city. Given her mother's sensibilities, as she like to call them, were a stretch from Norbie and Rudy's parents, Sheri was certain her mother would alienate the other parents over time. Instead, her mother was charming and said she was pleased to join in dinners with peers who had only good things to say about people.

Mona insisted rather than suggested they all eliminate politics from the conversations. All three mothers ended up in the kitchen making dietary suggestions for a slimmer more gourmet presentation and directing traffic. The first night had found Sheri stressed until Norbie explained to her it was not a fancy cocktail party and nothing had to be perfect. Giving up her OCD traits, Sheri found she really enjoyed their company and particularly some insights into Norbie she gained from listening to her in-laws in conversation.

Tonight, at Mona's, Lizette was informing all on the rules for French Canadian cuisine. Mona and Sheri both held their breath. Butter, bread, beans, potatoes, bacon, and lots of meat were all major components and were celebrated by all. Roland and Norbie's dads apparently had moved into this century when they agreed with each other that the old menus could be enjoyed by all today with just a couple of caveats: use smaller portions and sparingly use these recipes in their diets.

Later, in the family room, Roland explained he may not have been able to attend the dinner tonight. He thought a wake would be this evening, but MassLive, the local internet for obituary notices, listed it for the next night. Naturally he was questioned about the death. Roland explained, a good friend of his who was well along in years but very healthy was found dead along the roadside in Springfield on Boston Road. The police were searching for witnesses, because it appeared he may have been hit by an auto, but it could be he just fell and broke his hip. He'd been there, not easily seen, originally reported as twelve hours before his body was discovered. Roland was concerned, saying, "Lyle always took a walk at night in the dark but he was careful. He'd never had any trouble with falling. I'd kid him because he went to some yoga class to help with balance. He said I should do it. Rudy, can you just see me at yoga with all those women? No way. Besides, what good did it do Lyle?"

Norbie said to Rudy, "That's twice in a few weeks I've heard about an older person killed by a car on the side of the road. I don't think it's wise for them to be walking near major arteries like Boston Road in the dark. Balance is an issue for the elderly."

Rudy quickly responded, "No, Norbie, this is the third one I heard about or maybe the fourth death of an old man dead on the side of the road. I'll think about how many tomorrow. My MCU crew will have better memories than I have. Maybe the county could do a public service announcement. Older folks tend to listen to those more than our kids or us."

Rudy did not remember to question his detectives about elderly roadside deaths until a few weeks later. At an early morning meeting he posed the question. Rudy relayed the death of Herschel from Wilbraham and Lyle from Springfield to the detectives, who then reminded him about Ted's dad's friend Howie Blanchard from Russell found on the side of the road. Sergeant Lilly Tagliano said, "Don't you remember when Buck, a retired police officer from Palmer, was killed by a hit and run? Juan and I really liked him."

Rudy asked them whether it was worth calling attention to the series of accidents with a PSA (public service announcement). Ash was uncertain and wondered if the elderly would resent their night walking being focused on; perhaps the police would be stopping any elderly on the street after eight in the evening. With all this business about group rights, he thought there could be criticism if the wording was not carefully chosen.

Lieutenant Petra Aylewood-Locke said, "I don't think a PSA will hurt no matter how it is worded. I do think it's bizarre to have so many road accidents killing elderly men. Captain, you don't like coincidences and neither do I. Is there something going on here? We've four of them in a few months; how many do we not know about? Can you have Mason pull up all elderly killed by cars and left on the side of the road; and maybe all elderly unexplained deaths? Maybe we have a war on the aged."

5

Two Stories

Nursing training was the most wonderful opportunity for Chad; at least that is what he told his fellow trainees. There was a camaraderie he had never known before and he often told his mother he loved the training, the education, and his colleagues. Her response was always, "You need the training to support us. Do you ever think about me alone with the Olds, while you're enjoying your friends? You don't even have to study. I gave you the opportunity to learn early. You know I'm not well. I'll be joining the Olds before long and you'd better take better care of me then. You'll be a professional and will know how to treat me. I don't trust the doctor we have on call. You better get a job with health benefits. I need rehab from being on my feet all these years. I think you're getting selfish, Chad."

Chad often argued his side with his mother. He'd tell her how he'd handled the Olds well when he came home despite often being exhausted from training. One day, a gal in his class showed up with some notes he inadvertently left behind. He watched fearfully from the living room as his mother interacted with her. However, his mom was charming telling her how thoughtful she was to go out of her way for Chad. She did not invite her in and told her Chad was not there. Afterward she pulled a tantrum saying, "You're candy-assing around while I do all the work here. Don't think for a minute you can get married and leave me. With your luck your wife would leave you with kids and me having another caretaking job."

He thought, never would I let my kids near you if I ever have kids. You'll have to be dead before I ever have children. I won't let you vent your anger and depression on small children.

He often thought about how long it would take before she would die. Later, he'd feel so guilty about his thoughts as he cursed his father for disappearing and leaving him handling his mom on his own.

The year he graduated, he was first in his class. His mother did not attend his ceremony, saying, "You have your day. I have to take care of the Olds. There's no extra money to hire someone just so you can be a big man. I hope you get a good job, but I still have to keep the Olds until I see you will have the character to support us."

He did not let his mother take the shine off this day. Liz, the young woman who had come to his house, asked him why his family had not come. He explained his mother was sick. When she continued her questioning, he initiated the lie he would use in the future about his two sick grandparents who lived with him and who needed continual care. A year later Liz discovered his mother was running a care agency. She confronted him about his lying to her. She knew the patients were not his grandparents and that there were six patients. By this time, he and Liz had what he thought was heading toward a romantic relationship. It was not to be. She told him he had too many unexplained secrets which scared her. He thought, *I'm back where I was in high school and community college. People sniff the strangeness in me. I only lied to protect us from my mother; now Liz barely acknowledges me. I can't at this time promise her anything. Mom is still alive.*

Over the years, he acknowledged regularly thereafter that he had to accept this life until she passed, thinking, it's better than before. I excel at nursing. Everyone wants to know how I know ways to revive the elderly. I've been doing it for twenty years since I was a kid. Every time an Old died, it would take a month to get a new Old. Mom lost income and would bitch and complain. Other nurses and even the doctors treat me with respect. I get good haircuts now. I've put on some weight and don't look like a skeleton. I heard a woman doctor wondering why I was not married yet since I was intelligent, polite, and good looking. They don't understand. I have to wait until Mom dies.

Shirley Baker was working the post-operative gastro floor. She was new to this hospital in Springfield, but was already bored with floor nursing. She'd put in for the emergency room or for surgery and was a little put out she didn't get what she asked for. Her nursing school and previous nursing assignments at other hospitals in Indiana, Chicago, Erie, and Boston sent excellent references. From the scuttlebutt, she learned administration liked to try new nurses from other states in a typical setting before using them in a less controlled setting. She thought it was hogwash. The hospital couldn't keep floor nurses who were under forty because the pay levels were lower. The work was all paperwork; not what she loved about nursing. Shirley loved the rush of patients needing her for immediate solutions, not just fetching for every little need a patient might have. And some of the patients in this unit were divas. It was not a hotel.

However, Shirley was a pro and never, not once in her career, did she show impatience. She remembered the time a doctor's wife was under her care and would threaten to get her fired if she answered the call button a moment too late. The woman could have done it too, because the hospital was one of the last remaining private facilities in the rural region near where Shirley was raised. The doctor was a major investor and had a great deal of control over policy and his wife had a great deal of control over him. She decided then and there to leave her placement for a bigger area hospital. Now she was in her third major hospital placement. She thought, *nasty people are still nasty, but I'll never get fired from here.*

Her friend Elsa, who Shirley frequently lunched with, had given her a new listing of open positions. Elsa knew Shirley craved a change, although she did point out the lack of stress involved in working in gastro, saying, "it's a no brainer, Shirley. Administering meds properly along with familiarity with patient's history and calling in the hospitalist and keeping records of all decisions are things you do in a heartbeat. Other nurses don't understand how to cover their asses. They tend to want to be saviors or to be doctors and take it upon themselves to make decisions. Some are swayed by their patients to do what they're not supposed to do. Tully, our nurse manager on days, watches carefully for any type of bias. We have more patients to deal with than any of the other units. Your organization skills, Shirley, make you a hero here."

Shirley thought about the time when she was not celebrated as a hero. She could never remember getting a compliment from her mother; although her sick grandmother could not refrain from calling her an angel. Nana and Grandpa came to live with Shirley, her brother, and mother after her father was hit by a flash of lightning while coaching a Little League baseball game. Shirley remembered her moments with her dad at his shop. She so missed him but wasn't allowed to talk about him after he died. Later, her nana lost her husband, Shirley's grandfather, before Shirley was in her teen years. Nana's social security, pension, and savings greatly helped the family's resources. She thought, *And Nana was always available and always lovable. I don't know why she came to live with us. Mother was never easy to get along with and after Dad died, she was impossible. Grandpa and Nana could shut her up; in fact, they were the only ones who could. I loved taking care of Nana. She'd go with the flow. Later when I ended up caring for Mom; that was not a joyous trip. Oh, no, it was a living hell. I once asked Nana how someone who was so kind and agreeable could have raised Mom, who was never kind and always disagreeable. She smiled and said, "Genetics gives you what you get. Can't do a damn thing about it. You think your mom's difficult now; imagine when she was a teenager. She was lucky she trapped your dad. He was the best of the lot she brought home; he was a good man who didn't deserve his fate in marriage. Papa often wondered the same thing. He said his daughter was a throwback to the era of hate."*

Years later, after Nana and her mother and brother had died, Shirley shrunk away at first from her orphan status. The deaths themselves did not feel awful at first. Instead she found a sense of freedom from criticism. Her brother shared her mother's personality and when he was diagnosed with multiple myeloma, he would not listen to anyone. Oh no, he refused all care and died much earlier than was necessary. Still, she was alone.

Those years of caretaking almost brought her to a feeling of hopelessness. They died just in time. She now felt whole. She was enjoying life. She had friends. She was in a place where nobody knew her and did not know her mother and brother who were not regarded well in her hometown. No, they were not. And there was the incident at the hospital. Drugs were missing from the hospital. Her brother was an orderly there and had been seen, on camera, entering the larger room containing the locked pharmacy cabinet. Nothing could be proven because the camera was outside the main door and not just outside the cabinet; but it was generally accepted he was the culprit and she knew he was guilty of the theft. Shirley could not live with the subtle gossip always there behind her back. And she so missed Nana, who acted lovingly to her always. And how she had suffered. Good people should not have to suffer. Mama always told her good people should not have to suffer although Mama made her suffer. Am I not a good person was a thought she expressed to some friends who would always say, yes. Yes, this new situation looked good to her.

Shirley knew from her experiences at different hospitals that she was talented, could find placement at any hospital, and that she loved working in a hospital setting. This new placement in this western Massachusetts hospital felt like home to her and she wondered, *I'm ready to make a life here. I feel comfortable, finally.*

6

Mason's Ingenuity

A thoughtful Lieutenant Mason Smith entered the Pit for a morning meeting. He had several reports on different investigations, but an informal report on elderly deaths was in his mind this day and he thought it was explosive. He couldn't wait to share it, but had kept all the info to himself. He thought, *I do love a little drama. I blame all the vocal women in my family. Don't they add emotions to every situation, complicating all decision making? I don't do that, but a little theatrics are good for this unit.*

And his moment came. Lieutenant Mason Smith announced he had evidence of a plethora of questionable elderly deaths, and all of them roadway hit-and-runs. In the last year-to-date there were questionable deaths in the areas from Palmer to Russell to Chicopee to Longmeadow. The hit-and-runs numbered seventeen for men, not women, aged over sixty-five. Further, there were several hospital cases investigated; all were elderly men brought in from nursing homes, two in Wilbraham, three in Westfield, two from West Side, and one from Springfield. "Captain, there are too many deaths of the elderly; now I don't think for a minute all of them qualify as assisted killings. However, these numbers, if graphed, are a reason to call attention to criminal justice agencies or elder support folks or medical auditors, asking if they were aware of these stats. This mess needs, at the very least, a review from us or a referral to the District Attorney."

Ted, personally interested in Howie Blanchard's death in Russell, said, "You know, Captain, I'm a numbers guy. Mason's stats are frightening. More frightening is the idea someone may be selecting among the elderly who to kill. Of the four we've heard about, Buck in Palmer, Herschel in Wilbraham, Lyle in Springfield, and Howie in Russell, they were all hit-and-runs leaving their bodies on the side of the road. Sounds like the same murder weapon or four separate accidents by four separate drunk drivers or one driver selecting who to kill."

Juan was excited and said, "We've done it before, Captain. I'm willing, on my own time, to research their common associates and friends. I'll find out if they had health problems. You know, maybe they wanted to die and deliberately stepped out in front of a car. Lousy way to commit suicide, but a possibility to rule out."

Beauregard agreed and said, "Lilly can take the other hit-and-runs and map their locations. If there is a perp deliberately murdering old guys, we must know if there is a target location. If we are able to map the occurrences' settings, the result could lead to some info on the perp's residence. His hunting for victims and finding a source of particular victims to murder do not appear to be by chance. If there is a murder in any of these cases."

That afternoon found a frazzled Lilly. It took much longer to research all the accidents cases. There was the problem of different cities and towns where they occurred. She could follow traffic and accident reports but it took much more diligence to find the seriousness of the investigation by both traffic and homicide of different police departments. Not one program gave her everything. She noted age of persons killed and only took those where a pedestrian hit by a single car died. She then mapped the locations of the accidents. There was a previous one in West Side. She knew they'd never been informed and couldn't understand why.

Lilly visited Detective Mason Smith's inner sanctum; the only private office in addition to the Captain's and Millie's offices. Mason was a neurotic neatnik; still there were two tables piled with bricks containing files. He apologized for the mess which allowed Lilly to say, "I've never seen such a mess, Mason. You should be ashamed of yourself."

The trouble was Mason was ashamed when he heard her remark, and she realized she had wasted her sarcasm. Per usual, the result was Lilly apologizing again for being a wiseass. She said, "Mason, I sent you a map of all the accidents. I think we can rule out the several in Chicopee, Longmeadow, and East Longmeadow. You take a look and see if you come up with the same logic."

Mason, who loved detail and puzzles and especially challenges, studied the schematic which he did not think could be called a map. And then he saw what Lilly was getting at. Practically every one of the hit-and-runs were located on Route 20, the old Boston Coach Road to Boston. She eliminated several deaths because they were not clustered on Route 20. He then stated, "You have these accidents over two years, not over the past year. The data is more frightening this way. How'd you know to stretch the date time, Lilly?"

"You know me, Mason. I like research. I picked a five-year period because I wanted to see what the norm might be. One hit-and-run to me is too many. The norm in most cities and towns is small or non-existent for events of this type. Holyoke and Chicopee are eliminated because they are not within the cluster and not on Route 20. Notice,

Mason, the dates and locations on Route 20 where the accidents happen. Where there are multiple deaths in an accident, they occur on different spots, not on Route 20 in the city or town. The single deaths of the elderly are all clustered on this road. You'd think the public would be up in arms, but look, three were in Springfield and they were spaced by date by eight months each; all on heavily traveled areas. I know there have to be cameras on some of the areas because there are so many businesses up there. Maybe the Captain can access traffic cams through his connections with each police department. They'd know where the cameras are."

"You have two in West Side. We could easily start with those. Ted could look at the one in Russell. There are two in Westfield spaced-date wise almost twenty-two months apart. Wilbraham has three deaths with two spaced four months apart and the third just recently. That's a pretty small and active community to have those deaths go unnoticed."

"Mason, you know if there is a big public event, even death by accident becomes small news. Maybe these elderly have no one to speak up on their behalf. Palmer has two accidents almost twenty months apart. It may not have been noticeable. Frankly, I have to consider that some of these deaths may be just what they're called, accidental."

Chad enjoyed his new employment in the ER of a city hospital in Massachusetts thinking, I'm free from her and the Olds. Mom finally died, but not without some fuss. I did what she wanted, but never once did she think of me. I love what I'm doing here and my previous work knowledge is not wasted. So many new Olds come in by ambulance from nursing homes and assisted living, I can't help wondering why;

they look nutritionally deprived like Mother's clients. When there is a chance, I question the Olds. Their answers are often similar. They may be afraid of dying, but they're more frightened of living alone or having pain or not being able to get around. I wait to hear the words, "I'd rather die than go on."

Chad remembered when he was nudged by the ER doctor on call to help with a patient brought in by ambulance. He was seriously asthmatic and had the flu. Stabilization was most important and Chad knew the doctor came to him because Chad needed no direction. All the nurses in the ER were chosen mostly for their ability to handle chaos and to make quick decisions. The comments about this new nurse, Chad, were repetitive including, "He should have been a doctor. He knows so much about keeping them alive, etc."

He did like being needed and he had great respect for the elderly and children. He found himself sometimes impatient with patients who were in their forties and fifties. Many had lived unhealthy lives and blamed all their health problems on the medical profession. They'd rant and rave about stupid doctors and slow nurses and why couldn't there be more comfortable beds. All the world's social problems appeared in the emergency room. One could hear constant talk about racism, sexism, homophobia, and fear of people with obvious mental and physical disabilities. Chad often wondered where the religious and God-fearing patients were. Then a few would appear and appease his fears.

He loved this job. He had earned his nurse practitioner's license in another state and had to wait through the endorsement requirement in Massachusetts before he could work at that level. As a nurse practitioner he could prescribe most drugs for patients which made him more valuable when the on-call physician was busy. Chad acclimated to western Massachusetts. He often said to anyone who would listen how he appreciated the beauty of the Pioneer Valley. Whenever he wasn't working he'd take the old route and follow it all the way to the New York border. He could also go to Boston, but the scenery was exceptional going west. He loved that road. He always loved Route 20 and the idea of it; crossing the U.S. from the East to the West Coast caused a flutter of excitement in his heart.

———

Petra was apparently having some difficulty settling down at her desk. Her fidgeting alternating with her visits to the kitchen to charge up whatever level coffee she was drinking drew remarks. Ash said, "Petra, just what is up with you today? If you can't do desk duty, find something in the field worthwhile to do."

Lilly had cocked her ear to the conversation, jumped up, and said, "What say petulant Petra, we do a field trip on Route 20 and investigate the sights of all these accidents? It'll take the day. I've got minimum paperwork."

Both detectives looked around at their peers for criticism; instead they saw heads looking down at their desks. Ash looked up for a second and gave a wink. For Lilly, that was enough. The two decided to start with the one accident in West Side and then go east to Brimfield. Ash suggested they wait for reports on the West Side case. They reversed the strategy going east first. Petra jotted a list of items to be inspected at each site including: nearby nursing homes, public housing for over fifty-fives, small restaurants or bars, lack of lighting and cameras at the site, and the ability to drive unobstructed after the accidents.

There was one accident in Brimfield on a stretch of road near the Brimfield Fairgrounds. They were still awaiting the police report but

Mason had given Lilly a small article from an area paper, The Journal Register. It detailed the location and named the victim as Oscar Pokanewski. The text revealed Oscar lived in a home but was famous for taking two hour walks every Tuesday and Thursday along the road; often having dinner at a nearby well-known restaurant, Francesco's, which was his favorite for Italian food. Folks were used to seeing him and shared the thought that maybe he'd also go for a couple of beers after dinner at a little hide-away nearby. Lilly said, "I know the place. It's an illegal bar in an old guy's house. I was at the Brimfield Fair helping my friend who had an antique furniture stand. We busted up late with the help of some locals who told us to join them at Bud's place. We thought it was a bar and then thought it was some guy's home when we followed them. The bartender charged us and there were lots of older guys in there. Only a few there were women and they were all from Brimfield. Big secret in a small town but known to all. Perhaps the police report will show he was over the alcohol limit, but I don't think so. The paper says Oscar was just a nice sociable veteran liked by everyone. If he were drunk, there would have been some action from the town. Let's see if we can find Bud's place; although it's pretty early in the day to expect it to be open. Maybe it also does coffee. Serving coffee keeps these types of non-licensed bars open all day. One thing certain, Petra, is the patrons will all know about Oscar and how he met his death; and it won't be the party line."

Petra asked, "Do a lot of communities have unlicensed bars in homes? Do we have one in West Side?"

Lilly laughed. "Of course, Petra, over on Dunlap Street in West Side is this brick house built in the twenties. The original owner was a mason and there's a big yard originally used for his trucks and materials. Now visitors park there who are friends of the mason's son. He runs a clean little kitchen with a big table supposedly for his friends to play chess and drink coffee. It's all a crock of course, because it's now an unlicensed bar. Mayor Fischler was all in a snoot to close it based on neighborhood complaints. Really only one neighbor complained. He had built an enormous ranch house for a pricy tag about five doors down across Dunlap Street. He did not like seeing four or five older cars parked on a dirt lot near his home. If they'd been BMWs or Lincolns, it'd be different. Our uniforms would go there hoping to find enough to bring the bar before the licensing commission and sure enough, instead, would discover a brotherhood of old geezers all drinking coffee. There was talk about undercover when the mayor called it all off. Maybe the illegal bar owner gave a big donation. More likely, the mayor got an earful when he visited the senior center and housing complex. Petra, every community, especially ethnic communities might indulge in this practice. As long as it doesn't interfere with regular bar business, no one cares. It's kind of a thing in many communities to have a home-grown bar; think about the stills in the mountain areas in the South. People are all the same in most places; and these old guys can't afford a ten-dollar beer in our restaurants requiring a tip. This way they have their own kind of pork belly environment."

Petra said, "I love this job. Every day I learn something new I should have noticed before. I've been down that street many times and saw those cars, but never put it together. What else don't we know?"

"Lots, Petra, Lots we don't know."

Their drive to Brimfield did not take too long. They headed for the unlicensed bar. The Brimfield bar did not look like any bar Petra had ever seen before. It was a house turned sideways as if it had been constructed on a road perpendicular to the access street. She asked Lilly why anyone would build the house on its side like that. Lilly pointed out the age of the home and the possibility it had been built on a subsidiary planned road that never happened. She also suggested the driveway went behind the house and the entrance was in the rear. Although it was late in the morning, four trucks were parked behind the entrance which had a sign stating, "Welcome, Friends of Bud???"

Bud was not there. Instead a blousy blonde with a mass of sprayed hair, dressed in ripped jeans and a sweatshirt, stood by a counter. She graciously smiled at them. Five men were sitting at a long table with coffee cups in front of them. Silence prevailed. Lilly said, "Hey folks, I'm not here to cause trouble. I know you saw us on your camera and figured we were police. We're from West Side, not from the state or Brimfield. Just here looking for information. We are interested in an accident victim who was killed by a hit-and-run on this road. His name was Oscar Pokanewski. We heard he was a good guy. We're interested in hit-and-run deaths involving older men. We had one in West Side. We want to know if there are common things about their deaths."

Lilly noticed one man maybe in his late sixties moving around on his seat as if in distress. She addressed him. He said, "Finally, someone's looking at Oscar's death. We used to hang around together after his wife and son died. He was a little down then. He was a great guy and always helped anyone in need. He had such skills from plumbing to carpentry. No way was Oscar not paying attention where he walked. And he was fast for his age. He was antsy about working and helping people and joined a group of van drivers from Palmer to Wilbraham who drove the elderly to and from their medical appointments. He was alert and would not be careless in his walking. No sirree, he could move quickly. The hit-and-run driver had to be drunk and went off the side of the road, but those accident investigation cops didn't find a cause. Bullshit; they don't want us to think they can't control the drunk drivers."

And they all talked. They knew everything about Oscar. How he'd recently been let out of orthopedic rehab for a shoulder surgery causing them to be certain he was extra careful when walking. Lilly asked the name of the rehab and it was somewhere near Springfield. They said that a nice nurse became his friend and visited him at home several times. Oscar said she was single and pretty; he wanted to fix her up with Charlie's son who has this great job in hospital security. Charlie spoke up saying, "My son knew her from around the hospital. That's where Oscar met her. It wasn't at rehab. He said she didn't date as far as he knew and he wasn't about to waste his time getting fixed up with someone who wasn't interested or maybe had someone already on the line."

The blonde, still standing at the counter, looked at her cell phone and said, "Cindy, Oscar's landlord, is about to come in here for her late morning coffee."

Not one of the men made a wise remark encouraging Petra to think, maybe this is a coffee shop in the morning. They are a nice group and willing to help.

When Cindy entered, Lilly saw something transpire between Cindy and the blonde; what it was she didn't know. Cindy looked at the two detectives and said, "How can I help you, Detectives."

Since neither one called her, they assumed someone in the bar did; it was easy to decipher the culprit by the small smile on his face. Lilly turned to him and thanked him for helping them with this shortcut. He registered some surprise she knew it was him, but he wasn't embarrassed. Cindy was introduced to them and they soon discovered Cindy was not only Oscar's landlord, she had been his friend. She said, "I accompanied

Oscar for years in his career. I was a kid and thrilled to be on stage with the great Oscar Poski, his stage name. He was a Southern boy and a rather famous Country Western singer and songwriter. Imagine him settling in Brimfield but he loved this town. Said it reminded him of his home town in Mississippi.

"Oscar married later in life to my mom's best friend's daughter. Oscar and Shelley had a son who was surely special and the light of their lives. When the boy started second grade, Oscar gave up his career for a better family life. I went on to accompany some of his friends in their bands, but it wasn't the same, so, I came home here and became a social worker. Shelley and I were inseparable, and their family life was everything to them and to me. I'd avoided having my own family myself but probably secretly wanted one like Oscar and Shelley had. Never once did they not include me in family celebrations. A few years before his death, Shelley and Oscar, Jr. were killed, not immediately but later from injuries, in a train crash near Philadelphia. It took Oscar Jr. two months to die, while Shelley died in two weeks. Oscar was a basket case of suffering. So much so I was worried for him and insisted he come live with me. He had all the money he needed but he needed us; my family and me. That was in 2015. I'll tell you, Detectives, Oscar was a careful man. I think the driver was drunk. The road is dark when the fair is not there, but Oscar knew every inch of the road. He would typically have dinner on Tuesdays at Francesco's. Everybody knew him there. After dinner he was noted for walking a couple of miles before he'd come home. My house is past the end of the fairgrounds going towards Sturbridge. He'd have been on the sidewalk. The driver may have been texting but I doubt it; it was after nine o'clock on an early spring evening. The driver, in my mind, was drunk. I want him caught. The police got a piece of a fender. You can't tell me they couldn't find the car. They weren't looking. Oscar is famous in the South and he dies here where he lives and no one does anything to find the driver? I'm pissed. What can you do for Oscar, Detectives, what can you do? You're from West Side."

Petra's answer did not assuage Cindy; but she did not react, just sighed. Petra said, "We're investigating all accidents along this road. We had one in West Side. We think there has to be more effort expended by the police to help the elderly on these roadsides; at the very least give them public service announcements about safety. If we find the deaths are a result of drunk drivers, then of course, attention will be given to prevention."

Cindy, the blonde, and the men all snickered. Lilly pursued some questions about Oscar's health history and other associations. She specifically asked if they knew the name of the nurse who had connected with Oscar after his shoulder surgery. Cindy had met her but could not remember her surname, just her Christian name which was 'Shirley.'

The detectives moved to leave, were asked for their cards, and were told by the blonde, "Keep us in the know and we'll keep your visit quiet. The local cops would be all over you for this visit."

Petra replied, "No problem. Our Captain informed them before we came."

On their following Route 20 back, Lilly said, "Why'd you say that, Petra, the Captain didn't make a call, did he?"

"Maybe not yet. I'm calling him now. That group won't talk for a day. We have what info is available. I'm going to call the Captain now to rectify this situation."

Beauregard gave Petra some guff, but said he'd make the call. The visit to Brimfield had taken much too long. The two detectives decided to stop in Palmer for some lunch figuring they'd get their Palmer death site survey done and head home. They went past the site on their notes and had to double back. This site was located before they re-entered Palmer center. It was near the Depot Plaza on the north side of Route 20. They had notes on the death of Buck Gagnon, again from the Journal Register which serviced Palmer and several smaller communities. The paper said Buck was returning from getting some food at the Apollo Pizza House. He often went there and met friends, mainly towards the end of the week. This night was fairly cold and the piece stated he may have hurried as there was a wide driveway accessing a building and he was found on the east side of the driveway. The auto driver was going west and apparently mistook the driveway for road and hit Buck while he was still on the edge of the sidewalk.

Petra and Lilly could see how it may have been an accident; still they both thought the car driver may have been impaired. To be so far over onto the driveway meant the driver was not following the center line. The driveway was before the Depot Plaza. They both agreed it was slightly weird. The detectives decided to eat at Apollo's Pizza since it was right there. They checked the online menu and both liked the looks of the baked spaghetti dish which Lilly told Petra, "Maybe someone will remember that evening while we load our bodies with carbs."

———

Shirley was tested today by the overload of emergency room victims. The icy conditions outside brought in many slips and falls. Her colleagues, she knew, relied on her to cover when there was an overabundance of work. Dr. Teague, with whom the other female nurses sought to ingratiate themselves, clearly preferred to work with Shirley. It annoyed many of them, but they all knew Shirley was the best at battling in the trenches and her speed at every activity apparently pleased the good doctor. Most thought Dr. Teague, a single man in his mid-thirties and not gay, was ripe for the pickings; and they were confused when Shirley did not act on his obvious attraction to her. Her nurse friend, Dottie, asked her why she didn't just give him the nod and her answer was, "It's up to him to let me know. I don't make decisions in the shadows. Let him tell me about himself. Mainly, I don't know if he's ever been married or has some children. He flirts at work. I don't get that. Let him ask me out to dinner. We'll talk and see where it goes from there. Nurses dating every doctor in the ER will end up very disappointed. I don't need disappointments in life. I've had enough and they always involved people who I had a right to have expectations from. All were dashed. I'd rather be on my own and plan for my life with no one interfering."

Dottie insisted, "Shirley, you are living in the eighteen hundreds. The guy is shy. He needs a bit of an invite."

"Dottie, he's not shy when he's clearly able to flirt. What makes you think he's shy? What do you know about him that would be of interest to me aside from his cuteness? I don't want trouble in my life; my family life was enough for me."

"Dr. Teague is from this area and came back to practice here. That alone tells me he's not hiding. He did his residency at Beth Israel in Boston. He's good. Get out of your shell, Shirley."

"You did this to me before, Dottie. I dated that nurse who was handsome and a great nurse. I went with him on three dinner dates. He's really caring about the elderly, but something about him is strange. When I didn't go on the fourth date, he treated me differently."

"Shirley, guys don't like being rejected; that's what his behavior indicates. It's nothing more than that."

7

One Death Ignites

Mona Beauregard and Sheri Cull were volunteering at the West Side Friends of Community Association FCA. Sheri laughed at Mona who knew every volunteer, more than Sheri, saying, "You work full-time teaching at the high school, Mona, when do you find time for all this?"

Mona said, "I only returned to teaching last year. I've eighteen years of volunteering. You meet some of the best and kindest people; you also meet some who desire control. I hate it when that type of person is in charge. Alienation of helpers becomes the main outcome then."

The two were joined by five other women and two men working furiously on the St. Patrick's Parade project float for the Holyoke parade given the parade date was very close. Sheri had drawn the original design for the float meant to showcase the Colleen and her Court. The theme was "Roots of Ireland" and the Colleen and her Court were to be dressed in Irish dress sitting outside an Irish cottage replica. The volunteer carpenters had finished framing. The painters had finished also. Now this crew were laying fake grass and filling planters. They would use artificial flowers donated by Smythe's Flower Emporium on Main Street. They could not use real flowers because they didn't have a big enough workforce for any last-minute staging with real flowers.

The Court ladies would carry real flowers donated by the West Side Flower Shop. The group was content with the production in front of them, certain they may get at least an honorable mention for floats. They even used a created fake dog who resembled Buck in the new movie, "Call of the Wild." He was beautifully done by a bunch of college kids.

The major parade organizer who was also the proprietor of the Healthy Living Café, walked over to the workers and just stood and stared. Lance had tears in his eyes. They all noticed. Lance was not that kind of man. Mona said, "Tell us, Lance; what's up?"

He cried and couldn't get the words out easily, finally saying, "Stan is dead. Stan Korsecki is dead. Do you understand?"

Lance sat and continued to repeat his message. Mona sat next to him, hugging him. She said, "I know you were close. The standard Polish lover of food and you, the clean no gluten, no sugar, vegetarian. Tell me what happened."

Obvious to all present was Mona attempting to pull Lance from his depression by explaining what happened to Stan. They did not remember his being ill other than his short colon surgery hospitalization last year. They had not heard about related problems. But in their minds, you could almost see the Big C as a possibility. Lance shook his head and said, "What an awful way he went. Stan was hit by a drunk driver last night. He had just been outside the Senior Center. He'd helped the van drivers who parked their vans there to put on the locks. He did that three nights a week if he was around. You know we got new locks two years ago when those kids took the vans for joyriding and caused a lot of damage. The drivers have trouble with the locks, but Stan could do anything. What an awful, awful way to go. The driver should be shot."

Sheri and Mona looked at each other. Mona asked, "Lance, have they found the car and driver? It wasn't a hit-and-run, was it?"

"Yeah, and they haven't found the driver. No one's out that way that time of night. Other than the two houses where he was hit, there's nothing else out there and there is little lighting. He actually got hit after he crossed the street to walk home. He lived on a side street, not far from the Senior Center. Stan was right in front of those two houses. The car must have gone up on the sidewalk, because they found him on the sidewalk the next morning, today, early. I heard he was there all night. There was no one at home to miss him."

And Lance continued to cry. It took over a half hour before any of the group felt Lance could be left alone. In fact, Sheri begged him to come home with her. She suggested he may want to talk with Norbie about the accident. Lance said, "What can he do, Sheri? Bring him back from the dead? Stan's up there with his ladies. He's happy now."

Who could argue with that vision?

Rudy Beauregard was eating half of a salad from B Napoli's in West Springfield. Millie, MCU's admin staff, placed the order for the unit meeting which included all unit leaders and Chief Coyne. Major Crimes had the largest conference room in the department and one of the costs of this prized asset was that it be used for the monthly units meeting, which fortunately, based on an overload of policing problems, was only held bi-monthly. While the other Captains or Lieutenants in charge munched on pizza, pasta, and chicken marsala, Rudy ate sparingly. This caused an inordinate amount of comments from his colleagues. Finally, in disgust Beauregard said, "I am not blessed with a high energy metabolism and must use denial to balance out this DNA deficit."

The hoots and hollers following lightened the atmosphere as each unit department head gave reports. When Captain Murray gave his traffic report, there was a quiet in the room, unlike any such silence normally experienced at these meetings. Chief Coyne was the first to speak and he eloquently stated what the others were thinking. "Stan Korsecki is one man I could respect, and to die like this is a tragedy. Captain Murray has the state police accident reconstruction team report and the results are concerning. If Captain Beauregard said what I'm going to say, well, I would shut him down; but he's be right to be concerned, and Captain Murray is concerned. The driver of the car went way up over the sidewalk. There is a good curb there. The driver would have to be exceedingly drunk not to feel the vehicle was out of control. It was nighttime and even the worst of the cell phone nuts would have difficulty texting. Not that it couldn't happen, but if it did, in that case the driver would probably have felt it and corrected his drive. The tread marks show over a twenty-foot track from when the car accessed the curb before it hit Stan. That's a long distance. At any rate, it is, in my estimation, a drunk driving event or a deliberate hit-and-run. Captains Murray and Beauregard, I hope, are available to investigate this event. I want a report on my desk within ten days. I know you have other duties, but my office has been inundated with calls about Mr. Korsecki's untimely death."

The meeting continued for close to two more hours. Beauregard thought, this high-end lunch was scant reward for the endless detailing in notes the attendees were required to do. Coyne seems quite pleased with himself dumping this public relations matter on Murray and me. I imagine he'll tell all callers in the future he has two high level and respected captains investigating. He expects no results from us, but I am not so sure…I am not so sure!

Later, Captain Murray met with Beauregard in Beauregard's office. They'd each brought a latte in from the kitchen with Murray saying, "MCU is so important it has a commercial espresso machine. How'd you swing that, Rudy?"

"Easy, Frank, we all contributed to the coffee fund but brought in our own coffee supplies for six months; after that we had the money to buy the machine. It is the only socialist movement you'll see in this unit. So, tell me what you think about this getting you and me to work on a project without any definition, but with an absolute finish date?"

"It's all Coyne's bullshit to cover his back, but to be truthful, Rudy, I did tell him I thought there was a problem with this accident and the report. It wasn't a stretch to say the driver couldn't correct the trajectory if he was awake; even if he was drunk as a skunk, the car should have gone into the bushes at ten feet. What the Chief didn't talk about is that the skid marks show a deliberate correction toward Mr. Korsecki's direction. We did a quick check on him and his financials. Nothing showed up. Who, just who, would deliberately go after him is a mystery unless the driver just didn't like old men, or knew him in some fashion and didn't like him."

"Frank, do you remember a hit-and-run death accident involving an older man from West Side? I think it was an accident also involving an elderly man almost two years ago."

Frank Murray responded with almost a suspicious look, saying, "Rudy, how did you know I was looking at the early hit?"

"Because I know you, Frank. If you felt suspicious about an accident and couldn't confirm it was anything more, you'd do what I'd do."

"And what's that, Rudy, invent a serial murder case?"

"It never starts that way. I just don't create a case. The murders find me. But I know you. Spill the beans now, please, we've only got a couple of weeks. Time is limited and if there really is something to find I want to move on it; especially if it's not an accident."

Frank opened Stan Korsecki's file which was oversized for an auto accident event. Rudy studied the photos of the skid marks made by the auto, the auto's tire treads, and the body lying in situ. Frank patiently watched him noticing Rudy was in his own world. He thought, *this is how the big man works. I've heard about his concentrating abilities, when he forgets who's around him. He is slow moving and generally amicable but on the quiet side. Must save all his energy to brainstorm and focus.*

A long fifteen minutes passed before Rudy seemed to remember just where he was. He looked at Frank and said, "What was the older accident like? Did it resemble this one? You are oh so right, Frank, this was no accident. I'm totally baffled about who would want to kill Stan Korsecki; and kill him in this manner. The tracks went over him and they look like the car backed up and went over him again, when the driver would normally just turn his wheel to go forward to escape from the scene. The report is inconclusive with suspicion of a drunk driving event, but even a drunk would have just turned the wheel to the left. It stinks. I know the photo is a bit blurry, but this is what I see. Were you at the site when the photos were taken?"

"I was and I saw what you are seeing, Rudy, but it was clearer in reality. Accident reconstruction was made from these photos and a later visit to the scene. I was disappointed. The report said it was probably a driver not in control of his vehicle. Nothing was said about what you and I see; but then again, I thought maybe I was imagining details. Thank you for confirming my suspicions."

"Frank, it's there in black and white, but the body is facing the direction of the oncoming auto. Stan saw the car coming at him. Why didn't he jump over the wall?"

"He may not have had enough time. Also, Rudy, Stan had two knee replacements; they may have placed some limitations on his ability to move quickly. The wall is over three feet high and I question whether he could easily jump over it."

"I'd like Sergeant Ted Torrington to take a look at this. He loves to use details to solve problems. It's a real turn-on for him. You have the autopsy report?"

"I do. It's all in here. There are a few surprises in it. Stan had a bad ticker. Despite that, he volunteered for any non-profit out there. We all loved him."

"Yeah, Frank, and he dies without sharing his chili recipe. What about the other death? Does it also present some questions?"

"Rudy, I was transferred to traffic eighteen months ago. I have it here. It's really slim for a death. I didn't even know about it until one of the uniforms mentioned it on the day of Stan's accident. He seemed to remember it well. He told me Captain Spirito wasn't well at the time of the accident. In fact, he went on sick leave at about then. I came in later; the unit had a lieutenant filling in until an appointment was made. The covering lieutenant died seven months later of a massive coronary about the time the Captain also died of some heart problem. If you find anything suspicious, I can only say it fell through the cracks."

Beauregard took the two files, one heavier than the other, with the written name of the officer in the know, and thanked Frank.

———

Detective Ted Torrington was pleased with his two hours of paper investigations into the two West Side accident files. He thought, *there's no doubt in my mind. Stan Korsecki was hunted down. The driver, for whatever reason, deliberately went after him. The reason could be a kid who hated old people or hated Stan, but it was not an accident. I've made this list of Stan's friends and associates. It'll take a couple of days to make calls to them to hone in on who might really know something about his routine. The Captain insisted I work fast and I don't mind. I love the excitement of a little pressure; it pushes me.*

I'm lucky to have a record of Stan's routine from his pocket calendar found on his body. I guess at his age, he used a pocket calendar and his iPhone shows no use of a calendar. He probably didn't trust new technology.

Ted asked Ash to help him with calls. Since Ash had only paperwork ahead of him, he was delighted to assist; especially when Ted assured him this was the Captain's special interest case.

Petra and Juan were stuck filing away paperwork today while Lilly was chasing an interview on a suspected assault and battery case at a convenience store. When they heard a repetition of phone calls made by Ash and Ted who gave all the callers the same message, they insisted Ted and Ash explain what was up. They both wanted in on the project. Their desire needed no explanation; they were bored. The four detectives worked the phones for several hours and were able to schedule ten interviews; eight on Stan's accident and two on Ray LeFron's accident. Four of them were scheduled for this afternoon with two detective teams set to interview two each. They went back to their paperwork happily eating lunch at their desks. Petra was heard to say, "Finally, some action in a day that wasn't promising."

At two o'clock, Ash and Ted met with the owner of the home located at the Stan Korsecki accident site. Jay Parkins, the owner, had much to say. He'd heard the noise vaguely because the television was on and he was falling off to sleep. "This is why I didn't look out my front windows right away. I do have spotlights but they're aimed toward my walkways near my house. When I finally looked, a car was skidding onto the street, and I saw my stone wall was smashed. I cursed, but I didn't go out to inspect. When I did; well, I've never seen a dead body before. And I know him, or I should say I knew Stan. Detectives, please find out if he died immediately. If I could have saved him, well, I'll never forgive myself."

Ash answered the hanging question. "I'm pretty certain, from what I know from the police report, Stan was killed immediately. Don't go there, Mr. Parkins. It would be foolish to think you had responsibility for what happened. You didn't. What you can help me with is what your heard, what you saw, and what you felt at the time. I do want to know about your next-door neighbor. Your house and his are the only two within the area. I don't have that house on my witness list. Was he not at home?"

"He's a she and she's at her home on the Connecticut shore with her sister. She'll be home at the end of the month. I don't know why she goes there instead of Florida; it's as cold there as here.

"I heard a noise when he hit the wall; then I heard him back up to go forward; next the driver revved up to go forward. I saw the vehicle right after it hit the street. This is a main road, but no traffic dawdling over here, and I think a driver who might have seen something, in the dark, would just see a car when it pulled back out to the road. I saw the car then and there were no other cars passing at the time. In the morning when I saw Stan, I don't remember much. Sorry, Detectives, nothing else to tell you."

Ash and Ted headed around the corner for their meeting with Stan Korsecki's neighbor and friend. Derek Connor was waiting for them by the end of his condo's driveway. Derek was dressed in what Ted's wife Charlotte would call 'spiffy togs.' He was a friendly and talkative man who insisted they walk through Stan's condo, saying, "You have to see his digs to know about him." When they entered what they thought was a decent almost high cost condo, they saw the interior décor which tested their design sensibilities. Every wall held plaques representing awards of service from about every element in society. The centerpiece was a large needlepoint square. There was a message on it saying, 'MY LIFE.'

Every room had additional decorations aside from the master bedroom and two baths. Derek commented, "Do you now see what we've lost? When his wife was living, they occupied a large colonial decorated to the nines and none of these awards were displayed. He adored his wife. Later he met his lady friend, Lucille. She wasn't much of a house person, so he bought this condo. She decorated the walls with his awards. Lucille insisted he should see his accomplishments. He told me that no one came by and they would never see the lavish display. If they had a lot of company, he'd have put a stop to it. I have to say Lucille was a great gal. Naturally, a guy like Stan was in sales. In his office all his sales awards, many national, are displayed. He worked sales in several industries, a couple in technical parts. Stan was pretty bright and, boy, he understood people. Detectives, I don't believe this was an accident."

Ted asked about any recent associations Stan had. Derek said he had coffee with a nurse from the hospital where he'd had his surgery recently, saying, "He fought arthritis with vengeance. I saw him through two knee surgeries and he'd say the same thing every morning to me, 'I'm going to fuckin walk normally.'"

Ted continued. "What about the colon surgery; was it cancer?"

"He didn't tell me, but he wouldn't. I would not be surprised because he kept his connection with the nurse from the hospital. He said she was special. She had a friend who was a male nurse. Stan thought he was really professional at his job. He thought the two of them would make a great couple, but Shirley , the nurse's name, said she had reservations."

It took another hour of small talk all focused on Stan and his life before the detectives could start the goodbye process. Derek did not know Shirley's last name or the name of the male nurse, but stated they both worked in the emergency room at the hospital. He couldn't remember which one, but probably it was either Bay State or Mercy or some affiliate. Derek did settle the question on whether Stan had any enemies, saying, "Not a one. Stan could turn any negative into a positive. He was the best of salesmen through and through. I'm sales resistant but Stan could sell me anything. This guy was a good husband, significant other, neighbor, and friend. I only hope his death saved him from dying slowly of cancer. He'd never told me what the diagnosis was, but he was in the hospital for a few days and weak as hell when he came home. The hospitals keep you overnight for most normal procedures and another friend of mine had two stents put in his heart and came home the same day. I think those two nurses knew he was alone, facing a serious threat. No nurse ever came and visited me after surgery. These nurses were not VNAs."

Ted and Ash determined to investigate the identities of the two nurses, when Ash reminded Ted of the report on the Brimfield hit-and-run Petra and Lilly had shared. Ted agreed, saying, "The Captain doesn't like coincidences and neither do I. Shirley is not so common a name among younger people today. If it's the same Shirley, she would be the commonality for two of these guys. Commonality can be an indicator and connection is important."

The woman sitting in the conference room waiting for Lieutenant Aylewood-Locke and Sergeant Tagliano was a handsome brunette dressed in a very short romper; Petra thought, *she can carry it off, but if I were being interviewed by the police, I'd not wear it. The Desk Sergeant was effusive when he announced she was waiting. I see why. She doesn't look cheap.*

Petra initiated the interview with introductions and questions relative to Melody Burns' relationship to Ray LeFron. Melody answered in a sexy, husky voice in keeping with her dress. She said, "I apologize for my outfit, but I'm just back from a shoot for a TV commercial. I was drinking at a local restaurant on the outside porch. It was freezing, but the commercial will be run for the spring and summer seasons. I put my coat over this and had to race to make the appointment. The photographer did so many shots, I thought I'd never get finished.

"As to Ray, I grew up in the house next to his. He was the perennial bachelor. When I was young I'd watch him march different ladies in; most only lasted six months. Then there was Lucy. He must have been sixty and it was a love story. At least I saw it that way. This groovy guy was bonkers over a woman ten years his junior and she surely showed she felt the same. They never married. Since I always hung around Ray's house, I asked him why? He said it was strictly financial. If she married she'd lose her social security and her ex-husband's payments in lieu of a property a settlement or something. She did not want to be beholden to Ray. He said and I quote, 'A woman needs to be financially independent and it's most important in her later years.' And then Lucy has a major heart attack while sleeping. He was seventy-two then. It was four years ago. He tried to continue his activities, but he was hospitalized many times in the first year after her death from some lung issues. He used to be a smoker; so, I'm thinking the bouts were all from compromised lungs. Although I really think he was suffering from Lucy's death and never got over it."

Lilly asked, "Melody, you know quite a lot about his health. Are you in the medical field?"

"Yes and no. I work for a large healthcare agency in marketing and administration. They never say marketing; I have to be an administrator for a program for them to get reimbursed funding; marketing wouldn't get reimbursed. The modelling business is a side activity, just for fun. The agencies pay me well, but I do a lot of free work for non-profits for their advertising at a reduced rate. I'm aware, far more than I want to be, of medical issues. I could see Ray's color on his face change. It tinged toward gray and he was slowing down. He was hospitalized a few months ago. I met one of his nurses. She was very good to him.

"Detectives, Ray helped me. He paid part of my tuition for my last two years in college. My dad had died and because of a lack of funds, I was going to quit school. He wouldn't let me. He sent Lucy to explain to my mother it was okay for me to accept. Mom wouldn't trust any man giving me money. Lucy did that. Ray should not have died the way he did. What's worse was the driver was never found. He was killed a half-mile away from his home on the two-lane highway in town heading toward Westfield. He'd take nightly walks to settle down. It's all sidewalks. The car came over the sidewalk. The news inferred he wasn't killed instantly. It's not fair. He took over for my father. I loved him. He should not have died that way and I want the driver caught. I want to stop this driver from hurting another Ray."

Lilly asked her question. "Melody, do you remember the nurse's name who visited Ray after his last hospitalization?"

"I'm not sure. Maybe it's Shelley or Sheila; it's something like one of those names. I never met her. I did see her going in Ray's house one day. She was very pretty and in her early thirties. She has a beige Honda SUV and moves quickly. He told me she was very kind and worried about him. He liked that; Lucy worried about him and he felt safe again, I just think that, Detectives; I don't know it."

Petra and Lilly joined the other detectives and shared their notes. Ted agreed with the idea; finding Shirley may be important. He said, "She's been mentioned in three cases by name. Looking for a Shirley may not reap rewards, but is still worth investigating. The Captain does not like that type of consistency in facts in multiple investigations. I'll talk to him."

8

Fighting Romance

Shirley faced what she told her friend Dottie was her dilemma, accepting a date with Dr. Teague, who asked her to call him, Jesse. She liked the name, Jesse. The whole ER staff knew almost immediately the two of them, the nurse and the doctor, were to have dinner on Saturday night. She thought, *just how could they all know. I told no one. This place is a gossip sewer. Dottie said it was his extra smiling at me. If that's all it takes to assume I'm dating someone, I'm going to screw with them.*

And Shirley did just that. Not one other person picked up on it other than Chad. He did not notice her not smiling at others; only her not smiling at him. Chad's attitude was noticed by the other staff including Dr. Teague, who had major control in this ER and used it. Dr. Teague kept Shirley exclusively following him in all patient care, while Chad was the first on scene with each patient. The other nurses did not question the process because nobody was better than Chad in accessing seriousness of injuries. In addition, he worked faster than the others, and he was patient with language or aging or disabilities in a patient and/or relatives articulating their concerns. The other nurses were somewhat relieved to follow up after the first interview and setup. Only Chad and Shirley perceived the changes.

On Saturday evening, at the Frontera Grill located on Boston Road in Springfield, Shirley questioned Jesse Teague about the informal changes in process at the ER, saying, "You know Jesse, I do occasionally see Chad for dinner."

"Is it a problem for you that I like you too?"

Shirley's cheeks smarted. She answered, "No. It's not a problem, but I noticed you made changes at work. I need to be assured you won't let our having dinner influence staff assignments. I don't wish to be involved in work problems. You can understand, can't you?"

"Yup, I understand and I won't create any disharmony at work for any of us; okay?"

Shirley nodded happily when she saw him give her a big smile.

———

Ashton Lent was quiet this morning and all the coffee he drank did not help the situation. He was jumpy today; more so than usual. Juan, known as always attentive to the feelings of others, couldn't prevent himself from asking the question, "What's wrong, Ash? It's not like you to not embrace this investigation with vigor. You've barely responded to our insights."

Ash grumbled and instead of answering the question, asked another question. "The Captain has to make this right with the chiefs from other police departments because the sites of these deaths are not in our bailiwick. It's bigger than us. I know he's taken care of Brimfield, but if word gets out we're looking at what, five to seven other districts, he'll be in deep shit. Has he mentioned what he's doing about this?"

"Captain Beauregard never 'mentions' anything. You know that. He announces when he's ready, and has called a meeting for ten o'clock today. Ash, don't change the subject. What's up?"

Looking pale and decidedly distressed, Ash said, "I think Martina's in trouble. She's been to a heart specialist at MGH (Massachusetts General Hospital). She won't tell me how bad it is, but I know it's bad. She wants to get married. I've begged her to marry me many times, and now after this doctor's visit, she wants to marry me. She wants to make wills and says it's important for Elisa to realize I'm her step-father, not just Martina's boyfriend. I don't believe her. Elisa and I are good friends and she thinks of me as her father. Elisa wants nothing to do with her biological father. I just know Martina heard something serious from the doctor. She's planning to have a 'procedure' done and told me not to worry. I explained I would not let her go alone. We had an argument. Martina doesn't argue. Elisa wants to go with me. Martina's in trouble. She's always tired and her skin lacks good color. She gets out of breath easily when we walk. I know Martina is seriously ill."

Ted and Petra overheard the conversation. There was quiet in the Pit. Uncomfortable with silence, Petra said, "I think you may be right, Ash, but you also are required to respect her privacy. Jim wants to know everything about my health. Sometimes it rankles me. Could be what this is. If she's seriously ill, it doesn't matter what she's willing to tell you, your job is to support her. You and Elisa go with her for her surgery. Stay in a hotel near Mass General. There are several reasonable ones servicing the hospital. Eventually she'll tell you. It's so frightening when a patient's waiting for surgery; I think it's then she'll open up. Marry her. No matter what else is up, it's what she and you want. Have you talked with her parents?"

Ash replied, "Yeah. They know about her having a 'procedure' and they couldn't get more info either. Her mom is frustrated with what she calls Martina's insistence on suffering alone; she believes she's already caused too much trouble in life. She said, 'A lot of good Dr. Rodrigues did. He could never help her get over having a guilty conscience.'"

Ted stated hesitantly, "Ash, when you marry her, right afterward, insist you get a healthcare proxy for you or Elisa or her parents. She may not want to divulge anything, but the hospital will insist she state someone before she has surgery; and it sounds like it's a surgery and not a procedure to me. I'm betting she'll only trust you. Don't take any of Martina's attitude as a lack of trust in you. She sounds petrified and I think she is trying to find her way through this all."

Captain Beauregard walked into a room filled with detectives, and immediately seemed to assess the situation enough not to make any remarks. Petra thought, *the Captain knows something's up, but his sixth sense has held him back. Thank his cop's insight; Ash is not ready for more discussion.*

The meeting started as most such meetings with a review of the most difficult cases handled first. There were not many. Next on the agenda for discussion were the West Side hit-and-run cases. He'd reviewed the reports questioning whether there were some assumptions the detectives could make which would of course not be in the reports. Beauregard listened carefully. Petra and Lilly's report on the Brimfield and Palmer hit-and-runs became the new topic triggering Ted to ask, "How do we continue, Captain, without stepping on the toes of other police departments?"

The Captain announced the content of his conversation with the Hampden County District Attorney, saying, "The DA grilled me on the substance of our assertions when I said there is something more there. I did not use the term serial killings, although I think I could have, given the same weapon used and the similar profile of the victims. I believe

I convinced him when I discussed the Stan Korsecki case. He knew Stan; I guess every person in the county knew Stan. I told him about the shifting of the car and its backing up which I could not in good conscience call the work of a drunk driver. It shook him. He sounded emotional when he said he was horrified that an elderly man could be chosen for such a kill; and if there was some perp out there with that in mind, he would go to ends of the earth to stop him. I heard the DA has a wonderful relationship with his dad who is also well-known.

"Whatever his reasoning is, the decision is to put me in charge of a hit-and-run task force. It's fortunate all the deaths we're looking at are in Hampden County. Officers from the state police, Springfield and Wilbraham police, including two known as serious accident reconstruction specialists, will serve on the task force. This is a win-win for us. We are now authorized to investigate in any of the related towns and cities. He found your cluster map showing the location of the deaths all along Route 20 interesting. It's a go."

The detectives worked on assigning investigative interviews in the remaining deaths. Ted would concentrate on Russell and Westfield; Petra on Palmer and Wilbraham; Lilly on West Springfield; and Juan on Sturbridge. Bill would develop multiple murder boards and further investigate West Side deaths. Mason volunteered to man the phones for ongoing problems, with the Captain agreeing to fill in on dailies. Lilly insisted since she only had one town and it was nearby, she would pick up any slack. She said, "Captain, I don't know what the perp is getting out of these deaths. So far, I don't see, from the data we have, a financial motive. Normally we find some family members who want to get rid of a father for his house or money. I'm scratching my head over other motives for killing the elderly. Does some nut want to save Medicare costs? Maybe the perp just hates old folks? Like the Spider's son in the drug case who wanted to get rid of the established hoods, maybe the perp gets off on murder; or it could be mercy killing. If that is so, driving over them in a car is not a nice way to mercy kill."

Juan said, "We see mercy killing in victims' homes or nursing homes or rehab centers or hospitals; but by poison or smothering them with pillows, not by running them over."

Ash said, "Killing all these elderly men is not mercy killing. The perp may think it's what he's doing, but there's hate there. Imagine if that guy in Palmer or one of the ones in West Side were discovered still alive, which were distinct possibilities, how merciful would the resulting suffering be? Captain, you have a psychopath on your hands. He covers up his murderous work by stealing cars, choosing to kill at night from eight to ten, and leaving no evidence. He's smart choosing different towns and spreading the deaths over time. He doesn't want to get caught. He's not looking for notoriety. What is he looking for?"

A discussion ensued, stopped only by Ted who had observed there was an acceleration in dates between the accidents recently. He said, "What do you think, Captain? He's got a taste for this. He's going to keep it up. He thinks he's not going to get caught."

Beauregard responded, "He is going to get caught, Sergeant, and we're going to catch him. If there is an acceleration in his murders, he'll help us with a solution. Acceleration infers his emotions are getting in the way of his planning."

Chad took some advice from Dottie. He knew Dottie liked him better than Doctor Teague, or at least he thought she did. He was certain based on her reaction when the Doctor changed operations protocol and used Shirley as his follow-up and connected at the hip, nurse. She complained bitterly to some of the other staff. Chad overheard the complaints. "I thought it was a good idea for them to date. I like Shirley, but who wants to be a second-class citizen to Shirley. It's not even as if they've slept together yet; when it happens, we'll really be shafted."

Chad did remind Dottie that Shirley was also a nurse practitioner, and that status would always get a better position. Dottie said, "Chad, you're a nurse practitioner. We have two of you and a medical doctor in the ER. The initial work to assess seriousness should be divided between you and Shirley. Following the doctor to implement ordinary procedures is our responsibility. At least it's always been our protocol here when we have this level of staffing."

Dottie started having lunch with him. Chad got all the dirt from her. Although it forced him to learn far more than he wished about her domestic life as a single mother with two children. He thought, *I hope those kids have a better life than I had with my single mother. Then again, Dottie is not running a boarding house for the infirmed elderly. Dottie is a doting mother. She really tries to do right by the kids. She wants Dr. Teague to do right by us, but he's about himself. Dottie says I'm as good looking as Dr. Teague. I don't know; what I do know is any looks I have, came later after I got enough food in my belly to fill out. I hate to think about those days when I was always hungry. My shrink told me I do well because I don't often look back and reflect about the horror I had no control over. She told me to look forward to the good I do, and to focus on the possibility of experiencing happiness every day. I think it's good advice. It's not that easy to do, but I do try.*"

Encouraged by a more positive perspective, he again asked Shirley to dinner. Her response was interesting before she said yes. "Chad, you've been decidedly unfriendly to me until lately. What was the cause?"

"Shirley, it looked to me as if you no longer had any interest in other than Dr. Teague."

She looked sharply at him, but said, "I think when things don't go your way, Chad, you avoid confrontation and even discussion. In my mind, sometimes you show insecurity and I don't know why. I ask you a question and instead of answering me, you question why I ask you a question. This practice gets old fast."

He was silent for a moment. "Shirley, I guess it's not surprising you picked up on that. I have a habit of avoiding confrontation; which when I look back, I know it was a necessary habit to survive my childhood. Someday I'll explain it to you; someday. Don't think I don't want to directly face a person who has infringed on my good intentions. I do, but I am afraid of my anger, so I don't."

"Well, Chad, dinner looks good for me. What about we don't go to a restaurant on Boston Road. We could get some Asian or Italian food elsewhere; anywhere there is a beauteous setting."

Chad thought carefully, searching for a restaurant with a setting and finally offered a choice between a New England favorite, The Storrowton Tavern in West Springfield or the German restaurant called The Fort in Springfield. Shirley chose The Fort.

Chad was at first ecstatic Shirley agreed to dinner, but then, the ghost of his childhood clouded his mind with thoughts comparing himself to Dr. Teague. He came through as a loser in comparison. He reviewed his situation. He owned a very nice home in Wilbraham with a low mortgage, his own car which was paid for, and in addition to a pension plan he had accumulated a nice investment account. Still, he was a nurse practitioner not a doctor. The final problem was he had no confidence he could compete with Teague. Then again, he was having dinner with

Shirley on Saturday night. She'd already had her date with Dr. Teague, and still she was going out to dinner with him. Dottie's support was all he needed to keep faith.

Dr. Jesse Teague watched Shirley as she moved swiftly between two patient rooms. Today the ER was busier than normal, and this was the first opportunity he'd had to check her out. He'd heard through the grapevine she'd had dinner with Chad again. It looked as if he felt some sort of psychic pain. He was thinking, *I couldn't be jealous of Chad. Shirley's like every woman I've ever met. They all like to keep their options open until they get a ring or at least a promise.*

Jesse was nudged from reveries about Shirley and Chad by Dottie *who said, they do look good together, don't you think?*

He looked over and he wondered, those two are surely comfortable with each other. They're standing next to each other with their rolling computers talking. I thought we had an excellent dinner Saturday. She said she had a wonderful time and the restaurant was filled with Mexican music. I remember she giggled as we decided what to put in our guacamole. The serving gal was open to anything we wanted. I said, "Shirley, maybe not so much spice!" Her reply was a big smile and some remark about liking spice in her life. Maybe I have her wrong. Maybe she's a tease. No nurse here ever gossiped saying she's easy with her favors; in fact, quite the reverse. Dottie used to say she was one of the most uptight women she'd ever met. I'll have to watch this situation carefully. I want her. Besides, Chad isn't right for her. She'd live a quiet conservative life with him and be bored within a year. Going to save her from death in that kind of marriage; that is what I'm going to do.

Beauregard ordered a latte and cannoli at his favorite coffee haunt, Giovanni's in Agawam. The bakery had a side room allowing patrons to sit in relative quiet without disturbance. Better yet, Rudy was relatively unknown there. He thought, *why do I need food and drink to do my thinking. Too many things going on. I'm comfortable with the thousands of evidentiary details in cases; I can move through those easily. Strategic planning needs to be done by myself, alone. I can then bounce my results off my detectives.*

That nurse, she's in four of the cases; well I don't know for certainty the nurse is Shirley, but I think I know it. It will take some gumshoe work by MCU detectives; isn't it how we always solve out cases? A connection to these men exists. Maybe she discusses their situations with others. Perhaps she is a partner in choosing the victims. Could she be the doer; assuming she would use driving over her victims in a car; well, multiple hit-and-runs are not normal weapons for a woman. Maybe in the throes of revenge or anger a woman may drive over a husband or boyfriend. No, I don't think so, but who knows in today's world. She has a connection and therefore, she has information even if she doesn't know.

Ash is my problem now. How will I be able to help him? I just know in my heart Martina is seriously ill; more ill than she's willing to share with Ash. If she wasn't that ill, she'd share everything with him. She trusts him. She trusts her family. Her silence is a resistance smack given to protect her family from hurt. She knows she may be too ill. I'd do the same thing myself in that position; I would. How can I help Ash? I could tell him to work from home for a while. This COVID-19 is in all the papers. Boston has been hit. It's an international city; and there was a big Biogen conference which brought out of country visitors. It's claimed to be a source of infection for many cases of the disease. We're ninety miles away. Still, I'm hearing stuff on this disease as fatal to those who have health issues. Chief Coyne is having a meeting of all department heads on the potential impact of the COVID-19 epidemic on policing. Ash must work at home. Martina has a health risk. I'll tell him it's the prudent thing to do in protecting his family. That'll work. I hope these disease potential projections are overblown. I see nothing but trouble. How do I fight disease, the always invisible enemy?

The MCU detectives worked for several days attempting appointment setting. It was difficult for the older cases. Several witnesses had moved and Mason was searching for new addresses. Other unit work flowed in, leaving whoever was unassigned to continue the calling and appointment process. The Springfield cases had the least amount of witnesses listed in the victims' file. Mason determined the lower number may be based on the more congested housing in the larger city where residents often kept their heads down. He had grown up in Springfield and learned very early on the street to avoid any accident scene. Mason mused, *even when I make the call and the potential witness answers, I have to use all the public relations skills I have to be successful in getting them in for an appointment. The excuses range from their work schedules to babysitting the kids to lack of memory to they don't want to be involved. Thoroughly trained by my mama in giving guilt, my most successful strategy, I have an eighty percent success strategy. One from Springfield is a neighborhood watch freak and a motormouth. I pity the detective assigned to this interview. Hopefully it's Juan or Ash; maybe Ted. Bill, Lilly or Petra would not have the patience for this lady.*

The Captain joined Mason and listened to his progress. He informed Mason about his concern for Ash's home situation and asked if several of the set appointments could be changed to some form of media appointment. Mason was agreeable. He questioned whether most witnesses could be interviewed in that manner given several potential interviewees were senior citizens. Beauregard's phone rang. He listened for a long time. For Beauregard to listen and not reply on a phone conversation was unusual to say the least. Mason figured there was a problem. And there was one. The Captain said, "Take Ash off the interviewing. Petra's driving him to the hospital. Martina's crashed and the doctors are calling for immediate heart surgery."

9

Reactions

Waiting, waiting, waiting, after Petra's driving him like a crazy lady to the hospital, created some imbalance in Ash's thinking. Martina's mom met him at the Cardiac Surgery waiting room. She was stone-faced but hugged him, saying, "Thank God you're here. You're the only one she'll allow to know anything. If you didn't come, the doctors would just go ahead and we'd know nothing. Ash, my mother died of heart problems in her early thirties. I thought maybe Martina would not get those genes. Who knows, maybe not genes; my mother's life involved a great deal of physical work. She was a farmer's wife and believe me in those days, it was a very tough life. Not like what I see in magazines today with big beautiful farmhouse kitchens. It is not what I remember. I was young when she passed and soon after my father sold the farm and went to work for a large dairy. We moved to West Springfield. Later, when I married, we moved to nearby West Side. I could not protect Martina from what? She wouldn't tell me a thing. All I knew was she was thinner and pale and always needed to nap. Dad's gone to pick up Elisa who is currently working as an intern at West Side's music program. I never thought my healthy Martina, you know, would follow in my mother's footsteps. And our Elisa, not exactly like her mom, but you know, she plays a mean clarinet and sings. She has Martina's music gene. I believe you played a role encouraging her. Elisa loves you."

And while Anna McKay quietly wept, a nurse approached and asked, "Mr. Ashton Lent, are you he?"

"Yup, I'm he. How is Martina and what is going on here?"

The nurse identified herself and asked for his identification. After which, she was willing to speak to him alone. They entered a glassed-in smaller room. He'd been there before with assault victims' families taking statements. The memories weren't good. Further, the nurse said, "Martina is a candidate for immediate heart surgery. Dr. Petranus will be in shortly to explain the surgery. Martina has authorized the surgery. She is being prepped now."

Ash did not argue, although it appeared he was holding back. The nurse noticed, and said, "Mr. Lent, if it were my mom or sister, I'd want Dr. Petranus for the surgery."

Ash stayed in the glassed-in room and waited. Mrs. McKay could see him, but she did not join him. He did not believe she was obeying some kind of hospital protocol. No, he thought she was just as frightened as him and thought better not to know anything for the moment. He understood her thinking and wished he could avoid this next conversation. Dr. Petranus entered. What bothered Ash most was the doctor's extremely youthful appearance. He thought, *did they get this guy out of high school? He's younger than me and the nurse said he's got a stellar reputation as a surgeon. How many years has he been a surgeon? I'll check that out on the database. What good will that do? She'll be in surgery before I get an answer.*

Dr. Petranus introduced himself and explained Martina's problem. He said, "According to our files, Ms. McKay has been here several times for testing. We sent those tests to MGH in Boston. She's told us she has an appointment soon. The problem is she can't wait for surgery. She has problems with her mitral and aortic valves. Without immediate surgery, she won't last more than a day. She is young and we are hopeful. There are risks to the surgery."

Dr. Petranus outlined his approach to the surgery. He insisted she should have had the aortic valve insufficiency handled before, but Martina insisted she had few symptoms and she would wait. Included in his analysis was the complication in mitral valve surgery. Ash questioned at length but soon realized the doctor was hesitant in defining in absolutes his surgery. He did, however, list the risks and Ash caught his breath. Ash, who had never been sick other than almost being shot to death by drug mobsters, that he could remember, was unprepared for all this medical information. He did what he learned as a detective; he tried to slow down the process by asking questions and requesting drawings until Dr. Petranus quietly insisted, "Mr. Lent, you must let me leave. I know a lot, but in Martina's case, the expected surgical route is not absolute. What is absolute is she will die without this surgery and it must be soon."

Dr. Petranus left the glassed-in room. Ashton Lent, the tall and lanky musician/detective sat and cried. Anna McKay saw Ash, and she looked absolutely stricken. At that moment, Anna's husband and granddaughter entered. Elisa saw Ash through the glass and knew her mother was in trouble. She thought, *Grandma and Papa can hide their feelings, but not Ash. Oh Mama, fight, fight. I need you.*

Back at the Pit, Millie and Mason gave Beauregard and the detectives the news. Millie took the role of messenger. She explained, "Ash raced out of here so fast. He just said he was going to the hospital and Martina was facing immediate surgery. You know Martina was to see a Boston specialist. This is not good. This was not their first choice. I'm so afraid for Martina and Ash and Elisa and Martina's parents."

Mason got up and walked in circles. He did not like his people, a term he loosely used for his family and friends, to have troubles. In an attempt to get back to some sense of normalcy, he, perhaps inappropriately said, "Well the rest of you will have to do all the interviews. I'll reassign them."

No one questioned him. They knew Mason was adapting to bad news in the only way he knew by reverting to work and structure. There was a long moment of quiet. Juan couldn't take the silence and said, "We'll do whatever we have to do, Mason. Should any of us go to the hospital now?"

Bill Border, the last detective hired for MCU, and not noted for his over-sensitivity, was resolute. "Nope, the family unit needs to be together. We don't know how long this surgery will take. Visiting could be stressful for them. They'll have to be nice to us. Being nice to us is not their priority now. We can call and ask Ash to let us know how we may help. And we can wait for the results, just like they're waiting."

Captain Beauregard made them aware he agreed with Detective Bill Border's thoughts. He asked Millie to order some lunch explaining he'd just returned from a meeting with the Chief and the Mayor and all heads of the West Side Police units. The recommendation made by the Mayor and the Chief were to limit interaction with the public when there was no reasonable need by the public for a face to face, with the Captain explaining, "This new virus from China is now a threat headed toward western Massachusetts. We now have cases here and they think the virus is particularly dangerous for those who have compromising illnesses or are older. The suggestion is to protect ourselves. This unit is small with staff having specialized and perhaps irreplaceable skills in the short term. The Chief, in light of the hit-and-run cases, suggested we attempt to have tele-conferencing in place of face-to-face. I know you're thinking about the loss in information when you are not there to assess the person within their environment or even within our conference rooms. We will, however, do what we have to do."

Petra said, "I'm already on this. Carlotta's pediatrician has already read me the riot act. He wants me to stop meeting with other mothers and babies. He says his info is it's going to be big and to get used to staying home. I have such problems with staying in place."

Juan's mother, who was known by them all as an obeyer of rules told him, "I heard that doctor from NYC say there'll be recommendations for us all soon and this is big."

Beauregard cut them off with, "Schedule the interviews this way. Stay away from folks unless it's necessary to do your job. Chief Coyne has ordered special see through partitions for the Desk Sergeant. Juan, your mom's right; this will get bigger. Pay attention to your personal space. The Chief will forward some instructions to all police in an email. Look for it and read it."

The rest of the afternoon was spent with detectives making calls to change appointments. They were successful in all but two calls. One of those calls included a wheelchair bound person who had no internet. The woman was known by the police in her town of Wilbraham. She was a very heavy woman who fell several times and could not get up. She was told by the police she should not live alone, but she was an independent woman who did not want anyone living with her. She did agree to wear a monitor and her neighbor would be called when the police notified him.

It was reported that the neighbor was a retired Army sergeant, who said he was always available. Bill Border agreed to interview Sandra Adams at her home. He knew her from his volunteering in a disability program. This volunteer side of Bill Border was unknown to the other detectives and they used the opportunity to rib him. His answer was, "Inside of each evil one is a touch of the saint."

The other person not available for a tele-interview lived in a group home almost directly on Boston Road in Westfield. She was very hard of hearing and insisted the police come to her. She had a microphone they could use to speak with her.

Beauregard called Ash late in the afternoon hoping to hear some positive news. He did. Martina had survived the aortic valve surgery. Ash was told there would me another surgery in the near future, and the immediate concern centered around possible blood clotting. He did not sound at all like the ebullient musician Beauregard knew. The Captain shared his conversation with the other detectives and Millie.

Detective Bill Border approached the small old-fashioned home on Main Street in Wilbraham. There was no step-up to the front portico entrance which had recently been enlarged. He assumed it was made bigger to allow for a wheelchair. Maybe, the entrance was too modest to rightfully be called a portico. The home itself would not capture anyone's attention. He decided it was 'nondescript' The inside door was opened a crack which, given the outside temperature registering thirty-seven degrees, was a questionable situation. He announced, "Hi, Sandra, I'm Detective Bill Border from the West Side Police here to interview you about the hit-and -run death of Norman Carroll."

A loud woman's voice yelled, "What do you need, an invitation, Bill

Border, now you're a bigwig, a detective?"

Bill entered to find Sandra sitting in front of a large screen television with a luncheon tray next to her and three cats hugging each other covering the blanket draped over her feet. He thought, *this is the Sandra I remember. She finds comfort where she can. Look at the pile of books next to her. She's probably connecting with the authors by snail mail.*

"Well, Bill, what do you want to know? Norman Carroll was my neighbor. Well not next door, but in the area. I'd see him at church every Sunday; often he'd come with his van and pick me up. His van was wheelchair accessible. Norm was a good guy. He'd lost his wife. His two kids live in Texas and come up for Christmas. This spreading out of families isn't good for the elderly. Especially in my case, I had one daughter and she's a missionary in Africa. Lot of good it does me. She helps folks far away, but not me."

Bill attempted to keep Sandra on track, but she needed to rant. He listened and he learned that he had probably not been listening for years. Jessica, his lady friend, who he wanted to call a significant other, but couldn't, because she wouldn't let him, recently let him know he was a novice about relationships. Jessica explained, "Bill, you've never listened to others; perhaps you were fearful their needs would overwhelm you. Learning to listen, if you care to be loved, is the most important work for you. It's difficult; but for me to invest my future in you, listening is a requirement."

He remembered going home that particular evening and laughing to himself thinking, well, the shoe is on the other foot now. I'm supposed to be a stud and she won't even think of me as important until I learn to listen. I'm action oriented. She says that's very nice but not enough. She can hire someone to take the barrels out and clean the eaves. So now I try to listen. It's slow going. I guess this Sandra is a good test for me.

And Bill Border listened. Sandra cried. She explained Norm would call her regularly and listen to her problems. Now she just has her neighbor next door. She says he does a lot for her, but he is just not a good listener."

He could see that Sandra was getting anxious and he asked if she could call her neighbor. He'd like to speak with him. Sandra told him Otis Lambert offered to take her to the senior center luncheon today. "It's Wednesday, you know, and they have chicken with wine and lemon sauce. It has a French name, I simply don't know it. It's certainly out of character for him to so willingly offer to take me, but he knows I've had a difficult time since Norm died."

She continued her story that Norm and she shared an experience with a doctor at the ER. Norm had been stung by a bunch of bees on the same day she'd been taken by ambulance for what she thought was a heart attack. It wasn't; it was just severe anxiety. She was pleased to see Norm and while they were talking, Dr. Teague joined them. He was pleasant when he asked if he could interrupt. The doctor accompanied them both as they hurried back to their adjoining cubicles. Norm said, "I'll wait for you, Sandra, and when we're both finished I'll take you home."

While they drove to her home in Wilbraham which was a little ride, they agreed Dr. Teague was an interesting and amiable person. Sandra said, "He wanted to know all about my living conditions and my associations. How often do physicians want to know anything about you? They don't even look at you; they're glued to their computers. Doctor said he was surprised I met a friend in the ER. I told him all about Norm too. He felt badly that Norm was living alone."

The neighbor Otis entered the open front door and said, "You're the detective interested in Norm's death. I met him through Sandra; he was awful good to Sandra. You know, he just knew how to be nice to everyone. I'm not so good at being nice consistently. I mean to be, but I get involved in my own business and forget about others."

Sandra caught Otis up with her previous conversation, continuing with, "Detective, Doctor Teague did tell Norm he understood the loneliness in living alone; he was also lonely. He said they had a lot in common; Norm tries to fill his life with doing for others and Doctor Teague's whole professional life is doing for others. Sometimes you meet the good guys out there."

Detective Border asked Otis, "Had you ever met Dr. Teague?"

"I did. Nor before, but after. He treated some elderly friends I drove to the ER from the nursing home."

Sandra said, "You never told me you did that. I thought you hate nursing homes."

"I do, Sandra, because I'm afraid every time I visit I'll be in there next."

Sandra said, "Get over it, Otis. It's life. Most of us will end up there. You have no one. You help me. The only thing I can do for you is occasionally cook for you."

Otis went back to the conversation with Detective Border, saying, "I saw Dr. Teague about five times. One time, I was depressed and told him so. That day I met up with a male nurse who I would see pretty regularly; a guy named Chad. He asked me how well I knew the doctor. He said the doctor seemed interested in all the older patients. I laughed and said, 'you mean like you are, Chad. You know everything about us.'"

Bill asked, "Otis, have you ever met a nurse named Shirley or something like that name?"

"Shirley, she's the best. If anyone, disabled or older, hit the ER, she'd take them under her wing. And boy, would she follow through. If they had no one, she'd visit after their hospital stay and make sure they had services and food. I know she paid for lunch for a couple of the bad off ones."

"Otis, do you know her full name and what shift she's on in the ER?"

Otis smiled. "Better than that, Detective, I have her cell number and her email address. She is on the three to eleven in the ER at Wing in Palmer. She's super organized and used to be at Baystate Hospital in Springfield. I heard they're changing things around now with this virus from China."

Border looked quite pleased with himself when Otis gave him Shirley's information. Her last name was Baker.

Nina happily returned to work a month after her last surgery. The cataract surgeries were a breeze compared to getting a new knee and its troublesome required rehab. She thought, *I almost lost it. I was so traumatized by the stair exercises bending my knee, holding it, and counting, from the knee surgery, that I couldn't believe the eye surgery would be easy. I don't know whether I had an angel on my shoulder, but two good surgeries with no problems is a first for me. I remember Jon, my physical therapist for my two TKIs. He was so unemotional. When I swore one day, very loudly, he just told me life is hard but we have to live it; like I didn't know. I know it's hard; it's always been hard for me. The cataract surgeries were a piece of cake. I don't count them as stressful. I don't like wearing reading glasses around my neck all the time, but I sure as hell love being able to see clearly again.*

I'm to be Sister Althea's administrative assistant. A big job title; I'll try my best. She told me not to worry; she's really never had help or when she did, the help was helpless. I won't be helpless. Today we're having a prayer service and several of the van drivers were also invited to the after-service luncheon. Sister Althea and the Pastor both agreed with sharing their meal plans with those who helped the church. I like being part of this. It makes me feel worthwhile.

Pastor did not speak at length, but insisted God wished us all to be kind. He did say, "There's talk about this virus from China. From what I've heard we will need to be kind. It's very contagious and Sister Althea is instituting rules for our public luncheons and dinners. I will keep you posted; but right now, the practice is to wash your hands. We are using paper plates and plastic utensils. We hope that change will help. Our dishwashing staff will now service keeping everything cleaner than usual; we'll go from clean to immaculate. It's all our council of churches agreed was relevant. I will keep you informed."

Sister Althea led the attendees and two wonderful singers in a hymn, "We Shall Overcome." Luncheon was served. Nina sat next to Sister Althea, who announced her new position. Her table was then joined by the van driver Jerry La Follet. He said he was pleased to see Nina looking so well. The pulled pork was delicious; Nina knew that because Jerry took two helpings. She herself could barely eat one serving. With the corn pudding, mashed potatoes and buttered beans, Nina didn't think she would eat dessert. Jerry plopped a plate of coconut crème pie in front of her and a coffee. Nina ate dessert.

It was then that Jerry told Nina about two van drivers she knew who had died in addition to Buck from Palmer. Nina's reaction was unexpected. She said, "Those guys wouldn't put themselves in danger; all three of them were careful and always telling me to slow down. I don't believe it. I just don't believe they would all be run over. I know there are lots of drunks out there, my having been a drunk driver at one time; but, no, this is not possible."

Nina showed signs of her stress by banging her hand on the table and crying. Jerry and Sister Althea each tried to hold her hand, because it seemed she would hurt herself. Nina yelled, "I'm telling you! Those three were murdered. When I was a little girl, it's how they killed black men who were troublesome. But Buck, Herschel, and Stan were not troublesome. Why would they kill them?"

Sister Althea answered with, "This is not the old South, Nina, and these men aren't black. Life just comes at us sometimes."

Nina insisted the men were murdered and questions should be asked. She said, "Get men in blue to go after a murderer of old men. Nobody cares about old men or old women. It makes sense to me someone is murdering them. Three people I know. People who were good to me are murdered. Something's funny."

Jerry seemed thoughtful and, as Jerry often did, waxed philosophically, "I don't like these deaths, and the three of them going at once is troublesome. Nina, none of them had a whole lot of money. They were all lonely old men like me. I think it was their time and drunk drivers did the job."

Sister Althea said, "Before I found Jesus, a long time ago, I was on the streets and saw the cops chasing a serial killer of young working girls. Jerry, what if it's one drunken driver doing them all? Don't ask me why, because I don't know why. You know the cops in Wilbraham. Ask them about the case. Didn't you tell me you met that famous detective from West Side. If he told me these cases were just drunken driver cases, I would believe that."

Sister Althea and Nina looked expectantly at Jerry, who answered, "I can do that. I certainly owe my friend Herschel that. I miss him. Hell, Alice misses him."

And Jerry left the dining room for some quiet, thinking, I don't think Captain Beauregard will let me in for an interview. Cops tend to send you to someone lower on the chain of command to get info before I get to the big guy. I can call Norbie Cull, and get an appointment. I'll have to lie, because he's not going to see me for nothing important. He is a defense lawyer, but I heard him tell Captain Beauregard he loves business deals; especially helping small businesses get started and survive. Alice's sister is looking for help for a loan with the SBA for her woodworking shop. Yep, he'll give me an appointment for that. He won't turn me down.

10

Consult and Investigate

Sheila entered Norbie Cull's inner sanctum and looked around thinking, he's very neat for a man; well, other than his special corner for his awards with the Boys Club and athletic awards right up there with his 'Lawyer of the Year' award and other professional awards.

She'd tried several times to arrange them more ascetically but with no success. He'd informed her they were in the order of the time he received them and he liked them that way. Her reply was, "Norbie, Sheri's wedding picture is across the room and out of the time schedule. What about that?"

"Sheri is special. She's personal. She'd kill me if she thought, I thought she was an award. She insists she is the driving force in our marriage, and of course, she's right. Things are where they ought to be."

"Well, Norbie, I made an appointment for you with a new business client. He is from the tone of his voice an older gentleman; and unlike some who walk in here, he is polite. His friend is in a small business and he wants to help her get a small business loan; you know, help him with the paperwork. He doesn't want to talk to Charlene. I told him she was an excellent attorney and would normally handle this type of case. The potential wants you. I've scheduled it for eleven before your lunch."

Norbie noticed she did not say, 'Okay,' which simply meant he would meet with the new client and there was no negotiation about the issue. She placed an empty file on his desk with a legal pad and a typed sheet giving specifics from the client's phone call. He looked at the name and remembered, Jerry. Sheila said, "Norbie, I like the guy. You're a lawyer. Not every case is a big case. I hope you're not going to take only financially rewarding cases in the future. It's the normal clients who come here I like the most."

Before she left the room, Norbie reminded her, "Don't forget, Sheila, it's the financially rewarding clients who pay most of the bills. Not to worry, I won't neglect any client. I just had that hour before lunch scheduled in my mind already."

After checking with reception, Norbie entered the conference room for his new client's arrival, and he met Jerry LaFollet. He remembered him immediately and agreed with Sheila's assessment of this man. Jerry was not a man who measured what he said in nuances. In a most straight forward manner, Jerry said, "I lied to Sheila, your secretary. I didn't really want to fool her. She's a nice lady and certainly is interested in doing what you want, but I knew right away she would fall for a do-gooder story."

"Spit it out, Jerry, what is it you want? I would have seen you if you left a reference to where we met."

Jerry did spit it out including his recitation of Nina Mary's fears. He said it was all pretty suspicious. Jerry noted their age, living alone condition, all hit by drunk drivers, and the strangeness that they were all on sidewalks or at least on the edge of a curb when hit. He concluded with, "The police aren't that dumb to miss three drunk driving deaths and never finding the drivers. Listen, Norbie, the deaths I know about were in three different towns; but get this, they were all on Route 20. You know Route 20 is the longest east west transcontinental road in the United States, starting in Boston and ending in Oregon. I'm probably reaching there, but what if the driver has a thing for murdering on Route 20? I want you to look into it. I have a thousand dollars for a fee. I figure it would be mostly office work you'd direct one of your paralegals to do. If it costs more, let me know, I have some savings; not a lot, so don't go crazy."

Sitting back in the club chair, Attorney Norberto Cull seemed to be appraising the situation. He did not immediately react; the lack of which concerned Jerry who was thinking, *I've gone too far. He thinks I'm a nut case. Who else could I turn to, Captain Beauregard in West Side? He wouldn't be concerned with deaths in other cities; would he?*

Norbie spoke now. "You are asking me to do an assessment of three events in three different cities and towns labeled as accidents. You believe there is a killer out there who uses stolen cars as weapons. You're assuming the culprit is able to steal cars; chooses elderly male victims for some personal reason; and chooses murder sites along east/west Route 20. You assume a lot. Why haven't you called the police in each area? If you called enough times they would look into it and maybe connect with each other. If it's murder, then investigation is for the police."

Jerry replied, "I knew you'd think I was nuts, but I have a reason. I used to be an auditor for the state of Massachusetts. I was super at noticing details; well, not details but patterns. I'd look for what was repeatedly missing or repeatedly there. I discovered in the state college system, by auditing three colleges in one season, calculation formulas for disability which I'd only seen at those colleges. You know, Norbie, nobody can remember everything, but I had done another state college audit the year before and the accounting staff had quite a few newbies. It required me not to follow their process, but to test the process more diligently than we were required. I and of course the other auditor on the job found all kinds of mistakes but nothing deliberate. This was early in my career; no personal computers, just adding machines. The next year, I used the process I developed and it didn't work. So, my original process was faulty or the other colleges were using another process. I did some research. I looked at the union contracts and found changes. The colleges were using old rules for the calculation. It's just one example. I have a million more. Frequency of an unlikely event needs to be investigated. Same age and sex of victims is too coincidental to me. All these men were do-gooders; trying to help; Route 20 for all three victims. If I were to plan to murder a group of people, choosing different cities may help me get away with murder. I'm not nuts."

Norbie Cull answered, "I won't take you on as a client, Jerry. I'm sorry."

Jerry's face grimaced as Norbie stated, "I'm not the investigator you need. I will for my own purposes look into your concerns. I knew Stan Korsecki. Did you know he was just found dead, the victim of a hit-and-run in West Side?"

Jerry shook his head and repeated what he previously had stated. "Frequency of an unlikely event needs to be investigated. You must now see the need."

Norbie spent a few more minutes speaking with Jerry and promising nothing more than his best efforts. He said, "I will speak with the detectives in each of the cities where the bodies were found. I, first, would want to make sure they may be what you think they may be. If I agree, I'll do a bigger search. I won't use your name. I'll just say I have a client and I do."

"Norbie, you may use my name. Again, I'll pay you for your efforts."

"Not to worry, Jerry, I can't get paid by two clients for the same case. I thank you for coming in. You did good for your friends."

"It doesn't change things, being a good citizen now; does it? You can get killed maybe because you are a good citizen."

Attorney Cull made a call to Jim Locke, a principal in the Hunt and Find Investigators Agency. He particularly liked working with Jim, a former MCU detective whose wife was MCU Lieutenant Petra Aylewood-Locke. He asked if they could meet over lunch, saying, "I was scheduled to have a business lunch; but I'm cancelling to lunch with you. I thought we'd try Panjabi Tadka's today."

Jim replied, "You're bribing me with food. You must feel some urgency. I can't wait to hear. Your client this time must be in big trouble."

"Jim, you are oh so right. My client is me."

The family running Panjabi's catered to its patrons, but the waitstaff did not annoy them every minute looking for positive food comments. Norbie picked a table by the window knowing other patrons would have difficulty hearing their conversation. It was okay in their minds if they were seen in the window because at this time, the conversation was not about a high-profile case Norbie was handling. Norbie thought, *not high-profile. No one apparently cares if old men die from murder.*

'Rogan Josh' for Norby and Jim ordered, 'Chicken Curry' along with an order of 'Naan' and 'Raiti.' Norbie and Jim discussed Carlotta Locke, Jim and Petra's baby daughter, and pictures of the little beauty were shown. Norbie had pictures of his four on his cell phone, but they were teenagers and couldn't compete with the cuteness of Carlotta. The food arrived and the smell of the spices encouraged the men to quit talking for a few minutes before they approached the subject of the day.

Norbie tried to present the situation of each death and then collectively group them. He spoke of their commonalities until he realized this maybe was not new information for Jim; further, he didn't even play devil's advocate which he was wont to do on most cases they had in common. Norbie said, "Have you heard about this, Jim? Am I missing something? You're not telling me I'm crazy. Look, I have Sheila calling connections from Worcester to Russell for info about traffic deaths on Route 20. My gut tells me if there are four deaths with peculiar similarities, then maybe there are more."

Jim replied, "I can't talk about my source, but Norbie, there are more than seventeen hit-and-runs in several, I'm not sure how many, communities. And from my understanding Sturbridge and Worcester weren't included in the search, and who knows where the death sites end."

Norbie did not have to ask for Jim's source and wondered how they could investigate without stepping on Rudy's toes and putting Petra, Jim's wife in jeopardy. Taking a moment before he spoke, Norbie detailed what he thought; which relieved Jim's conscience for telling him what he should not have. He said, "Thanks, Norbie, I did speak out of turn giving you info I promised not to share."

The two men agreed on terms moving forward. Despite the small glitch in hiding the source of the number of victims, they believed every bit of evidence should be hunted for by all in the know. Norbie would be the go between Rudy and himself with no mention of Jim. Norbie shared with Jim his concerns for a blow-up in West Side, saying, "Stan Korsecki was a great guy. Sheri knew him and I met him at the West

Side chili contest. His recipe beat Lance's from the Healthy Living Café in West Side. I think there'll be a public reaction on this death. I just feel it."

"Norbie, you've explained what I just heard in the pipeline. Lance from the café is addressing the City's Board of Selectmen on the safety of the roads in West Side this Wednesday. He's aware of two other deaths and that they are all elderly. He has safety concerns. They tried to avoid hearing from him; the Mayor told him they were investigating the road safety issue, but he had fifty people who signed a petition to be heard. I got this, not from the police, but from one of the witnesses to a prior death site, who insists there is a road safety issue. When Captain Frank Murray, head of West Side's Traffic Unit, was contacted by Lance, he said something about, "All in good time. I'm looking at it and will notify you when I have the resources to follow this investigation further."

Murray did not placate Lance. He knew a political push would give Traffic's aptain Murray investigation resources. Smart of him; but there will be publicity. You may want to attend the meeting of the Selectmen."

Norbie reacted by saying, "This frees me. I'll go to the meeting. It makes it public. Meanwhile, you and I will do independent research. You have better searches. You can't be out there, and it is disappointing when Petra's job on an open case prevents my use of your talents. I'll tell you when I have specific computer searches needed to be done. Sheila, my assistant, and Rita who is one of the paralegals in my firm can do some preliminary stuff. I'm investigating this. I'll inform Rudy when it makes sense. Although, it sounds like Rudy is all over this."

The two men discussed investigation avenues and limitations while finishing their tea.

Back at the office, Norbie met with Sheila and Rita. Rita was hot to research, while Sheila wanted more specific instructions. He told them what he knew, saying, "West Side MCU is all over this, but we don't have access to what they know. We must find info legitimately. We can do that, especially if we have contacts in each area who may know the victims. Use the name of our law office and if anyone asks which attorney is interested, try to ignore the question. If, however, there seems to be a rich source of information, then give my name."

Norbie gave Rita and Sheila the Route 20 accident sites from Sturbridge to Russell to search for drunk driving victims who were men over the age of sixty-five and gave the time frame as the last three years. He explained he knew the police were looking at a two-year time frame and it might be sensible to search for one more year. If there are none in the third year back, he could reasonably assume the serial murderer started his dirty deeds at a specific date. He shared his thoughts that maybe the first death was the first murder or maybe the doer just moved into the area at that time. Norbie told Rita, "You've been a great researcher with your friendly and may I say gossipy style and technical skills. Go to it. Give it four hours a day for the next four days. Have Sheila connect with you if any clients who are potentials for interviews. Do it all by telephone if you can. Sheila can supply intros for you; they all know her if I handled cases for them or their relatives. It will all come out once you mention the law firm name."

Norbie left his office for the day thinking, if I talk to Rudy now, he'll interfere. I don't have to worry about city or town bureaucracies and he does. In the end, our work may be duplicate, but I can't not do something. All these dinners with Rudy and my parents have sensitized me to the importance of protecting the good people who were the Greatest Generation. All I have to do is pursue this plan.

Two hours later found Attorney Cull having cocktails with a group of Assistant District Attorneys. He'd picked up the tab, under the guise of enjoying life before he died of the corona virus. The ADAs all laughed and one said, "It's being called COVID-19 on television. There are all kinds of reports about wet markets in Wuhan or a virology lab there with funding from the US."

One of them, whose brother-in-law was well-connected in Washington D.C. said, "It's getting bad in California and Boston. Boston had some convention attended by lots of Asians and that's how it got here from China; it's the same with the West Coast. The President has closed the border for Chinese entering the country. The numbers are getting higher. Norbie, we won't be drinking like this in a week. Word is business will be shut down; all except what they decide are essential services."

Norbie answered, "Sounds like a sci-fi story. Besides, bars are essential   services."

He'd said it for laughs and got them, but was instantly sorry for his lack of discretion and continued. "Stupid remark which I don't normally make. How bad is it? What amount of disease would make us shut down business? This is a frightening thought."

ADA Philip Dodge said, "You've got your head in litigation, Norbie. Didn't you read about this and see it coming? The 24/7 news reports won't give up on it. I even heard they'll close the schools. My wife is up in arms at the thought. We have five sons under the age of nine-years. She'll go crazy."

Norbie laughed, saying, "What are you doing having five sons? Waiting for a daughter."

"Yeah, but we finally figured it wasn't going to happened, and we would spoil a girl. Maybe it's our karma to fill the athletic teams of the future. I've only one egghead. All the others were born with a ball in their hands and cleats on their feet."

Norbie and Philip had worked some cases together. Norbie was left with the impression he could work with Philip, thinking, he's a logical guy and not a buster. I'll lead into a discussion on hit-and-runs. He'll tell me about a couple of them, especially if the police are pissed at not finding the culprits. Philip lives in Wilbraham. Route 20 goes through there. Maybe I can bring up the one I talked about with Jerry; I think his name was Herschel something.

The two discussed sports, the corona virus, and Phil's wife's potential stroke and the thought of full-time childcare again when Norbie mentioned, "Hey, I was at a party in Wilbraham and one guy was late for the big doings because he'd been at a wake or funeral for a victim of drunk driving. I just heard from a friend of mine from West Side about Stan Korsecki getting hit the same way. Stan was a friend of my wife's and she's beside herself with anger. In both cases, the drivers have not been caught. I even heard there are more deaths like this and listen, Philip, all the deaths are of elderly men. What's up? Aren't the state's accident investigators doing their jobs? What gives?"

Philip grimaced saying, "You have always had your ear to the ground. Who let you in on this?"

"On what? Again, What gives, Phil?"

"Norbie, It's not well known because it's just in investigation stage now. I can't talk about it. The DA isn't certain there's substance; but Rudy Beauregard from West Side MCU brought some info about drunk driving accidents. He thinks they're deliberate killings. Sounds nutsy if you ask me because the supposed victims are old men. Lenny Hastings is the ADA on a task force. Several cops from other towns are on it, and Jones from the state police."

"Is that Cyrus Jones? He's the best accident reconstruction guy out there. He's not local. Phil, I don't think they'd waste his talent if there wasn't some evidence."

"Well, Norbie, the big problem is Beauregard. He has to be taken seriously because he is not a troublemaker or a looking for press kind of guy. He thinks there is something there. I heard the DA say, 'You have to take Beauregard seriously. He sees things and follows them. He's not a time waster. If he thinks something's there, there probably is.'"

Cull pushed, saying, "There has to be quite a few accidents involved. I know about maybe four or five."

Phil said, "I heard in the 'teens.' Keep it under your hat, because I got it from listening into a conversation."

"Phil, don't worry, it's just a matter of weeks. You simply can't keep this QT. Once witnesses get interviewed, it will be out there. Don't worry, I'll deny I've ever discussed this with you. You know defense lawyers go to their graves with big secrets."

The two laughed. Unfortunately for Norbie, he was stuck for two more drinks on his bar tab and would be late for dinner with Sheri and the kids. He thought, *I'll tell Sheri that sometimes you have to take one for the team. If I do say that, she'll hit me over the head with one of her three-hundred dollar frying pans. Now, I know this situation is big. Rudy is looking for a serial killer. I hope he's wrong. Doesn't matter if he's wrong, I know his instincts are superior in sniffing out a situation. So, I lose a few days. I don't like old men dying because someone else thinks it's their time.*

11

Public Airing

The West Side Board of Selectmen meeting was moved to the West Side High School Auditorium. It was rumored, so many citizens called the city about the latest hit-and-run accident, that the Mayor was certain a meeting held using the Town Hall space would not work because of the size of the hall. The Mayor had history with crowded meetings and was heard to say, "It makes for a mob mentality. We don't need counterproductive thinking now. Lance Colbert has some sway with all the high muckety-mucks. As a proprietor of this high-end healthy living stuff, he's a hotbed for gossip. This meeting's focus is to give a complete analysis of the facts to date. Captain Murray will explain unemotionally his concern over an open case investigation. He'll certainly state the importance of investigating drunk driving cases. He'll assure them the best accident reconstruction expert is working on Mr. Korsecki's death. I don't want Captain Beauregard up there. I don't want the public to interpret this incident as bigger than a simple and single case."

Norbie had heard the rumor but questioned whether Lance Colbert had the clout to have raised enough stink for the expected audience to be so large. There was a required movement to the high school auditorium. He thought, *good for him. Stan was a star among do-gooders. His death, by itself, deserves a quality investigation. I wonder if anyone will bring up the other deaths. If Jerry LaFollet hears about the meeting… Son of a bitch, I'll have Sheila call him.*

Cars packed the West Side High School parking lot when Norbie Cull attempted to park. He admonished himself for coming at the last-minute, thinking, *I'm always just on time, but community meetings get packed. I'm lucky if I can get a space and into the auditorium before the programming. They'll have all the community nonsense first; I'll be okay. Beauregard's car is here and it's his personal auto. Means he's not participating; but there is police presence; hell, I count five police cars with only one a cruiser. Civilians everywhere. Sheila had pulled the agenda for me and told me there was only one other item on the program and it would take at the most five minutes for a vote.*

Entering the auditorium required Norbie to run the gauntlet where there were wise remarks in place of weapons. He heard, "Who's your client?" "I didn't know you were close to Stan." "This is going to be a shit show, Cull."

He found a seat in the back but with a great view of the dais. In addition, he could stand and move around easily if he wished. The program began. What was interesting to him was the fact that the Chair of the Board of Selectmen turned the meeting over to Mayor Fitshler. Normally the board liked to maintain its distance from the mayor. Their constituents' votes were generally more important to them than currying favor with Fitshler. They were careful to show respect to the mayor in a public scenario with only an occasional rolling of their eyes when they disagreed. Since they often were at odds with the mayor, allowing him to take over a public meeting was not the norm. Mayor Fitshler read a statement expressing on behalf of the city his concern about the unfortunate death of Stan Korsecki. He detailed Stan's career and his recent service to West Side and its surrounding area communities. He spoke for a good ten minutes until the movement in the audience suggested he'd talked long enough. He ended with the issue of accident cases and the social issue of hit-and-run accidents often connected to drunk driving. He introduced Frank Murray, Captain of the West Side Police Traffic Unit. Captain Murray then carefully read a pre-written report from the Mass state police accident reconstructionist. Captain Murray's demeanor was in no way an invitation to disagree with him. He was authoritative but with an innocence and caring attitude which encouraged believability. With him was Sergeant Bobby Barr. The sergeant was noted in the community as a no-nonsense but fair enforcer of traffic rules. Captain Murray asked for questions. Again, this was a slight deviation from normalcy. The Board Chairman organized the meeting and would normally invite questions. Clearly the selectmen wished to separate themselves from any conclusions formed by the police and the mayor.

Norbie speculated, it's a wonder anything gets done in the political arena. I'm not even a specialist in the field and I can see all the players' hands. There's Rudy with Mona. Cool, he looks like a good citizen; not like the guy who is already investigating and serving on the task force which was not even mentioned. Fitshler knows this but he doesn't want the public to know this. Chief Coyne is also there with his wife and brother-in-law Sergeant Ted Torrington and his wife Charlotte. All look like good citizens. Every member of MCU are attending. Petra with baby Carlotta and husband Jim; all just interested citizens.

In the midst of Norbie's looking around and his reverie, Lance Colbert questioned the Mayor and not Captain Murray, saying, "This reconstruction report given by Captain Murray does not satisfy me or most of Stan Korsecki's friends and there are many of us. They will speak out after me. They will remind us all of his unstinting care for his community, our community. Stan could move like a young man in spite of his age. He was acutely aware of his surroundings. His friends will tell you he walked carefully on busy streets and always walked on sidewalks if available. If not, he'd move to safer turf. We don't believe these results. Further, there have been two other hit-and-run accidents killing other elderly but active men in West Side. Three deaths of fine men from hit-and-run accidents test believability. Are they really accidents or are they deliberate? We will not be satisfied until they are thoroughly investigated as a series. I've written letters to the Massachusetts Attorney General's Office, the Federal Government's VICAP program and the District Attorney. I want answers."

There were loud murmurs of agreement, and no reaction from anyone on the dais. And one by one twelve good citizens started to speak about the unfair loss of their friend and their disappointment in the city's reaction to the other losses. One woman unknown to Norbie was heartfelt in sharing the lingering death of Ray LeFron from West Side almost two years ago. Half the audience reacted with heavy sighing. They had not remembered his accident and now could account for one of the three accidents Lance Colbert had mentioned. Once the collective memory of the group was activated, disruption reigned. Helpless without someone keeping order, the mayor looked to Captain Murray who looked to Sergeant Barr who took the mic and with a few words of, "Let's hear what the others scheduled to speak have to say. We are all here to support a new investigation, when now we realize multiple accidents have occurred. We want any information you have. When you are through making statements, I'll do intake on your personal insights and schedule interviews at the station if needed. No conclusions will be developed tonight, just lines of inquiries."

An orderly process of speakers began again including two witnesses who spoke on the earlier accidents occurring in West Side. When the last speaker finished, the Chairman called the meeting finished. A line formed in the back to speak with Sergeant Barr and the Mayor escaped personal questions. Norbie thought, *Sergeant Barr has a future. He is wasted in Traffic. He should be the Department's public relations director.*

On the other side of the room, Rudy Beauregard had other thoughts about Sergeant Bobby Barr; so that's the guy coming over to MCU while Ash goes to traffic for the six-month service requirement. I want them both. Barr is not the stuffed shirt do-right guy I heard about. If he can deflect mob attention away while cooler heads reign, I want him in MCU. Today is a good day. Did Chief Coyne actually plan this. Ash will be in Traffic and could help with this exploding investigation while Barr will do a great job as a newbie; of that I'm certain. These placements are good for the department and good for MCU. Thank you, God; you've been watching again.

The next day, Sergeant Bobby Barr appeared an hour after Ash left the MCU unit following a farewell lunch attended by all. Ash, reluctant as he was in leaving, even for such a brief period, was appreciative of his new situation. He explained while they all ate the lush luncheon brought in from Auntie Cathy's Kitchen in Agawam. According to Millie, who typically decided where to get refreshments, it was a gluten free paradise of organic foods and desserts. Juan vowed he would never make fun of Ted's gluten-free diet again, saying, "These chocolate muffins are to die for and the egg and cheese sandwiches are the best."

Bobby Barr was invited to share in the leftovers. Like any cop, he loved his middle of the day repast. Barr, who was slim despite his broader frame, and fairly tall, piled his plate with two sandwiches and several desserts; enough to encourage applause from his new compadres. Lilly asked, "You're not even Italian or Irish, are you, Bobby?"

"Nope, you don't have a corner on the appetite market. I'm Scots and I was born hungry. I have two brothers just like me. My mom wanted us out of the house as soon as we graduated high school; she was sick of feeding us."

He laughed at his own remark. What Petra did notice was that Sergeant Bobby Barr, for his size and the size of his plate, was remarkably dainty as he chowed down. She thought, *I know he's not married, but Mama did a good job teaching the eating beast his manners.*

The Captain did not wait for Barr to finish. He spoke about Barr's addition to MCU in the most positive fashion and suggested he be filled in on the elderly victims of crimes case. He said to Barr, "This info is low key for the next day or two. I'm certain you already know about the DA's County Task Force. Nothing goes out of this room. It will be in the press soon enough. I want you listening in on interviews for today; after which Ted will assign you some interviews. If you have connections in police traffic divisions related to any of the accident sites not in West Side, let me know. You may have access to some facts; facts overlooked in the record but remembered by cops."

And the interviewing began again. Since it was determined in advance to do most interviewing by Facetime or ZOOM or any other method the subject was able to use to connect, the detectives had listed a summary of questions to ask. They were given some instructions for interpreting body language without the helpfulness of being in the same room to interpret nuances in movement. The Captain requested from Petra's husband a list of specific traits of a subject which could more easily be hidden in a tele-interview vs an in-person interview. Per usual, Jim Locke was on top of his game and gave the Captain more than Beauregard felt comfortable with on the spot digesting. Together they honed the different processes' results down to a few items. First, for teleconferencing there were the real and psychological barriers created by the technical requirements. Second, despite the ability in teleconferencing to visualize the interviewee, someone off screen and unseen by the interviewer could be making suggestions which may not be the interviewee's real experience, or the interviewee may be put off by the idea of how he or she may look. Thirdly and most importantly from a police perspective is the potential inability to build a good rapport with the interviewee. They believed the interviewed candidates in their own setting may not allow a relationship to build which could happen in an enclosed police conference room.

Interviews were limited by the availability of enclosed spaces. The Captain and Mason's offices were added to the normal three interview rooms. Beauregard instructed them to start with their (probably) least effective witnesses first; explaining they would develop better styles with practice. They would explain to the subject that a recording was being made. If it was not allowed, Beauregard believed an in-person visit should be made. He believed that the witness would allow a recording in order to avoid any inconvenience.

The detectives spent the day interviewing and writing reports. Eighty percent of the interviews were completed in one day. Beauregard thought, *hell, what a savings in time, labor, and auto costs. Perhaps there's merit in continuing this practice in the future; at least for some situations. I've always liked the face-to-face business. I believe I glean more from the interview, but as a manager, I see the possibilities in this.*

By the next afternoon all interviews were completed and the detectives met for discussion. The Captain had reviewed their reports before the meeting; at the same time as a pretty negative picture was being presented on national television about the corona virus, now called COVID-19. And the virus was the first order of business. New police procedures for the protection of the department were being planned. One was interesting. Only single Uniforms were allowed in cruisers. Interviewing by phone would be the preferred strategy. Some discussions were questionable, involving wearing masks. Juan said, "Cops will look like robbers. The public will have difficulty making complaints about any individual cop. New wave thinking, Captain."

Beauregard explained he would send updates by email on changes and suggestions. He instructed them to check their emails first thing in the morning, saying, "I think this thing is bad. They're reporting this virus emanated from the Wuhan, China, wet markets. Doesn't make sense to me. Those markets have been around for over a thousand years. No way are they the origin. We'll learn later some virology lab has been playing around and maybe then it infiltrated the markets; or maybe we'll never know the truth. China is a big country and makes a substantial amount of our products. I suppose we don't want to kill them with hard questions. They wouldn't answer our questions truthfully, no matter how important the answers would be. Globalization allows us all to visit everywhere. It also allows disease to spread. The government must know it's pretty contagious. One rumor is some states will be shutting down with the exception for essential services."

It took another ten minutes before the detectives' discussion could sensitively be ended. The Captain pushed the new subject by asking salient questions about circumstances surrounding the three dead elderly men. Detail by detail was examined and were either eliminated or put on the related murder board. Mason smiled to himself, thinking, *we have definitely decided these deaths are murders or there would be no murder boards. Good, some of these new details are convincing. These deaths are not accidental.*

Bobby Barr reported, "I interviewed Carolyn Aster, the live-in lady friend of the second man who was killed. She gave me her name on the night of the Selectmen's Public Meeting. I was fortunate to have met her in person and believe she is honest and savvy. Her insights into the second West Side killing, and she thinks it was deliberate, are on point. It was a nice Spring night. The victim was named Pete Proder. Do you recognize his name?"

When no one answered him, Bobby continued, "What about P. R. Proder?"

The detectives all knew that name. He was a local hero from the Vietnam War who had won all kinds of medals. Later he had a uniform business selling everything from school uniforms to plaques to military and sports related clothing. Bobby said, when he realized they all knew him, "Remember, it was called PRP Essentials. He ran it until fifteen years ago; when he was put out of business by the chains. He was ready to retire and did very quietly. Carolyn said she lived with him for the last seventeen years of his life after a disastrous marriage to her ex. She said he was the most charming gentleman and he did not like publicity. When he died, she went into a deep depression.

"I asked her why his death was so devastating for her when she was much younger than him and maybe could have expected him to go first. Her reply was he left all his assets to her. She is now quite wealthy, but in her mind, she lost everything when Pete died. It wasn't until six months after his death she felt well enough to ask questions. Our traffic unit told her it was an open and shut hit-and-run case. She asked if he were hit while crossing the road and was told no. That answer triggered her to insist on knowing exactly on what spot they had found his body. She couldn't understand how he could be hit when he was found way over on the sidewalk almost on the adjacent home's lawn. She could also not understand how the police could not find the driver.

"I never interviewed Ms. Aster at the time she first came to ask questions at the station; if I had, I would have been concerned. I reviewed the file when I reviewed the other files. He had a live-in girlfriend. He is the only one to have someone to care for him. It takes him out of the profile of the other victims. In the file the contents of his wallet are listed and included a business card for a nurse with her home number. Her name is Shirley Baker; the same woman Bill mentioned in his Otis Lambert report. This perp relies on his shrewdness in choice of a stolen car as a weapon and not leaving DNA evidence behind. What if he's a non-secretor blood type? In that case, we'd never get trace biological evidence on him. Only physical evidence of clothing residue or something falling out of his pockets or a tool left behind would assist. He hasn't in these three crime scenes left any. We need to have the other departments' reports. My guess is he's always been careful; but I personally think it's in our nature to make mistakes. He's not perfect. Still, I think the nurse is our only current lead."

The newbie detective was now well-regarded by his team. Captain Beauregard nodded his head, saying, "I agree. The nurse is the lead.

Mason, get the reports on trace evidence at the scenes of all the selected cases and look for anything out of the ordinary. I'm thinking of how these cars were so easily snatched. There are power amplifiers used to break into the new remote keyless systems. Nothing appeared to be stolen from the three autos used in our cases. I'm pretty certain, the killer is not interested in theft; but maybe if something stuck out he wanted, there's always that possibility. Other than that, I think normally a slim jim or center hole punch or porcelain would be used to smash the driver's side window. I've heard nothing about that yet. We don't know yet what his preferences are, new cars or older ones."

Mason replied, "Captain, the cars used in our cases were all less than ten years old and not normally chosen for car thefts. I'll do inventory on the other cases with other departments. I have connections from past cases. They won't require any paperwork and these cops will talk."

Lilly relayed a strange conversation she'd had with a woman interviewee. The woman said she was a member of a square-dancing club in West Springfield. She had called in the morning after the West Side public meeting. She was there and was uncertain if she had information worthy of a visit. "I scheduled a tele-conference because she only has a cell phone; she said, 'I've none of those unnecessary gadgets all the kids use today. If it is important I could get my granddaughter in with her computer. No, I'd have to go to her house, I think.' She found it difficult to articulate what she knew. She said, 'I partnered with Ray LeFron several times. He was quite a gentleman and good looking too. We had coffee with a group a week before he died. I think he liked me, but he also talked about two nurse practitioners who were very kind to him. One was a woman named Shirley and one was a man named Chad. They even brought him cooked dinners, all individually wrapped so he could freeze them and take them out, a couple a day. He said they had become important in his life. I believe, Detective Tagliano, he was very sick. On our last dance-class he had to sit out twice because he tired. So, I figured he may have contributed to his accidents. Maybe he fell down before he was hit by the car.'"

The Captain instructed Lilly, "Do a general look-in to this lady. What's her name? See if she looks normal. And find out just who Chad is; there can't be many male nurse practitioners named 'Chad,' can there?"

Lilly said, "Marie O'Connor. Will do a check on her and Chad."

Ted spoke up. "Look, Captain, I noticed something consistent in all the West Side deaths. Knowing we all hate coincidences, I checked out the deaths in West Springfield, because I have some connections there. Saw the same consistency. I then went to Wilbraham. One was not consistent."

Lilly, who hated to wait for info said, "Consistent in what?"

"The deaths all took place on the same day of the week; Tuesdays. The perp is not at work or at home on Tuesdays around 9:00 p.m. When we get a person of interest, this may help."

Petra asked, "Ted, which death in Wilbraham was not on a Tuesday?"

"Herschel Levine was killed on a Wednesday night between nine and ten in the evening. Don't know why it is different. The accident report looks much like the others. Could be Herschel only walks on certain nights. If the perp knew his walking nights, then he's a stalker. Could be the perp was busy that particular Tuesday."

––––––––––

Chad and Shirley sat at the hospital eating area taking a break from their work. Each had a not-bad, at least they agreed on that, sandwich in front of them. Chad's was chicken and Shirley had a steak tips special sandwich. They'd just been to an informational meeting and realized they would not be sitting together for lunch after the end of the week. Chad said, "This virus stuff is pretty serious for older people. I've heard it several times from two administrators. We'll be hunkering down. They think old people will not be able to fight this disease. It's bad enough we've lost so many from drunk driving incidents. Now they'll die from this virus."

Shirley looked bewildered for a moment She said, "You've noticed too. So many elderly men I've taken an interest in have died that way. I try to help the lonely ones; I mean the really lonely ones. I help both women and men, but most of the women have support networks. I think it's the people around them, but it could be they just connect more easily. I find men who have lost their partners later in life feeling loneliness more significantly. The death of Stan Korsecki really bothers me. Chad, you remember him. You helped with him. Dr. Teague was concerned with his long-term prognosis from his latest cancer. He thought it was shameful to have to go through the slow cancer death alone. I agree with Jesse. Dr. Teague suggested, what you and I know, the he is in for a terrible ordeal."

Chad thought while Shirley spoke, Jesse, Jesse, Jesse. Always Jesse! Let's stay on Stan, Shirley. Another one who didn't suffer the fate of their loneliness. Some of these guys who died have people in their lives who maybe love them but are distant or otherwise busy. Some have special others with my mother's personality. Better to be alone than have her. I have to remember not to put my mother into ordinary lives. She was not ordinary or nice or kind. I need to forget her.

He responded, "There have been a lot of deaths from accidents. It does boggle my brain, but could be God is saving them from something worse."

Dr. Jesse Teague joined them to Chad's distress. Jesse was charming as always. He said hello to them both and then directed all conversation to Shirley to the point of Chad's exasperation. Chad forced a return to his and Shirley's previous conversation about the deaths of the elderly men by a hit-and-run driver. He said, "Shirley and I have connected with some elderly men over the last couple of years who have died by being hit by drunk drivers as they were walking. We could recall a few of them with Stan Korsecki being the latest."

Jesse looked jolted and said, "Stan's dead? Killed in an auto accident? Maybe it's not so bad. I helped him thread his way through cancer specialists and surgeons; and I'm sorry to tell you he was headed for surgery next month and the prognosis was iffy."

Chad responded, "I saw him a few days before he was killed. He appeared to be chipper. He mentioned the cancer, but he thought he had a good chance. He was pretty happy on that day."

Jesse commented, "You kept a close relationship with a former patient? Do you do that often, Chad?"

Before he could respond, Shirley said, "Jesse, I don't think it's unusual. We're in the business of helping. Most patients have someone at home; but some of our older patients, who are not returning to a nursing home where the care is good, are living alone and often suffer depression when the loneliness kicks in. I talk to them after I meet them in the emergency room. I often follow them through the rehab experience and call them when they leave rehab. It's just a matter of being kind. I've noticed, Jesse, you are also often kind to the lonely ones."

Jesse took Shirley's statement as a hint, saying, "I suppose I do some of the same follow-through on the elderly. I did also check on Stan and a Nina from Springfield and I remember an Oscar from Palmer. They were all lonely. Except for Nina, who seemed to have a community within her church."

12

COVID-19

Dr. Jesse Teague spent his day in the emergency room repeatedly assuring patients about their safety from 'the virus.' He cursed the media for flooding inflammatory news, announcing shortages for nurses and doctors, and literally ensuring his day would be spent instructing and not in emergency care. He noticed the two Nurse Practitioners doing, what he thought, was a better job than he in the art of teaching. He found himself exhausted and quite distressed. Typically, he thought, *this kind of stress makes me go off my feed so to speak. I need some relief. I need to feel productive. I don't; not today. I'll have to do something; something to relieve this stress.*

Dr. Teague motioned Chad to join him. When Chad did not respond quickly, it let Jesse know something might be askew. Teague asked what was up and was told, "This man is the fifth patient I've seen today with virus symptoms that are not flu. I've tested for flu. They all attended a wedding held after the state notified on social distancing. That's one problem. The other is worse. I've been making calls on positive tests results. This virus is out of hand. I've made ten calls. Four of the patients who visited and got tested are now in other hospitals and not doing well. The other six feel better, but when I asked what their activities were recently and what their living situation was, I see some troublesome implications. Two of those patients continued to go out and party but have recovered. The other four were in bed for a bit but live in family situations. In three of the cases members of the family became sick and one was on a ventilator in another hospital. They came to us originally because most found it easier to access our emergency room. This is getting out of hand. You need to get this news out. I've been on the internet and the big hospitals in the big cities are on to it. I didn't expect to see this much potential trouble here."

Before Jesse could answer, Shirley joined them. She asked Chad, "You told him? Good. I thought Western Mass would be safer. We know from the press how Boston got hit with the big research conference held there; but here, we don't have lots of high rises and city living. If a wedding can infect so many, I'm worried. I've spent the day explaining to patients about the serious risk of contagion here. They all laugh at first and talked about some sci-fi movie I've never seen. I feel overwhelmed. I'm hiding masks for us all because we're short on them and the media says there is a national shortage. I don't want to get sick; how can I help if I get sick. I have a headache and I don't think it's from the virus."

Chad said he shared the same headache, saying, "It's just worry. I've learned that worry can make us react in negative ways. I'm trying to control that inclination in myself. We're also overworked here. It's Monday and they want us all on the Tuesday second shift. That's a night I've never worked."

Teague replied, "They'll have us working every shift if staff gets sick. Tayisha is out today. She has all the symptoms and thought it best to stay home. So, we worked with one less nurse today. We got tested yesterday; we won't know about your headaches until the tests come back or if you both get sicker. You'd better not. I'll be here alone. I didn't sign up for this. One thing is the elderly are disproportionately dying. One jerk over in radiology suggested it would help save Medicare money."

Juan Flores was dressed like a top business tycoon. That is what Lilly said to him. He ignored the barb, but shot back with a snide Hollywood type remark, "Listen, Babe, you don't look so bad yourself."

"So bad! You better think I'm the most glamorous gal you ever took to dinner. I don't go for the rooster looking better than the chick."

"I notice you steered away from the word 'hen.'"

"Glad you noticed. I'll never be a hen; even if I reach a hundred and ten. See, I can rhyme. By the way, Juan, where are we going to dinner in this area of informal Western Massachusetts, that requires us to be so formal?"

"My friends got us and some of my family in for dinner at the Lone Horse Country Club near Connecticut. We'll be in the main dining room and not in a separate room. I like it that way."

"Will your cousin Joe, the photographer be there. I'd love to have our picture taken in this getup. You like this dress? I think it's a gorgeous shade of petunia; nice and bright for my Mexican beau."

"You look wonderful; but you always do."

The drive to the club took a good twenty minutes. Lilly oozed over the stunning setting up on a hill. She'd been there before it had been completely rehabbed to this mega-monied structure; although the always perfect setting had not been changed. They entered and were directed down to the dining room. Lilly thought, *he's gone to a great deal of trouble and money to get us here, unless the whole family planned this for some family event. He didn't tell me, but maybe it's his parents anniversary or some birthday or one of the many relatives visiting from Mexico. No, not that, the President's put an end to easy entry from Mexico now; Mexico has also closed its border along with Canada.*

Juan's family including two of his aunts and their husbands, his two sisters and husbands and brother and wife along with Mamita and Papi, and the photographer cousin and wife were sitting waiting for them. A loud, "Ahhh! Finally, the two cops are here and three minutes late."

Juan laughed, saying, "I'm never late. It's the first time you've all been on time. I think you like the glamorous setting."

Mamita answered, "No, Juan, that is not the reason. I don't have to cook. I'm out of the kitchen and your Papa says I can't have Mexican food here. He doesn't know I love all kinds of food. I make Mexican for him because when I don't, he complains."

A debate ensued but apparently it was an ongoing discussion and no one was taking offense or sides. Lilly thought, not that different from my Italian and Irish family; although my family shouts out to take over the floor. It's all in good fun. Good thing, I'm used to constant interruption. Although when I talk in the Mexican family groups, nobody interrupts. I'm still the visitor and they are showing respect. I like that.

For the next two hours the gathering appeared to enjoy the food and drinks and the many toasts. Papi mostly did the honors; one toast after another. Dessert was chosen, but they were informed a couple of dishes would take twenty minutes. Juan took this opportunity to excuse himself and Lilly. They were to take a tour. It was cool outside requiring them to retrieve their coats and they enjoyed the beauty of the grounds. They stood by a wall, leaning against it. Juan said, "The state's closing things down soon. It may be our last opportunity to be out and about in public places."

Lilly said, "I know. Tonight is special; it'll be all take-out sitting in our cars from now on. You just can't plan on anything in our world today, Juan."

"I don't agree, Lilly. We can put some things in place. Some security for the bad and good days; a home for instance and folks we love. It's the only insurance against the world's troubles I know. By the way, I thought this was a good setting for decision making. Will you marry me, Lilly Tagliano, I truly love you; and this ring, well I've been carrying it around for a week?"

He took her hand and placed a very large diamond on it. Perhaps it looked large because Lilly's hand was so petite, but Lilly knew diamonds and she didn't think that was the reason. She paused and said, "I wasn't prepared for this, Juan. I didn't expect it. It's a beautiful ring. You don't have that kind of money. You can't spend this on a ring for me. I thought because you are hesitant in the romance department, you would take much longer to get to this point. I don't know what to say."

His look at her brought her to a new reality; one she was confounded to have creep into her heart. She thought for just a second, *he needs an answer. He's one of the good guys. I feel safe with him. I can't disappoint him ever. I just didn't' expect this so soon. I thought I had another year before deciding. Hell, no, I've already decided. Who else could I ever love after him?*

"I'll marry you, Juan, but you'll have to return the ring. We can't afford it."

A happy Juan, now recovered by what he thought was going to be a negative from Lilly, kissed and hugged her and said, "The ring stays and thank God you said 'yes.' The family's waiting to congratulate us."

"You mean they knew before I knew. Hell, Juan, that practice stops here; you get me?"

"Probably will, but understand, they want me happy. They knew you were the only girl I ever brought home. It was to be you, Lilly, or no one."

"What about that high school girlfriend who's now married with all those kids?"

"She lived in the neighborhood. I never brought her home. She'd just show up."

The two looked over a section of the beautiful maintained green golf course and kissed and talked and hugged until Lilly shivered from the cold. They returned to the dinner. From their happy faces, the family knew then their Juan got his answer, the right answer. The noise they all made was slightly embarrassing to the lovers, but then dessert was served and the waitress wished them a wonderful life ahead. Lilly said, "She knew too. Juan, who else knows?"

She thought she saw a blush but was uncertain with his darker skin color. He said, "Your parents and siblings, Captain Beauregard, and the detectives, and Millie. I think they're the only ones."

A flustered Lilly sighed and said quite loudly, "Juan, I'm going to have to teach you about keeping secrets."

Papi stopped the question of secrets and started what turned out to be toasting by every dinner guest.

———

Lilly and Juan entered the Pit to the tune of a wedding march playing on Petra's cell and a view of crazy pictures of Hollywood stars who had married recently. Applause and laughter filled the room and of course morning pastry was also served. Lilly was continually bombarded with questions on a wedding date, type of wedding, would they all be invited, who would be the best man and maid of honor, venue, music, wedding shower, etc. Lilly was exasperated and shouted loudly enough to be heard over the noise, "If you all don't shut up, we'll elope."

Ted laughed. "Won't happen, Lilly. Juan would tell us the location and the world will show."

The Captain said, rather quietly, "I'm pretty certain it won't happen until, at a minimum, the autumn. The state's going to close all but essential businesses. We're in the essential business description and we are going to have to make changes. No wedding venues for you, Lilly and Juan, be happy; it gives you time to reconcile yourselves to your future. Now while you're noshing, let's talk about how we'll be doing our work when the Governor slams his hammer. Chief Coyne is sending some thoughts down in a memo to all later this day, but I think we should have our ideas ready on safety issues. Think about the hit-and-run cases. If there is info a potential witness might have, bring them in now before there's an excuse not to leave their homes."

Some shuffling of folders occurred before Bobby spoke. "We have got to get Shirley in here by tomorrow. Maybe we should visit the ER where she works and talk to other people there. We could say it's to see the state of mind of some of the victims, but also check up on her as well."

Bill agreed and offered to accompany Bobby to ER on the same day Shirley was scheduled for an interview at the station.

The rest of the day was spent in planning case investigations given the potential COVID-19 interference with work product. The detectives amazed themselves with their ability to find ways around physical interviewing. They joked as they found potential solutions. After a couple of hours of detailed work, Bill Border said, "If they close non-essential business, we'll have to cook at home or if it's allowed and restaurants will do it, buy takeout. I'm dating. I can't hang out at her house all the time.

My place is lonely as hell."

Bobby quipped, "No problem for the newly engaged and married folks, they can all rub noses together. No being lonely for them."

Petra, not to be outdone, said, "Bill, you can take Baby Carlotta for a few nights. You won't be lonely and I'll destress."

They all remarked about Petra's continuing desire to share her baby until Petra said, "I love her; honest I do. But, but, I was meant to adopt an eight-year-old. I'd be great at playing games. Jim is the icky-sweet daddy, oohing over every smile. Although she is, I must admit, gosh darn cute."

Into the room waltzed Lieutenant Ashton Lent as if he still belonged in MCU. One remark after another, however, reminded him he was now a visitor. He disagreed, saying, "I heard from Millie there were pastries from the bakery here. It was an invite. Go fight with her."

And of course, no detective would ever argue with the Duchess of Admin, Millie Banks. Ash waved a folder, saying, "I have some good info for you. You don't get it if I can't get pastry and cappuccino. The coffee sucks over in Traffic."

Petra asked about Martina's health and the smile left Ash's face. He explained there was some doubt about Martina having a full recovery. There was some damage to the heart muscle and there may be a need for a second surgery. She was to take it easy. Ash wanted her to quit work, but she told him, "My brain is my biggest enemy, Ash. I imagine horrible results when I'm not busy. Music and you are my saviors and work is my structure."

"What can I do; just ride it out. I have hooked her up with a bio-feedback therapist. She balked at the thought at first. When you think about it, it makes sense. It does nothing but desensitize you from the thoughts and feelings about which you are sensitive. Martina is overly sensitive. Can't hurt trying. She went along with me on it. I'm grateful."

The Captain thought Ash looked strained from the conversation. He said, "Back to business you guys. What brought you here, Ash?"

"I checked about twelve of these so-called accidents reports. Being in traffic sets me up for discovering info from every traffic unit in affected departments. These guys love to gossip. They know who all the bigwigs are who were given a pass for driving under. I've learned a great deal. One thing I've noticed is that all but one of these accidents happened on a Tuesday evening. I don't think it's a coincidence and will be useful later."

There was total silence. Ash got the picture quickly and said, "You knew this already, didn't you? This is not new info to you? Hell, I'd better scurry away with my pastry and coffee or you'll take it from me."

Everyone talked at once until Beauregard shut them up. "Thanks, Ash. Ted is diligent in noticing details; he caught it. We agree and thank you. We, like you, know it will be important for corroboration when we get a suspect. What else have you seen in the fifteen reports you've looked at and may we have a copy of those reports if they came through a legitimate process?"

"They're already on your computer, Captain. I had to work one of the departments for honest access, but discovered the Chief was more amenable to sharing than the Captain of Traffic. I have not gone over all the reports, but Bobby, you are known for seeing problems with traffic reports. You'd be better than me at that."

Bobby Barr smiled. "In a month, Lieutenant, you'll know what I know, but I love this stuff. I'll be pleased to do a fine combing."

Ash left the room. Beauregard caught Millie as she was snagging a pastry and coffee and said, "Can you print an email on my computer from Ashton Lent, please?"

Stuffing the last bite of pastry in her mouth, Millie nodded while whispering, "No respect for a working girl here."

Lilly said, "Watch your language, Millie. You may have a great shape despite eating desserts all the time, but 'working girl' has a different connotation for the police."

"Aw, you all go on. I'm a Southern Girl. We eat pastry. We live for rich desserts. You Northerners give me a compliment while you correct my word usage. You all would not survive in the South; I can tell you that. It's not the issue of your manners, but you don't know how to restrain your mouths."

And with a harrumph, Millie left and then returned to the room with the reports in record time. Millie could slow down or speed up and transition easily between the two in seconds. Beauregard thought, *she's a gem. Hope the Chief doesn't try to pull her upstairs. His assistant is getting ready to retire.*

Mason grabbed them and said, "Let me do a spreadsheet on detail with Bobby. We'll not miss anything."

And the two retired to Mason's sacred office space which suited both Mason and Bobby well. The other detectives, not including Ted, thought the office was just too perfect to get any work done.

The detectives were busy today, scattered away from the Pit to do as many in person interviews as possible. Lilly and Petra were visiting Marie O'Connor, Ray LeFron's live-in. Bill and Ted were to hit the ER out of town where the Nurse Practitioner Shirley Baker worked. One of their objectives was to locate the other nurse practitioner Chad. His last name was unknown but they assumed he may work with Shirley since both nurses had visited at least one of the elderly victims together. Bill asked Ted, "Would they have two nurse practitioners together in one unit on one shift? Seems like a costly item for the hospital."

"All depends on the number of patients and any rules requiring a doctor or nurse practitioner to be present at all times. They have to eat and take breaks. Can't assume anything, Bill. As Charlotte says and I think she stole the phrase from the kids, 'It's not my monkey. Don't ask me.'"

Bobby Barr and Juan Flores had decided to assist Mason Smith with his calls and cataloging facts from files he was starting to receive from other departments, when Captain Beauregard interrupted. He changed their direction, saying, "Mason only needs one of you. Bobby, if Mason has trouble with any department, you can use your contacts in traffic divisions to find the best way around the problem. I don't need three of us out interviewing. I want Juan and myself to visit Springfield's traffic division. I've talked to the Chief there. She's on the task force and is open to our visit. Juan speaks Spanish and that division has several in the unit who will be open to Juan quicker than myself. One of the victims in Springfield was a friend of my dad's. My dad asks me every single day if I discovered more facts on this case. He never asks me for any help. I can't deny him."

Bobby and Mason found themselves working really well together. Mason said, "Bobby, I thought only the detailed Ted Torrington was a threat to my position. Both of you are good with computers. Not surprising since you're both a bit younger. You are fast, Bobby, and very neat. That's the highest compliment I can give."

They listed every stole car in each case. Mason made calls to the various departments' stolen car divisions in nearby cities and towns, when he knew someone, and Bobby made calls where he knew someone. They were startled when they realized they covered all accidents with the exception of the one in Russell. Mason said Ted's father knew the victim. "It's such a small town. The Captain knows the Chief well. He'll call on that one."

Four hours later, including an organic food break, the two detectives had a piece of astonishing information which made the dog work well worth their efforts and would bring a smile to their captain.

13

Making Headway, Maybe

Norbie Cull and his assistant Sheila were reviewing copies of police reports she'd received for ten accidents. She said, "More's coming but it was a bitch. I tried calling some connections I had but apparently there is some attention being given to these reports. Not one of my friends wanted to later testify about the reports being handed out willy nilly; especially to me who works for the super pushy defense lawyer."

Totally ignoring the jab, Norbie asked, "How'd you get them, Sheila?"

First, I went to the newspapers for reports on the accidents after I'd checked with obituaries for two years. You asked for more years, but it was difficult enough to get two years. Why can't your buddy, Captain Beauregard, help you out here?"

"Don't go there, Sheila. The line has been drawn. I have no client in these cases. I'll be getting one for certain soon. Remember Jerry La Follet? You made me see him. Well, I wouldn't take money from him when I was unsure about the facts involved, but I think now I'll take a hundred dollars to solidify my representation. I'll play the card if I'm hired by him when it becomes helpful or meaningful. He'll go along. He called me yesterday. I must have given him my cell. He and a friend called Nina have more to offer. Back to your research process."

"Norbie, once I got the name right from either a news report or an obituary notice, I called for police reports. When they're not new reports, I had to wait for them. I agreed to pick them up to make the process faster. A couple of the towns only mail them out. At first, I thought they looked normal. I wouldn't if I were in those police divisions look at them twice. I see tons of police reports in this office for accidents. These wouldn't stand out."

"Yeah, Sheila, you're dragging your feet. What did you notice?"

"You've taught me over the years, Norbie, to look for inconsistencies. I guess you taught me the reciprocal. They are almost carbon copies of each other from multiple police departments. Weird, don't you think?"

The two examined Sheila's notes and Norbie agreed with her assessment. In every single file she pulled, ten in all, the men were on the sidewalk and not near the street sidewalk edge. In two sites, the killer car had actually backed up over the body and then continued forward. He thought, *the killer car driver was ensuring death. Rudy must know this. Ten files and I'll bet the rest of the files all say the same thing. For certain, we have a serial killer of elderly men. I don't want to die this way. What the hell is the motive?*

"What do you think the motive is, Sheila?"

"Well, they are all unmarried men according to the reports in the papers. People left behind were not spouses. In one case, there was a significant other. So, they're not killed by their wives and they're too old to be killed by their moms or dads. Norbie, each obituary listed quotes from neighbors and friends celebrating the attributes of the deceased. I don't think it's likely one person was alienated by all of them."

"Good thinking, Sheila, and I agree. Is it possible a killer is doing some form of mercy killing? Were they all sick and facing hardship?

Maybe the killer thinks elderly men need to be removed from society. But why only men and if just men, would that notion imply a woman killer? Still, a car is not a normal weapon for a woman."

Sheila thought it may be a Medicare employee who was fed up with the amount of medical support given to the elderly. Norbie did not think a general thought, like reducing medical care costs for the elderly, had enough passion in it to sustain so many deaths. Each death required stealing a car, picking a victim, stalking the victim, coldly driving over them, and then dumping the car. He was convinced there was a more personal motive involved. He said, "In the end, we will find a killer who has a history involving the elderly; history could be good, Sheila, or it could be negative. Think hateful, getting even, or mercy killing them at a certain time in the victim's life."

Before he left for court, he asked Sheila to search the where, when, and how the cars were stolen.

Beauregard and Juan were greeted openly by Captain Kurt Shroeder in Springfield's Traffic unit. Having the Chief on the Task Force was helpful and ensured Shroeder would not hold back on the investigation. They went through the three files including Beauregard's dad's friend Lyle Pilon. All sites were on Boston Road and not near cameras. Captain Shroeder voiced his view about the perp. "He's familiar with the road. It is loaded with cameras and yet this guy's found three sites with no cameras. He has to be cognizant of how we put them up. Many cameras are barely noticeable even if you know to look for them; especially since tree work hasn't occurred yet."

When they asked about the location where the cars were stolen, they were given three addresses. Juan said, "Captains, two are on two of Bay

State Medical parking areas and one is on site at Mercy's new building where I did some rehab for my shoulder. It's a good source for choosing a car to steal, but all those sites have cameras. Couldn't you see the theft on camera?"

Captain Shroeder smiled. "We looked, and carefully. The owner in one case was unsure of the location where she parked her car. We found it leaving the space based on her description, but we could not get an identifying visual of the driver who was wearing a hood and dark glasses. The car, all the cars, were stolen near seven in the evening of the deaths. The perp had some unlocking device. We don't know what. At first, we thought the first car was stolen by a friend of the owner's, but that lasted a minute until we looked at her background. The other two cars were parked under a tree and the cameras did not catch much. We could see the cars being driven away, but in both cases, the cars were parked between two vans. The guy knows how to cover his activities. And, Rudy, there was absolutely no forensic evidence. We are now submitting dirt and debris to a more intensive analysis. I don't think they'll find anything."

Beauregard asked, "Where were the cars found and when?"

"Again, Rudy, each was found on a used car lot on the next day when the lot owners came into work. The perp had to park his own car nearby; all three cars lots are on busy streets. We checked camera footage near the lots. Each lot had its own cameras. One was not very helpful, but the other two showed the perp driving the car in and walking away. There is nothing distinctive about him. Here, I have them for you to see."

Beauregard was very interested in viewing them, thinking, he could have held them up for the task force meeting or ask me if I was interested in seeing them. If I expressed interest, he could have said it has to go through all the steps through his chief, etc. Instead he's inviting me to see them. Pretty fair of him, but I've enjoyed a good relationship with this department.

It took a bit of time to find the section of each tape. The three men nodded and agreed the perp was the same in each one. Juan said, "He's not Mexican, Black, or Puerto Rican, I can tell you that for certain. His color is too light. You can see the edge of his face and his hand. Look at the walk. He is a college graduate. He walks like a nice college boy but older. The sweats are not his; they're not sized for his body. He stole them or bought them for these activities and the sweats are different for each theft. He's not worried about money. See the label on the sweats on the second tape; it's a Nike label. He dumps them afterward; probably at some Savers or Goodwill box. He has means to dump a set of sweats costing close to a hundred bucks; I say he has a job."

No conclusions were verbally stated, but the potential profile of the perp registered with them.

Captain Shroeder asked, "So can we rule out a woman? Maybe she could be an accomplice but not in stealing these cars."

Beauregard answered quickly, "Not so fast, Kurt, how tall is our thief? I don't think he's taller than five foot eight or possibly a little more. And Juan says he walks like a college boy. It could be a woman. It's a graceful gait for a man. The sleeves are covering the hands in most of the shots like a teen girl wears those long sleeves down over their hands. Some guys do too, but not quite so often. A woman is not off the hook yet."

"Rudy, women don't rob cars normally. They are not the normal thieves I see."

"Kurt, with all this electronic stuff out there unlocking car doors and we see no damage on your theft cars to show a jimmy, it could be another entry mechanism. Also, look at the owners of the cars. The reports show they all worked in the facility where they parked their cars. What did they do?"

Juan said, "I noticed a few are cafeteria workers. You know the café workers know everybody and everybody knows everything about the café workers."

The Captain and Sergeant Flores left Springfield. While driving, Juan asked the question, "So are we looking for someone who works in the hospital, Captain? If so, we'll have to pull in all the owners of the cars and see if they are connected in some fashion to the victims. Or more likely, find out who they talk to and if there is a common employee to all the stolen car sites. It's a gumshoe investigation. How we going to do it with the Governor shutting down the state?"

"Work for you, Juan, when we're back at the station. Seventeen calls! You have Springfield and West Side info. Mason will have fifteen of the sites probably open to you by tomorrow morning. Review them. Set up interviews if the conversations get iffy. Other than that, talk about their work. If at the hospital, in what area is their work, and who do they regularly have meals with. Some may not work at the hospital, but just get free parking at the lots. And maybe all the stolen auto sites are not medically related. Could be parking for associated medical professional offices. Also, pay attention to where the stolen cars are found in other cities. We should have complete details soon."

Looking in the killer's mind's rearview mirror left the killer quite satisfied with the killing activities. The killer at this time referred to self as a 'you' thinking, *yes, thinking as always, I'm a you, not a he or a she, or not an I, a her, or a him. Using, You, helps push the action on the other. Something*

I learned in the chaos from the cast of characters of my childhood. You have done well, You. Yes, you have done well. Twenty killings on my beloved Route 20 and no one has a clue. How could they? You have been smart. Never make killing personal. It is not killing for personal motive but to do good. You know the importance of looking at the picture as a photographer would. You see in your sight like a motion picture camera: the view of the elderly man's needs, the vision of the car theft, the auto accident, and return of the stolen vehicle. Because it is you looking at the killing action script; you do not personalize the play. You are the spectator picking the play apart.

I remember telling HE about the few totally accidental encounters which could have screwed up the play. I may have been frightened about discovery, but I was able to correct the script. I told HE, you will have to be more careful in selecting the old men in the future. HE has gotten lazy. I think HE listens well except HE killed one man unnecessarily. The man had a good and loving caregiver. She would help him leave peacefully when the time came. This man was not alone. HE will have better opportunities for selection by visiting some senior center. HE can find persons who are not immediately connected to hospitals; just in case a smartie starts investigating. I hope HE hasn't missed some detail. I've checked. I don't think so; but why are two West Side detectives coming to the ER today? HE perfectly executed those actions. I don't like West Side detectives involved; there is the Detective Beauregard there who finds serial murderers. This death should be investigated by traffic division and not by murder investigators.

I really can't wait to discover what they want. Criticism is important for the artist. I'm rather excited about meeting them and the staff is excited. Nothing is kept secret in a hospital setting. HE may have been in error, but I trust HE will show more insight into HE's eagerness in the future. I can see HE is getting jumpy. I don't understand why. We've talked about it before. There must be some period of time between actions. HE must always consider consequences. HE's not a child. The last one was only ten days ago. HE must consider a good site for the next one in another town. Maybe further east out of Hampden County. No one will be looking in another county. HE must better research. Take more time before the next one. Find the poor soul who needs this help. Society doesn't understand how to take care of its good ones, the venerable, and give them ending comfort. HE must get busy.

He needs to remember past history. The history, both good and bad, belongs to HE. It is HE's purpose. Kindness is HE's purpose. Life has not been kind to these men lately. HE must want to be kind to these elderly men and help them to a better world. HE is doing the righteous thing. Why do I have to remind HE of our destiny? Why does HE quarrel with me? Yes, it is HE, HE who is my partner for the future.

Beauregard and Flores identified themselves and were greeted with a smile by the ER information kiosk staffer whose nametag said, Linda. Linda apparently was aware of their visit this day. Captain Beauregard said, "I hate to bother your hard-working staff. We think it's important or we wouldn't be here."

"Not to worry, Captain Beauregard, we were told to give you all the time you need. Are you looking into a murder? You're from West Side, not from this town. I've read about you in the news. The staff is ready for you. We have an extra doctor on for several hours if you need to talk to our normal resident physician, Dr. Jesse Teague. I know you asked to interview two of our nurse practitioners, Shirley Baker and Chad Roswell. They are great people and I'm certain they'll help you if they know anything. I'll show you to the interview room. It's awfully small, but we don't have a lot of extra space. It's the staff break room."

They walked to the room after Linda found coverage for her station. She chatted all the way about when the police brought in a patient and the accompanying required accommodations. They were offered bottled water but said no, and then were left to wait for their potential witness. It took ten minutes before a handsome brunette rushed into the room and introduced herself as Shirley Baker. She gave a big smile and apologized for making them wait, introduced herself, checked their badges, and asked how she could help. The detectives were slightly surprised at her asking for their badges, but forwarded their story on hit-and-run auto accidents being investigated by a task force and their interest was in the victims, their state of health, and those who may be able to give more information on the victims' abilities to take care of themselves. Beauregard hoped it sounded harmless and non-threatening. Shirley told him to fire away and both detectives relaxed their posture signaling a comfortable environment for all. Juan started the conversation as planned, saying, "Ms. Baker, do you remember Stan Korsecki, an elderly man who recently died in a West Side hit-and-run accident?"

Shirley answered, "Won't you call me Shirley, Detective Flores? Yes, I do remember Stan. How could I forget that dear, very sweet man? There isn't anyone he wouldn't help with their problems. I first met him before he was sick when he'd drive patients to the hospital from various facilities for treatment. He'd come visit us asking if anyone needed rides back. He'd do this even when he wasn't driving to the ER, just the main hospital for the drop off point. You know he had some health problems? Perhaps his death was timely after all."

Juan remarked, "Timely? Do you say that because of his cancer issue?"

"You know about his cancer, Detective? He generally kept silent about his health. Yes, he had advanced lung cancer. It was discovered when he went for a small surgery on his colon. There was no option for additional surgery on the lung; just chemo and radiation but it had spread. Like many of the old timers he was a long-time smoker, gave it up about fifteen years ago, but ignored a hacking cough. He told me he wasn't afraid of doctors and hospitals until he lost his wife. He suffered terribly from loneliness after her death. He thought she was the most wonderful woman. I quote, 'How do you ever feel excitement equal to when you had a perfect partner. And she tried diligently to live for me; but instead we joined in to prolonging her agony. She said if she was to die, my job was to go out and volunteer to help others. That's what I do and I do it for her.'"

Beauregard asked her how often she saw Stan and was dumbfounded to hear she saw him at least fifteen times including lunch and coffee breaks during his frequent trips to the hospital. She explained both Chad Roswell, another nurse practitioner and Dr. Teague all thought highly of Stan. "We worked to keep him chipper; each of us in our own way. Detectives, we are in the caregiving business and despite what you have heard about the medical profession, some of us truly care."

Beauregard discovered Shirley knew where Stan lived and had even been at the Chili contest. He did not remember her but the contest took most of a day and he was not there the whole time. He did query to himself, *why wouldn't I remember such a pretty lady?*

Juan wanted to know what was most distinctive about Stan and his habits. Her smile included a laugh about his fear of dying slowly like his wife and his insistence on taking good care of his sick body. When questioned about what type of care he took, she related his absolute dedication to walking each evening. Shirley thought it was a sign of a man conflicted; one who was hoping God would reward him for staying the course even while he wished not to. She added, "We all were affected by his death here in the ER; particularly Chad and Dr. Teague. He should have been taken more mercifully by the heavens. Tell me please, did he die, instantly?"

Within a second, Juan nodded his head leaving Beauregard thinking, she does look as if she is truthful, but why would Juan share any detail when we are in the business of getting details, not giving them. This Shirley is a perfect example of a woman who presents herself with grace, charm, integrity, and kindness. Is she too perfect? I always measure against that standard. Too perfect is not always necessarily a good trait; it can imply evidence of a manipulative sociopath. I can't say that particular word aloud to my MCU detectives. They'd respond saying I was back to my favorite subject; but I also can't ignore my experience. The major problem involves our lack of investigative timing. One only knows if her good traits mask a killer by watching the related actions. She does purport herself well.

The conversation continued. Juan carried it well with lots of touchy-feely sentiments for Stan Korsecki. When he finished documenting her recollection of the approximate dates and locations of her interactions with Stan, he asked if she met Stan alone. Shirley reported when she met with Stan at the hospital, both Chad and Dr. Teague would also congregate because, "Stan was the most charming and endearing man, but we all could see he craved our company and good conversation. He gave more than he got in that regard. He liked to talk, as many of our elder citizens do. They have so much to share. We loved his visits and he'd always look around the ER to see if any of his regular clients he drove for were there. If so, he'd interact with them."

Beauregard asked, "Shirley, tell us about two other West Side elderly men who died in the same manner. They are Ray LeFron and Pete Proder. Both men died in the same way. Did you connect well with them?"

"Captain, I knew Ray quite well. I was a floor nurse in the Springfield Hospital when I first met him, and later got to know him well when he'd come in here. He suffered from a chronic lung condition and I mean really suffered. But Pete Proder, I didn't know well at all. I mean I heard through the grapevine later he had died, and I believe I saw a memorial set up on Facebook, but no mention was made about the cause of his death. I even read his obituary. It mentioned making donations to the cancer society. I'm saddened by hearing his cause of death. He was a dear man and much loved and I'm told he never complained about suffering."

"Does it matter whether the man has a loving caretaker or is alone, Shirley?"

"No, I don't mean to insinuate or to minimize the horror of death by being struck by a car, but the other two men were very lonely. Pete was not lonely and he would have had any procedure if it promised him continued life. He was different from the others; Stan and Ray."

Juan documented Shirley's visits with Ray and Stan and questioned her if Chad and Dr. Teague were friendly with the two as well. Her yes answer required her to remember dates and times of their visits. She named some dates but assured them they may have met at other times with Ray and Pete. She was asked if it was unusual for a nurse, even a nurse practitioner, to visit patients in their homes. She answered, "I don't date them, Detectives, but I do try to drop some pastries to them when I get a feeling one or another are down in the dumps. Sometimes they call me with a question about medication when I know there is no ignorance about meds there. It's really my social life other than an occasional date I might have. I'm not married. I have time for charitable visits. I'm what you call, a part of the unpaid do-gooders. My grandmother had these same qualities. I'm carrying on the family tradition."

Shirley gave them a most winning smile; a smile to fall in love with, but which left them more uncertain. They ended the interview after she answered questions about the three men's walking and balancing abilities given their advanced age and illnesses. She assured them she never had to help them and they never asked for physical assistance.

The Captain asked Shirley how she found time for other activities given her penchant of spending time helping all these elderly men. He answer was interesting to him. "Captain, I'm a runner and join all the 5K races for good causes. I've stopped recently because I've been busy adjusting to my new home, work, and now the impending virus. I'll get back to it."

A final inquiry about the men's schedules in the evenings was answered with great sarcasm but with detailed information. She willingly told them about their tendency to walk on some or all evenings. She went further, explaining the tendency of older men to enjoy an evening stretch while most of the older women she knew walked in the morning and rarely alone.

They were left alone while Shirley notified Chad they were waiting. It was ten minutes before he showed. Chad Roswell was direct with a forceful handshake. He had the build of an in-shape construction worker with a kind smile. Beauregard's first thought was, *I like him already. He's not a slacker and smiles as if he means it; but his eyes are wary. I suppose he's not used to being interviewed by detectives… I don't know about those eyes though. I'm thinking like usual, suspecting anyone who looks too good.*

Chad chatted away about his being delayed by a patient who was overwhelmed with her injuries, and added to her distress was the fact her daughter had not yet arrived to help her make decisions; and there were decisions to be made. While he chatted, both detectives were obvious in their checking him out. Chad stopped chatting and said, "Did I say something off? I feel like you're about to grill me."

Juan spoke softly. "No, Mr. Roswell, you are not what we expected. We heard from others, friends of some elderly men who died, how comforting you were to them in their loneliness. You don't look like a caretaker type, despite the fact that nursing is in the caretaking business. You look like an ad for a project manager on a construction site. Right, Captain?"

Annoyed at being brought into Juan's soft touch conversation, Beauregard still nodded in the affirmative. He said, "It is true. I think you must have been a welcome treat for the men we're here to discuss. They would trust you. I'm certain Shirley took a moment to explain our mission. We're interested in several men who died in hit-and-run accidents in West Side: Ray LeFron, Stan Korsecki, and Peter Proder."

With a smile, Chad said, "Yes, she did tell me and very quickly so I wouldn't make you wait too long. We do, much like cops, take care of our fellow colleagues here; much like the old blue line. And I did know all those men, but I didn't know Pete Proder was killed in an accident. The men, Captain, were all strong in mind and spirit. They loved talking with us and if they occasionally expressed their dissatisfaction with their loneliness, we were all open to some conversation. It's what we do here."

Juan asked, "You certainly can't give every patient the attention you gave to these men. We were informed you came to visit them in their homes. Is it a normal practice?"

"No, Detective, it is not what you call a normal practice, but it's not also an abnormal practice. I get the idea you are looking at me and I can't imagine why. I liked these men. I wanted them to live forever. Ray and Stan both had problems with their lungs. I don't know if Pete had any major problems. Their company was the best. Most of the patients I see are not particularly open to discussion. When I meet one who is intelligent and worldly and easy to get to know, I enjoy the moment."

"I have a few questions; I'll throw them all at once. Can you tell me more about them? Were they open in telling the world about their schedules? Were they depressed? Pete had a significant other and one would think he would not have great loneliness?"

Chad said, "Pete was not lonely, but he had so much to share about his business. His lady friend, well, I'd love to have somebody who loved me like she loved Pete. Pete was a seriously scheduled guy and quite open about his life. I never heard he was depressed; no, not to me did he ever say he was down. He and his lady friend were some couple."

Beauregard questioned Chad about Pete's lady friend Carolyn Aster. "Pete left all his assets, and they were substantial, to Carolyn. What did you think of her?"

"I just told you. She was wonderful to him. She loved him. So, he left everything to her; she wasn't interested in money. She wanted him alive. They had such good times together."

Juan said, "You're knowledgeable about medicine, I need an answer to a question I don't understand. Many of these men had some form of disease like cancer. Probably they were taking chemo or radiation or at least chemo pills and yet they were all known for their habit of taking long walks in the evening. Seems unlikely to me and I'm young. If I had cancer I may not have strayed far from home on long walks."

"I think, Detective, it's precisely because you are young. You don't understand. These men did not give into themselves. They'd work through pain. A couple had military backgrounds. They were philosophical about end of life. It's not unusual for patients to enjoy the majesty of the outdoors as a refuge at this time, when they expect the end impending. Our day will come, Detective. We'll think the same way when the time comes."

The Captain showed discomfort as if he himself had been chastised and he responded, "You may have something there, Mr. Roswell. On the other hand, I live in a more fact-based world. If you don't mind, can you think of anyone these three men could have rubbed shoulders with but not in a good way?"

"No, Captain, and I don't think anyone else will tell you differently. Unless they'd been in a road rage situation, I can't even imagine their inspiring anger. They all drove a van or small bus for patients and not one complaint have I ever heard about their driving. Sorry, I can't help you."

Juan asked, "Mr. Roswell, you do not have a regional accent, although Western Mass citizens believe they have no accents, but I can tell the difference. Where'd you grow up?"

Chad answered, "My life is an open record, Detective, I grew up in Ohio in Lakeland which is a small town. It's a nice town."

"Did you do your nursing program in Lakeland, Mr. Roswell?"

He answered, "I did my nursing degree but not my PA there. Nursing is all I've ever wanted to do. It was a great start."

They were interrupted by Linda from the ER info desk saying,

"Chad, they need you in there. Shirley's off at lunch and this is the only time Dr. Teague is available."

Before Chad could leave, the Captain asked, "Are you a runner, Mr. Roswell? You're in very good shape."

Chad smiled as he replied, "Nope. I could never do after school sports in school. My mom needed me at home and by the time I got to college, there just weren't enough hours in the day. I do some weights and cardio at the gym. What about you, Captain. Are you a runner?"

Beauregard laughed, saying, "Do I look like a runner? I wish!"

Chad said goodbye and it took five minutes before Dr. Teague entered the tiny room. Juan thought, he looks like a TV doctor. Must be a heartthrob for all his patients and nurses. No wedding ring and no mark showing he took one off. Can't see his type taking an interest in old men.

He introduced himself as Jesse Teague, while Beauregard introduced himself as Captain Beauregard, and continually addressed Jesse as Dr. Teague. There was the usual discussion about the ER and its patients and their various problems before the subject of elderly men dying in accidents was approached. Dr. Teague had no problem discussing the issue, saying, "God, it was just the other day when Shirley, Chad, and I realized we had treated several elderly men who were later found as victims in road kills. It's a lousy way to go, I guess; but I've seen worse ways to leave this earth in the form of long-term suffering."

Juan asked, "Which elderly men were you friendly with or assisted to some of their needs outside of the ER setting?"

"Well, probably quite a few, but I'd need a name to remember a person. I do remember Stan and Oscar. Shirley and I talked with Chad about their deaths."

Beauregard quizzed, "Dr. Teague, tell me about the walking habits for old men, in general, I mean."

Teague easily answered, "Well they're like all of us, Captain. You have the energetic and the sitting folks. Time has forced them all to compromise in some manner. It's interesting how the internal spirit forces some of them to fight all the way until the end of life. Some walk and run into their late nineties; they understand they have to continually move. Golf is a great game for elderly men, and women I suppose, as long as arthritis hasn't affected their joints too much. Most of the walkers pay attention to their health. You know, they eat right. Some elderly are just mad they're getting old and plainly give up. They're the ones waiting to die. Medically, I can't do a thing for them. Often, they just want more anti-anxiety pills. It's a bitch to be their doctor when they won't try."

Juan questioned, "Doc, do some of the elderly wish for death?"

Teague shot back, "If you think we help them die you are wrong. Besides, why would I help anyone who won't help himself. No way. I respect the walkers who fight the good fight all the way to the end."

The Captain offhandedly said, "You look like a runner, Doctor. Did you ever compete?"

"Thanks for noticing, Captain Beauregard. I ran track in high school. I was a sprinter."

Earlier, Beauregard had noticed Teague's phrasing of putting Shirley's name with his own and as a twosome when speaking with Chad and thought, *he's got something going with Shirley, I'm certain of it. A background search on all three of these goody medical folks is in order. And now, he likes the walkers. If he's the perp, why kill the ones he likes? Makes sense if I buy into the mercy killing idea.*

Juan questioned where Jesse had been before settling in Western

Massachusetts. Dr. Teague graduated from medical school in Chicago, interned in Ohio, and came to Boston for his residency before taking this position in Western Massachusetts. He said, "I've never been happier than I am now. I hope it lasts. I'm sick of moving."

The Captain gave the same statement as was given to the others before informing Dr. Teague they may be back with more questions. He added, "Doctor, what do you think about this virus? Is it going to be a big problem?"

Teague appeared solemn, saying, "We have already seen a few cases and one was tough. We think we've seen more of them but the patients were not too sick. We've been told not to plan too much, but in the ER, we've already set up a questionnaire for patients and two beds in isolation. Myself, I think we are in trouble. The next few weeks will tell us. If you need me or Shirley or Chad later for questions, I think it will be difficult."

"Why, Dr. Teague, are you going elsewhere?"

Teague gave the Captain a quizzical look, smiled, and said, "No, Captain, I think we are going to be in over our heads with this virus. I've read all the reports from Boston. If it hits us hard, our facilities and staff will be stretched; no, I mean over-stretched."

"Not to worry, Doctor, if we need a conversation, we'll find you at your convenience. Meanwhile, if you remember other older men you knew well who died later in car accidents let us know. Ask about others here who may have their ears to the sounds of the broader community."

Teague looked startled, saying, "You think there are more, don't you? There can't be that many more, Captain. There just can't be. Good luck, but don't mind if I hope you are wrong that there are more of these deaths."

The drive back to West Side forced the detectives to search for an oasis with food and enough quiet to allow a private conversation. They took Route 20 west. The Captain said, "What is the magic in this road? It's an old road. It hides its history. All kinds of new development happened and made this major route west almost a secondary road. Sometimes it connects to little side roads and other times it's part of an interstate or major state road. Why murder only on this road?"

Juan said, "If all seventeen murders are connected to one person, we may have to consider other killings off this road as part of his forte, Captain, too. Seventeen killings makes him a person who passionately, deliberately, and with some hidden motive, murders elderly men on this route. I know you like to hold on to this route as an element to motive, but maybe it's not."

Beauregard looking at his iPhone, said, "Head over here, Juan. We'll hit Russo's Steakhouse in Palmer. I'm hungry. My stomach is making noises which interfere with brain function and Mona is having salmon and salad. Every week, once a week, it's salmon and salad. Not potato or rice or bread is even put on the table. Healthy eating is killing me. I can't wait for the nutritionists to tell me salmon and salad isn't good for me. I remember when eggs were bad for your heart. I never listened to such advice. My Canadian parents have eggs with their oatmeal every day and they are in great shape for their age."

Juan said, "Mona is just trying to keep you alive. I'm like your Mona, Captain. My parents have corn and wheat with everything. I try to slow Mamita down on the carbs. We don't have many older people still living in my immediate family. Mamita tries to change the diet, but my Papi wants traditional."

They pulled into Russo's. The smell was wonderful. Both ordered steaks, although one was a rib eye and the other a sirloin with mashed potatoes and a salad. Halfway thought filling their bellies, Beauregard asked Juan, "What do you think of the three of them?"

"I don't know, Captain. They don't look or act like dirtbags. Chad's eyes are watchful. The Doctor looks unusually aware, but he is an ER doctor. They may all be extra focused. Shirley is charming and has a beautiful smile. I'm not so good analyzing pretty ladies who act nicely."

Beauregard laughed at his sergeant. He said, "Who is, Juan; you tell me who is? But she's in four of the victims' lives and I'll bet my paycheck she's in more of their lives. I want backgrounds on this group of ER medical folks. Why would Teague come from the big leagues in Chicago for here? Maybe he didn't get an offer in a larger city or there's something negative in his background; although I forget that BayState Medical is one of the larger hospitals in Massachusetts. Did these three know each other before here or were they in a common work situation? Does Route 20 go through the areas where they grew up? I want to know about their childhoods. Were their backgrounds loaded with trauma; particularly were they raised by older parents or grandparents or foster parents? Three professionals going out of their way to give support to elderly men without a particular medical requirement is not the norm. I always have to question deviations from the norm. The norm in childrearing is problematic enough without complications from moving away from the norm. I feel their need to help may be based on their childhood, and issues born then. I feel there is something."

Juan said, "Captain, they are all runners or exercise buffs. Pretty smart of you to follow that observation, but the answers keep them all in the same boat. A different answer from any one of them could lead to evidence, but didn't. I don't know, Captain, when you start feeling without evidence, you worry me. Your instincts are notorious for finding trouble. I'll go with them, but I'm a touchy-feely guy, less instinctive; and I only got vibes from Chad. He kind of blocked his feelings out for a few seconds. His eyes tell everything. So maybe there is something in his background. I don't get anything from Shirley. She seems like just a special lady; you know nice and all that. The Doc seems too smart and quick in his answers. But why would a guy who has everything want to kill?"

"Killers all have a motive. Most often the motive is difficult for us to get. The problem, Juan, is, we ordinary folks can't easily understand the distortion in their brains that allows them to take a life."

14

Cull as a Busybody

It took Sheila a few days to bring Norbie her report along with Jim Locke's investigative report. She told Norbie, "I smell something too, after all the stats came in. You are doing some good here, Norbie. There is a killer out there, looking for his next victim."

Norbie told Sheila to hold his calls and started on the reports. Between the two reports, he saw the commonality of sites from which the cars were stolen as well as where they were dumped afterward. He had friends in low places, not just in high places and decided a personal visit to each car dumping site was in order. He'd contacted them all in the past for clients' various legal reasons and thought, *there's no reason not to visit them again.*

Cull took the list and headed for the closest used auto shop which was in Agawam, thinking, the killer didn't hit Agawam, but knows where it is. Is he a native of Western Massachusetts? I don't think so. If he were, there'd be older evidence of this stuff. I'm no shrink but the deviance of this killer's choice of victim and weapon must have been growing in him for years. Unless he's mentally damaged from an accident or disease; hell, I don't know but I'll find out.

He spent his first two hours at three sites, one in Agawam, one in West Side, and one in Springfield. No luck! He moved to the next one in

East Longmeadow, Polan's Autos, and met up with an old friend, Lucky Polan, the owner. Lucky, known as a veteran but lucky gambler, was in a good mood and was available for a discussion on any topic saying, "I'm bored, Norbie, and I never get to see you at the club now. What's up? Is Sheri controlling after all these years."

With a smile, Norbie responded, "You haven't seen me because when MGM opened in Springfield, your attendance at the club was spotty. How come the casino hasn't thrown you out yet, Lucky? You must be marked by some of the casinos. The word gets out."

"Not yet, but if I hit another big one I'm a goner. I try to keep the wins within the daily limit, but their computers will find me soon; then they'll watch. Too bad because I like the feel of this location. So, what's up, Norbie, I may be available for gossip, but you're missing a thousand bucks an hour talking to me."

"Did you forget this is Springfield, not Boston? Legal fees are affordable here. I do want to gossip about a stolen car left on your lot a while back."

"Which one, Norbie? It happens about one or two times every quarter."

Norbie gave the date and make of car. He knew these guys in the car business were aware of each auto profile, more than they knew about their wife's birthday or anniversary. He often marveled at their memory when sitting over drinks with his insurance agent, who totally agreed. It took Lucky about thirty seconds to pull the auto data from his mental computer, saying, "Yeah, I remember the car. It wasn't the normal kind of stolen car. The thief had to be digitally knowledgeable. He'd got in with one of those gadgets. If you have a remote to start your car from inside your house, the gadget can access your car. It's called a relay attack device. It only works on cars that have a keyless remote and push-button start. It's useful on cars produced after 2010 and before 2018. I told the police this is how it was stolen if it was locked and it hadn't been hardwired. The thief is professional, Norbie."

"What about camera footage?"

"Of course, I have camera footage and the police got it, well most of it. My sales guy talked with the police the day they came and offered what he thought was all of the videos. I don't tell him about two of the videos playing remotely for me to see what he's doing. I took a look. They cover the side street and back of my building. It gives me a longer view. I'll show you. Maybe you can see something. I did see a country club type dude running like a team runner, not a street guy."

Norbie took a look and agreed, thinking, not a hood, though wearing a hoodie, but ducking down like a runner. Definitely he's a runner. He's pulled his sleeve to check his watch. Why no cell phone? Of course, if caught, the police could check his whereabouts. He pulled up his sleeve. I'll bet I can get the make of the watch if I can get Lucky to give the tape up.

Lucky gave it up. Mainly because Norbie played his role as not too interested except having a desire to appease his client. His thinking was, *I'll have to give it to Springfield police eventually, if I find something on it. I'll pretend it's no big deal. If I seem to need it Lucky will exact a price and not just dinner at the club.*

Norbie walked away with the video, but also with an offer for dinner at the club. Both men were pleased with the exchange.

———

HE is gaining control. HE wouldn't agree on the rules. HE is worse than working alone. I hope HE won't think he is the planner. I'll have to pacify HE. HE will go along with what I want as long as I give a little. I don't like to think of myself as manipulating and controlling, but like in all things in life, use of a bad trait is sometimes necessary. It's better than being manipulated and controlled. HE is looking at a person who really is not a candidate for dying. I think HE was thrown off course by the patient's attitude on God. HE absolutely hates God, but goes to church every week. Talk about an anomaly. I have explained to HE quite often, God does not like HE's insistence on sending patients home before God desires. I mean, how silly is this idea. You either believe in God or you don't. HE, I think, really believes. I'm uncertain about believing in unproven, unscientific concepts, but I must say history has never been completely able to prove the non-existence of God. Then again, who can prove the existence of God?

This potential victim HE has chosen is unacceptable. I wonder why HE has insisted on his dying. I can't always be there with HE, when HE is making a decision. I am able to be with HE when HE is distracted; that's when I know what HE is thinking. But I believe HE deliberately shuts me out when HE is thinking about going against my wishes. HE is like a naughty child in many ways. I do like HE. HE has been with me for a long time and has saved me from attacks. HE sees what I don't see. HE sees evil in other's thoughts quicker than I do. HE has done some dirty deeds to protect me and often is more astute than I am. However, HE is a risktaker. I'll have to be careful.

I often wonder if HE knows what is on my mind. Is HE like me? Does HE have to wait until I'm distracted before HE can figure what is inside my brain? How do I give my thoughts away to him? I'll have to test for that. I can play games too and now my understanding of HE's abilities is important; I can protect us both. HE sees only what HE wants. We both are at risk. I must stop this particular mercy killing. I think instead it's a hate killing or just a lust to kill.

———

Chad was having a quick supper in the café with Shirley. Things were heating up in the ER. Despite it being Tuesday his day off, the regular staff had been called in to a management information session. He thought, *foolish, it's just a waste of time. We all know what's coming down. Just look at what's posted on FB or is in Google or Fox or CNN. I've never seen so many info items all interpreted differently. It'll be interesting to see what the top docs here have to say. I know Jesse is speaking. I already know what he has to say. Shirley thinks he's in the know. Teague goes to great lengths to impress her; my only route to her is in showing my adherence to morality and kindness. It would be the kiss of death in our relationship if I showed any jealousy. I am jealous; I just can't show it. Teague gets credit for any medical issue he goes on about.*

Shirley joined him with trays for them both as had been previously agreed. His favorite on Tuesday's menu, when he was here on a Tuesday, was always American chop suey. It was the one meal his mother made in excess because at that time ground beef was pretty cheap. It brought back a memory of when he ate dinner and was full afterward. He never got a dessert on those nights then. It would be gingerbread with cream. The 'Olds' would always want seconds of anything sweet; none would be left for him. He greeted her and thanked her for getting the supper trays. She said, "Chad, you always do it, and tonight we're so rushed. We were all called in today to work. I checked in two suspicious virus cases that tested out to be flu. What about you?"

Before he could answer, Teague appeared with his own tray. He had a super double cheeseburger with lots of onions on top and fries. Shirley remarked, "Big calories tonight, Jesse, you need nourishment for your speaking engagement?"

Jesse answered with another question. "I noticed you got Chad's meal but you didn't offer to get mine."

Shirley did not defend her actions. Surprisingly she said, "I don't respond to questions about my actions, Jesse, you ought to know that by now."

After a moment of discomfort for them all, Jesse continued with a discussion on the virus and his expectation that all their professional and personal lives were about to change. He relayed a summary of what he had heard, saying, "Stuff's going back and forth all the time. I say stuff because I question the validity of the info. Politics, science, and economics are being rolled into one big question. The question is, 'Do we force people into isolation?' From what I've heard, China has not been quite honest with us. They had it earlier than what we were told. They closed Wuhan province, but let many Chinese leave Wuhan and their country. Boston, Milan, and Venice received a great many Chinese returning home. Now we hear deaths totaling big numbers. The United States is a big country. I don't know how we'll contain it. I've worked in several states and the rules related to medicine are different in each state. It sounds like a virus similar to SARS but may be more contagious. I'm afraid some of us working here will get this virus. Tonight, they'll be giving us new rules for the ER. Those rules will just make our lives more difficult."

Shirley commented, "Jesse, we'll deal with it. We always do. What will be a problem is dealing with more death! Depression hits me after I've been nursing a patient who just died. I know I don't do as much on-patient care as a nurse, but when a person touches my soul and I lose them, I find myself in a kind of emotional feeding frenzy. That feeling I get pushes me to do something risky to save the world."

A concerned looking Chad answered, "Shirley, I've never seen you show emotion, at least the high level of emotion you just described. I'll watch out for you in the future. Thinking and feeling together can create great anxiety and we know anxiety often leads to depression. We see it happening with the elderly who have few personal connections."

Teague appeared frustrated by this conversation and responded, "Shirley and Chad, I've never seen a nurse, nurse practitioner, physician's assistant, or doctor with a more consistent attitude of positivity in their job as you, Shirley. I don't go along with this discussion. What happens mostly happens for a good reason. The patient dies! The patient may die for all the normal reasons. Poor health history, diabetes, physical organ deficiencies, mental health issues, abuse at home, and chronic systemic disease all play a role in patients' background leaving them less capable of fighting infection. This virus is supposed to be like the SARS virus, but more contagious. Yup, there will be more deaths. Tears and sympathy will not help. Good medical care might, and I say might, because I don't have enough information to be certain. I can't stand anticipation of the negative; it doesn't help. Some of those dying will be people whose lives are currently unlivable. This is especially true amongst the elderly. Not such a bad end in my mind. A short illness may be preferable to two or three years of suffering."

Frowns and fidgeting in their seats were the first symptom of the other two medical providers' discomfort. Shirley and then Chad heatedly argued against Jesse's lack of emotion and acceptance of death. Thankfully, they were prevented from continuing by another doctor approaching them who reminded them they'd better get moving or they'd miss the lecture.

———

Back at his office, Sheila uploaded the file, enlarging the picture of the arm with the watch. The watch was an iWatch in stainless and black faced. Sheila said all the older ones have black faces unless touched to see whatever gadget you wanted to see. This one showed the face a minute after the man looked at it. Sheila said, "Go to the Apple store or even Verizon, Norbie; they'll immediately know the make and the size."

"Sheila, it looks pretty big to me; can't be a woman's."

"Norbie, my sister has one and wears it all the time and it looks to me like a man's watch. You can't be certain. Even if Apple says it is a man's watch, some ladies like them oversized."

Norbie growled, saying, "Just when did women decide to change their dress style to men's clothing style."

Laughing, Sheila said, "Sydney, your daughter is in high school, Norbie, and the last time she came in here she had her hair slicked back and was dressed in jeans and a man's Red Sox T-shirt."

"Well that's what all her friends are wearing. And her hair may be slicked back but she has added a fake hairpiece in the back. I think it's cute."

"Oh, so as long as she has a feminine touch to it, it's okay? You're not homophobic, I hope."

"I don't think so but if any of my children are gay, well, I think it's a different way of living. I'll help them out, but I can't say I will totally understand their choice. I'll do my best, but my gay clients seem to have more baggage. Maybe it's from their parents or teachers or friends who don't understand; I don't know."

Sheila laughed and said, "And from their lawyers?"

Cull spent the morning on the phone calling more auto shops. He had more success with three who he'd helped in the past. One was out in Westfield, another in Palmer, and the third - another one in East Longmeadow. He now knew how to approach the owners with a question about video on the back of the shops not shared with the police. He thought, *if one of these operators has secret cameras unknown to employees, I'm certain others will too. It's a small club of used car dealers in this area. I know they exchange cars to sell. Fancy used cars have a different market from the low-end ones. If it's not in their market they exchange to another dealer adding a little premium for themselves. When it comes to calculating cost differential from holding a car on the lot for six weeks to maybe giving up a sale profit for a kickback, they know when to fold. I'll ask for other cameras after we play the game of friendship, my client, or their troubles.*

An hour later, Cull had additional tapes from two of the auto dealers; one from Westfield and the second from East Longmeadow. The two had been his clients in some serious criminal business facing the local AG's office in Springfield on a consumer fraud investigation. Cull had been able to get one case dismissed and the other case's payment reduced with no triple damage penalty. They were wins and the auto dealers wanted to keep Cull in their pockets for potential problems in the future.

Sheila set the film up for viewing and said, "I've got some microwave popcorn for the movie, Norbie." He told her to stop being a wise-ass and she responded with, "No way. You had two assistants before me and both had to have babies to quit. You're so agreeable, but my job requires a sense of humor; I have to be a techie, an actress, a gossiper, an expert in real estate, criminals, drugs, keys, and on and on. You need me. No one else will last with you plus Sheri says you love popcorn."

The films were good, actually having cleaner views than the other one. There was better lighting that didn't distort the action. The killer had a habit in each as in the first of glancing at his watch on his left hand to see the time after he parked the car. Sheila said, "Whoever the killer is, he's OCD. He drives well. Notice, Norbie, he shuts off the car's lights and still backs into an empty space in the middle row of cars as if he knew already it was there. I think he knew it was there; it's just too perfect. He has gloves on. Norbie, they look like surgical gloves. Look, he rolls them off, doesn't pull them off. I worked as a hospital candy striper when I was a senior in high school. I watched doctors who removed their gloves in the same way. I can't really see the size of the hand, but it's not a large hand. What do you see? And he's probably right handed since he's wearing the watch on his left hand."

"Sheila, I see a smart and agile perp. Look how he moves in the small space and then runs. His legs are strong but not heavy. His build is difficult to assess. The guy is wearing a big sweat shirt in all the videos, but wearing slimmer sweats in this. He's no taller than five foot eight or nine inches. No hair showing because the cap is pulled way down. Over on the East Longmeadow video, he parked his car in the restaurant parking lot next door. It's loaded with cars. He's a brazen bastard to unload a murder vehicle in front of a full lot with people going in and out. I can't see the make of his car. It's black or dark gray or dark blue; a sedan. Scan the film again. Maybe you'll see more."

"Hell, Norbie, if it were a lady's body, you'd want to do the scanning."

"I pay you high bucks for your ingenuity and resourcefulness, Sheila."

"It's time for my evaluation and I'll remember to put those adjectives in my request for an increase."

Norbie groaned as he left his office thinking, Sheila would make a great auditor. She sees more than the average person. Now I'll try the hospital parking lots. It's Tuesday and I hope the same security staff will be on. The killer only stole from five lots. He's familiar with those lots.

Armed with a take-out grinder and a seltzer from Mom and Rico's in Springfield, he headed for Bay State Hospital. The police reports had seven of the cars stolen over the two years. He noticed the cameras' excellent and strategic placements. All seven of these thefts were in late fall, early winter, or early spring. He thought, *seven in the evening would be dark enough. It's close to seven now. What do I see? I'm a lawyer. I don't do this kind of investigation unless I have a questionable accident case. I've done enough of those; I should be able to understand the thief's motivations for stealing at these times and for leaving the cars later in another city. That's the easy answer. Cars stolen from here, when discovered, would have the all-out search by Springfield police in the immediate area of theft; although the surrounding city cops and Staties would be notified with auto descriptions. Still, the thief had a better chance to dump a car further away, having left his car at some faraway site.*

He searched for all the particular sites as stated in police reports. Surprisingly, the thief stole three of them from the same area and two from another area, and the remaining two from separate spaces further apart. He stopped for a minute and thought, *I'm an idiot. The thief's car is over by the dumping site. How did he get here? Did he use Uber? Are there two involved in this fiasco? Does he have two cars; one parked here and expected to be here, and the other parked over at the dump site. How did that car get to the dump site?*

He located the security guard whose service involved his continual driving around the lot looking for break-ins or drivers who were having a problem with their cars. The security service was well known and the owners lived in Ludlow and were known to him. Norbie thought, *if I have a problem with this guy, whoever he is, I'll call John. Even if I have to make a trip to Ludlow it may be worth it.*

There was no problem. The driver was a long-ago client he'd represented in a domestic dispute. "Hal, I didn't know you were in security?"

"I wasn't until last year. My company was going bankrupt. I saw the writing on the wall about two years before the ship sank, grabbed my pension and got out. We'd saved, and life was good, but I'm really too young to retire. John, the owner has been good to me; lets me choose the hours I want to work. He knows I'm honest and will keep his clients happy. It's a great gig. I work with some retired cops. They keep me informed on what's going on in the city."

"You still with Alicia, Hal?"

"What a great memory you have. No, I tried for another year and gave in to her divorce demands. It was either agree or get dragged into court on another phony 'he hit me' charge. You got the first one dismissed, but if she did it often enough, I'd lose. And, Norbie, she was using the kids. It was my eleven-year-old daughter Kit who told me to give up; that her mother was never going to change. No, I met a great woman and married her as quickly as I could get her to agree. Actually, Gail made me wait until I was divorced for two years. She insisted she needed time to figure out if I was over my marriage and whether my kids would like her. Thankfully, it worked out. The kids are grown, know their mother is nuts, and truly like my Gail. I had to learn patience during those two years. Now what do you want?"

"So cynical, Hal; what makes you think I want something?"

"Cause I'm good at this security stuff. I watched you doing a double around the lot and you were not looking for a space to park; you could have been waiting for someone, but why not park in the circle. No one's going to question an Infiniti owner."

Norbie was grateful and congratulated Hal for saving him a lot of bullshit. Showing Hal the seven theft sites and their dates, he asked if Hal worked those evenings. Hal noticed all Tuesdays were listed and said he was present on site with the exception of one Tuesday which happened to be his wedding anniversary. He had talked to the Springfield Police about all of the theft dates and said he thought they occurred between 7:00 and 8:00 p.m. Seven in the evening was when he got on shift. He was to start his drive after the other guy made his rounds and sometimes there was a fifteen-minute space in time where the lot was uncovered. Hal said, "Norbie, even without that space in time, when I'm circling I can't see every location on the lot. It happened seven times. After the fourth theft, we had double coverage all the time and no one thought to just do it on Tuesdays. Believe it or not, I didn't think Tuesday was the only day. Right in front of me and I didn't see it.

"Still there were three more, but they were in another area than the first four. The thief, I think, knows a lot about our cycles. And more importantly, when we changed our routes, he picks the three most difficult parking spots to see, even if you were only fifteen feet away. In all those three cases, the stolen cars were parked between vehicles much bigger. How did the thief get here was my question? He didn't come by bus. The timing was off; I checked. He could have walked, but we checked the cameras for both entrances a half hour before the thefts. Nada! It's either an employee or a visitor. After the fourth theft, we matched the tapes for all the theft times. Some people exiting the facility were common to two of the nights, but not all four of the nights. We checked the emergency room exit but had no luck. There are several other exits the public would not have access, but it's all shady and we only saw some known staff. Security questioned them but they were on short breaks and returned to work within fifteen minutes. There is the connected doctors' office building. We didn't check that one. It's free to park in the day for patients, staff, and doctors, but locked up after office building hours at about eight. Maybe you can think of something we missed."

"Just tell me if later we find the killer, can the police come back and check tapes for staff and doctors and admin's consistent attendance on those days? Please keep the video."

"Don't worry, the hospital keeps all video. They are security and video crazy."

Norbie left to visit the other nearby hospital. Fortunately, he knew one of the sisters who was still connected with the place. She'd been his third-grade teacher, but often told him she liked him better as an adult. She would say, "You weren't a bad child, but you were always looking for trouble. I guess as an attorney, trouble finds you."

Sister Margaret Flaherty was pleased to see him, saying, "How can I help you, Norbie? Is one of your accident victims or maybe a criminal in here. You know I can't give you info about them; so, don't ask and save both of us a lot of time."

Norbie explained the situation and Sister Margaret's eyes lit up. She brought him to a room he'd never been to before and after checking his dates pulled the videos. He thought, *she's in her late seventies. She didn't have those skills when I was in third grade, but she did repair the mimeograph machine for the other nuns.*

When Norbie commented on her expertise she gruffly replied, "You think your generation and thereafter are the only ones in the know.

I learned both platforms for Apple and Windows when nobody but experts could develop code for integrating the two. That was a long time ago. Young folks today think it's always been easily integrated. They don't know history any more than you did."

"Sister, I was only in third grade. Give me a break."

"Why should I? You did well; you could have done better, but you were too busy fooling around. I don't know how many times I was required to stand up for you with Sister Lucy. What was that all about; you and Sister Lucy?"

"I thought Sister Lucy was a 'nutter' and nosey, too. She'd tell me she would tell my parents. I wouldn't flinch. She didn't like when she couldn't control. She was pretty sneaky for a nun."

His remarks were ignored, but Norbie thought he saw a slight smile on her face. Sister played the video from the first date he gave her. He did not know about this lot. He saw when he pulled into the lot today, there was new construction in the back. The problem was there were many videos because there were actually four lots a parker could use. He watched all the videos. The killer knew what he was doing. Sister Margaret said, "Must be one of my former students; a snake in the grass."

After he laughed with her, she also pointed out the killer knew where there was a camera. "That is astonishing to me, Norbie; as we had a specialist determine the best camera coverage, but he left some dark spots. Could a layman see quickly what a specialist in layout could not see? I think your thief knows these lots intimately."

Sister Margaret supported her reasoning, impressing him with her logic. Her observations allowed him to ask the pertinent question. "If someone works here, how can we see when they enter and leave?"

"I was just thinking about who could get in the lot and not be noticed.

Both cars were taken from lot 2 which has two parts: the emergency room and the lot for additional parking for staff and visitors. At seven in the evening, there still is a guard in the shack serving until eight. Your thief is nervy and not afraid of being noticed; hiding in plain sight like they say."

Norbie grabbed her remark and used it to answer. "You're thinking what I'm thinking. Staff or doctors would not be noticed."

"Yes, but it is still a risky proposition for the thief. In the first instance of investigation, staff and doctors will be the last people to be suspected of car theft. However, it you think you have a suspect, do come back. Our videos would let you know who was on campus around the time of the theft. I know about every staffer or doctor or admin who have been here over two weeks. Let's look and see who walked through out entrances. How long a time period before the thefts should I use, Norbie?"

"I don't have a perfect answer for you, Sister. I think a couple of hours would be enough."

"I can scan the videos and make some guesses quickly, but to be of real help, I need some time. Call me tomorrow and we'll talk. I can't send paper, you understand legalities and all that, but consistency of being here for any staff, not regularly on duty, can be noted."

Norbie left thinking, enough for today. Sister Margaret will see something if it's there, and she is such a sly one. She'll check with legal, a nun or an attorney, before she calls me back. I love shrewd folks but sometimes their smarts slow the process down.

This killer has a whole consistent MO for all the killings except one; so why did he choose one victim who had a significant other? Norbie pulled his car over to check his own Cliff Notes on the victims. The victim Pete had a girlfriend Carolyn Aster. Did the killer have a problem with a happy older guy with a girlfriend seventeen years younger than him? All I've found from this wasted day is a field for searching backgrounds when a person of interest is found. I've got to get this material to Rudy and listen to him chastise me on interfering in an open investigation. I'll see him tonight at my house; this week is our week for the family dinner. Sheri and Mona were both free tonight, so it's tonight. Doesn't matter if it's convenient for Rudy and me. I won't talk to Rudy about this tonight. I'll wait a few days. No fireworks in front of our parents. They won't understand Rudy and I playing 'cat and mouse.'

15

HE vs I

"HE, you must be more selective. I can't imagine why you're in such a hurry. I've explained the plan over and over, but you rush it all the time."

I speak loudly hoping HE will pay attention and listen. It's still too early for another accident. I've told HE that the police are actively investigating some of the kills. I don't really like the word 'kill.' It is a deranged misstatement of the necessity of these accidents. Instead I like the phrase 'Sleep Assistance' albeit a long sleep. I have a deep sensitivity to and respect for the Great Designer, whatever or whoever it may be. I would not be involved in a plan if I wasn't doing good. I did not choose Peter to sleep. Why was HE so insistent? I remember the stress in my early years. Nobody listened to the old man in our lives but me. The old man begged to escape the torture of existence on this planet. Did anyone listen? No! Just I!

I still find it slightly funny when all the do-gooders load the elderly with drugs to keep them quiet. Mostly, all the patients want is conversation, but no one wants to listen. HE believes we should be doing more of these 'to sleep' activities. HE sees himself as a crusader and thinks I'm just worried about the police. HE is wrong. I know I can fool the police if HE will just work according to plan. I'm hopeful the police will investigate Pete's lady friend, Caroline Aster. She inherited a big-time estate. She'll have an alibi; actually, I know her alibi, but this is a juicy type case for the police. They don't like a hit-and-run when the guy is leaving all the money to a girlfriend who is much younger. I met the famous serial murder investigator, Captain Rudy Beauregard. He didn't seem particularly quick to me. He probably got his great reputation from summing up what his team found. The Mexican detective appeared more intuitive. Still, just because Beauregard isn't the classic six-foot tall Adonis seen on television doesn't mean he is a complete dodo. It was his slow movements. I know he thinks about every word spoken. He let Detective Juan carry the ball so he could watch the action. Maybe he can't do two things at once. His eyes would be what my mother would call 'penetrating.' She did not like penetrating eyes; of course, she wouldn't!

HE wants a 'to sleep' tonight. Too soon, too soon! HE's picked a guy with a girlfriend; AGAIN. She will be upset just as Carolyn Aster was upset. I told HE, our plan was to help, not hurt. HE is angry with me. I can't always control HE. I hate not being able to control. I don't know why I can't control HE when my life is perfectly orderly; just as I like it and HE has repeatedly told me my organization and planning is worthy of respect. HE's acting out is similar to a child's acting out. HE almost says, "So, whatcha gonna do about it?" I can foil HE's plan. I will. I will keep HE under control; I must do it now, before it's too late. Attention is spotlighting near me. I don't want the spotlight. I will make HE see the danger.

The parents dinner at the house was noisy with howls from the kids and grandparents telling outrageous stories about the middle generation. Norbie noticed he himself was not reacting to stories he wished were left unsaid. His ego appeared to cave since he did not disrupt the blasts from the past. He responded with, "When you're a great son and father, small things are exaggerated by those you love."

Rudy was not left out of the ribbing. His two sons who were present compared the normally slow-moving dad to the man who could outrun any of his boys. Jeremiah said, "I'd try to sneak out the back way through the back door and come all the way around the house to escape chores. I'm fast, but he'd get me every time. He probably outsmarted me by figuring the angles he could cut to block me off at the pass."

Sydney had the most to say about Norbie. Rudy asked why her brothers held back on conversation and let a girl lead. The Cull family's laughter led Sheri to say, "Rudy, this is a talking family. You just have a couple of magpies; we have all three guys and Sydney; but Sydney even talks in her sleep."

Conversation tended toward the topic of the day, Corona Virus, now commonly called COVID-19. Norbie's dad turned on the television to hear the news on the virus. Roland, Rudy's dad and Sheri's mother joined him. Sheri asked Lizette and Norbie's mom, why they weren't as interested in this topic as her mother. They were interrupted by Liam and Delia, Rudy's brother and sister-in-law. This was the first night they were able to join the parents night. Norbie's siblings were either out of town or had conflicts.

Liam with a quick look realized the group was split; one group chatting and one group tied to a news program on COVID-19. Within seconds, Liam directed all their attention on himself as the virus guru. He announced, "We're all going into quarantine and soon."

Rudy questioned how did he know? Liam's client apparently was in the know. Everyone had heard some inklings a couple of days before on quarantining, but thought quarantining would only happen in a few places in the U.S. Liam said, "This is serious stuff. Actually, there's going to be a whole lot of disagreement about this. And the medical info is being politicized which doesn't help, especially when the doctors can't agree on what the right thing to do is. Masks, gloves, wipes, social distancing, stay in your home, clean your grocery bags, blah, blah, blah. We're in for a rocky ride; mainly I'm worried about the economy. I don't know what to do with my clients' funds; how not to invest them with all this uncertainty. Travel and tourism related investments will suffer. Retail investments will also suffer and more.

"Tonight, I don't think all of my business worries are important. Delia and I were coming back from an appointment in Boston and decided to get off the Pike in Ludlow. We took the road out to Route 20 in Springfield and were required by traffic to wait ten minutes. I talked to one of the cops there."

Delia interrupted. "He did. He is so not shy. I'm afraid to do anything when I'm near an accident site. The cops demand you stay in line and follow their instructions. Not Liam, big as life, he pulls over and uses your name, Rudy, to get some answers. About the accident."

"Jeez, Liam, don't do that again. I have to get along with Springfield cops and I don't want them thinking my family thinks they can do their own thing; that they're special."

"We are special, Rudy. We're your family. Now, listen to this, an old man was hit by a drunk driver... the guy was walking near an entrance to a small strip mall which was mostly closed. We were late for dinner. This was about eight-fifteen. They said he was well known all around the area, but lived in Wilbraham. His name was Jerry. The Supervisor came over to see why I wasn't leaving. The cop told the Supervisor I was your brother and he said to me, 'Wait till tomorrow. Your brother will know all about this case, but knowing Rudy, you won't get a word from him and no more from us. Get going.' He was not too nice at the end of our little tete-a tete."

Rudy quickly said, "You're lucky he didn't give you a ticket for interfering with the police, Liam. Cripes, you are one big buttinski. You didn't get his last name, did you?"

Rudy mentally absorbed Liam's answer but his face evidenced a disagreeable look, causing his son Luke to say, "Are you sick, Dad?"

Norbie said, "Rudy, it's a Tuesday night. The accident may not have happened at nine o'clock, but it is a Tuesday. Can you call and see if it's LaFollet?"

Liam realized the party was over for his brother and Norbie. To allow their escape to Rudy's kitchen, he shifted into entertainment mode. A natural comedian, he made fun with the thought of quarantine for the kids. Mona, Sheri, and Lizette showed less interest in Liam's comedy show. Lizette said, "Bad news. I think they got bad news. Do they know this old man?"

Sheri replied, "I hope it's not Norbie's client."

The kitchen location for conversation was a good choice with the slight humming of the dishwasher as background. Rudy said, "I'll call Detective Mark Spaulder over in Springfield. He's a friend of Jim Locke's, Petra's husband, and he's been a good source for us in several other cases. He'll tell me." The call took ten minutes to connect and the conversation took less time. Norbie did not have to be a mind reader. Rudy was upset; it had to be Jerry LaFollet.

Norbie's eyes misted and he slammed his hand. "I listened to him, Rudy, but I didn't think he'd be at risk. He knew about the killings. He knew how they were killed. If you know, why would you even walk on a Tuesday night. And he knew about the Route 20 connection? Why would he walk along Boston Road; it's Route 20 there? Rudy, he had a lady friend. We both met Alice at the Wilbraham party. Why would he take a chance? You can't win with a car driving at you. You can't identify a hooded driver coming at you. Why? Why?"

"Spaulder said there was a gun found at the scene and two shots were fired. Norbie, he was being a vigilante."

"Shit, do we have to say anything about it? He had a service record. Let's hope it was a licensed weapon. I wonder if the killer's car was hit."

Rudy said, "Not my investigation, but when they find the car, they'll know if the bullet hit it or the person driving. One drop of blood would help. I love forensics, but they need evidence to be helpful."

The two joined the boisterous group and tried for a moment to forget their new information.

Captain Beauregard was busy first thing the next morning. Calls were made to Springfield's Traffic Division Captain Kurt Shroeder and to the guru for accident reconstruction for the state police, Cyrus Jones. He received a call from ADA Lenny Hastings attempting to push some pressure on the investigation now that there was a new remarkably similar death. Hastings called for a Task Force Meeting giving Rudy two days to do a preliminary investigation. The District Attorney would hold off the press until then. He said, "Don't think, Rudy, you're off the hook, because this is another Springfield case. The word on the street is the 'Expert Serial Murder Solver' is on the case and that is you. Rudy, you!"

In a few, Beauregard met with his detectives. Several knew Jerry

LaFollet. Rudy said, "We'll have to watch out on this one. Jerry was a friend of Attorney Cull's Uncle Ed. Ed Cull is a retired federal prosecutor. Keep information close; Cull will be doing his own investigating if I know him and I can't have any mix-up in information. The last thing I want to do is have the DA required to call Attorney Norberto Cull as a prosecution witness."

Mason's offered one of his typical answers. "Why not, Captain? It would make a great television murder mystery serial finale."

Beauregard ignored Mason and directed Mason, Ted, Juan, and Bobby to get on the phones and research the two nurse practitioners, Chad and Shirley, and the doctor, Teague, saying, "I want to know their lives from birth to when they came here. Do not miss any previous employment, education, criminal or civil court or police records. Find work associates and neighbors who will talk about them and do it all with a sense of support for them as witnesses to a hit-and-run accident. If the person thinks one of these untouchables is just being looked at as a witness, the result may be more fruitful. Use terms for elderly and their kindness to older citizens. Ask what kind of background would make them go the extra yard for a patient. Move the rocks; there's a bad growth under there for at least one of them and maybe more than one."

Millie interrupted the meeting. She past a typed note saying, "Attorney Cull says he needs to see you today. I knew you were meeting Cyrus Jones this afternoon, so I told him to come right along."

The Captain did not grimace which relieved Millie. She rarely would make an appointment for the Captain without his ok, but she knew the Captain and Cull were tight now. If it ever changed, Millie's behavior would also.

Back in his office, Beauregard welcomed the illustrious defense attorney, saying, "Remember, Norbie, the rules about an open investigation. It's a one-way street where you give me info and I thank you. Not ever is it the other way around."

"Thank you, Captain Beauregard, for the kind welcome."

Beauregard nodded and with a serious tone in his voice said, "The killer is out of control. The DA is calling a task force meeting and it means the FBI will be up here. There's no use running away from their assistance; and I am pleased to welcome them."

"Everybody who didn't suspect serial murders will now. Rudy, the world knows Jerry La Follet. He was the original do-gooder. My Uncle Ed called me this morning. He is livid. He remembered when we were at the Holbrook's party in Wilbraham and our conversation on Jerry's friend who was killed by a drunk driver. This will blow up. Sheila called me while I was waiting for you. She said a woman named Nina Jones called the office. Apparently, she was a close friend of Jerry La Follet. She told Sheila, Jerry was a walking saint. Nina also said I was Jerry's lawyer and she wanted a meeting with me. He told her to call me if anything ever happened to him. He didn't think Alice would handle things well. Who's Nina Jones, Rudy? Sheila, of course, the ultimate gal Friday set up an appointment for me tomorrow at eleven. She does this when she likes someone. I'd like to fire her sometimes, but I couldn't run our practice without her. Lawyers are all about the case and timelines and Sheila is about making everything balance at the firm. She has the other attorneys and staff coming to her for all management decisions. It just happened. She told me it happened 'because any void is always filled.' The implication is I left a management void."

Rudy knew enough not to touch that issue. Instead he said, "Don't have the foggiest idea who this Nina Jones is, but if she's a friend of

Jerry's, she's another one saving the people. You gonna be stuck with her, Norbie. Don't stick her on me. Now, you would not have wasted a visit just to tell me about Nina, so what's up? And why didn't you confirm with a phone call today that Jerry La Follet is dead and was your client?"

As if he were a politician, Norbie did not answer the question. Rather than ease Beauregard's nosey desires, he relayed his investigations into the auto robbery and dumping sites. Rudy started to complain about Norbie and open case violations, but backed off when he heard new information. Cull explained his conclusions, saying, "Rudy, the killer is or has been in and out of both hospitals and knows the parking lots well. He also has chosen dumping sites near busy restaurants. I think he may have frequented these restaurants socially, and became aware of the used auto lots nearby. He is a risk taker, meaning he measures risk but doesn't normally gamble. Think about his practices. He or she passes as belonging wherever they are. Implies no complete body tattoos or freaky dress. Unusual apparel or appearances would be noticed. The restaurant parking lots had shrubbery with exits facing the auto lots. Even if a person got out of the car and looked around, nothing much would be seen. Only risk would be smokers and they normally stay by the outside of the restaurant door."

Beauregard said, "What now, is Attorney Cull a private investigator or a wannabe cop? You spent some time. Why, Norbie?"

"I liked Jerry La Follet. Sheila and Sheri like Jerry. My Uncle Ed likes Jerry. It's enough for me. I liked Stan Korsecki. I'm going to be an old man someday. My dad is getting up there. This has to stop."

Chastened and surprised, for he thought he was misunderstood by his friend, Rudy agreed and said, "What else did you learn, Norbie?"

"I'm thinking the killer has changed his MO. Two kills were out of the norm. The old men had women who loved them. I'm not you or an FBI profiler, Rudy, but it tells me the guy is escalating. He likes what he's doing for whatever goddamn reason he's doing it; and the timing? It's a little close in time from what I know but I don't know all of the kills. You do.

"It has also occurred to me the killer is just too familiar with hospital lots. The killer looks normal. The killer does probably frequent good restaurants. The killer is well regarded to have been able to ingratiate himself with the victims and not be noticed. I think the killer is a medical professional at some level or a counselor or even a van driver like Jerry."

Rudy laughed. "You got a line into my conference room? We're looking along those lines. Anything else you can help me with?"

Rudy listened as Norbie detailed his conversations with Hal and Sister Margaret. He shared Sister Margaret's reticence about making conclusions on the spot and his inkling she would come up with some possible suspects. Norbie said, "You will have great avenues of circumstantial evidence to explore once you find a suspect. I can keep what I have or give it to you. Maybe, Rudy, I should hold on to it. The FBI may come in and run all over the place pursuing identification from the hospital cameras before you are comfortable with a person of interest. You don't have anything if I don't give it to you. Your big question is how did the killer get back to his car after the murder or get to the theft site; one and/or the other would require transportation unless there are two killers. I can't follow Uber or taxis. You can. The killer could come back any time after the murders; not necessarily right away. Could be the next day."

Rudy said, "Did you ask what cars were there on the lot overnight? The physicians' garage should be checked. Most of those cars are gone.

The ones left could be traced. We'll do that and more. Thanks, Norbie, you've been helpful. Not to worry, I want this guy."

The Captain joined his detectives. Instructions on tracing Uber and Taxis on dates of the killing for hours extending to the next morning through noon were to be followed. He suggested next, a directive asking if the restaurants, adjacent to the two or three auto lots Cull had visited, had kept credit card receipts for dates of the car dumpings. His final request was, "Check the history of all the victims for surgeries within two years of their deaths and hospital visits. How many ever came through the ER he and Juan had visited? Do what we do best. Listen for every connection. Look for common names. Don't be totally focused on Chad, Shirley, and Jesse, but do look for their connections to all the victims."

I was disgusted with HE. What do you do when you can't trust? I can no longer trust HE. How do I counteract HE? This last death was too risky and it doesn't fit with our mission. When I questioned HE, did I get a reasonable answer? What I got was the sign of an addict. I knew it. I just didn't want to really believe it. HE needed a death now. I told HE, it is not about needing a death; it's about our good work. This death may not have been a good work for Jerry La Follet. Mr. La Follet liked his girlfriend Alice. They got along. At this time despite his diagnosis, Jerry had a companion who would see him through the journey. HE said I was a missionary and did not live in the real world. The real world was filled with temptation.

I ranted at his gall. Did HE agree? No, HE argued against Alice's ability to understand and endure the dying process; Jerry would essentially be all alone. I countered with, "How do you know? Alice and Jerry were good together."

HE's answer was cryptic and historic and earned my rejection. I answered, "You think I don't remember what happened earlier. I remember my past very well. You were not there then at the time. This mission is not about my history. Nothing could make up for my childhood."

HE appears to know all about my childhood; if you can call it a childhood. I must have been careless in what I've said. Even if researched, there is no easy connection to negativity about me; my family, maybe. The mission is to do good. I think, and I explained to HE, that deviation from the plan brings these actions away from the divine good. Deviation invites Satan. I think HE is truly afraid of Satan, and why not? Satan was the overwhelming villain present when I was… I just can't go back into those thoughts. If I do, I'll stop being careful. And where was HE's God then when I needed saving?

When I told HE about the possibility of being discovered by the police, I was laughed at. I then pointed out the lives we currently lead and how wonderful they are. If discovered, HE would be denied the right to act as the Angel of Death. I said, "What would you do in prison, You? Every moment of your life would be monitored. In that case, any killing done in prison would not fit our mission at all."

HE calmed down. I reiterated the agreement terms. I wrote them out as I have all instructions. I'm not always certain I get through to HE. I think HE rereads what I write several times. I noticed I didn't write about Pete and Jerry; that must be the problem. HE thinks if the death occurs before I write, it's authorized. I will talk to HE later tonight, when there is quiet at dinner. I will write down on paper before dinner the following: "HE, you can't be an Angel of Death until I write the story."

Control, yes, I think I can control. As for now, diverting the police is the issue. I can probably do it one more time. Any deaths in the future must be spaced further apart. That is a problem. HE likes a convenient schedule. Distance makes implementation of the plan more difficult. Perhaps a vacation in another area on Route 20 would allow HE an easier time for this important work. I'll not only say the word 'vacation,' I'll also write the word down for HE to see I am not limiting our work, but assisting in a solution. There is always a way.

16

Jerry La Follet

Alice Meade did not answer her cell forcing Detectives Barr and Aylewood-Locke to drive to her home. The two listened to the COVID-19 news on the radio and both agreed ordinary in-person interviews may be a 'no' on Monday or soon, unless there was an arrest or an acknowledgement of death or injury. Petra wondered, "Maybe we'll be better in our judgments when we're not looking at the person."

"Someone else said that before; maybe it was you, Petra, but that's bullshit. Watching a person, in-person, gives vital clues. You know and believe in observation techniques. You gave a class in it at the Academy. You downplaying your own personal history now?"

"No, Bobby, but I keep an open mind. Could be I'm fixated on my training. Could be there may be a more efficient way to interview. All the big businesses looking to hire middle and upper management positions are doing two and three phone interviews with the same candidate and then a ZOOM interview and sometimes a final real interview for hiring managers. Works for them."

"Petra, murderers are not MBA's."

"Some are. I'm just exploring interviewing perspectives, Bobby, not making a decision. Looks like Alice Meade lives in a petite hideaway. I think it's kind of cute if we can get up the walkway with all the bushes hanging over."

Bobby didn't answer. Petra looked up from the bushes to see a woman in a long skirt and short caftan styled top with Western boats and her head wrapped in an African turban. She was not African. Her blonde and gray hair straggled down her neck unleashed from the headscarf. Alice Meade may have looked like a hippie, but if so, she was quite a handsome one. Tears filled her eyes as she invited them inside the cottage type home. She offered tea. It was obvious she had prepared for them. Three china cups and a tray of homemade ginger and chocolate cookies decorated the quaint hand-carved coffee table. The sitting room was Home and Garden all the way with chintz drapes, lace curtains and pillows with herb designs. Petra commented, "Alice, thank you for the little feast here. This room is lovely."

She sat, ate a cookie, and laughed. Petra said, "Chocolate chips and ginger in the same cookie and it's great. These are definitely homemade."

Alice said, "Jerry loved them because he thought they combined his two favorite flavors. We can thank Jerry. I'd never made them before I met him; never heard of putting these two together before. There are many things I never tried until I met Jerry. Detectives, when someone thinks you are wonderful and tells you all the time; well, there isn't anything you can't do. I believe what I just said with the exception of my losing him. I do find it difficult to accept. I thought this morning I couldn't cope. I don't want to accept his never coming back to me. And his dying in that manner like the other older men is unacceptable. I hope you will find this killer. Jerry knew there was a killer out there. He hired Attorney Cull to look into it; that's how certain he was and Jerry never threw his money away easily."

Bobby talked calmly to Alice about her loss of Jerry. He asked if he had friends in the medical community or in the hospitals. Alice explained Jerry often brought patients from nursing homes or their homes to the hospital. Some of it was paid by the nursing homes through Medicare and some of his driving was voluntary. The detectives noticed Alice brightened up as she detailed Jerry's everyday life; she was most impressed with his ability to find joy in doing for others. During the conversation Alice also mentioned Jerry's current concern about his health, saying, "He would not tell everything, but I know he met with a pulmonologist in this area and then scheduled an appointment with some doctor in Boston. He went to Boston three more times. He gave up smoking a number of years ago. I never heard a heavy cough, but he couldn't walk more than a half mile recently. He claimed he was aging. I believe he had a problem and I didn't push it. It was important to him to be able to keep me happy. It may sound selfish, but I was willing for a man to feel that way about me. If he was going to die, cancer wasn't a disease for Jerry. I'll tell you Jerry did not sit down often and would not be a good patient. He had friends he made over in all the ERs he transported patients. Dr. Teague had dinner with us here. I met a couple of nurses with Jerry. He really liked them. They weren't regular nurses, but nurse practitioners. It's all different now, Detectives, with the medical community. I don't often see my doctor except for my annual check-up; unless I'm very sick. I see other licensed medical practitioners. It's all new to me, but Jerry had help in deciding what to do about his condition; of that I am certain."

Petra asked, "Alice, what was Dr. Teague like; I mean his relationship with Jerry?"

"Strange you would ask me this question in that way, Detective. Jerry was… Oh, I was going to say 'is,' but he 'isn't anymore, is he? Jerry was very smart but down to earth. Every person he met, even those forever talking old people, were worth listening to. Dr. Teague is very nice, but I think he is a bit of a snob. I know Jerry told me the doctor was very well liked by all the patients and he was particularly kind to older patients. Doctor Teague spoke kindly about them to me, but his eyes did not smile when he talked about them. Eyes tell the truth. He just wanted to be thought of as caring. Jerry argued with me when I told him my thoughts on the god doctor; oops, I mean good doctor. He insisted my personal history with my ex-husband colored my thoughts on professionals. He was wrong. When Jerry brought the doctor here for dinner, Dr. Teague looked over this little house and actually asked me why I didn't buy a bigger one. One question on top of another question. Why do you decorate in this cottage style? I like bigger rooms. Like I care what he likes. Jerry stopped that talk with, 'I like the hominess here, Jesse. I need to feel connected to be happy and this is one place on this earth where I feel totally accepted.'

"Well, Jesse didn't challenge Jerry's value of my home. In fact, he kept asking Jerry why he needed to feel accepted anywhere when he clearly was his own man and constantly helped others. Jerry went on to say, 'I believe in the community in which we all live, wherever or whatever it may be. Community prevents each of us from being overwhelmed by our individuality. Now don't take me wrong, Jesse, I'm a Western individualist and proud of it; but people need other people to help show them when they go wrong.'"

Alice then said, "Jesse didn't like Jerry's philosophy and basically gave him a long dissertation on how community could never control him, since so many in any community were clearly intellectually inferior.

I remember that dinner. I did not like Jesse, although I must admit not many young professional men have dinner with elderly men. I don't know who was doing the missionary work in their relationship; Jesse or Jerry. Shirley and Chad, the two nurses, well, they related to Jerry with respect and interest in why he was such a supporter of others. They were not snobs."

Petra and Bobby spent more time with Alice. She gave a fuller picture of Jerry. She gave a longer answer to the question about Jerry having a gun with him at the accident scene. Jerry was Army, all the way. He'd been a paratrooper and always had a gun properly stored in a locked container separate from ammunition in his home. He rarely carried, however; maybe if they were walking in the woods. Alice said, "It was normal for Jerry to be walking on the section of road where he was hit. It was a little later than usual. He was hit at night, but was it still dark? I don't remember the time. If he had a reason to walk on a dark highway and knew he would be walking there, then of course he would carry a weapon. How come he didn't shoot at the car? He was an excellent shot. I went target shooting with him and he drew respect from the other shooters."

Bobby questioned what would happen to Jerry's estate. Alice said, "He said most would go to his family, but there was a little something for me and some money for his friend Nina. I'm not interested in money, Detectives; I have plenty to live on and I'm conservative about spending."

Bobby persisted and asked if she knew if Jerry was well-to-do. She said, "Jerry did not spend easily and most thought he may have been short of money. Have you seen his home? It's very nice. His kids are all well-to-do. He has a state retirement and I met one of his friends who says he's loaded, but Jerry and I never spoke of money."

Alice offered them a view of her property. The sweet little fairyland-like house sat on seven acres of land. She shared her history of buying the home with her divorce settlement. Her ex-husband laughed at her purchase and told her she was leaving the high life to live in nothing, but Alice said, "This house has given me such comfort, and I hope enough to help me through this loss."

Petra and Bobby agreed on something while driving back to the station. Alice's house and land were gems and could be quite valuable. They truly liked Alice, and wondered why she wasn't upset Jerry was leaving a little something to another woman; and who was this Nina? Bobby said, "The Captain will be interested in Nina; especially if a little something left to her is really big. I wonder if Jerry's estate is big. Money is always a motive. Petra, even fifty thousand dollars to some people could be a motive to kill. But then and again, the weapon used is not normally associated with a woman."

Attorney Cull welcomed Nina Jones as he entered his small conference room. Sheila had set Nina up with a tray of desserts and coffee. Cull had missed breakfast because of an early meeting with his client before going to court for an arraignment. Therefore, he welcomed himself to some coffee and a great looking crispy croissant and some cherry jam. One of his favorite and oft cited views was, "It's best to handle problems on an empty stomach. No reason to invite indigestion when your adrenaline is up." This view was constantly attacked by his friends in the medical know, but it worked for Norbie and he was staying with it.

Nina asked, "Attorney Cull, where did you get this cherry jam? It is not store bought. When I was a kid my Mama made cherry jam because we could get free cherries up the street at Mrs. Holt's house. I know this taste."

Whatever Nina's story would be, the look on Cull's face turned warm and kind. He was notable for responding to simple thoughts and truths from his clients and in this case an investigative witness. Nina shared her story and Jerry's story and her eyelids held back tears causing her to blink repeatedly which showed clearly on her light chocolate skin. The lady took an hour in her tale insisting Attorney Cull must understand the kindness Jerry La Follet offered to people and specifically to her. She ended with, "Someone is killing these old men and so far, they're killing just white men. I don't think it's racial, Mr. Cull. Jerry thought it was mercy killing by some deranged person who thought these men's lives were not worth living. I can't imagine Jerry was right about the motive. I mean none of these men were in the hospital suffering. Mercy killing, I told him, was done by nurses and doctors to patients under their care or by wealthy family members looking for an inheritance. Is it merciful to run them over with a car? I don't think so."

Cull asked Nina about some of the other elderly men who were killed. She knew some through van driving, saying, "Mr. Cull, my main job was driving a van for my church in the Mason Square area of Springfield. When not needed by the church for its people, they'd arrange for me to drive for nursing homes, care homes, and agencies who helped the elderly. My church work was mainly in the Afro-American community. When I drove for other agencies the riders were all colors. It was then I met other drivers out of my community. I'm not driving vans now; I'm administrative assistant to Sister Althea at The Holy Spirit of God Church (HSG). It's the best job I've ever had.

"Jerry and I had supper at the church not too long ago. He smoothed an emotional outburst I had that evening. I thought I knew only three men killed, Herschel, Buck and Stan. Later that night Jerry told me Oscar Poski from Brimfield died in the same way. I drove Oscar several times. He told me he was a van driver and then I remembered him from one of the Council on Aging dinners. Poski was his stage name. In talking with him, I caught a little Southern in his voice. He said he was a Country Western musician for years. His regular name was a long Polish name. I can't remember it, but a nicer man would be difficult to find. He had much to live for; plenty of money and people who really liked him. I picked up his music on YouTube. Community is what he had. Not like my community which is church-based. He had rural community with a place to hang out and folks who waited for him every day. I'm old, Mr. Cull, a little younger than Jerry, but old nonetheless. Jerry helped me find a path to live and move forward and so did Sister Althea. I don't want to die like Jerry, Stan, Oscar, and Herschel did. Who is such a monster who can think we older folks don't want to live? Help me, for Jerry, Mr. Cull. Who's going to drive the vans and be nice to the elderly?"

Nina's honesty moved Cull more than he wished to acknowledge. Rather than emote, he questioned her knowledge of each of the men's routines. Her answer almost made him laugh. "Mr. Cull, we're all old. We go to doctors, dentists, other specialists, rehabs, and find places for community. Those men and I thought we were the lucky ones. We had jobs driving vans. We met new folks every day. We were challenged by others' infirmities. I can work any kind of wheelchair or assistance device. I know how to safely let riders out of my van, how to avoid accidents. I've learned all hospital rules for entry and exit, and every other agency's rules which often change weekly. I know where the free lunches are and other free products for the elderly. My mind was busy.

We were lucky and some devil decided to take that luck away. Their routines start this way. We all rise early, unlike other elderly people at home. We rise early because our services are needed. We go to bed early because we are needed early the next day. AARP and all the Councils on Aging insist exercise is important for the old. Van drivers get in and out of their vans and I think even with all the bone replacements, we are more limber. Still we all agreed we must walk to make up for sitting on our asses driving all day. Those dead men were all getting their healthy walk in and were killed while walking. Someone knew their schedules. I have a schedule now and never had one before when I was young and drinking. That's all I know about them."

Norbie Cull walked Nina out to the waiting room to exit. She stopped him and asked, "Where do I pay, Mr. Cull? I want to continue your representation. Jerry told me he paid you to investigate."

Turning pink, Cull told Nina he would work on the matter but did not need payment and could not assure her of successful results. She stopped in her tracks, looked straight in his eyes and said, "I'm from the street, Attorney Cull. If you won't help me, tell me. Jerry was going to go to a Captain Beauregard in West Side if you didn't help. He said he was certain you would. I can pay you a hundred dollars a month for however long it takes. If you are not interested, I'll go to Captain Beauregard next."

Cull directed Nina back into the conference room and kindly explained to her the difference between attorney representation and police assistance. He said, "I'm a lawyer, Nina. There is not a legal case here for you. You are not a wife or mother of any of these victims and neither was Jerry, but I will help. I promise. I don't want your money. I'm doing this because I truly believe as you do, there is something wrong here. I also think if you can get in to see Captain Beauregard in West Side, you should do it. You and I need all the help we can to protect future potential victims. I hope, Nina, we are both wrong about these deaths, but I don't think we are."

Nina said, "I'm trusting you, Mr. Cull. If Jerry believed in you then I believe in you. I am glad this guy doesn't murder women. It seems to me most murderers who kill many people, and I think there is a name for killers of multiple people of a certain type, mostly kill women for sex. These murders are weird. The word I'm searching for, Mr. Cull, is serial murderer."

Cull thought about Nina and her fearlessness in going the distance to attempt to pay him to investigate. He called Jim Locke, his go-to Private Investigator and scheduled coffee for later in the afternoon. Meanwhile he headed for the West Side Police Station figuring he'd walk in on Beauregard. He knew the afternoon mid-week was often Rudy's favorite time for reviewing cases. He was willing to chance the trip today. Getting there quickly, he was escorted to Beauregard's private office by Millie who'd been informed by the Desk Sergeant. Greeted by a surprised Rudy, Cull actually apologized for not making an appointment. The Captain laughed and said, "You must be off your feed today. Apologies from you, Norbie; you must want something. Have a seat. What's up? Do you have a client I'm going to hear about who maybe killed someone?"

"Rudy, I had a visit from Nina Jones this morning. I remember telling you last night. She was a good friend of Jerry La Follet. He helped her out many times in the past. Nina knew Jerry had contacted me and, according to her, was my client. She wished to retain me. I explained I was an attorney and not an investigator. I told her to go to the police.

Jerry said you were the policeman who was the best at solving serial murders. I think she may be coming to you next, especially if I don't get enough evidence to close these cases. And, Rudy, as far as she is concerned, these are murder cases. She knew four of the victims. She is amazed a serial murderer, my term not hers, would murder only men and old men at that. She believed because they were all white, it was not racially motivated, and inferred the killer was white. She insisted the killer knew these men, because who else would know their nightly walking patterns. She doesn't connect the dots perfectly, but I'm with her on her conclusions."

"What did she say about possible perps?"

Norbie answered, "She inferred, again, my word, that someone knew them well enough to know their habits. She said as a van driver, she knew all the ins and outs of all the hospitals and nursing homes and often had meaningful conversations with her riders. She'd get complete histories from the repeaters. Everything screams of the medical community. HIPPA doesn't always prevent someone from examining paperwork submitted in a day. Access to paperwork could give a lead to a murderer looking for certain types of victims. He could then find a way to get to know them better."

Rudy said, "So you think the killer knows a lot of elderly men, picks mostly men without a special friend who are lonely, picks only white ones, knows they walk in the evenings, further knows they walk on Tuesday evenings, then steals cars, kills them, and dumps the cars. He does this all with great success. Norbie, she is not the only one missing connections. She has an excuse, you don't. You're a professional. I ask you, how could the perp know for sure if these guys decide on a Tuesday night, not to walk. Maybe the victim is feeling lazy on a night chosen by the perp and doesn't walk. The perp's stolen a car for nothing. Alright… you win. You want to know if stolen cars were found on the same lots on a Wednesday morning but not connected to a death. I didn't think about this. Maybe my detectives did."

While Rudy made a call and held discussions with the detectives occupying the Pit today, Norbie mused, how many more times did the perp try to kill. If there were several missed but planned nights, can a timeline for the killer's desires be established? Rudy will see this possibility. I won't have to tell him. Even with what little we know, the killer is possessed with a desire to kill. I don't care what an old man did to him when he was young, he is a psychopath, not a mercy killer. Killing satisfies his desires and I see no self-control exercised by this guy.

"Well, Norbie, they took a minute to pull the files. They've researched fifteen of the auto thefts and dumps. Two extra thefts in medical facility parking areas and used auto site dumps listed occurred on Tuesday nights. One occurred a week before Peter's death and one two weeks before Jerry's death. Do you see what I see in that?"

Norbie answered, "I don't know if it's what you see, but I see a killer with an increasing need to murder. In both those cases, Peter and Jerry were not his typical victim. Why not? It's plausible, Rudy, the killer had a victim in mind who somehow was unavailable to kill. Could be the potential victim died, or was hospitalized, or didn't go for his walk on the chosen Tuesday night. Then he went for the next available old man he knew, straying from his choice constraints."

"I'm thinking about psychopaths and how they think. Norbie, I agree with what you just said, but I am also confused with the direction I'm taking and our current choices of potential killers. They are all highly educated and charming people who have somehow ingratiated themselves with their elderly victims. Now I have great esteem for our elders and their ability to see when someone's bullshitting. I know these men were all lonely, but out of seventeen, wouldn't one of those old men question the attention he received; especially since it's a rare commodity. I suppose if my current potential killers are all in the medical field, the victims may think the attention is just good medical care. I don't know, Norbie, my dad Roland would not fall for any of this stuff."

"No, Roland would not, but Roland is not lonely. Roland would discuss any attention he got with Lizette; and she'd be meeting the caretaker and questioning the hell out of him with an emotional analysis of the guy."

Rudy said, "I always read and now I have Mona reading psychological reports on narcissists, sociopaths, and psychopaths. Generally, the psychopath, for instance, shows a focus on one person and does what's necessary to keep that one person in line and under control. He may use flattery, kind deeds, gifts, and generally a lot of attention and later withhold it. Narcissists put on emotional masks to give their victims what they need. I've interviewed my three potentials and the masks they wore for me were ones of caring medical professionals. I think I need more info on their victims; in this case maybe we can find the two potentials the killer didn't get. We'll work on Jerry's case. Just who two weeks before was in my medical people's care? Maybe the person's out there. The big problem is the location of the killer's sourcing. Was it in the emergency room in which all my potentials worked? Did the killer source in many places? I'll have to work on the connections."

Norbie then spoke in a quiet voice, which always signaled to Rudy he was up to interfering in Rudy's work. He said, "Don't go berserk on me, Rudy, but I have some opportunity to ask questions without the attached stigma of police investigating. I'll be considered a lawyer looking for a great and rewarding accident case."

"Stay out of it, Norbie; it's an open case. You hear me?"

Norbie heard him and nodded, but Rudy didn't believe he would stay out of it. He thought, we have worked against and for issues for years. Norbie will find some former client who knows all about the ER out there and all the elderly patients. He's made it a mission. Hell, I can't blame him. Catching this killer is my professional work and is also my mission. Mona told me last night I didn't have to join her for Luke's teacher's conference; I was to work on catching this despicable human being. Luke's conference is related to his half-hearted efforts in math and English. I think he is just being a male teenager who doesn't yet see their relevance. How can he be bad at math when he calculates engineering equivalents for his science project on space, like a whacked-out sci-fi type? Best I'm not there. I get touchy when they describe Luke as deliberately inattentive. I remember last year, "Mr. Beauregard, Luke's IQ is one of the highest in the whole school, so it doesn't make sense for him to pull a D+ in English. I resent when he writes perfect papers for Science and Social Studies but won't put in the effort in my class. It's especially annoying when he teaches the other kids grammar. He must learn to give effort in all his classes; not just in his 'faves' as he calls them."

He's a kid trying to figure life out and a good kid. Immature, maybe, but he is a good kid. I want to scream for them to just wait until he is twenty. I think guys grow up then.

Rudy met with his detectives and explained the essence of what Norbie had learned and what he himself thought. Bobby and Bill wanted to move back out to the used auto shops and pick up video on the two cars left in the lots in the one or two weeks before Pete and Jerry's accidents. The Captain reminded them to make certain they get all the cameras because the owner of one of the lots held back a video on a previous accident.

The Captain and two other detectives spent their time making further calls on the backgrounds of the three potentials, saying, "There has to be something in their backgrounds to differentiate them from each other."

Millie put through a call to Beauregard from Chief Coyne. The call was relatively short for the Chief and left the Captain with a grimace on his face. He motioned for the detectives to leave what they were doing pronto; which did not mean pronto, but instead meant ASAP. Petra was the last to be able to leave her call. Beauregard said, "We're in a box. Governor Baker will be issuing a stay-at-home order. We saw it coming. They'll be closing the schools, but the Chief says nobody really knows what's ahead. He says masks and gloves are next. There will be daily briefings from the President and state governors. The Chief is issuing cleanliness advisories. Maintenance will be in soon to do a cleaning. One thing he said makes sense. Don't use each other's desk phone or computer; or if you do, wipe all the surfaces."

Amid groans against compliance, Lilly said, "Like being in my grandmother's Italian house. Wipe, wipe, wipe everything after anyone touches something. I never saw her without a 'mopina' in her hand. We can do this. We probably will have less sickness that's not this COVID-19. It's all very mysterious and spy like. Think about a virus from China infecting the United States; infecting us in West Mass. Wow! You should hear the conspiracy theories out there about the Chinese taking over the world. I am afraid for my parents. My dad has a heart issue and Mom has rheumatoid arthritis. They're always spouting about co-morbidities making recovery from the virus more difficult."

Beauregard, who had tried to overlook all, what he called 'blather,' on the virus suddenly paid attention. He thought, Lizette and Roland are at risk. I know they are older parents, but they live so sensibly. I can't imagine a virus taking them out. Old men are being murdered and this virus takes more elderly out than any other group.

Ted said, "No one and I mean no one will let us in their houses for interviews and unless we threaten to arrest them, they won't come to the station. Definitely will put a crimp in investigations. Thank God for computers, Facetime, phones and ZOOM."

Mason said, "I've been tracing the good Doctor Teague. He was in three foster homes before he was adopted at age nine. Kind of late for adoption, I think. The social worker who handled the adoption was pretty young at the time of the adoption, is retired now, but I am told is reachable. I'll work on her. Then I'll trace all aspects of his resume. I've tried to get a contact number for his adoptive parents, but so far, it's a bust. There was a name change, both first and last name, when he was adopted."

Ted reported that Chad had a very straight forward upbringing, saying, "His dad left or died. He lived with his mother while going to Lakeland Community College and later transferred to a nursing program at Cleveland State University in Ohio. He worked for a few years. After his mother died, he moved to Albany and got his practitioner's training at SUNY. I'm checking licensing in Ohio, New York and Massachusetts. There doesn't seem to be a lot here. No police records. No driving offenses. The guy's a regular Boy Scout."

The Captain responded, "Early life, Ted, is important. 'As the tree is planted, so grows the tree' is a quote with some merit. Although, I hope it doesn't have meaning in my case. I want every detail. Are grandparents involved? Why did the dad leave if he did leave? Did Chad have any contact with him after he left? Was the mom on drugs or a nutcase? Were social services ever called? Worm your way into the Lakeland community. I know one thing for sure; the pathology behind these killings was grown in a negative environment."

"Captain, if we find nothing in his background, do you really believe its absence removes him as a suspect?"

"Yes and no, but I firmly believe early experiences have great impact on future actions. I also believe some personalities are born with a lack of sensitivity to the needs of others. We've talked before about some studies of sociopaths and evidence of differences in their brains. Given these thoughts, we don't assume no negative history in Chad's life as a sign of innocence. We always have many lines of investigation. His choice of victims inplies a lot."

Juan asked, "What about a partnership? All the planning necessary to kill seventeen men, all elderly, with the same weapon which requires successfully stealing and disposing of seventeen vehicles and having knowledge of seventeen behavior patterns smacks of a partnership of conspiracy. Captain, no evidence in the cars was found. The only evidence of the perp is a glimpse of a watch which we are in process of identifying more fully. The video Cull found also links the killer's habit of removing gloves in a particular manner as used in medical situations. Other than different cover-ups for clothing, there is not a lot. Seventeen crimes, Captain, and not a lot of mistakes. I'm thinking two heads are better than one in planning."

Beauregard agreed. "Possible, but if two are planning these, why would two men be murdered whose profile differed from the other fifteen? Two heads would not allow such a mistake; unless the one doing the killing is out of control. Let me know when info on the guy who wasn't killed two weeks before Jerry's death is found; if it ever is."

———

Chad was overwhelmed by the amount of work required in dealing with COVID-19. He thought, nursing was difficult enough without all the changes necessary for stringent cleanliness. Dealing from one patient to another required complete changes in smocks as well as gloves and masks. Try practicing this social distancing in the emergency room. It's a laugh. We'll all have it before long. Can't help lapses when we have so much to deal with. We now have separate COVID rooms. We work in a quasi-military space with rules, new rules written every day. Shirley looks exhausted and stressed. Teague, well, the good doctor, lets nothing bother him. Though, I have noticed he never misses a break now. A big change in behavior for the image of the big 'doctor on call.' I do admit he looks like one of those television doctors. He is the doctor in charge of the shift when he's on and with the increased load we and he are supposed to cover some days on another shift if required. We're going through staff, but Teague refuses to take another shift day. Administration argues with him, but he insisted his constitution couldn't take on any more. Granted, he is good and it's why they allowed him to stay with his regular work, but the rest of us would lose any argument of that nature. He's set himself up as a god here and they all fall for it. We, the nice guys, finish last.

Shirley approached him in great distress. A nurse called in for tomorrow. It was her second call out and she said she had all the symptoms. She told the Nurse in Charge and was directed to Jesse. She had expressed surprise because the nurse in charge would normally be handling scheduling nursing staff. She informed Jesse who blew up, not in fiery anger, but with an almost snide sarcasm the nurse had never experienced from him. He was now headed to the medical admin office, and she and Chad were to handle all medical decisions. Not a problem for them, it was often their role when a doctor was not available; as long as they documented and called on any iffy stuff to any doctor on call. The policy was to have a doctor on call in the event of incapacitation or unusual overload for the acting doctor in charge. Shirley said, "I have such problems with outbursts like Jesse's, Chad. I heard them all through my early childhood. They terrify me even to this day. My stomach's in knots and the remembering impedes my performance. I need a cup of tea. Could you cover for me until I calm down?"

Chad was not averse to helping Shirley out, considering she may find his attitude more pleasing than Jesse's sarcasm. He'd take any opportunity to magnify Jesse's flaws in comparison to his. Still, he wondered how Shirley's background could be so negative to have this effect on her when she was experiencing pressure. He had noticed and asked Shirley before why, when new rules or guidance were given to the medical staff, she would always appear stressed. Later, Shirley would be the best at adaptation, but clearly, all noticed she did not like surprise changes. She negated any offers for a birthday party and when she was surprised with one early on she did not enjoy herself, and it was evident. He thought, *something's off in her childhood. I know all about that stuff. Now, she talks about her grandmother, grandfather, and her father; all of which she refers to fairly regularly with wistfulness in her voice. She barely mentions her mother. There is a brother, but she won't discuss him. How bad could it be? She is normally an even-tempered person; not one who shows evidence of abuse; although she holds her privacy right as strictly as anyone I've ever known outside of Mom.*

Chad had often asked Shirley about her education. She said little, but he gleaned she grew up in Gary, Indiana near lower Lake Michigan. She inferred she lived in a little better than marginal area saying it was 'like all Gary, Indiana.' She attended Indiana University Northwest for her nursing degree and later gained a nurse practitioner certificate from a program at Case Western University. She loved her experience at Case. She'd finally left Gary and her family and felt free. Free from her work experience at a small hospital near Gary that left a bad taste. She would not say more. He had checked this with a clerk in personnel who shared information too easily. Shirley never complained about money and she attended good schools.

———

HE was not acting normal, as if, I think, HE ever acts normal. HE's antsy. I see it and feel it. HE's vision in the mirror is at times almost distorted. HE's not aware I can see him then, but when HE walks by a mirror I see the reflection. HE needs to find another 'good work' to do. Does HE believe it's good work when the man chosen to die does not fit the criteria? When a man has hope and an interested partner, there is every reason to wait for God's judgment. We act when God is too slow. HE knows what our role is. I've lectured HE about filling HE's own need versus the elderly men's needs. HE has CLAIMED UNDERSTANDING, but I am afraid HE sees only personal singular needs and wants, and is yessing me to death. Partnerships are like marriage; it's not until you are in one, when you see all the small contractual details missed in entering the deal. Perhaps if I had a love interest for a partnership, I would not feel this stress with HE and HE's actions and maybe I could get out of this relationship.

Killing Jerry was a major mistake. Captain Beauregard is not stupid. He may know about the victim selection criteria. HE will have to also discover the process of finding new potential victims. I don't like the word victim which is Beauregard's term. I like to think of them as social work clients. We are very good social workers. In the end, most out there do not even value the person who was killed with the exception of Pete and Jerry who left people who occupied their daily life with them and are now there to mourn. The public's interest does decrease eventually. Good citizens have their own lives. After a while, they lose interest and just say 'too bad.'

I'll have a conversation with HE tomorrow; maybe take HE on the previously mentioned vacation for two days for a slow-down. If HE isn't too needy HE will choose a victim nearer Boston; we'll still be near the same route. Route 20 is the source of our energy. It was there HE and I first met.

———

After five views of the video for the stolen car from two weeks before Jerry's accident, Sergeants Border and Barr looked at each other. They had agreed beforehand to make several views before commenting. After the third view, Bobby pressed Start to view again with no argument from Bill. Bobby spoke first. "Could be one of the Captain's 'Ahaa' moments. Did you see what I saw?"

Bill replied, "I don't know, Bobby, but I saw two things. I saw the watch again. He's not so smart, is he? He wears something distinctive when on his escapades. He always looks at the time. He probably has a list of time requirements for every action. He's a planner, Bobby, but why change his choice of victim profiles. Unusual, according to all the books

I've read on serial murderers. I saw the series on the development of the FBI Profiling."

"What else did you see? We can talk about the other stuff later. You are a talker, Bill."

"Not according to Jessica Taylor, I'm not. She thinks I avoid all difficult discussions and try to control the conversation."

"Yeah, you do, do that sometimes, but she's just trying to train you for your future relationship figuring maybe she might want to keep you around. You're lucky my friend, she is beautiful and accomplished; not one to throw away."

"I did once, Bobby. I was young and stupid, let her go. I'll make changes, whatever changes are necessary. The other item I caught on the video was his wearing one of the designer athletic outfits he wore before; the Nike one. Could be it's a different one, but it tells you about his choice. He has good shoulders, solid, but is slim and lithe. If he walks into the conference room I may recognize the stance; that is if we ever get him in the conference room. What did you see, Bobby?"

"The neck has always been completely covered before, but not totally this time. There is enough of a view to see he doesn't have a bull neck. He also did exactly the same here as in the other video we have at this dump site. He went around the back of the sales office up the street. This guy is working all territories he is accustomed to visiting. If we went to that restaurant consistently on Tuesdays we'd probably see him."

Bill responded, "Well, why don't we grab the charge slips for those Tuesdays when the killer wasn't committing murders on the weeks before these murders were committed related to this dump site?"

"You think, Bill, he goes to dinner at the restaurant the week before he kills to scope out changes or problems with the car dump site?"

"I'm trying to put myself in his place. Think about it, he's probably picked the mark. I think Tuesday nights are available for him to dine out. if he's one of the medicals the Captain's got us looking at, there's not a lot of leisure time. According to their notes, they all have Tuesdays free. There was another night free, but it wasn't the same for all. Let's go with what they all had. Of course, the killer could scope sites in the morning, but they're like us. They have daily routines, don't you think? When I'm working I don't want to do stuff before I go to work. I mean if I'm stuck with testifying in court, it's work. If I need to see a dentist or doctor; well that's different. Humor me, let's just check."

"Bill, I'm laughing. You think the killer has habits just like us. He's a serial murderer. I don't like the comparison."

"Wrong, Bobby, he is human and it's his human habits I'm interested in. They will trip him up. They always do. We know more about him."

17

A Vacation to Murder

I promised He, I would book us into the Canyon Ranch in Lenox for a few days. I haven't told He they were completely booked. He'll go nuts. He knows my work schedule. Yes, He does. I can't lie about work. Look at the news from our Governor. Everyone's insane about this virus. We die; we die. Natural selection at work. HE and I are working to perfect natural selection for these elderly men. It is a kindness we both promised ourselves when we were younger; just a few years ago. We would protect them from the life of loneliness and prejudice intrinsic in the lives of elderly men without partners. Years of nothingness after lives of service. I understand HE's need, after all, I chose HE; but we have to survive. How will I tone down He's need to kill?

Ah, government at work is finally helping!

HE and I had a conversation about the vacation. I did not tell HE I couldn't get reservations. No need. We watched the news and while we watched, I gasped and said, "I'd better call Canyon Ranch and see if they're affected by this."

Right in front of HE, I called and with a little drama of disappointment in my voice, I said, "Are reservations already made, now cancelled?"

Oh, how devastated I looked when the answer was 'Yes.' HE believed me. HE wasn't angry but did make a sad face. Normally, HE tries to make me happy knowing how difficult it is for me to accept unhappiness in my life. I am the original pink bunny of happiness. HE thinks I need HE to play a role; one that is to please me. Strange, because HE wasn't worried about pleasing me when HE chose Peter and Jerry for an early death.

I think the beast in HE is quiet for now, although HE asked me how soon we could go on vacation. In appeasement, I called Canyon Ranch and made tentative reservations for the Christmas Holiday. It would be lovely; and whatever HE did then would never be noticed. I am safe for now.

Shirley was stressed again for the second time this week. She was not the only one. Her friend Mary-Ellen, a CAT Scan operator, was truly frightened. She told Shirley, "I visit with my granddad who lives independently nearby; in fact, insists he should live independently. He brought me up, but he is not feeling well and has been like that since my mom, his daughter and only child, died. I can't seem to find common ground with him. He shuts me out. Remember, Shirley, he was in here in the ER a month ago with some type of infection never diagnosed. Virus was the final guess. He is weak and morose, and I've been working longer hours, have my two kids, and I'm a single mother. I don't have much time for him. I try, but it is just not enough time to give him the attention he deserves. He takes a walk every night for 'stamina.' And he is stronger than when he came out of the ER, but is acting depressed."

The two were interrupted when Dr. Teague set his tray on the table. Mary-Ellen grimaced. She had explained to Shirley before that doctors thought they were always wanted. Shirley gracefully said to appease Mary-Ellen, "You took a big chance, Dr. Teague, sitting down with women when you were not invited."

Turning beet red, Dr. Teague said, "If I'm butting in on some important conversation, I apologize."

Both women smiled, but Shirley stated, "Not really, we were discussing Mary-Ellen's grandfather who is quite along in years and feeling lonely. He does well physically, but is acting down. He walks every day, which is the best thing for someone fighting depression. Is he out in the sunlight, Mary-Ellen, when he walks, and is the route he takes, safe?"

Mary-Ellen said, "He walks at night after the sun goes down. Granddad won't go in the sun at all because of his medicines. His doctor told him not to be out in the sun. I tried to explain that going out at six at night would be better than going out after sundown; the sun rays are much lower then; but he insists he will do what his doctor tells him to do."

Mary-Ellen directed both her gaze and her voice at Dr. Teague and said, "Doctors won't take the time to explain a directive more fully. Older men need some exposure to sunlight for their bones. In this case sunlight would help with his depression. Why didn't the doctor inform my granddad strong sunrays are harmful but some sun is important. Oh no, takes too much time. He's in his eighties. He needs explanations given maybe two or three times, but they do not bother."

Jesse Teague did not argue with the women, maybe because Shirley nodded her head in agreement. It was understood by all the professionals working in the ER that Dr. Teague rarely found something to criticize in Shirley's actions. He did ask further questions about Mary-Ellen's granddad. His interest pleased her and she gave detailed information on his daily schedule, including where he lived, how he had made his living, what assistance was given to him in his home, and how often he took his walks. The women were impressed with his caring manner. Dr. Teague said, "Mary-Ellen, he qualifies for some visiting nursing and house cleaning. Why haven't you applied for assistance?"

Mary-Ellen laughed, saying, "He won't tell me anything about his finances. His generation believed they could take care of themselves. When I told him how much I make, he was flabbergasted. He'd never made the equivalent of my salary in his life, but owns his own home without a mortgage and lives on a small pension and social security. I want to help him. He could move in with me; my home has a separate apartment I don't use with a separate entrance. Any money saved could be used to pay a male companion to play cards with him. They could travel around town together. Oh no, he says, 'Mary, (he always calls me just Mary. Says it's the Blessed Mother's name and I don't need any other name to make me special.) Mary, you're getting all my assets when I die which won't take much longer. There's no reason to make changes now; too disruptive.'"

"I can't help him if he won't let me. I think he's in pain. I saw prescriptions for muscle relaxants and Ativan. He moved the bottles after he saw me reading the labels. There were two more bottles I didn't get a chance to read. I'm hoping they are just blood pressure and cholesterol meds."

Chad Roswell stood over them, saying, "I was told to fetch you. They're having a meeting right in the ER now. Something big about COVID is going down."

———

HE is feeling the stress. I am stressed. The new COVID measures introduced today are even more cumbersome. The News is overwhelming and HE responds to every nuance as if it's valid. I know what will happen. I know HE. What do I do now? HE has offered me a new potential. I told HE, the choice is too risky. HE name-called me accusing me of acting like a silly girl. Imagine HE saying to me I'm too uptight. Who taught HE everything? I did. The new possibility is from Three Rivers. I think it is a section of Wilbraham. Maybe could be a go, maybe?

Jesse Teague exhibited a great deal of impatience after the sudden meeting of the emergency room staff. He thought, did the brass tell me, senior physician about the changes before the meeting. No, why bother? Admin knows what is the best medical practice. This whole virus thing is a shit show. You have daily announcements to the public at odds with our instructions. What the hell are they thinking? We go home to our communities and say one thing and we're told another from the national and local news. Everyone is frightened. Even Shirley is off. Chad has developed a nervous twitch when I'm around. He doesn't know he has it. I resent that he agrees with everything Shirley says and is oh so protective. There is something off with him. I should know. I lived in a foster care home with every kind of crazy. The parents were the worst. The mother was the pervert, which is not the norm. She was after us boys. I was a bit young, but she tried. I stuck with the old man. He pretended he didn't know about wifey, but he did. He let me hang around him to make her jealous. Oh, I know all about those crazies. She caught me only once. I hate her. My grandpa I met later listened to my stories and wormed his way to get me to tell about the sex abuse. He was the only one I told. He could be trusted with a secret. Then he dies with my secret and never talked despite his suffering. God, I loved that old man. I liked my adopted parents, but they were so easy to please, it got annoying. Chad's annoying. He plays the perfect young man, but I will prevail. I had no competition before him. I wish Shirley didn't get so uptight at a little stress. It seems to be her only flaw. She'd make a great doctor's wife. She is not clingy. I don't want a wife who tries to own me. I need time to myself. She'd agree to our having separate lives. She has told me she understands my needs. I know it. I just have to get rid of Chad and soon. Or I could just set him up to fail. That works too. He interrupted our perfect relationship. Why does she go for him, as if she's known him for a lifetime?

Attorney Norberto Cull used his relationship with a security guard at the ER where Rudy's persons of interest worked to get some info. The guard, Al, was more than happy to chat with him, but said, "I've got to be careful, Mr. Cull. Security is tight here because of the virus, and it's going to worsen starting this weekend. The virus death stats have gone up. They're shutting down the hospital for all visitors. Only emergency medical procedures can be done. The ER is for patients only and you will have to call ahead if you think you've got the virus. They've promised there will be constant changes. Good thing you came today, Mr. Cull."

Cull questioned Al's familiarity with some of the elderly men who died; specifically mentioning Jerry LaFollet and Pete Proder. Al remembered Jerry well but his recall on Pete was hazy. He explained, "Pete's death isn't recent, Mr. Cull. He was an important man. He was also fun to be with. You know he was famous as a Country music musician. I've heard him in concert. Funny, they both were hit by drunk drivers. Bad way to go."

Cull asked, "I'm interested in elderly men who were in and out of the ER several weeks before their deaths. Here are the dates of their deaths to jog your memory. Also, what van drivers were pulling in here often during that time? Can you help or ask around, but don't ask the doctors and nurses? They'll shush me out of here because I'm a lawyer."

Al went behind his stand-up desk and pulled his clipboard containing notes for the past month. He said, "Mr. Cull, these are my notes and far more reliable than my brain. They don't belong to the hospital. I'll give them to you, but I don't want to be in court telling a judge about these notes. They may be my notes, but they were written while I was on the job and I guess I don't own the rights to them. Am I right about that? You take them and don't throw them away. You can be my attorney. I have a right to give my attorney stuff; right?"

Cull laughed and said, "Where'd you get your law degree, Al?"

Al never answered. Cull continued the conversation directed at interpreting Al's notes. Al took great pains documenting his everyday work. Lists of van drivers with patient names connected were organized by time of delivery or pickup. Unusual activity was also listed. Cull thought, *Al has earned his keep. He should be a paralegal; not only does he not miss a detail, but he documents everything. What a witness in court he'd make.*

Cull thanked Al and asked if there was a place to sit to analyze the data; given that he thought he might have some further questions. Al responded, "Could you go outside, Mr. Cull? I'm only supposed to direct patients to the waiting room before intake. You can come back in to ask questions. Nobody will catch that; they'll just think you're a new possible intake. This virus stuff is keeping us on our toes."

Cull went outside and found a bench about thirty yards away. Fortunately, it was shady and he could see Al's notes clearly. His scanning took about fifteen minutes before he came across some interesting data.

He thought, *Jerry LaFollet brought two elderly men from the same rehab home to this ER four weeks before his death. He brought one of them home to Three Rivers three days later. Al can give me their personals if he's willing. If not, Rudy will be able to get them. If not, Jim Locke, my go to private investigator, can talk it out of someone here. Cripes, even Sheila, my office manager can work the phones on this one. If one of these guys fits the bill for a victim, then I've really been lucky. Never that easy, but could be this time. Sheri says I am the king of happy outcomes. Hope so this time. This killer has to be stopped. No one has the right to decide who lives or not; just no one. And Rudy needs this data even if he won't like that I was quicker than his guys in the retrieval process.*

An hour later, Norbie had coaxed names and addresses, but no health details, from Al. He promised him Red Sox tickets. Al, who lived in Springfield, could pick them up at his office. A quick call was made to Sheila to get phone numbers for the two men or their nearest neighbors. He told her to explain he was calling to see if they needed further services paid under their insurance. Norbie knew he could tell just about any insured person about additional health insurance benefits they did not know existed for them, and get a positive response.

He grabbed a sandwich from a small Mom and Pop shop in Palmer and listened to their worries about being closed down. He commented, "You have groceries here. Not to worry, you deal in essential services and I'm pretty sure the Governor's going to allow essential services. I think you'll be able to stay open."

Mrs. Dudek said, "If we don't stay open we'll lose this business. We have enough to carry our expenses for six weeks but no longer and we have children to feed. I hope you're right."

Her worries stopped Cull in his tracks as he realized what the economic impact would be if the Governor did close most businesses as was anticipated. He also wondered about this more rural city. He did not think they would be as severely affected. The sandwich was quite good and it was not one he would normally order, but then again, he thought, *how bad could steak and cheese on a fresh grinder roll be?*

Twenty minutes later, with telephone numbers of both men available to him sourced by Sheila, Cull arrived outside the first address; this one was on the Springfield/Wilbraham line. He thought, *this is a no-go. First it is not in Three Rivers and there's a handicapped ramp. If the guy needs a ramp he's not going to be out for a nightly walk, now is he?*

Cull's knock on the door resulted in an elderly man answering so quickly, Cull almost fell off the small stoop in surprise. Mr. Wyatt greeted him and Norbie noticed he had no trouble walking. On the pretense he was representing Ray LeFron's estate, he was let into a sunny living room. A woman in a wheelchair loudly welcomed him. Her voice was strong and she motioned him to sit on the chair to her right, saying, "That one's for himself. He needs some comfort taking care of me all the time. Rod, come join us. I heard you say your name, Attorney Cull. I've read about you in the papers. Tell me what you need. I'm the talkative one in this marriage. Rod is the thoughtful one. It works as long as we both are alive, but when one of us goes, the other's going to be in trouble."

Norbie noticed Rod did what his wife asked and waited for her to develop a conversation with the new guest. It evolved, the conversation that is, over time and it was not to be rushed. Mrs. Wyatt was not to be hustled in any manner. When she settled on his request for information about Jerry LeFron who drove Rod to the ER, she said, "I'll have Rod tell you about Ray, but I can certainly say he was a wonderful man. Rod's experience at the ER was all good. He met medical staff, the like of which he says he's never met before; right, Rod?"

"Margie says it like it is, Mr. Cull. Ray picked me up when I fell at the Senior Center. We were having a big luncheon honoring a new manager. Right there, I suddenly couldn't talk. They said my face drooped on the right side. I knew it was a stroke. Just as I fell down, a minute later, Micky Leary had a heart attack. Ray did not wait for an ambulance. I walked into the van as they carried Micky. We were there so fast and while on the drive, Ray called and asked for Shirley or Chad to warn them. They were there waiting for us when we arrived with Dr. Teague. Good people, they are all good people. Micky is alone. If he'd had the attack at home he'd have died. Instead I was out in seven hours, while Micky was monitored overnight and sent home after tests and with medications. It was my first time at the ER. I never had a problem before, but Micky was in there a couple of weeks before with digestion problems."

Margie butted in with, "Best medical team we've ever had. It took me three hours to get a neighbor to take me to the hospital. I was met by the Nurse Practitioner Shirley Baker. She couldn't do enough for me. Chad, I forget his last name, well, he joined us. They kept my spirits up. I need Rod, but right then, Rod needed me. They told me early on it was a minor stroke and he'd do well. He just needed tests and medication. He's still getting tests and the meds are upsetting his sleep and appetite. Look how skinny he's gotten."

Rod stopped Margie cold. "Enough about me, Margie. I don't want you to go on and on."

Margie stopped talking. Cull next expressed interest in Micky Leary. Through a lengthy interview mainly with Rod, accompanied by Margie reinterpreting the information occasionally, Cull learned Micky lived nearby in Three Rivers. Cull pretended it wasn't important, but said he was interested in men like Ray who had no one to care for them. Rod told a typical story of an outgoing man blessed in marriage to a stay-at-home wife who cared for him. There were no children nearby. Rod said, "Not a lot of employment in Three Rivers and the kids were ambitious. Both went to Austin, Texas. They made it big in some manufacturing business, come home at least once a year. Micky was lost when he didn't have a little lady to go home to."

Cull asked, "I know if he was outgoing, he could keep himself busy, but Rod, he was older. What did he do at night?"

"I've met him a few times for lunch out at the Burgundy Brook Café. Good food. He was a foodie. I don't know where he ate supper, but he would tell us about these great gourmet meals he'd make for himself and some neighbors. Then he'd go for walks. He walked all the time; you couldn't keep up with him. I was astonished he had the heart attack, because he was in decent shape."

Cull asked, "Do you walk at night, Rod?"

"No, Mr. Cull. I'm an early riser and get all my exercise in early in the day. Margie and I eat home most nights. It's easier; we are in front of the TV by eight. Every night is the same. We talk. Sometimes we play Scrabble. We have visitors. Doesn't sound interesting to you, but we appreciate our life and each other."

Norbie left the Wyatt home and headed for Three Rivers. It didn't take too long before he was in front of a very modern home next to a very old farmhouse. Incongruous was the first word that sprang to mind. Micky Leary lived in the modern home. Micky certainly could see any visitors coming into his triple size driveway through the enormous windows on the front and left side of the home. The driveway ended in a four-car garage connected to the home by an enormous breezeway or addition. He was used to calling connections from garages to homes as breezeways, but this one was an addition. The modern home was not quite a ranch. There was a second story with peaks and valleys on the roof but covered only half of the structure. A man walked out his front door down the walkway to the drive and introduced himself, saying, "Rod called me. Says you're a lawyer looking for info on Ray LeFron. Come on in. I'll make some java."

Norbie looked around the kitchen which opened to a large living room and dining room. All were separated by lower ceiling moldings but there were no impediments for movement built in on the floor. He thought, *really a nice place here. It's well designed and furnished, but there are jackets and bags left all over the place. Micky is a slob or maybe he cleans once a week. I'll have to tell Sheri I appreciate her housekeeping. I can't credit myself; I'm gone so much. I wonder how I would do if keeping up the house was all left to me.*

Micky put mugs of coffee down and pointed to the cream and sugar saying, "Only real stuff in here. Nothing is low calorie. I've some coffee cake I've made for the center; actually, two of them, one for the center and one for me. I love to cook, but I have to stop eating the rich stuff. While I get the cake tell me how I can help you. Rod said it was related to Ray. He was your client?"

Cull gave his story on Ray's death and his handling of Ray's estate. Micky did not go into a discussion as easily as the Wyatts. Micky couldn't understand how he would have any useful knowledge to contribute. Norbie shared there were some questions about the accident; whether it was an accident or not. Micky then showed some interest, saying, "You mean someone was out to get Ray. Can't be. Not Ray. He was one of those soldiers in life who always contributed. Who would kill Ray?"

Cull maneuvered the conversation to Micky's knowledge of the goings on at the ER, saying, "I know Ray brought you there after your heart attack. Can you just bring me through the process of admission, your stay, and your exit? I want to know just who you gave information to, and who was particularly helpful to you. It is important. I can't tell you why, but it will help in settling Ray's case."

"It's not about Ray, is it, Mr. Cull? It's about me. Don't bullshit me. Do you think I'm in danger?"

Try as he might, Cull could not get out of this one. He summarized some of his suspicions that Ray may have met somcone at the ER who noticed him, disliked him, and sought to kill him. He explained the family asked him to investigate and maybe there was nothing there. Micky said, "I don't quite believe an attorney of your notoriety would waste his time investigating details. More likely you'd have a regular investigator do this type of info chasing. Ray had some resources, but was there that kind of money to pay for a suit like you?"

"Yeah, there is? I'm doing it for no money though. I liked Ray. He was a client. His friend is also a client and she thinks there is something wrong with the accident scene and so do I. I'm working on a 'wing and a prayer' here, Micky. Would it hurt you to share info with me?"

Micky's attitude did a one-eighty as he detailed his emergency room visit. He said, "He was frightened in the ambulance but better on admission. Dr. Teague, Shirley Baker, and Chad Roswell met the ambulance. Arriving in the ambulance let him bypass intake and all that 'crap' was how he stated it. Shirley did intake and she wanted to know his whole damn life. Micky said, What did I eat that day? What did I do that day and the week before? All my meds, foods I normally eat; that was a hoot when I told her about my French cooking and the amount of butter and wine I cook with. She and Chad actually remembered me from an earlier visit I made for digestive problems. They probably should have done an echo-cardiogram at that time. They might have found my blockage then. I have no complaints since I've suffered no heart damage. Chad and Dr. Teague were prepping me while Shirley asked questions. They were listening intently for what I thought was boring. Chad, he's pretty well-built, wanted to know about my exercises. When I explained I walked every day, I was asked how long I walked, what was my route, and what time of the day I walked. I complained it was none of their business, but Shirley is a sweetheart. She said, 'How many miles, Mr. Leary? I see you have an iWatch on, so how many steps? Do you walk mornings or evenings and do you walk on sidewalks; I mean is it safe where you walk? Do you walk alone?' Before I could answer, Dr. Teague explained that these questions are asked with the hope they would get truthful answers and that I was of a certain age and perhaps would not be able to rationally explain my habits. Chad inferred they needed to understand how cognizant I was at this point in time. So, I told them everything, which is not what I normally would say. I don't share my life with people."

Hope rose in Norbie. He said, "So how many miles, what time of day, and where do you walk, Micky, and do you still have the same habits now, after your heart attack and surgery?"

"Pretty much. Took me until about ten days ago to get back walking. Why?"

Cull lied and without guilt said, "A friend of mine is not doing that well after a heart attack. I just wondered."

"I walk up Boston Road. Been walking that way since I was a kid.

Lived in this area my whole life. Met my wife in high school. Life was great until she died. Rod Wyatt is lucky. He still has his wife; she may be handicapped, but she's a good companion for him. I don't have that anymore. I told that Dr. Teague to get a wife. Going alone is tough. Think about it. It's tough for me and I'm outgoing. Imagine a guy whose lifestyle was always being at home. Really tough aging alone for those guys."

Cull added, "What time of the day do you walk?"

"Around seven-thirty or later after I've finished the dishes from dinner. I walk even when I have company. My friends know my schedule. We eat at six in the evening. They leave after we all do the dishes. I'm no maid. I cook; not so good at clean-up. I walk close to four miles, sometimes taking little walks partway down side streets. I hit Mr. B's on the Wilbraham line before I go home."

Cull questioned Micky about the medical team and whether they ever called him or visited him after the surgery. He said he'd seen Dr. Teague in the ER for a short visit later when he was hyperventilating thinking he was having another heart attack. The doc told him it was common to feel frightened after a heart attack and surgery, and, "What I was enduring was simply some anxiety. I've never been anxious in my life and I argued with him. Shirley called after I returned from the first surgery and Chad called me a day after the second ER visit. Got the best care there. Love those people."

Cull left the house after sharing with Micky that nothing appeared to be of assistance in Ray's case which seemed to please Micky. Just as he was leaving, Micky asked for his card in case he remembered more about Ray other than seeing him around a lot.

Driving back to his office in Springfield, Cull made two calls; the first to his wife Sheri to tell her he appreciated her. To which she asked if he had several cocktails in the middle of the day and laughed. Next, he connected with Rudy and confessed. Rudy gave him the usual lecture about interfering in an open case and it would do no good in court later. "I know, Rudy, but this guy Micky Leary may be at risk in taking his walks if he's been marked. I don't have all your information, but I don't like it. If you need my help, I can pay Jim Locke to follow Micky on his walks for a few nights until you've assessed any danger. I don't want any old men mercy-killed if I can help it. It could be you and I, Rudy, if our wives leave before us. It could be Roland. What would he do without Lizette? We, guys, are fragile in old age."

Rudy said, "I have funds for Locke, just ask him to keep it down. Should only be a couple of hours a night for a week before I can figure this out. And, I hate to say this, but thank you, Norbie."

18

Personal History

First thing the next morning Rudy assigned Petra and Lilly to use a personal car to tail Micky Leary on his walks on certain nights, saying, "Make sure you are on the same side of the road far enough away not to be noticed, creeping, but close enough to speed up if a speeding car heads toward him. Do it starting next week, on Tuesday nights, for the next few weeks. Today we'll review all the background checks. I'm hoping a motive can be guessed from this medical group's childhood experiences. I can't rule out two people committing these killings. If there are two killers in partnership, then how did they find each other? I heard in the interviews that both men, Chad and the doctor, may be interested in Shirley. I don't like any of this, but my gut tells me we are on the right path. I think it's one or more of these medical folks. We haven't evidence or any inclination to consider any other potential."

Mason Smith reported first. As usual, he told the detectives what he personally thought. "No fk'n good, whoever's killing these old men. You don't get to decide who lives or dies based on your personal history. Don't go from the specific to the general. Don't people take logic classes today; they need to. I'll tell you what I've discovered and you tell me if any of it would direct someone to murder seventeen people with such consistent zeal. The guy doesn't make mistakes."

Petra was the only detective, now that Ash was transferred to Traffic after his promotion, who could stop Mason from further philosophizing. "Get on with it, Mason. What have you discovered?

"Dr. Teague was named Jake Lorenz by his birth parents and taken from his mother three months later when the police arrested her and her boyfriend, who was not Jake's father. The birth father was long gone and never showed up later. Teague or Lorenz was placed in a good foster home and the people tried to adopt him, but the mother wouldn't give up the child. When Teague was three he was moved to another foster placement that wasn't so good and removed a number of years later after the foster parents were arrested for drugs. The third home lasted until the foster mother suffered a stroke. She did not die, but was out of the foster mother placement. He was then adopted by the Teague's who had been in the process of adoption. His birth mother had died of a drug overdose and there were no longer any legal impediments to adoption.

"The social worker handling the adoption agreed to speak with me. She is retired. She felt this was as good a placement as she could have gotten for Jesse, saying, "He was always a good boy. I was around for all his placements. His last one was the best. She was a caring and good woman; she did complain that Jesse had been exposed to some pretty sordid stuff in his second placement. I knew nothing about any problems at that time. I'd make my visits, all by appointment. There were no signals. The house was immaculate. Maybe that in itself is a signal of pretense, but I got no hint from the placed children who were well-behaved. I had the highest caseload in my unit and it was the policy then not to have extra visits unless there was good reason to suspect a problem. You know foster mothers have to gear up to have us come to their homes, and our visits were a disruption in their structured childcare. They shouldn't be, but the mothers said the kids go antsy when we would visit; they were afraid we'd take them away. Now I think the perfection in that home was the signal I missed. When we moved the children to other placements they all had problems; it wasn't just Jesse. The Teague's had executive positions; the wife at a large non-profit and the husband was a vice president at the electric company. The husband was a real nice guy who volunteered for all types of community events. His wife was more conservative and maybe shy, but a good lady. Jesse bloomed in their home. I'm so proud of him now." She felt he certainly was one of her big successes in placement.

"The Teague's both died within a year of each other. Mr. Ralphie Teague died suddenly but was suffering from a debilitating disease. He had pancreatic cancer and was expected to live a year or two more, but died. It was thought to have been treated early enough to give him a longer life, but this was a while ago. The wife had breast cancer and was very sick during her husband's illness, but she lasted a year. Doesn't look suspicious to me. I spoke with Mr. Teague's sister who said the Teague's were good people, but older when they got Jesse. Jesse was named after her father. She said her dad loved that boy as did her brother and his wife. They spoiled him terribly trying to make up for any suffering he had been subjected to. She described them as, 'Over attentive parents trying to smooth out Jesse's path in life.' She also said, 'I have five children. You can't give kids everything. Jesse sucked all the air out of room when he was with you. He was handsome but needed all the attention. Other than being the archetypical only child, he was okay. He's not close with us at all; not even with one of my boys who is the same age.' That's all I have for you, Captain. He sounds self-absorbed, but nothing explosive in his background."

Bill Barr reported on Chad. His report was shorter, but perhaps more interesting to the detectives. "This guy is a Boy Scout. I got hold of a high school teacher who gave him a recommendation for college. I didn't know community colleges required a recommendation. The teacher said he was a skinny kid who was not well treated by his peers, but was tops in the class. He said Chad's mother ran some sort of old age residence in her home and Chad did most of the heavy lifting. Chad's mother was disliked by most people in the community. She worked in nursing homes. Staff not only did not like her, but in two cases caused her dismissal. She was competent but not patient. Chad's grandfather lived with them when Chad was small. The mother got state funding for him, and that's when she made her home into a care agency. The grandfather took care of Chad until he was five. It was then the grandfather had a stroke. The teacher knew all this from another teacher whose father was in Chad's mother's care. Chad was not treated well at home, but he stayed around until his mother passed. She said Chad took good care of his mom until her death. The rest of his story shows high grades in graduate school and stellar performance at his work. If there's a problem it's from his mom, grandfather, or being forced to babysit elderly people when he was too young for that kind of responsibility. I don't want it to be him; I think he's endured enough."

Lilly responded, "Lousy life, Bill, but if he kills, then I have no sympathy. There's enough in this report, Bill, to make me wonder."

Petra reported on Shirley. "Talk about a goody-two-shoes; Shirley must be the eighth wonder of the world. Not one person had a negative comment about her. However, her mother and brother were, and I quote, 'The meanest and most untrustworthy of people.' It was said she had a wonderful dad and maternal grandparents. The dad died young and her grandfather lived sometime thereafter. She took care of both grandparents. Shirley was a scholar with many friends. I spoke with her supervisor from her last position before she arrived in Western Massachusetts. She said staff and patients raved about Shirley and her work but she kept great distance from any knowledge about her personal life. She had few dates and after two or three, she would shut herself off from the guy. Shirley explained to one friend that she didn't trust easily. I think her brother got into trouble from the police and perhaps her mother also. I heard this from a nurse who worked in a hospital with her."

The Captain thought there was little new information on Shirley; just confirmation on what they already knew. He asked what, if anything of importance, had been discovered. Mason referred to Bobby for a report they developed. He said, "We have astonishing information which we think assures us we are on the right path with these three potential perps. All three lived, worked, and were educated very close to Route 20 in various areas from Indiana, New York, Ohio, and Boston before posting out here. This information, we believe supports the direction we're working towards, but is not much help in discovering which one is the perp."

Beauregard replied, "I asked before to search for auto accidents killing elderly men in other states on Route 20. Did we get results yet?"

Bobby answered, "Lieutenant Lent thought he could do better on that issue, his being posted head of the Traffic Division. He said he'll have something tomorrow. He and I both think if there is even one case, we may know who to look at more closely. One problem I see is, all three were generally in the same areas before coming here; not necessarily at the same colleges or hospitals, but close enough."

The Captain said, "You know how I like a matrix to spell it out. Get it on my desk when you hear from Ash Lent. Start is now."

———

I thought HE seemed particularly antsy today. I certainly understood why. The stress we suffer working under the COVID-19 umbrella is over the top. All these changes in policy based on constantly changing direction from the CDC have created constant fear. I have to remember today, just what today's policy is, and forget what I learned yesterday. And the patients are so fearful. I find it difficult to have a personal relationship when I can't see them unmasked. HE told me a break was needed. HE arranged for a day off since we've worked six days a week for the last two weeks. Naturally HE chose a Tuesday. I will have to watch HE's actions very carefully. I reminded HE of the off choice we made in determining the weapon to end these lonely men's lives and allowing them to seek Nirvana. I remember discussing the method for helping Venerables to their deaths. It was not an easy discussion. HE thought as medical professionals, we could easily use too much medicine or pillows and get the desired result. But I forced HE to read all the literature on mercy killers and how the police caught them.

More importantly, I informed HE about the horror of their families' existence after discovery of their being killed deliberately, making them victims. HE agreed discovery of death by auto would seem an unaccountable act of God. HE did say at that time, I was too cautious but nevertheless agreed with me. My problem is two-fold. Discovery would prevent our good work. The big impediment was the devastation and last-minute fear our patient would feel being choked or realizing an injection given by a caregiver was the end. The thinking experience could muddy the movement on. When HE first mentioned a road accident as a methodology, I said a decisive, 'No.' I could only envision the trauma, and the question of 'How could we assure ourselves instant death?' I want my gentlemen to meet the light cloaked in white embracing the freedom we give them. HE gave me an answer. It made so much sense; yes, it did. HE said, "Birth is traumatic, but the infant does not look back. The infant goes to the light; there is almost always a sharp cry, but then the comfort of the mother makes it all worthwhile. Our men will go to the light and be embraced by the All-Knowing One. Our men will not regret we took this action. The physical pain will be short. I'll make sure of that."

HE did kill our men instantly, except in one case where it was required to run over the body several times to effectively kill the man. Perhaps that man did not want to die. We do make a judgment the men are ready. We think it through; or we did. HE is ready to fulfill his mission. HE is faithful to our cause; I know HE is, but HE is getting careless. HE doesn't know I will track HE. HE's off Tuesday. It is difficult for me to follow HE. Getting access is difficult and how in the last minute can I shut HE down? I've only done it once successfully. I saw HE checking Micky Leary's record. I know where HE will go. It could work. I'd attempt to stop the act, but may not be successful. It would be a whole lot better if HE at least went to Worcester County for the next one. We had to move from one hospital early because HE brought two men to God within a month within abutting or nearby towns. Even HE agreed it was a careless move.

I feel so good after a death. I see the man's soul walking in white in the light no more to fight the world's delights; ready to assume white nights forever. I love poetry. I write it all the time. I would have left poems for each of my lovely men but the police love evidence like that. I don't care how smart you are, many detectives work on these cases. If there is any evidence left behind, forensics will trap you. We have left absolutely no evidence.

When I was a child, I saw the goodness rubbed out of my grandfather by disease. My family called him the 'old man.' Oh, how he begged to go. I was too little to help, but I did try. I was stopped before I was successful; I suppose in time. Grandpa whispered to me, a thank you. Grandpa understood. I think I carry his wishes out, even today, with my mission.

It is absolutely necessary to have a mission in life; something you know is important to society and you feel such joy in your accomplishments. HE and I agree and even when HE steps out of line and acts, I do forgive. HE is fulfilling our mission. Still, we must be more conservative. I think I know who HE has chosen for our next one. This killing must be stopped. HE has always wanted immediate gratification. I've explained planning is most important and will allow us to continue our charge. I could call HE's mark and tell him to stop walking at night. I'm familiar with his health and there's enough in there to support my warning him. But, if HE learned about my action, and HE seems to be able to predict some of my actions, at times, HE would not forgive me. I need HE. I'd better not.

———

Lieutenant Ashton Lent was happy today. Martina felt better. They cooked a really healthy but spicy to their tastes dinner last night and were alone to enjoy it. Better yet, they both had finally come to terms with Martina's limitations if she wanted to stay healthy. He thought, *I never knew about the mental round-about a patient with chronic disease faces. Martina, and I, if I were to be honest, go from embracing life for tomorrow to exhaustive fearfulness. She is doing well, but is scheduled for another surgery in three weeks.*

Martina gave him a stunning smile and quietly asked, "Will you marry me, Ashton Lent? I love you."

He thought, what can I say? I want so much to marry her. But is she marrying me because she's afraid she's on death's door? That is not romantic. What's the matter with me? She wants to marry me. I want to marry her.

Ash looked straight into the irises of her eyes filled with glistening tears spilling over the lower lids and said, "I love you. I'll marry you, but don't you die on me, Martina. I don't think I could recover."

After she hugged him with great force, Martina said, "We'll get the license tomorrow and marry in ten days before my surgery, okay?"

"Okay, as long as you're marrying me for love and not just to take care of your estate affairs if you die."

"Nope. Ash, I have an estate attorney already. In fact, you can sign all the documents once we marry. That includes all the powers to give you access to everything. I want you, Ash, only you."

They turned on the television news after cleaning up and heard the state would be shut down. The news was a repeat. They had ignored the news for several days. They both wondered how this shut-down would affect their plans. Martina asked, "They might not do my surgery for when we planned. It's okay. This time it is not emergency surgery. Let's get down to City Hall tomorrow for the license. With our luck, they'll be closing City Hall soon."

Ash asked, "Who's going to marry us, Martina?"

"I asked a witness from one of your cases."

Ash said, "Which witness? How did you meet her? I'm assuming it's a her although there are lots of male JP's."

"Ms. Lavender James of the purple hair in the psychotherapist case is my choice and I stand by it, Ash. Do you not remember the night we met her and her significant other at the Casino in Springfield?"

"Yeah, I remember, we met in the South End Marketplace. You did get along, but how did you get her number?"

"Ash, you guys were talking sports and when you do, you see nothing. She gave me her card. We need a little purple hair and excitement in our lives. Elisa will love her."

And their plans were made.

19

Preventing Murder; Maybe?

Ashton Lent had spent days on the phone calling cities and towns on the Route 20 cross country highway. He was able to narrow his focus after Bobby Barr gave him some specific locations. He tried Lakeland Ohio, Chicago area, and Boston area. The first results were disappointing. He then asked them to look for accidents along Route 20 and he was awaiting search results. He called Bobby Barr who had worked Traffic and asked for advice for the search. Bobby did some work and found areas on Route 20 in his search areas which showed small townships with separate police forces. Ash sent out refined search requests, but did not cancel his previous one.

Later in the day, his automatic printer spit out accident reports for several deaths; three matched his prescribed descriptions. Two were in the same area; outside of Boston. The other was in Chicago on Lake Street/Route 20 west side of the city. All were on Route 20. They occurred within a year of each other. There were no major investigations into the accidents other than the usual drunk driving with a stolen auto. No camera footage was listed in any of the accidents. Ash was waiting more complete reports.

Ash called Beauregard who asked if he had time to come on over to MCU. An hour later, the two men were both growling in frustration.

Beauregard said, "They were all working in the areas when these accidents happened. This is not as helpful as I thought. I'd hoped we could rule one of them out. Perhaps we can. Were they working those nights? They might all be working the same shift here, but it's unlikely their schedules would match in Chicago and Boston. They also told us in our interviews they met each other in Western Massachusetts on the job."

Ash asked, "Captain, Petra worked Boston as a young cop. She has always been the best at getting around. Maybe she has connections in the hospital where they worked. I know getting work schedules is a no-no without a warrant and we don't have enough for a warrant. Even if some judge gave it, it would get around. We would get nothing more out of the perp; if the perp is one of these three."

"The perp is one of these three, no question about it. How to figure which one is a dilemma for me."

"Do you have any ideas outside of Petra and her connections?"

"Ash, I'll try everything, but right now we have a potential victim to protect, with info relating to the possibility that one of the three suspects wears an iWatch on his or her off-hours matching our video clip, and some assistance with a personability profile developed on our perp by Jim Locke. I'm in contact by phone with FBI's BAU agent John Abbott. He's doing an analysis for me based on the files we have. Normally, he'd be here, but with travel restrictions from this virus, we do phone. Works better for me. I've asked him about search warrants if we found any of our suspects were in another area during other similar accidents along Route 20. He said he had some contacts and maybe legal formats would not be necessary. He inferred the warrants could be gotten later, saying, 'Rudy, don't want to wake the dead if we don't have to.'"

"Did you say it first, Captain, or did Abbott?"

"Me, but he was quick to agree."

———

Rudy Beauregard and Jim Locke spent several hours together discussing the seventeen killings. Jim was being paid for his work which kept the two from chit-chatting. Jim was, by nature, a talker and today was no different. Rudy was a listener and organizer, and focused. Rudy did not particularly like profiling and he relayed this concept out for Jim, who laughed, saying, "Nothing's changed since I worked in this unit, Rudy. I don't disagree with you. Profiling uses our history on killers as a lead to the future. It is just helpful in giving direction. Even you must agree, it does do that."

"Jim, you and I have chased sociopaths and psychopaths. There are no rules with them, just guidelines. If you have a sociopath with an objective to do harm, and who is smart, all the rules meaning nothing, absolutely nothing. You know I'm right."

"Well, Rudy, there are some valuable guidelines. You know, as well as I, this killer is organized. This killer plans. This killer must be intelligent to consistently leave so few clues. This killer normally abides by a set plan. Right?"

Rudy's answer aligned completely with Jim Locke's thoughts. "A profiler would say the killer is most likely a male because of the weapon used. The killer is most likely educated. The killer looks quite normal because there is no evidence of an unusual type of person in any connected areas in the seventeen murders. Each murder has three sites: site of auto robbery; site of accident; and site of auto dumping. Lots of opportunity for people to comment on strange folks hanging around; but nada!

"This killer is lithe and moves gracefully. This killer has knowledge of cars and how to break into them; he knows about used car lots. This killer steals cars from hospital related parking lots. This killer drives well given the maneuvering noted by forensics at one of the accident scenes. This killer has a fixation for Route 20. So, a profiler would say and has said the killer is male, between ages twenty-eight and forty years of age, could be a medical professional, has lived or worked near Route 20, maybe feels a connection to mercy kill on the road, and was related to an auto guy or he himself worked with autos. We are not there yet, Jim."

"No, but your choice of potential serial murderers is good, Rudy. And you have only a few possible routes to discover the bad actor here. You can hope he'll make a mistake on this next one and that I or one of your detectives will catch him in the act on a Tuesday night. You can re-interview the three and maybe catch one to one or two lying, but I don't think it will be easy since I suspect one or two or three may be brilliant sociopaths. You could background check each locally and see how people feel about them. You've interviewed them, Rudy, and those close to them who already thought these three were sent from the Almighty to do good works. You've not interviewed their finance people, their friends and neighbors, and their work colleagues. You don't really have a fix on what they do for downtime."

"Right on, Jim. We'll check gym memberships; I have connections with many of them. They'll show me times and lists. Petra and Lisa are gym rats. They could find commonalities there. Backgrounds are the way to go; work colleagues at former positions if in the midst of this virus stuff, I can get medical people to speak with us. Always good to speak with you, Jim. I miss you being in MCU, but clearly, you've not forgotten me. Bill me for your time."

I can't believe the police have gone this far. Questioning Alice Meade about Jerry LaFollet's death infers they are being extraordinarily diligent in solving these accident cases. I told HE, I told HE many times; "You must stay with the plan. The plan protects us." I knew Proder and LaFollet's deaths would be the focus. The police must have a criminologist or whatever they call them from the FBI. I've read all about their profiling techniques. When we changed our choice of victims, just what information does that give them? I know they now know we have gotten careless.

The police are now expecting more mistakes. I watch police shows. I know how they work when they ask questions; will they try to contact my family? I say good luck to them. HE must understand there can be no more mistakes. I've got to let HE know when HE is listening - they've gotten too close. HE mostly avoids reading the papers and is not concerned with what others think. If Alice hadn't come into the ER with poison ivy all over her, I wouldn't know how deeply they were investigating these deaths. I think HE heard Alice, but maybe not. I must make HE understand the risks.

They know our choice of victims, and therefore know our choice of methods. How long will they take before they are following HE? Not long, I bet. I've read books on the details of police following a mark. The mark is sighted. Normally two or three officers in plainclothes and maybe two cars are used. Captain Beauregard is in charge of the detectives who questioned Alice Meade. He would not have enormous assets to use. West Side is a small city. Yet, the news reports in the past have said he is relentless. One said, "He waits and waits and then gets the bit in his teeth and never lets go."

Maybe his department is working with other police departments in the area. Not good…not good! Means he has greater than normal personnel and cars at his disposal. The trail of the stolen cars and methods of dumping them are like a tell in a gambler's face. I think the biggest risk is in the dumping of the cars. They can't possibly know who our next elderly man is, because we haven't chosen him yet. Unless HE goes off the deep end and goes for Micky Leary in spite of my objections. Raises the risk, but how could they know about the elderly men we don't kill? They probably know we like elderly men with no connections, which is why they questioned Alice on Jerry's death. That death was a mistake. They know it was out of plan. They know organization, which is how they define serial killers, and break down when there are mistakes in major areas. Those two deaths were not minor forensic mistakes. No, they were serious out of plan errors. HE, oh why did you not listen to me; not just once, but twice? Would HE be so stupid as to do it three times? I shouldn't worry so much because Micky has no connections, but it's too soon and he lives in an area being reviewed in these cases. How would they even know about Leary? They wouldn't. I just don't like sloppiness and killing Micky Leary at this time would be sloppy. I will rant at HE, although HE often shuts me off when the message is not palatable.

———

Captain Beauregard was closeted in Detective Mason Smith's tiny, neat, but crowded office questioning him. "Have you searched Facebook on our cast of characters, Detective?"

"Facebook, Messenger, Twitter, Instagram, and some others, why?"

Rudy answered, "What about complete history searches? Do I have to have the Feds do it?"

"No, Captain, I can probably get them from Google without a

warrant. If you are just scanning to assure you are on the right inquiry and you think it won't be needed for a trail of evidence, tell Jim Locke. He probably employs a hacker. I don't know how far back they go. Maybe you don't want to go there."

"I'll go where I have to go. See about the process with Google. We want data on three suspects. I'll talk to a criminal profiler."

The Captain left Mason's office. He did not call Jim Locke as had been suggested; he had a better idea, thinking, I'll have Vargas hook me up with his IT guru hacker, Maurice. I don't even know his last name. He found my father; he can find anyone, and he is an unknown. Luis will help connect if it means getting a killer off the streets. You have to know who are the good guys when you're moving off the rails. I don't like having to do this. It is just for information; not to railroad someone. But, but…an old man is getting designated for death; I can't let that happen.

———

Luis was quite willing to meet with Rudy in an hour. A short explanation about his back being against the wall was enough for them to meet at the Mary Meadows Rehab Parking Lot in Holyoke. This site was Luis' suggestion; his auntie was there and he was to visit her sometime today. His being there would not be suspicious.

Rudy slipped into Luis' police sedan, having parked his own car twelve cars away. There were not many vehicles in the lot. He suspected they were mostly staff, but enough so his car would not be noticed. Luis had a reason to be there. He did not.

Luis said, "Explain, Rudy. Must be important to want to see Maurice again."

"I didn't tell you I wanted to see Maurice. How did you know?"

"You forget, I'm a detective, Rudy. What do you need? I won't ask you why you need Maurice. If you want him you have a good reason and if I want to never testify in court, it would be best for me to know nothing. You want Maurice. I've already called him. He says he'll be jogging on Riverdale Road in West Springfield in a half hour by the Thai Restaurant. Pull in the driveway and he'll get in your car. By the way, he'll have no cell phone on him. You two meet for five minutes. Do you know how to shut down everything in your personal phone as well as the police call?"

"Thanks Lu. I do. For your question, I've got three possibles for multiple murders and I need more background information on them to determine which one or two need further investigation. I have every reason to believe a new murder target has been chosen. Is that good enough?"

"Works for me. Good luck, Rudy. I know this was a difficult decision for you."

Maurice was behind the restaurant when Rudy pulled into the parking lot. He tapped the car. Rudy unlocked it. Maurice looked as wormy as before allowing Rudy to consider something he'd not thought of before, *Maurice is not just a hacker. He's police or former police or PI. He moves like one. He's not street druggie, not that I think he's clean. Maybe is a reformed criminal with the way he looks out of the sides of his eyes. Maybe military training or has been incarcerated. No one will remember him even if they directly look at him. I have trouble remembering his face. His slouchy movements keep you away from him. He's good. He's unnoticeable. Takes a lot of training and discipline to look and move like this.*

"What's up? How can I help you?"

Rudy explained his need for complete background and social profiling and email correspondence on three people. He gave him names and work locations and addresses. Maurice did not write anything down. Rudy questioned whether he was taping it; for how could he remember all of it? Maurice replied, "I don't use names when I talk to you, but I remember, verbatim, everything you say. You've heard about photographic memory, well I have something called for want of a better term, 'Procedural Memory.' It is not brilliance, not that. I think it is learned. It started at home with my mom, who insisted I repeat word for word every conversation with every person I met each day. It was her form of preventing me from connecting with the wrong people for very long. She was a tiger. I got good at it. I can wrap up what was said in this car today and in three years pull it back. It has made a career for me. Who knew; Mom didn't know. She doesn't like my work, but I do. Don't worry I haven't missed a word. I'll call Lu when I have answers. He'll contact you. If I am not available, I'll send some paper to your home address with an "Edison Home Supplier" return address. Don't throw it out as trash."

Maurice jumped out of his car and started jogging down the busy street. Rudy realized he was in racing jogs and although skinny, he had long and lean muscles.

Petra and Lilly's plan was to visit gyms this day. Their first visits were to those located nearest the home addresses of the three persons of interest. If no luck then, they would hit gyms near hospital parking lots, used auto dumping sites, and Route 20. The two detectives were dressed in their most used gym clothes to look as unlike police as possible. Once they got the lay of the land, Lilly would try to gossip with one of those mainstays who stay at the gym half a day. Petra and Lilly were certain they could in five minutes get the lay of the land. Petra would stand at the desk and pretend she was looking for her colleagues who were in the medical field. Her conversation was to include her supposed introduction to the gym by any of the three names. She'd show disappointment if they were not members and she had the wrong gym citing her desire to get some COVID-19 info from them. The gyms were to be closed shortly along with everything else.

Lilly's outfit, although clearly worn, was more revealing than her partner's. It was so, by design. They had no success at the nearest gym to Shirley's home and were now at a gym close to Chad's home. Lilly approached a total jock at the weights who stood up at attention when she walked in. She recognized his full body stare and thought, *he's the one. I'll have no problem with him.*

Her conversation with Vic, the stud, was as expected. He wanted to know why he hadn't seen her before. Lilly's story included a tale of wanting to work out with the right kinds of people. She said, "Vic, I can tell you have a good eye. When I'm at the gym, I want to meet people who have jobs, places to go, and other interests; I'm not interested in gym rats. You know the kind. I can just tell; you take your body seriously. You're not just hanging about. One of my friends told me his work mates go here, and he was certain I would like it. Maybe you know him. His name is Chad Roswell."

"I know Chad from another gym. Planet Fitness in West Springfield. At least I used to see him there. I go to a few; you know to keep my workouts from being boring. What kind of group is it? I mean where do they work? That would help. I'd really like to help you, Lilly. You can be sure I'll be wherever you choose."

Lilly thought, I bet you will, but Buddy, you are going to be so disappointed. If I see you at my gym, I'll be out of there!

In contrast to what she was thinking, Lilly asked, "Vic, you are really in the know. Shirley and Jesse are two of the names. I can probably drag last names from my brain if necessary, but those two names aren't that common. If you've ever heard them, you'd remember. I mean, I don't know many today with the name, Shirley; do you?"

"I know Shirley. I don't know if it's the same Shirley, but she is one difficult woman to get to know. She only talks to women here, and not even women like her. Maybe she doesn't like competition, because she doesn't mix with the real beauties. Most of them like to gab about the latest in health and beauty. Shirley gets along with the dull looking ones. Strange because she has one awesome body hidden in sweats. I know Jesse. He just came here recently and I think he's trying to make Shirley. She is nice to him, but he can't take any license with her. Her body language is, 'I'll take the lead. I don't follow.' She may have it all, but she is not worth the effort you'd have to make. You know what I mean, Lilly?"

"Oh, I surely do, Vic. So many stars in the sky to chase, why waste your time with the distant ones."

Vic laughed and said, "Profound, I like that in you, Lilly. We're going to get along. I hope to see you here soon."

Lilly left him with false ideas about her potential return. She joined Petra who also looked pleased with herself. Back in their vehicle, Lilly said, "Vic thinks I'm profound. How come no one else ever told me I am profound?"

Petra answered, "Because Vic is a special kind of philanderer who is stupid. Most of your friends are smarter than that. 'Profound,' what a joke. Now tell me if he gave any info other than trying to get in your pants."

"Petra, Shirley and Jesse belong here. Chad goes over to Planet Fitness. That gym is in West Springfield; not that far away from the hospitals. What did you discover?"

Petra said, "Sue remembered that Shirley came here, but she did not mention Jesse. Sue shows no interest in men. She is, however, interested in Shirley and apparently Shirley trusts her. Shirley shared stories on her relationship with her brother and mother; said they ruined her early life and it took her years to come out from under their negative influence on her life and reputation. She adored her grandfather, grandmother, and her father. Sue told her it's normally the other way around; when the male figures ruin our lives. Shirley did not agree, but said she doesn't trust easily and is not fooled by men who do not have that soft and kind side."

"Nothing about Jesse, though, Petra? Too bad, we get a feel for one, but not the others. Let's hit West Springfield's gym. Someone will know Chad; he is a hunk. I suggest we talk to a female. He must have been noticed."

An hour later the two detectives were having latte and dessert at Lattitude's Restaurant practically next door to the gym. Lilly said, "One of the perks of this job; we get a visit outside the workplace to all the best and worst of food services. This is a good one. This pistachio cheesecake is to die for. Seems Chad worked for his mother's care agency and told one of the girls it was a horror show for a kid's life. That's all I got. I saw you talk in depth to the serious tall gal. What did she have to say?"

"Toni just loves Chad. Says he's a gentleman who likes some companionship. He shies away from the aggressive ladies. He is not a wise guy with the men, but they like him. Toni said, 'What's not to like?'

"She continued with his story of finding life in nursing; not just a career but a path to living a full life. According to Toni, he thought he had found a special person for a long-term relationship with her, but she was a bit gun shy. She had not turned him away. No, she had not, but another guy was also after her. He told her the competition was stiff and he was generally not a competitive person."

Lilly said, "Our cast of characters, personalities and needs are filling out. Let's go back and review what we know. Both guys are after Shirley. Both compete in a game where the winner is unknown. Maybe it's important; but we are assuming Jesse is the other competitor in this trio of love. Pressure creates stress. Stress pushes action for motivation and release in the sociopath. I've heard the Captain say over and over, 'Stress causing the serial killer to act can be very small: just someone laughing at him or her; a slight of word given by a colleague; feeling he or she is unappreciated, and more. That's all it takes sometimes.' I also think if there are two of them as partners, it's not the two men together. They are at odds; unless it's to fool people. Could they be that smart?"

20

HE — Out of Control

HE can't seem to relax. I feel it. My brain tells me I'm in OCD mode and to just relax. I can't relax when I remember my history. I saw my father's face frozen in fear for me and himself. I didn't see what he saw. How could I? I was too young. He had my interest; he surely did. Some of the others didn't. Look what happens to the good people. They get no respect. I try to instill some little fear in others to ensure respect. I do it subtlety. I feel compelled to do good as my dad would do. Keep everything to yourself. You can't trust people. Look what happened when I told my mom I would be living with Dad. HE, like my dad, is on my same trust wavelength, but I don't think HE ever felt the same; didn't connect in any relationship. HE likes the adrenalin fix of killing and feels no guilt; or doesn't show guilt. I believe I am at fault here. I have trained HE in the safety of doing good as a backdrop for HE's skill in killing. The problem is HE seems to have missed discipline training. How could HE miss it? Being a kid is filled with the 'No's' in life. I understood early on what I could get away with. I only made one mistake and it was a biggie. Sensitivity training was not considered in my home as a child and not even in school. I remember Mrs. Sterner, my second-grade teacher, who told my mother I was a strange kid. Did my mother care? Absolutely not! She told me to wipe the smugness off my face and smile like the other bratty kids so no one would know I was weird.

The rumors that the state of Massachusetts was to close all restaurants, clubs, schools, stores, leaving only essential services open were getting stronger. The West Side Police along with City Hall were inundated with questions. It did not take very long for suicide hotlines to light up as not had been experienced in quite a while. A call must be placed for authorization to visit the Emergency Room unless brought in by ambulance. Doctors' offices were to be closed for all but the most necessary appointments for chronic disease and those appointments were put off if possible until the Federal Center for Disease Control understood more about this virus and shared it. There was talk about a distance requirement: six feet away between two human beings walking outside, but it was so cold in this section of New England, practically no one was walking for pleasure. Auto traffic was expected to decrease. The detectives anticipated the roads would be a pleasure to drive on, but where were the destinations. Air travel, in the words of Detective Petra Aylewood-Locke, "Sucked."

The nearing shutdown caused great concern for MCU. Leading the concern was the task of finding some good take-out food joints for their often brought in food. Captain Beauregard told them it was time for them to brown-bag it from home, since he thought all their investigations required appointments and there would be no 'hurry-up and missing meals' excuse for draining the slush fund built up over time. He said, "Pull in your belts, it's time for us all to learn clean living."

And because he was certain they would rebel, the Captain quoted their favorite Beauregard family member, Mona, saying, "Mona insists we use this difficult time showing our behavior as examples for leadership in this social purgatory caused by this pandemic. Wisely shop; show no fear; be considerate of the six feet spacing; wear masks even if it makes your work more difficult; keep your eyes and ears open for new kinds of problems. We are Americans and we have faced problems before."

Mason grumbled, "Hell, Captain, I love Mona, but she is waving the flag and leading the charge for all this stuff when I haven't figured out if the CDC and those doctors on TV even know what the hell they're talking about. I'll try. My wife will keep me in good shape with her cooking. I'm not sharing with you riff-raff. Do your own cooking. Time to learn how to turn on the stove, Bill Barr. Either that or marry the lady and maybe she can cook for you. She's already telling you how to live your life; may as well marry her."

Barr gave Mason a look and said, "I only wish. This gal is not going to the altar until I have passed all her tests. I don't even have a study guide."

"You never get a study guide, Barr. Women change the course test without telling you. You couldn't print new study guides fast enough."

Lilly yelled, "Stop the misogynistic crap! I've made a few calls. You can order ahead at these few restaurants. I've been told other ones are gearing up for take-out. I am not going hungry and I don't have Mason's wife to cook for me."

Lilly handed out copies with emails, apps, and telephone numbers of ten restaurants not that far from the station, who were advertising they would be open for take-out during the scheduled shut-down. Settled in with their needs addressed, the morning meeting began with Captain Beauregard saying, "We had no elderly men killed in a drunk driving accident on or near Route 20 this past Tuesday. Just a small favor from God; He or Satan held this psychopath back. I do feel the killer's need to move forward and kill again. The stats support his chomping at the bit. Mason and Ted have a graph to show you. At first, we didn't see it, because when it was initially completed, we only had about seven killings. Now, it is obvious. Escalation over time; not overly fast, but there. Then if you look at the two problematic murders, it is difficult to avoid seeing the killer was rushing. He or she needed to murder. The killer was under stress at the time and moved forward when he or she couldn't control his or her passions."

Petra said, "Sorry, Captain, you know I think women can do everything just as well as men, but this scenario smacks of male, of testosterone, and not of women. Why can't you let go of the possibility it is a woman? The FBI profiler says it's a man."

Beauregard smiled, saying, "No, Petra, the report from the FBI profiler states it is most likely a man."

"Yeah, so why don't we go with the most likely and not waste our time?

Bobby Barr answered, "If we are not certain, then we can't eliminate a woman. It costs us in time if we chase one line of inquiry when two or more are possible. I don't need certainty in investigating; I only need certainty in charging. Sometimes, we don't have that."

The Captain thanked Bobby for his insight and practicality. He insisted they keep the possibility of a woman as a potential, saying, "Several things bother me. We have three potentials; two men and one woman. The weapon used is not out of the realm for a woman, although it usually would inspire men. One of the reasons to use an auto accident with stolen vehicles would be the elimination of forensics. This killer is extraordinarily careful. We found no scents, no creams, no dropping of makeup or anything. I find it quite remarkable. Think about who are the greatest in cleaning up their environment. Your answer would be medical people. They did say the cars were wiped with a common Clorox wipe; not identified as some specialty hospital wipe. No trace possible for ID. Then we have to consider motive. It is in viewing the killer or killers' two mistakes, that make me wonder. Is the killer on a mercy path? What joy is it to kill elderly men who are quite close to death soon? The killer does not get notoriety in the horror of it except in his or her bad choices in victims. There is no writing notes to the press on his or her successful kills. The killer normally kills those who have none or few connections. Twice the perp killed men with loving connections. We think these killings were in error. If so, who has a motive to mercy kill elderly men? Who has a relationship with automobiles allowing familiarization to unlock the cars, steal the cars, and dump the cars? Next, we remember the lithe way the killer moved at the auto dumping sites. The killer is in great condition. The killer is comfortable around medical parking lots. Reinforces our choice of three potentials for suspects. Finally, what drives the killer to kill on Route 20? Mason has other kills on Route 20 and not in Western Massachusetts. Route 20 is somehow important. I checked all the interview notes and there's nothing in them about Route 20. None of this is new information. It is only now that we can see it all connected."

Lilly said, "Captain, you said killers. Do you really think two perps are working together to mercy kill, if that is the motive?"

"Don't know about any of this, Detective, but it is what we've got. Can two killers have the same crazy perspective they buy into; yeah, it is possible. Group think is always possible. I hate group think. If there are two or more involved in these murders, one theory would be group members have had similar experiences in their backgrounds and one of them is a powerful and charismatic person capable of leading.

Now, add some stress and the pressure of helping these old men with their lives and maybe, just maybe, a moral dilemma arises assisting in the occurrence of murderous groupthink."

Bill Border agreed. "We saw in those sado-masochistic murders we solved, the grouping together of two unlikely killers through a kind of groupthink. One may be in on it for the thrill of control; you know, the ability to snuff the life out of someone. The other may have this grand mercy-killing plan. Together, they reach harmony for each. Fuckin sick of human nature sometimes, Captain."

Beauregard answered easily, "One of the most negative aspects of being a cop or a social worker is the skewing of the population we see. Like in the whole criminal justice system, we see only the most negative of events. After some time, it would be easy to bring that warped thinking home to your spouse and kids. You could start thinking your kids are up to no-good and maybe also your spouse when there is a little push and pull at home, but it is the job talking. Every single cop, you detectives included, must watch yourselves. Prevent your minds from going in that direction."

There were serious nods in agreement given.

———

Lieutenant Petra Aylewood-Locke headed to Boston. She'd arranged a sit down with two old friends. It had taken days for Petra to sort out which friends worked in the Boston hospitals matching the work dates of the three potentials. It had not been an easy task and involved several hours of contact once she'd sourced the people to call. Sourcing them had also taken several hours. She did wonder whether she could get worthwhile results, thinking, *how do I know any of my matching contacts will remember any important information? I don't know.*

I'm probably marching down a dead end; but this is my kind of policing. Pound the pavement and see if anybody or any item jumps out. When it does, the adrenalin fix is better than an espresso.

Caitlin O'Neil said, "I won't hug you, Petra. We're nuts about protocol now. I wash my hands so many times a day, they're sore. You look great. A baby girl named Carlotta for you, congratulations. I have two girls; did you know?"

"No, Caitlin, and I would never have known if I didn't pick up the phone looking for info. We both have been all about living life and not looking back. Now, I think it's a mistake not to look back a little. Look at you! You look happy. You make me remember some great partying nights."

"I remember you always stopping us from going too far. You questioned all the guys who came around. Petra, you were the most suspicious friend I've ever known, but thanks for spotting that idiot Brad Long. You saw right through him. He's in jail now for a felony charge. He stole all his live-in girlfriend's money. It could have been me."

"Then you know how important it is, Caitlin, to catch up with felonious punks. I need your help. My boss, Captain Beauregard supported my coming to Boston to inquire and to pay for lunch; that means a cheap lunch, Caitlin; okay?

"I'm looking for background on three medical personnel, one doctor and two physician assistants who worked two hospitals while you worked them. Even if you don't know them, I'd like you to ask around. I want to know both the good and the bad about them."

The counter guy from the cafe brought over their coffees and turkey croissants with chips. The day was beautiful and an umbrella protected them from the sun as the ladies attacked their lunch with vigor. Caitlin said, "I get so hungry. I'm at work at seven and I swear the growling in the gut starts at eight. What are their names?"

Caitlin's eyes lit up at Dr. Teague's name. She said, "He's a hottie. He took my girlfriend out. She was crazy about him, but she said he was unavailable emotionally. She thought he was wonderful with all the elderly in the ER, especially elderly men nobody wanted to bother with. Can't tell you anything more. He never made a pass at me; I can tell you that.

"I do know Shirley. Shirley is a perfectionist at her work. Despite that, she is very easy to work with. Every once in a while, when she's pushed she gets her back up, but snaps out of it pretty quickly. She is antsy when other staff try to control her in any way or talk over her. Not for Shirley! She accepts more critiquing from men, but never, ever flirts. Kind of unusual since she is really good looking. She always kept the men at bay. As to Chad, I worked with him and would have dated him, but he is slow to ask. I met my husband and that was the end. You know my husband, Petra, Jeffrey Brodski."

"No, you married Brodski? He's a great guy. You didn't tell me you married a cop."

"He came into the emergency room, one too many times. I started looking for him and he noticed, and that's it."

Petra pumped Caitlin for the next hour and got nothing else out of her with the exception that two of the ER patients treated by the staff later died in auto accidents. They were hit by drunk drivers and both were elderly men. Petra questioned the location of the accidents and dates. The dates coincided with her employment data for the medical three, the name Petra had started calling her potential perps. Caitlin remembered one accident was in Weston and the other in Brighton.

She had no idea if those area accidents were on Route 20, but said the Boston Post Road goes through Weston. Petra explained the old Boston Post Road was Route 20. She was now satisfied her murderer/s were active then too. Petra would check to see if the Boston Post Road was called Route 20 in this area hoping it was as in Western Massachusetts.

Petra's second interview of the day was with a security guard at the emergency room of the same hospital. She knew him from the old days. He was happy just to have a coffee with her and catch up as they sat outside drinking the Dunkin' coffees she brought. She asked about her medical three and he squirmed his face into a tight unhappy grimace. Tim Fortin said, "Those three, it's funny you ask about those three. All their touchy feely with the old men. Look, Petra, I'll be retiring soon and I want people to treat me well when I'm old and have some problems. I do, but this group enjoyed exploring all the icky sweet invasive stuff with the old men. They weren't that way with the women. Well, not quite true, Chad was overly nice to all elderly.

"That Shirley, she was like this teacher I had in school who always wanted to know what was going on in your home life. My mother told me to stay away from nosey teachers. She said they were all reporters to social services. My mom was a single mother and paranoid her kids would be taken away from her. My dad was a drunk. In those days, the family would get a reputation and Mom thought no info to anyone was the best strategy. The doctor was full of himself, all nice and caring, but I didn't get a feel from him that he felt emotional about anyone. Cold; he was cold. Shirley was sugar. You'd get diabetes hanging around her."

Petra responded, "Tim, you're from New England and you question everyone. Did any of these three ask to look at records after an elderly patient left? I mean you have access to dailies. They'd have to go through you or the admin person to see dailies, wouldn't they?"

"We don't call them dailies anymore. Everything's on computer now, but I could easily go in to see who was treated when and what cubby hole the patient ended up in and the staff involved. Happens sometimes. I don't think the medical people would be able to do that. We change passwords daily. But if asked, I'd look up a patient for any cockamamy excuse."

"Did you ever for any of these three?"

"Petra, I really can't remember and I'm grateful I can't. One of them is a problem for you and I don't want to be remembered for helping them. You understand?"

"Tim, I'm looking for a bad dude, feminine or masculine. I don't know. What I do know is everybody needs to help when we're looking to put the bad guys away. I just want to know particularly about two elderly men who were later killed by drunk drivers. Were any of the three names I gave you particularly helpful with these men?"

"I don't want you to think I can't help you, but these three are all, kind of over the top, nice to all patients. My Boston background makes me think that kind of consistent sweetness is suspicious. I don't look through rose-colored glasses, Petra. Thinking about it and if I were looking for trouble, they were too interested in the elderly. Now that is not always bad, but it is not normal. Everyone is interested in kids and stars and middle age people with stories. The elderly are not often interesting even to me and I am on the cusp of joining them. I think they searched out the elderly for special care. I can't give you incidents to prove it, but I think it. About the elderly men killed by drunk drivers, I saw every staff member upset. The two guys killed, who I barely remember, were not difficult elders to deal with. I think that's why we all thought it too bad;

not that we'd wish that kind of death on anyone."

Petra thanked Tim and headed back to West Side.

I don't really think Captain Beauregard thinks one of us is the killer. It is just that he knows in his gut the victims are connected to medical facilities and unfortunately, the victims all were here. I'd forgotten how easily authorities could discover who was where and when. It is like being in communist China. The damn hospital has records on everything. I got a call about my parking permit at the lot at Mercy Hospital. Admin there asked, "Do you want to keep it now that you're not here that often?" I do go to many meetings there. I am certain the call is a response to Beauregard's investigation. If the police have visited all the stolen car sites, dumping sites, and then connected all the murders, they are too close. I have to be careful though, I don't give Captain Beauregard too much credit. He may know nothing. Mercy Hospital is attentive to parking details. Still, HE must not move forward. I have explained this dire situation. Hold off on all killings for a few months; just a few months was what I insisted. HE explained COVID is creating stress. I know HE can't take stress; we are all having problems with stress. I tried to get some time off. No way now. We are like indentured servants. I could go out on sick leave, but I need a doctor's note. That wouldn't stop HE. I have to be aware of HE's movements every minute of the day. It creates more strain on my psyche.

I do think stealing the cars will be chancy now; more so than before. I've an idea. There is a lot not used before. Dumping is not quite so easy. I think I'll have to use the middle of a large parking lot with no cameras. There are a few. It won't be medical related, but will confuse the heck out of the Captain and that smart-ass attorney. I don't like deviations from original plans that have worked so well. Still, I and HE will make necessary changes. The venerable who have lived so well and now are alone, well, their needs are paramount. I will address their needs. No more loneliness. They will approach the white light and be greeted by their loved ones who have passed. I look forward to that day, but I have work to do first.

Captain Beauregard received a call from Mona. "Rudy, I've saved a thick envelope with a return address 'Edison Home Supplies' for you as you requested. It doesn't look important. What are you trying to buy?"

"Business, Mona, for the office. I'll be home shortly."

Shortly thereafter, back at his office, Rudy read the reports disguised in the 'Edison Home Supplies' envelope. There was a summary on a single page for each of his medical suspects supported by pages of printout data. Mona probably thought there was a catalogue in the envelope; it was so stuffed. He glanced at the first sheet. Chad Roswell emailed just about every one of the seventeen victims. Rudy was surprised, and thought, *how come all these elderly men have email addresses? My dad doesn't; then again, if it were needed for hospitalization, Lizette would make sure they had the technology. It's surprising though. He's really nice to these men. He writes well and warmly. His only other emails are in confirming dates with Shirley and an email to a friend or relative back home, I think, about putting flowers on his grandparents' graves. No social media posts. He does troll and answers occasionally. No Twitter and no Instagram. I'll have someone follow up on the grave-decorating friend who may know more about him. No mention of decorating his mother's grave. Hmm!*

Beauregard studied the info on Shirley. She was an emailer and often posted on Facebook. She answered all emails about confirming dates with both Chad and Doctor Teague. She also corresponded with seven different nurses whom she had worked with at other hospitals. They were chatty emails, but mostly discussed sad cases they had witnessed. The Captain wondered, *she is clearly respected by all these women. They hold on to her statements as if they are the last word in medicine. She is respected by her colleagues. No one is laughing at her. Her Facebook posts were many but always medically related and giving good information. She posted no pictures of herself and no identifying photo. Her public persona could have belonged to just about any woman. In fact, despite her warmness in her emails, there was no real sense of who she was. I get nothing really about her at all from any of this.*

Dr. Teague's social profile was perfect for a handsome, available, and talented professional. There were no candid shots. All were studio photos. His emails were cursory. There were many to the victims. Beauregard could not find fault with them, but they contained none of Chad's warmth. There were several posts on Route 20 East to West with sites of important places to visit along the way. Teague posted every auto repair shop within five miles of the route. He corresponded with five different men on the merits of this historic road. Beauregard checked Wikipedia for matching information. The men knew much more history on the road than Wikipedia or any of the states' internet sites. Rudy thought, *Route 20 is central to this man's hobbies. How important is this fact? It's not in the others' profile. We need to check on all the men he corresponds with about Route 20.*

21

Missed!

Sheri was serving her famous wings with blue cheese and celery as an appetizer. The Culls were hosting tonight. The Beauregard's brought dessert and vegetables. It had seemed fair when the three families first decided to do the elder dinners. Sheri did not think it so fair now, remarking to all, "These dinners were meant for us to be together with no work for you, Mom, or Lizette, or Roland or Darla or Neil. Each of you have brought special treats; that is if you call a collection of dietary delights including home-made potato salad, French meat pie and beans, lemon meringue pie, and chocolate cream pie, treats. Together, they are a meal. I don't know why I cooked chicken francaise and linguini with a Sicilian salad. It is redundant."

Sheri's mom laughed and contrary to Sheri's view of her mother's normal interest said, "Sheri, Lizette, Roland, Darla, Neil, and I like to cook. Could be we are trying to demonstrate we appreciate these dinners. Sometimes the kids are here and sometimes they're not. Sometimes your siblings are here and sometimes they are not. It seems to me a little extra food in case there's a full house is helpful. Don't interfere with a good thing, Sheri."

Roland's brother Liam, who was a much bigger man physically than Roland, said, "Sheri, there is never too much food at a family gathering.

If you're worried, I'll make a concerted effort to eat more." His wife told him no and he was to content himself with normal portions, saying, "You're getting rounder in the middle, Liam."

The conversation continued through dinner on reduced caloric intake and the loss of taste. One of the teens was heard to discuss the theory that for every hundred calorie reduction in a recipe, there was a two hundred percent reduction in taste. This statement was immediately challenged by Sheri and Mona and the other ladies. He proved his source as from a French Chef's book on gastronomic delight. Mona was thrilled her son even read such a book but her balloon was quickly burst when his brother explained Luke's new girlfriend told him about it.

Laughter was diminished when Sheri's mom brought up COVID-19. She asked, "Can we continue to have these dinners? Will they place us older folks at risk?"

Mona was the most informed of the group; the others thought it was because she was a teacher and school was to be at home supposedly starting in two weeks. She said, "Thanks for bringing the subject up, Debbie. I think we will have to limit these dinners. Norbie, Rudy, and the children and our siblings will be out there and the exposure is threatening to elders. I think we could plan on dinners but smaller. I'd have to think about this more; there have been some crazy nursing home deaths because the elderly are lumped together and have what is being named comorbidities. The data suggests that even people older than sixty with no other illnesses do not do well with this virus. This may be our last regular dinner."

Darla spoke up. "The last thing we need is to be confined to our homes. For Neil and I, it will be okay because we have each other and lots of at home interests to play around with; but you, Debbie, you are alone. I don't see why we elders can't have a dinner together once a month if we promise to obey all the other restrictions which is not easy since they change daily. Getting together for us will be easy. We don't have to go out for business."

Rudy's cell rang with the small static sounds his son had chosen for his ringtone. He moved to answer it and without an excuse, said he must leave. Norbie asked if he could help and was turned down. Norbie immediately moved towards the restroom where he could contact a police friend to see if there was an accident in town. He got a 'no' and joined the families again. He thought, *something's up. Rudy is the least dramatic guy I know. He walks out on a family dinner without excuse. Only business and serious business could be the reason. Not an accident and not a killing or I would be informed. Still; some important event is up.*

At the 'almost' accident scene, Petra and Lilly had doubled back to meet the Captain after losing the almost killer car. Lilly said, "Captain, he almost got Micky. We were parked with no lights going in the direction of Micky Leary's walking. We thought we could stop any vehicle that suddenly veered over on towards the sidewalks. There are walks all along his route. Foolproof, right? Not on your life! The killer was driving along at a normal speed; must have known the best place and time to hit Micky; because he suddenly moved in at the curve. You know I react quickly but I was uncertain at first. I started our car. I could not have stopped the car, so I beeped like hell to make Micky move over. He did. Damn, he's fast. The driver missed. This driver's reflexes are the best. He moved right back on the road. I let Petra off to help Micky who fell in the bushes, and I then followed the vehicle. Son of a bitch took a right on a connector road I'd never seen before when scoping out the area. We should have seen this was a great spot for an accident. I chased, but the connector road has several turns and streets running off it. I knew he was headed back on the highway. I had three numbers on the plate. It was a green Toyota and I radioed it out. I lost him, Captain. I shouldn't have but I did."

"Have you called hospital security for a search for missing cars at the hospital parking lots? What about the parking lot for the hospital the three work in? Might be a new choice for stealing cars, although it would direct attention to them. Are there any other parking lots near Mercy and Bay State we didn't check before? I believe they would be used as a source before the killer would move further out. What about used auto lots? There have only been four used so far."

"I did that first thing, Captain. Nope. I'd hoped we'd catch him dumping the car. They're asking Wilbraham and Springfield and Ludlow police to check all parking lots."

"Good, Lilly, but hit the two West Springfield big parking lots. This killer is white and would be more noticed in a lot with many minority parkers. He was not here that long and probably knows little about Ludlow. Wilbraham and West Springfield seem more likely. Remember he has to get to his own vehicle. Find the dumped car. Find cameras. Find traces of Uber pick-ups. The perp did not plan this."

The Captain approached Lieutenant Aylewood-Locke who was holding Micky Leary's hand. He did not seem to be in distress. Rudy asked if he was okay. Micky answered, "I am now, but I was frightened. I'm surprised I could move that fast. More importantly I thank the good Lord for giving me great hearing at my age or I wouldn't have been so shocked at the loud honking of your detectives cars. You knew this might happen, but you didn't tell me. You should have told me."

Rudy thought, he's goddamn right I should have told him. I used him as bait without his permission. Cripes, how do I explain that I really didn't think we were right; it was just a far out guess? Did I really think it was an almost impossible idea? Honestly, no. It was an educated guess from experience. I knew there was a profound need to kill I've seen before in my psychopaths. I'll just tell him the truth; carefully.

"Micky, we wondered about you as a potential person at risk. You are not the only older man we are looking at. When you said you walk every night on Route 20; well it triggered our minds about your habits being a match for what has been happening. I notice you have some service experience. Can I ask you what kind of work you did in the service?"

"How do you know about my military service?"

"Perhaps the medal over in the bookshelf the day I was at you home, which I assume is yours, gave me a hint."

"Damn, Detective. I don't talk about it much. Lost two good friends over there. Remember, Detective Beauregard, I was married young and left my wife here when I served. Mostly I was military police, but we came under attack and I barely made it back. I still have some problems with my right leg; it was injured when our truck was blown off the road. Some of it landed on my leg. All I could think of was my wife Janelle and that when I got home, if I got home, I'd stay in Three Rivers. It may not be exciting enough for my two lads, but for me, it is home and I love it. I may be lonely, but I'm in my home and I am relatively happy."

"I knew you may be police, Micky. You have the disease. You questioned our knowing interest in your life."

"I question how you know as much about me; I think you're in cahoots with Attorney Norberto Cull. I didn't fall for his bullshit story about investigating accidents. He didn't show me he was chasing a buck.

Attorneys don't do that. I checked the news articles in the library and guess what I found; Norbie Cull and Rudy Beauregard have worked on cases together and opposite each other. Funny relationship for a defense attorney and a police captain, don't you think, Captain?"

"Yeah, it sure is. Micky, did it ever occur to you chasing justice brings all types of birds together? Bet you can't imagine a cop and a lawyer both in the pursuit of justice, can you?"

Micky laughed and said, "Touché, Captain! You are not defensive at all, are you? Guess a real cop can't be. My experience has been cops hate to be questioned. So, I am going to question you. Am I in danger after tonight? This killer of old men, he's the one who tried to get me tonight; right?"

"Don't know for certain, but suspect it to be him. As to a continued risk, I can't answer you, but I think you need to change the time of the day you walk to mornings."

"What put you on to my being a potential victim for this guy, Captain, and don't tell me you can't talk because it's an open case. I hear that on television whenever the police are being interviewed."

"I'll tell you some occurrences which interest me, but your repeating them would leave me to infer you were impeding a police investigation. Maybe it's best you don't know."

"Nope, Captain, I was a sitting duck tonight. I figure you owe me."

The Captain, cornered by Micky, thought, how much to tell him? If he has an old man's loyalty to folks who helped him, he may not take our interest in the three medicals as valid. He may warn them; as if tonight, alone, isn't enough to warn the killer.

It was as if Leary knew what the Captain was thinking. He said, "You think I don't want justice for Ray and myself and the other old men. I do. Nothing you say will leave my mouth. You're looking at the Doc and Shirley and Chad; that much I know. I've been thinking before you came over here; they all know all about me. I'm not a big talker about myself; never had to be. I told them everything thinking it was needed for my health. I tell you I was frightened when I had the heart attack. I remember giving them my walking schedule. The doctor asked my route, and Shirley asked the time of day I walked. Chad later questioned why I walked at night when older folks mostly walked in the daytime. I told him if I didn't walk after dinner in the evening, I'd have an extra cocktail and fall asleep in front of the television. My wife told me to walk at night; otherwise I'd be comatose at eight in the evening. She was correct, but until you catch this guy, I'll walk in the afternoon. I do think it would be too dangerous for this crazy killer to come after me now unless he gets obsessed with his choice of victim. I know all about obsessed people who can't let go of an idea. Do you think I'll be safe now?"

"Frankly, Micky, I don't know. I think you were one of the chosen, but it is really too early for the killer to move now given all of our focus on you. It is also too soon for a rational person to act; trouble is, he has done a couple of killings that take him out of the concept of a rational killer. He is a serial killer; he or she, we are not convinced it could not be a woman. Once a killer, who is a planner, deviates from plan a couple of results occur: he gets careless like tonight or he becomes compulsive and kills more indiscriminately. Right now, you fit his victim pattern. He will now know, we know, how he picks his victims. Our question will be, until the next murder, will he choose a different kind of victim? I don't think so. He is wedded to a kind of mercy killing."

"Why mercy kill me, Captain? I have a great life and if I take care of myself I have years left. I have plenty of money and loads of friends. Why kill me?"

"Micky, do you have a lady friend?"

"No, Captain, I have many lady friends. I like being a couple, but living together? I'm slow to go there. At my age, I could pop off quickly. Why subject a lady to that kind of grief. I like life, but not every lady even fifteen years younger than me wants to go all the time. I don't know what you know of my lifestyle, but I am a social animal. And although I truly miss my wife, I love life. How dare this pervert decide my life's not worth living. It is."

"How much of your lifestyle did you share with Doctor Teague, Shirley, and Chad, your healthcare supporters?"

"I think quite a lot, except I did not tell them about the ladies. Good men don't talk about ladies, you know that, Captain. Is my having lady friends important?"

"My instinct, Micky, is he wants to choose from the unattached. My feeling is he thinks the unattached elderly male wants release from this world, especially if the person is facing health problems. Do you have a major health problem in addition to the heart attack?"

"When I was in the hospital, they found a lump under my arm. I was tested for some kind of Lymphoma. Turns out it was nothing and went away by itself. They did all kinds of blood tests, but I didn't get the final tests back from the specialist in Springfield until this week. No one knows about this dark cloud I've been living under until now."

Beauregard said, "You fit the profile until now. Discovering you don't have cancer makes you an imperfect candidate. I think your records did some talking, while the final result was unknown. Don't walk at night."

There was a lull in the conversation making the Captain uneasy. He could see Micky Leary grimace until a big smile broke on his face.

Beauregard had seen looks like Micky's before. He said, "No! You hear me? No, I'm not using you as a patsy. First, it won't work. He'll be gun shy to try again. Secondly, tonight I did not expect to be fruitful. I just put a precautionary car on you, in case. I'm as surprised as anyone he tried."

"Come on, Captain, it will work. I can go back to the hospital and say my tests were positive. I had them at Mercy. My specialist is at Mercy where they are not affiliated. The people you are interested in at the ER; well, it is not connected to Mercy. They'd believe me. It would make me a perfect chump for them. Set them up. Put cars on each of them. What say?"

Fortunately, the Captain was interrupted by Lilly. He listened and then excused himself for a few minutes. Lilly was pleased to tell the Captain the stolen car was discovered before it was reported stolen by the owner. "A bully for them" was Lilly's evaluation on the quick recovery. They traced the car to its owner only to discover it was stolen from an alternate lot from one of the hospitals in Springfield. Lilly told Beauregard, "Captain, they found the stolen vehicle right at one of the places you had specified in West Springfield. The killer, even though almost caught tonight, is foxy. He leaves the car where he knows the territory and must have left his own vehicle close by. We're moving on the cameras there, but I bet the only vision we'll see is a guy in a hoody jogging away to Riverdale Street. There are many businesses on that street without cameras and back alley exits to short streets and connectors to main roads. Many of these businesses are closed after six."

Beauregard remembered his meeting with Maurice and knew if Maurice chose Riverdale Road as a location then the killer was wise to do so as well.

He said, "Try. The killer was caught off guard; we can only hope he has made another error. He was smart enough not to go to one of his regular dump areas. He now believes we know their locations. He didn't know we had dump site knowledge, but guessed it tonight. Smart man to suspect so quickly. He changed course and did what I would have done. For sure he had previously thought about strip mall parking lots as a possibility. The one he chose tonight is a great choice. If you find no direct camera on his dumping, you should have enough on all the entrances in a variation of fifteen minutes after an estimated time of arrival from Three Rivers. He was smart not to stay close to the drive-by site."

Lilly agreed to follow through on the cameras she found on the shopping strip's multiple lots and particularly on the entrances. She would also check cameras on the street heading toward the highway. She asked, "Captain, we should have had cars on the three potential perps. We didn't. Do you think the perp is so obsessive, he will attempt to try killing Micky again; I mean, would he take that kind of chance?"

Beauregard answered, "If he were logical the answer is no; but he is a psychopath who thinks he is doing God's work. I don't know. Just in case, we need to watch Micky. Lilly, check on the three medicals' schedules and make sure Tuesdays are still their off nights. Check for a second night off on the weekend. With this COVID-19 business, the hospitals are pulling staff in whenever."

As Lilly left, Micky Leary took it upon himself to walk over to speak with the Captain, saying, "I don't need your help. I'll be out there walking my same route. Further, I'll be prepared. If he goes after me, he'll be done. I don't want old men being killed and me doing nothing for them.

This is not vigilante justice, Captain Beauregard, it is self-defense and taking the rubbish out."

Beauregard, to his credit held his temper, but still gave a thousand reasons why this would not be a good idea including the fact that Jerry LaFollet had a gun on him the night he was hit and it did him no good. Leary must have had some debating experience, because he had an answer to all Beauregard's problems. When the Captain suggested Micky may face legal problems for setting up a situation where violence could foreseeably be used, Leary insisted, "Your problem, not mine. If you say nothing and I get this guy; no one will be the smarter. If you do say you knew about my actions, you will be the one in jeopardy. Just pray your killer is sick of me. I don't think you believe he won't try again."

The Captain said, "Micky, please don't walk; just for three days. I'll call you then. I need time."

"Okay, Captain, you got three days. And you are safe. Tuesday is a week away; that's if he stays with his plan." Rudy's eyes lit up. He thought, *selfish, I am totally selfish, but what's wrong with using a non-police information source. We do it all the time.*

"Micky, would you be able to contact any of the three, Teague, Chad, or Shirley to see when they will be working in the next two weeks? It would save our going through all the permissions to get schedules. I'm hoping their days off will continue to coincide; but if not, you and I need that information."

"I see your point, Captain. I'll make a couple of calls. I'll stagger them; that way if one of these is the killer, he or she will think I'm discombobulated. I'll rant a little about being sick and almost being hit by a car. I'll tell them I don't care, no one is going to interfere with my walking schedule. I can say I need a few days but I'll start walking again on Saturday. It will sound legitimate. They know I often have friends over Saturday afternoons and need my walk to recover from having a good time. I'll say it better when I talk to them. I used to be a Toastmaster. I know how to say things."

Beauregard responded, "I did not say the killer is one of these three; please don't think it. They may be part of a gossiping conversation at the hospital letting information flow beyond normal sources. Don't think beyond that thought. We don't know who the killer is or we would be following him or her night or day."

"Yeah; right. I'd hate to think it was a woman. I'm old. I hold women on pedestals. Most of the women I have known could not, would not, take a life; except in self-defense, which I believe is justified. You haven't fooled me, Captain, you think it's one of these three. The killer must really hate or love old men; must have had some sick experience to go off kilter like this."

22

Virus Adaptations

Three MCU detectives were out sick. Beauregard did not appear pleased with playing house mother to incalcitrant sick detectives or living with their non-presence in MCU. He demanded the three get tested immediately for COVID-19. He experienced medical dragging of the feet. His detectives lied about their symptoms. He did not have healthcare proxies for them. Contrary to his normally friendly management style, Beauregard came down hard. He reported them, and the Chief took over. They were required to get tested. Beauregard was impatient with the medical process, thinking, *a lot of good this does me. It'll be a couple of days before we get results. I've talked to Ash, Juan, and Lilly to discover their contacts; contact list includes me and my whole department. We're all being tested. Meanwhile, Mason is trying to work from home. The others are limited until we get controls on their computer use. It is a mess. Tuesday is coming up. The whole world is topsy-turvy and I have a serial murderer who will be taking advantage of the situation if he knew about our predicament. I have put a silence out on our risk, but people notice when business is conducted differently.*

The results came back. Two tested positively for flu and Lilly just had a fever. Three days were lost. The Captain felt he should have known it was okay. His detectives had been pretty careful after the virus directives for prevention of spread had been handed out. He called a special meeting for a Saturday. Lieutenant Aylewood-Lock complained vociferously. Normally she would be jumping at the chance to return to work, but not this day. Jim had arranged with several mothers a playdate for the babies. The pediatrician had suggested it would be good for them as long as precautions were taken with separate dividers for the children and all toys and food kept separate. Since only Carlotta was walking and not that well, the parents thought they could control the event. Petra said, "I'm the mother and I miss out on this event. Jim will be the only father there. The other mothers will think I don't care and what is Carlotta going to think about me later?"

Mason said, "Good detective, bad mother; can't have it all, Petra."

To which she threw an eraser at him. Called to order by an impatient Captain, discussion centered on the coming Tuesday night. Beauregard had received a call from Leary with proposed schedules for the next two weeks. He explained, not giving complete details, Leary's decision to walk at night. Juan said, "Set it up with the Wilbraham police again, Captain. We need to take turns nightly for a bit. I heard through the grapevine all the departments in the area knew we were hit by the virus. We weren't, but they got some scuttlebutt we were. Could be the killer heard it; if not, maybe the word should be shared."

Beauregard said he was uncomfortable with this whole deal, but said, "Micky Leary could tell the security guard there. Norbie says his name is 'Al.' Al would take care of Micky if he thought he just wanted to make sure he came in when the 'good' staff was there to help him. Bobby, call Leary and ask him to call Al at the ER. Maybe he can get the info on our illness directly and now. He says he's a great actor. We'll wait on Leary's results before we formalize a plan."

New information had come in on the three potentials' backgrounds.

First, a neighbor of Chad's home when he lived with his mother had filed a complaint with Lakeland social services about Chad's lack of nutrition. Nothing came of it. The neighbor said, "Chad's mother knew I made the complaint and she never spoke to me again. She told Chad he couldn't talk with me. It's too bad. It was right after Chad's grandfather died and Chad was a little guy and needed a friend. I could do only so much. He did good even after his mom kept him inside all the time. She didn't want me telling him secrets about the long-lost father. I don't know how she pulled it off and I don't know how Chad put it all behind him and became successful. He has a lot of his father in him despite her trashing the dad."

When the neighbor was asked about the dad, his response was, "She probably buried him in the backyard after poisoning him. Don't think she wouldn't have done it. There was trouble in the household and then he disappears. He would never have left that boy. He was crazy over him. The grandfather was sick when he moved in with them. The dad and grandfather, both, were good people and would have protected the boy. Chad loved them both."

Bill Border, who interviewed the neighbor by phone, explained his response. I said, "Are you telling me you think Mrs. Roswell killed her husband and nobody asked questions? There was not an investigation? Did you report your suspicions to the police at that time? We're talking over thirty years ago."

"We did. My wife and I both did. The police went to the house and interviewed Chad's mom. She said he walked away from the responsibilities of fatherhood. She cried and carried on and they took her word for it. It does happen. They looked around the home. The thing is he left his car there. It was registered in his name. She had a hell of a time getting it in her name. She declared him dead after a number of years to collect fifty thousand dollars in life insurance. Doesn't sound like enough to kill someone now; but then it was big bucks."

"Captain, the neighbor says Chad would know nothing about this. He always told the neighbor his dad deserted the family and the neighbor said he would never tell a kid his suspicions because he'd tell his mom and she might do away with him too. In my mind kids always know if there is a secret. They may not always discover the secret. But it's inside them and creates an approach to living life always searching for what is not said. I think this from my experience as a witness to my parents' marriage and their remarriages."

There was an uncomfortable silence until Juan directed them to new info on Dr. Jesse Teague. "I got hold of one of the kids who was with the doctor in the group home the social worker later discovered was not what it should have been. This man, Melvin Carter, has not had a good life. He is in AA now and has addressed his issues. He insists Jesse, who he thinks is a good guy, is capable of just shutting the door on bad experiences and going forward. Their foster mom would beat them and the next day Jesse would pretend it never happened. Melvin thought it was why Jesse was so successful. He said this and it bothers me. 'I could let go of our foster mother's meanness. I thought if you had power over someone you could be mean and it wasn't until I hit rock bottom, I realized meanness was wrong and destructive. AA has saved me. I'm kind of in a good spot right now and want to stay in it. Jesse could just forget; I had to learn to forget.'"

Bill butted in, saying, "I don't believe for a minute you can close the door on experience. Bullshit!"

Ted responded, "Bill's right. Melvin's experience is Jesse's experience and I don't think Jesse could erase completely the connections between the power and brutality experiences Melvin felt they both had shared. Not an early positive history. Let's have a look at Shirley. Mason. You have her report, don't you?"

"Yeah and I didn't get much more than what we've already have. Great father and grandparents and lousy mother and brother. Great work record but left two good jobs for no particular reason. Her job in Boston paid really well. I don't know why she left Boston for Western Mass; then again why did the other two do the same? Maybe they all didn't like Boston, but their moving into and leaving about the same times makes me wonder. I don't like it. Coincidence, with her and the other two making the same decision about the same time, I don't believe it.

"What is most interesting is this med group, all, worked or lived near Route 20. I don't think all three could be involved in a partnership of mercy killing because I don't think, just like you, Captain, that a threesome could maintain the consistency of details for so many murders; but it makes me wonder. Shirley told her nurse friend, Dottie, Chad always took her to restaurants along Route 20 and she asked him why. He just changed the location for the next night out. She also told Dottie that Dr. Teague took her to a restaurant on Route 20 for their first date. She questioned him, but he said he just thought she'd like Mexican."

Beauregard summed up their thoughts in a nutshell. "We haven't moved an iota. We know one or two of them are most likely our perp or perps, but which?"

Bobby answered his cell phone. He smiled and said, "Captain, Leary's fast. He's already called Al and told him about how the virus has hit our detectives screwing up our investigations here. Al also had heard it from the grapevine. Leary says he's a born gossiper. Your med group will know within a half hour. He did say the work schedule for all of them is the same as of today."

Beauregard responded, "So Micky Leary is on as a patsy. What other days are the meds off and is it always the same day for each?"

Bobby said, "Captain, they each have Sunday off. Leary said if any day would be changed it would be Sunday."

Beauregard reminded his detectives, "Captain Murray and I were given two weeks to solve Stan Korsecki's case. We are way over that time line. I hate to say thanks to COVID but the virus has brought the whole city to another consciousness. So many dying of virus, one hit-and-run seems less important; but the magnifying glass will be on us soon. We have to figure this case out."

Chad and Shirley agreed to meet at Stanley Park in Westfield on Sunday morning. They both thought the beautiful park would allow them to have a breakfast picnic in the fresh air. Jesse Teague had heard of their plan. He asked if they could make it later in the day so he could join them. Chad could not hide his disagreeable look, but still said an okay for him. It was Shirley who said, "No, Jesse, I am busy in the afternoon. I'm co-writing a research paper on the typical co-morbidities in the elderly, by race and geographical area, which could create an impediment to recovery from this virus."

Jesse, acting annoyed, answered, "Forget it, Shirley, it's been done."

Shirley reacted. "Don't tell me what I should or should not do, Jesse. I don't like being limited and reduced in stature by anyone's personal opinion. It is just your opinion. There is data on disease in the elderly and some of it is by race and by geographical location, but data for research on illness is for populations under seventy years old; and most of that data has been developed by pharmaceutical companies pushing particular drugs. My cohort and I have a grant for this paper. I thought I told you, but perhaps you don't retain what I tell you. Perhaps it is not important to you because it is not about you."

Chad appeared to suppress a smile, while Jesse's face reddened at Shirley's unexpected verbal assault. He attempted to explain but stumbled over his words in an almost stutter. Shirley did not attempt to soften her stance. The result was Jesse apologized and had the grace to tell them both to enjoy their Sunday morning.

Jesse later approached Shirley apologizing profusely and blaming their work stress as a reason for his inattention to her needs. Shirley did not back down. She insisted he must learn to respect her work, her choices, and her wants. The explanation referenced her childhood. He asked her to share her problems so he could better comprehend why she felt such a strong insult from a slight remark of his. Shirley said, "There you go again, Jesse. Your remark was slight according to you and my reaction was too strong. You were wrong saying what you said. You must admit the error was yours not mine. There will be no future in any relationship we could have without you learning to respect others and their opinions as well as mine. I say this for your own good, Jesse. You are quite self-absorbed. I am quite certain others have questioned your narcissism before."

Jesse must have decided not to defend himself. He paused and waited. Finally, when Shirley did not fall for the "who speaks first, loses" concept, he quietly said, "I'm learning about you, Shirley. I will try to take your hints better. Forgive me if I've tread carelessly; I want to be what you want in a man. I always have."

Jesse's statement appeared to unnerve Shirley. She responded, "Just don't tell me what or how to live, Jesse, and we can go on."

Jesse went back to his work, but he appeared to almost hibernate through the rest of the day.

Sunday was going well for Chad. Shirley was in the passenger seat of his car talking happily about some muffins she'd made for their breakfast. He responded by telling her how thoughtful she was to bake for them. Chad was to pick up some hot take-out coffee nearer Westfield. He'd also packed water bottles, wipes, fruit, and some egg, cheese, and bacon frittatas cut into squares. He'd made them earlier this day when he first rose. He thought, *she'll know I went to some effort for her and the frittatas taste great. I'll pick up coffee and pastry nearer the site.*

Chad stopped at a coffee shop in Westfield that was offering take-out. It did not take too long. When he returned to the car, Shirley said, "I think we are going to be frustrated, Chad. They've closed the park earlier than most for anything other than walking."

Chad took a moment before stating, "We'll have our picnic in the car over in the Westfield Shoppes Parking Area. Pretend it's another time when a big day was going to a car-hop. We'll eat in the car leisurely without any bugs and then walk the park. How's that sound, Shirley?"

An absolutely brilliant smile spread over her face, when Shirley nodded a yes and said, "You asked me what I thought; you didn't just assume. We'll have a great time."

Chad's day was not ruined by breakfast in his car. He thought, how could my day be ruined despite the change in plans. Shirley is happy. Jesse is left to fume about our date. The sun is shining. This close date with Shirley would never have happened before COVID-19; before we both realized the disease is seriously contagious. I would never have dared to plan a picnic with her. I would have thought she'd want dinner at a good restaurant and see a movie or attend some musical event.

———————

I am not amused by HE's reaction to Sunday's events. Drama and lack of insight exists everywhere. HE thinks the whole day was a charade. HE said, "What a joke! Doctor and nurses all discombobulated by COVID thinking a picnic was the way to go because it was outside. Two guys trying to get into a girl's pants. Same old story."

HE has no social graces and doesn't understand romantic efforts. HE is a snob like some others in my life appear to be; the difference is you can ignore them, but not HE, who decides and then implements without permission. HE hovers as a part or outside the group of three. HE is an add-to yet separate and still one. HE must learn to think about the trail involved in planning. HE certainly understands the Route 20 trail across the United States. For HE, it is everything. I don't remember when I first met HE. It certainly was a while ago, but HE is important to my plans to help those in need of early crossing. HE, from the day we first met, understood my quest. I don't remember our first conversation about my mission, but I do remember HE needed little description of what was necessary. Before HE, I took personal risks which I now see as dangerous to my well-being. HE is my answer to a safe practice; until recently. HE acts and I have to guess what his actions will be. Never before did I have to ask. HE always did what I said was the plan. Just what made HE stop listening; no, HE always listened, but now is something of an outlaw. If HE is going to continually put me at risk, I will have to take action. Action is more difficult for me. Planning is my forte. I think it is the stress of our work and the overwhelming fatigue brought on by COVID. He, I think, wants to relieve our work stress created by this virus. I know it, not think it. HE is aware of the relief I feel when we have helped an elder to pass. Such relief. I know I have been feeling the stress; no different from the other staff in the ER. I will just have to watch HE tomorrow. I should be able to see what HE is up to if I am diligent. HE is trying to control the whole process. I will not allow it.

MCU detectives busied themselves as Juan, Bobby, and Billy debated. Contrasting aloud to each other data on the three probable perps, the detectives demonstrated their exhaustion. Billy spoke a few expletives, "Too many similarities in their backgrounds and too little data."

Ted and Petra joined the group, adding ideas which the detectives immediately rejected. Bobby said, "I'm sorry but you're adding imaginative ideas I feel are not needed. Data and information are needed, not new theories."

Not to be put off, Ted said, "What about the resistance we've all had about two perps maintaining all those murders? It makes sense when we wonder how the killer gets home after dumping a car. Before we assumed maybe a two-car theory or a single car requiring just a hop to a hospital for business and use of its adjacent parking lot for the theft, with the killer's own car parked near the used-car lots. If we use that theory how did the killer get his own car to the used-car lot? He'd have to get a ride there."

Petra agreed, saying, "Last Tuesday, did we check on cars parked near the used-parking lots previously identified? I don't think the Wilbraham police did and I know for a fact we didn't. The killer would not have then known about our surveillance of Micky Leary. I think we should go and interview the restaurant staff near the lots. My guess is he'd have used the lot nearest Three Rivers. Maybe a car was left until later and was noticed. Restauranteurs worry about abandoned cars in their lots and take numbers down. Happens all the time."

Juan insisted, saying, "I think this killer has a sixth sense about our investigation. He was so quick to go all the way over to West Springfield from Three Rivers. He probably got on the turnpike entrance nearest the connector under the bridge from Wilbraham and cut over to the exit in West Springfield. I don't care how smart he is, that would be a pretty brilliant instant decision. Unless, he had originally decided to dump the car there."

An observant Captain overheard the conversation from his spot making cappuccino in the kitchen. He answered, "Good policing; now get on with it. Do we have video from the pike for Tuesday? We should have it by now for the road from Three Rivers to West Springfield. Get out now and talk to restaurant staff at the car lots. I think the one in East Longmeadow and the one near Boston Road in Springfield are your best bets."

Juan sighed. "How we going to do that, Captain, the restaurants are all closed?"

"Call the owners. They'll be happy to have something to do besides worrying about lost revenue. Get going."

Petra said, "I received the video from Mass DOT on Friday. Let's take a look.'

Crowding around Petra's computer without consideration of COVID restrictions, the Captain yelled at them to wear their masks. They noticed he'd put on his. Bill thought, *he surprises me every day. He hates wearing the mask, but he thinks we may be at risk and he will do whatever is the prescribed protocol for our protection. I think I trust him to do right by me and every other detective; but I do hate wearing this damn mask. The closing date is almost here and we have practiced for obeying the latest from the doctors.*

It did not take more than a couple of minutes to ID the stolen car. They followed it from one camera site to the next. Petra pointed out some weaving of the car, saying, "The driver is nervous or a bad driver. We know he or she is not a bad driver. Also, in addition to the weaving, the driver hugs the left side of the lane, no matter which lane he is in. We should follow them all driving and maybe we can pick which one is the killer. We need to choose one of the three to hone in on."

Bill laughed. "With our luck, they all hug the left side of the road. I do think you have something though, Petra. I went to a driving ed psychological class put on by a police support group and this nutty psychologist tried to give insights on the type of driver we were following before a stop. He insisted their driving could tip whether it was an aggressive driver versus a non-risk taker driver. It was for our safety. He specifically stated that hugging the left side of the lane indicated: drunk driver; non-risk taker; car out of alignment; old lady or man; new driver; or maybe deliberately avoiding police. This driver was not drunk, is not old, not a new driver, and can't be risk adverse. This driver in my estimation was frightened he was almost caught and his safe hugging the left side of the lane was his reaction. I don't think West Springfield was his brilliant sudden choice. I think he was scared out of his friggin' mind."

Petra said, "Congrats, Bill, you didn't say it was a woman for sure. Still, if any of them drive like this normally, it could help us. Why not follow each one; not for long. Wouldn't hurt, would it?"

Beauregard said, "No, it wouldn't hurt. Go ahead; just drive time in the afternoon when they would be the most stressed after a tough day for each of them. Try tomorrow."

Juan said, "He is not a poor driver. Look at how he exits on that long three sixty turn. He's a wheel man. He knows the area. He stays on the lanes of his direction early on; doesn't wait for lane marks to signal. He knows West Springfield and must go there often."

Ted insisted on a discussion on the possibility of two perps. He asked the Captain his thoughts on the issue. Beauregard said, "I don't rule out the thought of two perps, but we have no evidence. The timidity of this killer's driving after his attempt to kill does contrast differently from his aggressive driving to kill Micky. I find that most interesting."

Petra's ears perked up. "You mean one of my husband Jim's nuts, Captain; some sort of dissociative disorder?"

"Well, it's not the first time we have been faced with mental illness. I don't get into particular disease names and the mental health differentials among the various mental diseases for one reason: they change them constantly. If they know all about it, how come they reassign symptoms, names, and treatments almost yearly? I do know about some potential risks for mental disease or at least acting out: early childhood trauma, attachment problems, and persistent neglect of a child especially in the early years – all contribute to problems. Some children, subject to ongoing problems, can develop, what they call, an 'alter' or co-consciousness. It is not exactly like that famous movie "The Three Faces of Eve," but does involve the person having one or more identities. Sometimes they talk to each other. Sometimes they don't. Sometimes there is one identity in control. I think it's called the gatekeeper. All I know, when the condition becomes more pathological, we in the criminal justice system must understand all the identities. Psychiatrists used to call it borderline personality or multiple personality disorders or split personalities and now have a new name for it which I can't remember. Jim Locke would know all about it. For us, we need to sift through these persons of interest. There would have to be something there. We know the killer has a mission and in his or her mind it is a mission of mercy; but if there is a second person involved, whether real or one of these 'alters,' that person may be the more heartless one. Maybe the 'alter' thinks his or her role is to kill to make the other happy. Who is in control? To me, the 'alter' is now in control because the act of killing has become more important than the choice of victim or safety of the killer. This is all guesswork and not evidence. Again, we need evidence."

23

Frustration and Inquiry

Finding her choice of a Justice of the Peace in the COVID-19 pandemic was, at the very least, problematic. Martina tried several times to reach the dancer Lavender James, but her phone was no longer reachable. She drove by Lavender's home and from the changes outside the house, she knew the design perfectionist no longer lived there. Summoning her courage, she knocked on the door. A pleasant older lady answered and was happy to give Lavender's forwarding address. Lavender had moved to West Side of all places. Using her GPS, Martina found herself sitting outside a very large home embedded in a hillside of wild flowers, the likes of which Martina had only previously seen in garden design magazines. She thought, *dancing must really pay well. This house is worth a million at least.*

A truck backed down from the long driveway and a man got out. Martina recognized him as Lavender's boyfriend and in turn, he also knew her. She congratulated him on the beautiful house and he laughed, saying, "Yeah, that crazy murderer thought I was a loser. I kept my cards close to my vest. Even Lavender thought I was just an employee in the trucking firm; fooled her, I'm the owner. I didn't tell her until she agreed to marry me. She almost called the wedding off when I did inform her. She's the best. How'd you find us? We try to keep her location a secret because she is still dancing at the club until the end of the year. Doesn't bother me because with this virus shit, she won't be dancing anyway. How can I help you, Martina? It is Martina, isn't it?"

"Good memory, Jimmy. Ash and I want to marry and soon. I have a health issue and am having surgery. I'd like Lavender to do the service. I know many JP's aren't performing weddings now because of COVID, but as long as my parents and daughter come, we're fine with any precautions. I also need to know which towns have kept their clerks' offices open."

Jimmy's response given with a huge smile was, "Lavender will love this. You can marry here and bring the whole detective bureau. The living room is forty feet long. Lots of room to spread out. Lavender is not here right now but give me your number; she'll call first thing. Congratulations to you and Ash. You're the best."

Ten days later, West Side MCU detectives with their significant others including Jessica Taylor, Bill Border's lady, entered Lavender James' large living room and appeared overwhelmed by the décor. Martina and family arrived with Ash. The Justice of the Peace was, probably for the first time in her life, dressed conservatively for her role as Officiant. However, her long dress was colored lavender matching her name. Its style, although simple and to the floor did display her curves. Unfortunately, social distancing was not practiced well as Lavender hugged everyone explaining, "I've barely been out of this house for three weeks. I am not contaminated and kisses belong at a wedding. That is the reason weddings in general are not being conducted now."

The bride did outshine the Justice on this date if for no other reason than she glowed with happiness. She wore a long white sheath with long sleeves made of lines of lace spaced between silk shantung fabric.

The sheath flared somewhat at the lower hip line allowing a graceful look. She wore a large bunch of greens and Queen Ann's Lace flowers. Mona identified the flowers for all. Martina looked stunning and her normal hesitancy in her social actions was gone. Lavender read beautiful poetry and quotes, and the vows she chose for them were a match for the couple; to which the post ceremony conversation testified.

Lavender arranged a lunch at her home for the couple which was a godsend, since there were no venues open and Martina's condo was too limited for a crowd. Ash insisted on paying for the food and labor. He thought Lavender was too easily convinced to accept his payment. Later he would discover why. Lavender had purchased a beautiful vintage piano for them as a wedding present saying, "Normally, I wouldn't be able to have a find like this, but I took over selling the assets in an estate for a friend of mine who played in all the local bars but wrote music for some big names. He made a ton of money and found this piano twenty years ago. It's been checked out by a tuner and it has never had a hard life. I hope you like it. Jimmy will move it for you when you're ready."

Lunch was served and its delicacy fit the bride Martina; although Ash would have been pleased with a corned beef sandwich. Mona, Petra, Lilly, Charlotte, Jessica, and Mason's wife Jerusha agreed the wedding feast matched the designs in all the best magazines with a wedding cake filled with a truly tasty lemon filling and frosted with mousseline buttercream. There was no evidence of a pall over the celebration despite all knowing Martina was scheduled for additional heart surgery soon. All present welcomed this day with great joy. Added to the joy was Martina's bouquet giving a direct hit at Lilly. She did have to reach up for it, but the athletic detective was clearly unwilling to let it fly past her.

Having assigned the Edison Papers' info on Dr. Teague to Sergeant Mason Smith, Beauregard was not surprised to find Mason's list of Route 20 friends from Teague's contact interviews summarized on his desk. They apparently were talkers and the notes were long. Some of the men, and they were all men, had diverse interests including one who knew every detail of the history of changes to each section of the road in its laborious trip cross the U.S. Another collected a list of sites to see along the road. Mason had checked it against Wikipedia and some of its states' listing; this guy knew quadruple what was on the Wiki. Scanning the voluminous documentation, one page struck home for him. Jerold P. Klein was a former state cop from Ohio who had attended the aftermath of accidents and his retirement efforts were focused on accidents along Route 20. To read his reports, Route 20 was a dangerous road. Beauregard tapped his fingers on his right hand. Fortunately, he alone occupied the office. He rose and created the first excitement of the morning, entering the Pit saying, "Where in hell were those non-area accidents on Route 20?"

The three suspicious non-accidents listed in the Unit's records matched Jerold Klein's lists enabling Beauregard to feel some confidence in in Klein's work. Mason said, "You thinking what I'm thinking, Captain?"

"Well, Mason, if you're thinking we can look at every place the three have lived and worked and really know the extent of one-car accidents, and we may find something, yeah. How far did this guy go?"

Mason's smiled, saying, "Geez, he only went back as far as the fifties because most department records were not available before then. When it was too small of a town, the guy visited the town personally to get data. He's kind of like the 'Diner' people who spend their vacations visiting a section of the country and searching for and eating in diners that still exist. Jerold visits police departments and of course their sections of Route 20. Got to have a hobby, Captain; mine is eating my mother and wife's cooking."

The Captain shared the lists with the detectives. Mason had shared a map of towns and cities near each potential perp's home area, college areas, and work areas. There was quiet in the Pit for a short time before Lilly yelled, "Got a 'like' here; meaning I like a problem here. What was Shirley's dad's name?"

Juan scrambled looking for the name. It was in one of the interviews of Shirley's professors who mentioned Shirley's father was struck by lightning. Shirley said, "It was in all the papers at the time. He was managing a league baseball team. His name was Bruce Baker."

Lilly showed the detectives an accidental death of Bruce Baker, an automotive garage operator, most probably killed by a drunk driver, on Route 20 outside of Gary, Indiana. The date in 1973 coincided mathematically with Shirley's age as a young child. They all jumped on it. Mason summed up their statements. "If he is her dad, he did not get struck by lightning, which is why I never found a report of the death in the Gary, Indiana newspaper. We need the file. Why would she lie about how her father died is my question?"

Beauregard said, "It is what she told us in her interview. We do need the file, Mason, get on it. It's been a while; they probably haven't backed it up digitally. Have them copy the paper and send it. Tell them it's important for a homicide investigation. Shirley would be too young to have murdered him, but the mother may have been a bad actor. Shirley, by all accounts, was much loved by her maternal grandparents and her father. Find people who knew the family when Shirley was young. Any other deaths?"

Ted answered, "Well, yes and no. There was an accident near Lakeland, Ohio, near where Chad grew up. The guy's name is Bernie Halder. It happened about the same time Chad's father disappeared. The accident report showed serious discrepancies in determining how it happened. Someone hit his car, but he was not killed immediately. His death came from a blow to his head after the accident. No weapon was found. The police looked for the weapon in his home and at his work at an auto repair shop, which was owned by a Charles Roswell. The police theorized it was from a ball peen hammer used by mechanics. A worker at the garage said a hammer was missing. The police investigated the worker. Since the report showed the police looked for a Charles Roswell, owner of the auto body shop and he was missing, they found nothing and decided it was most likely a blow from the accident."

Beauregard insisted he wanted that file too and for Mason to re-interview the neighbor who had filed a complaint with the child safety organization in the state, saying, "I want a file picture from the police of Chad's father. He left his car at home. By itself, it would have raised suspicions. Why didn't the workers at the auto site ID the body as Charles Roswell if he owned the shop? The Registry will have a photo in their records. Let's hope the police pulled it out. Although I would think they'd have matched missing persons photos with accident victims. We need the accident report. Now we have two of the suspects who had fathers in the automotive business and both were killed in Route 20 accidents. Blows my mind but doesn't help us choose one of them."

I think HE has some of my mother's characteristics. Don't know how HE got them. HE may know some of my history but certainly not all my early history. I feed HE bits of information and never too much at one time. HE seems to have a wonderful memory and remembers verbatim every memory I share. Sometimes HE assumes and tries to match my emotions, to such a degree I am almost taken in. At those times, I distance myself and regroup. I have had to live with unbearable knowledge of evil. If I were not doing the good work I do today I would perhaps have difficulty living with my past. Lying to the police. Hell, I've been lying to every teacher, neighbor, friend, and police since I was a kid. The police really believe they can make a kid tell them the truth. Kids are smart and I was a smart kid; smart enough to know how to protect myself. If I had told the police the truth; Ha, just where would I have ended? The answer: probably in the morgue next to my dad. I sat at my father's knee and learned everything from him. I learned only good things. My head hurts thinking about the past. No more. I have enough of a problem with the present. Tomorrow is Tuesday. I will wake early. I've told HE nothing about my plans for the day. Normally HE would be badgering me to find some interesting place to visit. It's not normal when HE isn't pestering me for action of some kind. It's eerie to be in this empty place without HE badgering me. Two of us have always operated with precision. We have been the equivalent of two souls with an innate connection.

I worry about what I don't know about HE. Is HE more fragile than I thought? Perhaps HE would cave under pressure. HE has put us at risk. Doesn't HE know they will be watching today? I've explained over and over, I have respect for the collective skills of the police. I am not fooled by Captain Beauregard's doddering ways; he is a sly fox. I've met his like before and because I recognize inner slyness, I've always been able to defeat devious plans meant to get in my way; and most never know I was the architect for their failures. I mustn't let my ego get ahead of me now. HE will not be able to escape them twice if he goes after Micky; it's a fool's journey. If I were Beauregard, what would I do? Who is his suspect or suspects?

———

Beauregard authorized some detectives to follow each of the potential perps on Tuesday, while two others were tracking Micky Leahy during his Route 20 nightly walk. The medical groups' schedules showed the usual day off type activities; shopping, gym, and several trips back to their homes. Dr. Teague went to dinner alone at a busy restaurant on Boston Road for take-out. The restaurant was near the Wilbraham line. But in Springfield, and diners could eat in their cars. Petra and Mason were on his watch and quickly realized he had parked between two buildings in this strip of businesses and could easily walk out of the area unseen. He was dressed in sweats and both detectives excitedly agreed he could be the killer.

Meanwhile, Juan and Ted followed Shirley who also was dining with takeout at the Route 20 Bar and Grill. She also was dressed in designer sweats. They thought she looked too handsome to be the killer, but did notice she left her vehicle near the back entry of the restaurant. It was difficult to see her and stay in the parking lot near other vehicles. It forced Juan to walk circling the restaurant to get a visual of the back.

Bill and Bobby followed Chad who hit two closed bars before settling on a quick takeout dinner at Crazy Jake's in Wilbraham. Meanwhile, the Captain and Lilly were parked in a protected grotto near the site of what Beauregard had surmised would be the best section to hit a person allowing a quick escape. A Wilbraham detective was parked inconspicuously on a side road to the turnpike connection. Another one was a floater ready to go to whatever site his presence was needed. Two other undercover Wilbraham detectives were spread along Route 20. For sure Wilbraham police would be joining West Side in the arrest, if there were an arrest. Bill Border called the Captain and said, "I think it's strange, Captain. All three are having takeout dinner alone in their cars at restaurants on Boston Road. It is just too coincidental. Maybe they are all working together; hell, they're all dressed almost alike."

And they waited, and they waited, and they waited. Micky Leahy finished his walk. Between eight and nine o'clock, all three potential suspects left for home alone. Beauregard called them off for the night.

***

HE kept to the plan. I hold my breath sitting outside this stupid restaurant trying to keep my mind at rest. Recently, HE has made me on edge even when we are having a normal discussion on tactics. I can feel HE's not listening to me; I just feel it. I don't like not being in control. HE is not the planner. HE must understand I am the planner. HE is the executor. I don't like that I've used that word. We are not executing; we are assisting in the crossover to the light for the alone and suffering. HE is making me feel our mission is one-sided, but tonight HE listened. Tonight, we are in sync.

But – I am again in stress; what about next Tuesday? It would be just like HE to think a missed week allows business as usual. I have such a headache.

***

Mona Beauregard listened as Rudy went over the details of his evening; foiled by the killer was how he explained it. As the kids would say, Rudy was on a roll and to her it was a depressing roll downhill. She tried to reassure him, saying, "Rudy, I trust your gut. Why are you second guessing yourself? You have every reason to believe one of these medical people is guilty and don't tell me you've told me nothing about it. I've heard you on your cell. I see and hear some of your discussions with your detectives. Don't shut me out. Tell me about their personalities. Maybe I can help you."

A grumbling but grateful Rudy developed his logic for his suspicions. When Mona asked about the other detectives and what their instincts were, he gave her detailed descriptions on each of their thoughts and choice. Mona immediately pointed out what he already knew, saying, "Rudy, the killer sounds OCD and obsessed to be able to perfectly enact seventeen murders without forensic details involving stealing cars. I, personally, doubt I could do any event consistently seventeen times without some deviation. That alone suggests an intelligent person. His getting away from your detectives on this Micky Leary attempt speaks to an ability to make instantaneous changes when necessary. I find that surprising and not with my idea of an OCD person but does fit with experience as a nurse or doctor trained in emergency medical care. The whole extra interest in the elderly patients is truly unusual. The ability to steal cars so easily speaks to me of a background by hobby or training in cars. Normally, I'd infer that background to be found in men and not in a woman, but today, I could not rule a woman out. Other than hoping the killer will act out again on a Tuesday and your detectives will be able to intervene, your best hope is a diligent scrutiny of their backgrounds. I know you must have done it already, but I'd go back again. Just sayin', Rudy, just sayin.'"

"Well thanks, Mona, for the summary. I agree, but I can't put Micky at risk again. He is going to walk and I can't guarantee his life. I'm telling you, I feel the urgency this killer feels, Mona; I feel it. Do you think I'm going nuts?"

"Rudy, could you use a dummy walking on Boston Road; not actually one who runs? I mean how far away is the driver when he first sees Micky? It is fifty or a hundred feet? Could a dummy be planted at a spot with something interesting to look at that would make him stop moving for a minute or so? When I walk, I often stop to look at a pretty garden or a hawk overhead."

Rudy sat erect and with the broadest of smiles said, "You are one brilliant wife, Mona. Why didn't any of us think of that. I know just the spot on the road where it would work. And we will do more background checks. Thank you."

Mona laughed. "I want dinner out this weekend. Okay? And don't rule out a woman for your killer yet. Norbie Cull's daughter Sidney is taking a course in car mechanics at a community college. She is frustrated because it's been called off because of the virus and there's no assurance it will run again. Girls know about cars and everything, Rudy. Just because you have three sons and a brother is not an excuse for ignoring women's full reach into all fields of inquiry. Get your nose out of the police station and take a broader look on life. I won't be married to an old geezer."

The Pit detectives were working the phones. Ted had developed and posted a matrix of each potential suspect's information and contact numbers. The matrix was coded with references to interviews with teachers, neighbors, social workers, suspects' past colleagues, and police. There were four detectives on the phone while Ted and Mason handled ordinary police calls, and Petra as conference colleague documenting and assigning newly discovered material to the matrices.

Beauregard, meanwhile, was in his office designing a plan for location of a dummy on Boston Road. He remembered, the department has three life-sized dummies previously used in a drug raid. I'll check them out for size to match Micky Leary's body measurements. Micky is well-built and of average height. He wore sweat pants and a hooded windbreaker on the almost accident night We can duplicate that. I drove to the area most interesting for a secluded accident before coming to the station this morning. It's perfect except but for a large street light not far away. I don't think we can get it turned off for three hours from seven to ten that night. I'll call the Wilbraham Chief and see if he has some pull. I don't; not for a town I have no juice in.

The Captain set his accident plan in motion with the assistance of Ash and the Wilbraham police chief. His heading the traffic department gave Beauregard some skilled assistance from the unit's personnel and a good connection to the Wilbraham police department's traffic division.

Finished with his planning and looking more settled, Lilly said, "Ready for what we've learned, Captain? I can tell you've finished whatever you were doing. You look smug."

He growled, "Smug? I am never smug. I am never satisfied, but I do like short actions I am able to plan or complete. I guess you're right, Sergeant, I do feel better. Now, what's up?"

And the information, limited somewhat, was shared. Nothing in Chad's life other than his non-truthful tale of his father's death was suspicious. Maybe he didn't know what happened to his dad. His father had not left the family, but Chad perhaps did not know it. He was too young when his dad left; so, it was not a lie. As to his father's death, it had now been characterized as a homicide by the area police. Mason had shared their understanding that Charles Roswell was really Bernie

Halder. DNA was being matched, but the dead man Bernie Halder's bank account data showed a deposit on its opening from Charles Roswell's account. There was every reason to believe he was running away, but not too far away. Additional support for their theory came from the neighbor who told the police, "We tried to tell you then, Charles would never leave that little boy. He and the boy rode their bikes one day around the time he disappeared and the boy came back alone with his mother. We didn't know exactly when Charles disappeared; it may have been that day."

The police did not know whether Chad was told to ride his bike home alone by someone who met them; it was now up for discussion by the detectives. Their conversation ran the gambit, including maybe the mother met the husband after he put Chad in his new car, told Chad to drive home on his bike, and then killed the husband. Since their discussion was not based on evidence, they got tired of it.

Shirley's history had some interest. A contact with Joan, Shirley's former apartment roomie in their nursing program, gave some insights. Joan told Juan that Shirley's mother had been questioned in her husband's death. Shirley thought she remembered walking with her father toward the playing fields and stopping at the variety store at the corner when her mother showed up in the car and told her dad and her to get in because there was a lightning storm. She explained her mother drove her home and then left with her dad to help him get the kids off the field. Shirley was little, but remembered her father was reported dead from a lightning strike. She said she was lost after his death, because she had spent most of her time with her dad at the auto shop or at the playing fields and that her mother was not motherly.

Dr. Jesse's history stayed the same, although Ted thought his negative foster home history was still pertinent. In conclusion, Bobby stated what they were all thinking, "Pick one and go after the one. I bet on Chad."

Petra and Lilly both said, "We bet on Shirley."

Beauregard responded, "Not how it works, Detectives, and you know it. You think these two are working together? My gut says it's one or the other. There are childhood issues for all three to be potentially acting out. Sounds to me Chad and Shirley are either ignorant of the facts of their dads' deaths or in denial. Even if we knew the facts about the dads' deaths, they wouldn't explain why they wanted old men to die. Chad has history with old people and probably saw a few die on his watch. Makes him a bit more interesting. Shirley had a bad relationship with her mom and brother. All three were very close to their grandfathers. It's that relationship I am interested in. How did the grandpas die and were they there for the deaths? Meanwhile, we follow both of them on this coming Tuesday night. I want Petra and Lilly on Shirley and if she goes to a restaurant, one of you go and watch the process. Dress unlike a cop. The other stays in the car. Bobby and Billy go after Chad and do the same. Ted and Mason, go after Teague. I'll be alone with a car at the potential site. I hope he or she bites."

———

Plan in place found Petra and Lilly following Shirley as she made stops to drop off laundry after leaving her gym. She appeared to be going to the same restaurant on Boston Road as she had two weeks before. Petra said, "I tell you, Lilly, there is something about this woman. I was never a good little girl and maybe that's my bias, but she is too good to be true and so structured in her behaviors. It is her structure thinking, I'm targeting. This kind of thinking is perfect for planning seventeen murders."

Lilly said, "Yeah, but it takes two brains to carry this out. Does she have the skills to steal cars, to drive wildly when needed, and to change planning at the last minute? Her driving is like an old lady's. Not once has she gone over the speed limit."

Lilly had forgotten the Captain was listening in. He replied, "What do we know about smart drug runners, Lilly. No matter their risk-taking inclinations, when they are on the roll, they always drive within the speed limit."

Meanwhile, a similar conversation about Chad occurred. The problem was different. Chad was not a consistent driver tonight. He again stopped at two closed bars and the owners came out with a forbidden by the Governor takeout drink and stayed a short while. His driving was reminiscent of Bill's teenage years. Bill said, "He passes on the inside lane when there is a car in the passing lane going too slowly. He speeds and slows down. He is a good driver, but not if you measure him in regards to driving rules. Would you stop at two bars if you were about to commit murder?"

Bobby had an answer. "I would. I'd have to be drunk to kill someone. Maybe he has some guilt issues about his mercy killing. Maybe it's more of a need than a want."

Following Teague, Mason Smith told Ted, "Teague's not the killer. We're not following the right car tonight."

Ted said, "How can you tell, Mason? It's not I don't believe you. You have instincts, but I can't tell that yet. His driving is normal. He's on his off-day errands. There is nothing unusual about his behavior."

"Yeah, there is, Ted. All he does is look in the mirror at his hair and keeps fluffing it. He started it after leaving his gym. The Captain may call him a narcissist, but I see just plain old vanity. If you were going to kill someone, your hair doesn't matter. He'll never put the hood up on his jacket; it would muss his hair. It's the little things, Ted, always the little things."

"Wish we could introduce the little things as evidence to the District Attorney, Mason, but we can't."

24

Error

Beauregard waited in his secluded spot, thinking, all our money's on these three. I've ruled out one of them already based on my gut feelings. I could be completely wrong. What if it's not one of these three, then it's a good thing I've used a dummy. And if nothing happens tonight, the Wilbraham Chief won't support another night.

Petra texted, "I'm going in the restaurant. Shirley's dressed as before. Are they all in the same type of uniform; all with hooded name brand sweats? That's suspicious."

Mason called, "Captain, Teague's a bust. He's heading for home without dinner and not via Boston Road."

Beauregard told them to follow him home and if by eight-thirty he had not left his home, they were to then go to an area by the entrance to the Mass Pike. And they were to wait.

Lilly called and said, "Captain, Shirley drove around the back of the restaurant to park because there was already a car parked in the spot she used last week. Petra just came out from behind the restaurant. She nor I saw Shirley leave, but her car is still there. The lot is loaded with cars and I think she may have gone further over and avoided us. Here is Petra."

"Captain, she must have scooted right around the next building before I got around to have a view of the back door. I did see an olive colored Jeep SUV leaving the lot as I tried to see where she went. Didn't get the plates. She's got to be in it. No person or car has moved out of here but that one. And, Captain, it must mean she's going to come back here and dump the Jeep on the other side of the lot. Risky, very risky!"

Beauregard said, "Follow the Jeep. You're way behind but you know where she's going. Don't get to close to her. Her behavior is not normal and if she's going to dump the Jeep back there, it's not risky, it's stupid. Maybe she's working with Chad."

Beauregard called Mason and told him to head over to the restaurant and sit by Shirley's car near the restaurant explaining his theory. "She may be dumping the stolen car there and getting into her parked car. In case we miss her, get her then and arrest her on attempted murder of Micky Leary."

"Captain, it's only attempted murder of a dummy; even though she's tried twice. I guess you're right."

"Mason, have Bill and Bobby call Micky Leary. In fact, have them go over there. I don't want our potential killers to see him for the next forty-eight hours. I want no one to see him. I want Shirley to think she's maimed him and if we were to have the dummy die, we'll arrest her for murder. Got that!"

A second later, Bill reported, "Chad has gotten a second cocktail from the last bar. Bobby went to check. He texted me. Chad is drinking and the owner or manager is enjoying one with him. So much with closing the bars for alcohol. They must be buddies and I can tell you he's in no condition to murder anyone successfully. Should Bobby buddy up to him?"

Beauregard agreed and told him to be careful. And he waited for the green Jeep, thinking, it can't be this easy. It can't be Miss Molly Goodie

Two Shoes or whatever that name is. If Chad is drunk and Jesse's at home, it's Shirley. Given that, then Shirley is more complex than a kindhearted lady with a soft spot for old men. Did we see anything in her background for church? I saw nothing about mercy killing. Lots of kids lose a loving father and don't kill old men. Her father didn't suffer. Whether her mother killed him or not, he died instantly. Must be the grandfather figure who took over the dad's job of loving the kid, but got sick. Could his suffering make her want to do this? Running over old men seems a heartless way to kill. Nurses normally smother with pillows or inject with something. Although when you think about it, smothering a helpless person with a pillow is just as heartless. Her father did auto repairs; was she old enough to learn from him about cars? She is supposed to be very bright; but he died close to thirty years ago. No. She may have decided to love what he loved and he loved cars. Did we check to see if she took an auto course for fun or as an avocation? No, we missed again! And there's more we miss every day. She could do an auto-course over the internet. Although Maurice did not find that on her recent internet activity. This generation learns everything on the net. My son Luke doesn't read directions to put an appliance in; he uses the net. I'm old. I like paper.

Beauregard saw a car coming on the inside lane. Most cars on this street were in the travel lane and there was not a right hand turn for at least three hundred yards. When the car speeded up just as it passed him, he knew it was the killer. The driver headed for the dummy who had been put on stable digitalized rollers and was being moved by a Wilbraham police officer stationed in the bushes. From where Beauregard was behind the Jeep, the dummy walking looked real. The killer veered over on the curb hitting the dummy and tossing its body over into the bushes against a high wall. Beauregard thought, *the Jeep's taking off like a bat out of hell, and Shirley Baker is not obeying the speed limit. She is headed for the restaurant and she doesn't know I am after her.*

He paced his car, but kept her in his sights. She had slowed down, not to the normal speed limit, but not much over it. It was two miles to the restaurant. His heart was beating fast. A car passed him on the inside and pulled out in front of his. He could no longer see the Jeep, but thought he knew her destination. The car in front took a right hand turn and the Jeep was nowhere to be found. He looked back and saw a hidden left turn. She could have taken it. There was no traffic coming that way. He thought, *it's what happens when you think you know where you're going when you really don't know. Cripes, I just made a rookie move.*

Beauregard made a U-turn and went down the hidden street. He realized there was a turn halfway up. Taking it, he found the Jeep. There was a scarce wooded area and it was next to the restaurant parking lot. He did not wait, but drove through an opening of brush through the wood to find Mason arresting a defiant Shirley Baker and reading her rights. Several police cars joined them having been radioed in. They had their killer, but they only had circumstantial evidence; although there was substantial circumstantial evidence. Petra spoke to Beauregard, saying, "We need her confession. There are seventeen murders. I think Lilly and I should do it. She trusts women and not men."

The Captain responded with agreement and said, "Look for that watch. I hope the hell she was consistent and is wearing that watch."

———

The station house had a buzz despite the fact the time registered at eleven p.m. The Assistant District Attorney on this case would arrive soon after he finished a speaking engagement. Shirley Baker was booked.

Despite Beauregard's insistence for 'silencio' the word was already out. Shirley was reread her rights and asked if she wanted her lawyer. A composed Shirley Baker said, "Why would I need an attorney? I've done nothing wrong."

Juan had her sign her attorney refusal and acknowledgement she had been read her rights. Petra and Lilly entered the interview room and sat with the prisoner whose demeanor expressed a blend of earnestness and confusion. Petra asked Shirley, "Do you know why you are here, Shirley?"

"No, I was arrested as I entered my car. I don't remember why I was arrested. I had a nice takeout from the restaurant and after dumping my food debris and then leaving, that officer arrested me for attempted something. I didn't get it all. I paid my restaurant bill. I'm certain I have a receipt here."

Petra heard a buzz in her ear from the Captain who told her to offer the prisoner coffee or tea and come out to get it leaving Lilly to do small talk. She did as requested, but was upset when she spoke with the Captain who was sitting in the room behind the one-way glass. "What are you doing to me, Captain. I was just starting and you saw the bullshit story she was giving me. Why did you stop me?"

"Petra, did you look at her demeanor when she spoke? Her voice was a sing-song presentation and her eyes were flat."

"Yeah, Captain, because she was lying through her teeth."

Beauregard said, "Think about it. Shirley is intelligent. She doesn't know she did not hit a person but a dummy. She's not arguing that. She's saying she was nowhere but in the restaurant dining. Ask her about her sweats and does she always wear them. Ask her what she had for takeout; she can't answer that because she didn't get takeout. Ask her about the time stamped on her restaurant slip; she doesn't have one. Ask her about her watch which is a match for our video, but it is not an exclusive item. Describe a camera on Boston Road with video of her driving a Jeep SUV. Ask her what she thought all the police cars were doing at her arrest site. Work the evidence. Booking found brambles on her sweat pants. Tell her they match the woods between the adjacent street to the restaurant parking lot. Create confusion and then get more assertive. Watch her demeanor as she answers. There is something off with her in addition to her being a serial murderer."

Assistant District Attorney Thaddeus Miller arrived. Informed about the circumstances, he agreed with Beauregard's theory for the interview, but asked him, "You are thinking a mental health issue, Captain?"

Beauregard responded, "No, not in the traditional sense, Thad, but maybe two personalities in one person. Her complete denial of wrong when I know she is observant and bright tells me she's either a great actor or she has an internal accomplice who has not shared with her what she's done. Get what we can and then she can get analyzed. I'll call Jim Locke. He'll know how and who to handle a mental health exam. Right now, we have evidence of her hitting the dummy and wearing a similar watch as in the videos of the other murders and nothing else. We need more. Petra or Lilly, however they want to conduct this interview must go through all the deaths and I think they should talk about the great suffering each elderly man killed had to endure. For sure, Shirley is the personality behind the mercy and we must shock her into the realization she has done great harm."

Petra nodded her agreement, saying, "Our plan was for Lilly to go through each murder. That won't change. She is a stickler for details and can interview for hours when she's after the carrot at the end of the stick. I'll do the first part."

Beauregard, ADA Miller, and Detective Torrington watched the interview. The subject's demeanor did not change despite Detective Aylewood-Locke's consistent logic in presenting facts such as, "Shirley, why did you drive a Jeep SUV, park next to the back entrance of the restaurant, and drive over to Boston Road to Three Rivers in a stolen green Jeep, make a U-turn on the road to return to the restaurant, park the Jeep on the adjacent street, run through the woods, and approach your own auto?"

"Detective, I did not. I would not. You have the wrong person."

This version of a one-way conversation of one person presenting facts and the other party denying them with absolute innocence continued. She said she had a nice dinner but could not remember what she ate. She searched for the takeout receipt, but could not find it. She said she thought she may have thrown it away.

Detective Tagliano detailed all seventeen murders. Shirley cried a little and shook her head in a no response. Lilly, disgusted, started voicing, when reaching the facts of the eighth murder, with a deprecating moral tone, "Oh come on, Shirley, how stupid do you think we are? We know it was you, thinking you are God limiting the lives of all these men. Elderly men who loved their lives. Elderly men who had maybe ten or fifteen more years to live. Do you really think you are God? There is no mercy in killing an old man with a three-thousand-pound automobile. Just tell me why you think your actions are merciful. You are a vicious and miserable human being. You are a criminal. If not, why would you hide your deeds? Why on earth would a woman whose everyday life is conducted with kindness and grace hide her lust for killing old men under the guise of mercy? What happened to you? Was your old grandfather abusive? You admit your mother and brother were terrible. If you didn't kill these men, then why did we catch you at it? Why aren't you killing women and young men?"

Shirley said, "It's not me. I could never kill. Do you understand. I want these men to not suffer. Don't you get it. Their dying avoids all their loneliness and suffering, but I can't kill. I just can't. I saw my grandfather alone and dying. My grandmother was sick and my mother treated her horribly. They both protected me from my mother. My grandfather tried to protect me too like Grandmother and Father did, but he was too weak. He told me, 'When a man is old and can't take care of his loved ones, the pain is too much to bear.' He asked me to help him leave. I tried to smother him but I was too small. Grandmother stopped me and told me Grandpa must wait it out. Why wait it out if you're ready? At least Grandpa had Grandma and me."

Beauregard and Miller held their breaths. Miller whispered to Beauregard, "You know, Captain, the murderer is them both, don't you? You knew before they started this interview."

The Captain nodded and shrugged his shoulders, saying, "Don't say another word. I know nothing. You know nothing. My two detectives are getting the answer now."

Detective Aylewood-Locke, playing good cop to Tagliano's bad cop, said, "You know who did the killings. Tell me about the killer. Just when did the killer come into your life and why did you let the relationship happen?"

Shirley's innocent blue eyes, previously filled with tears, changed. She said, "HE just appeared when my brother and mother were screaming at me. I was all alone; my grandparents had just passed. HE saved me. HE took over and does now when I am stressed."

"Who is HE, Shirley? Why would you, such a savvy and accomplished woman, let a man take over? And this Savior, where is he now, Shirley?"

In a savage but low voice, unlike Shirley's, the detectives heard this: "Savvy, she's stupid. All she can do is plan and be a nurse. Even then, if a patient is about to die on her watch, I have to take over. She could never drive like me. But, Detectives, it is her plan. I'm not covering for her. She's on her own. You saw her. She blew it. Foolish, fearful, stupid woman. She should have known the police would be there. We could have taken an old man in the hospital, but she says (mimicking a high-pitched Shirley voice) 'It's too much of a risk.' Does she think I want to be buried in her life, forever? She's not alive. Shirley, no risk Shirley, does not know how to live. She's too stupid to even realize I've been taking over. She tries to keep me in the closet and just let me out to talk with when she's ready, but I am now too powerful for her. Shirley should not exist. She is so weak."

Petra asked, "Are you HE?"

"She calls me HE; just another way to avoid parts of herself. Approval is important to our little Shirley."

"If you are not Shirley, what is your name other than HE and are you a man or a woman?"

"You think I'm going to discuss gender roles with you, Detective? I am what Shirley thinks I should be, but Shirley is interfering with who I am. I guess I am about to be Shirley."

"Then, if you are not Shirley, whatever your name may be, did you kill seventeen elderly men by running over them with stolen cars?"

HE answered, "I'm going to let Shirley take over this conversation and confuse and deny everything. Screw you, Detective, I will love where we're going. I will so enjoy coming out and taking good care of our Shirley in a setting where I can control. Little Shirley is in for an interesting change in circumstances. She won't control, but I will."

The detectives saw a visible change in posture and attitude in Shirley's face. She said, "What did HE say? I know HE. He told you stuff. I can always feel when HE has been here."

"What do you think HE said, Shirley? Are you afraid of what HE may have said?"

The next hour of the interviewing process was not productive. Shirley cried over and over and said she was not responsible for HE. HE was always saying outrageous things and doing terrible things. She said HE killed her brother and mother and she was glad. She shared that she could never do such terrible things; after all, she only believed in helping the good cross the chasm early. The evil should stay here and suffer. Shirley continued in the guise of the best behavior of a professional lady. She stopped crying and asked when she could go home, saying, "I am really tired and my shift tomorrow is longer than usual." When she was told she was not going to be allowed to leave, that she was under arrest, Shirley explained, "You must get me my toiletries and a change of clothes. I will need my medications too."

Lilly pushed. "Shirley, tell me what medications are you taking? I'll get our pharmacy to get them for you."

The answer she gave with a relieved sigh was, "I take Abilify sometimes and prochlorperazine. If I take Abilify regularly, I don't feel safe and need to speak to HE, but can't. When I stop taking Abilify, I can talk to HE."

Shirley stopped speaking other than to now ask for an attorney.

ADA Miller rubbed his forehead with both hands while shaking his head. "Arraign her, Rudy, and we'll order a mental health exam. This is not good. She's admitted to trying to kill her grandfather, but she didn't meet HE until after her grandmother died. These kinds of cases never are easy. Just who is killing these men – Shirley, or her alter, HE? Doesn't matter to you or me. We want her off the streets, but I don't know if the concept of Shirley differentiated from her alter HE is innocent at all. She physically killed these men. We don't actually have a really good confession from HE. She says only the elderly good men should die. Shirley says HE killed her brother and mother. A good defense attorney in court will create havoc with this one."

The Captain and his detectives were putting the case to bed. The paperwork for the ADA included the results of further information garnered by Mason Smith, who said, "The deaths of the mother and brother were surprising to their doctors. Both had seemed to be doing well on their chemotherapy. The brother's future would not have been for very long, but the doctor had no idea why the mother did not fare better. Neither death was investigated. There were two doctors involved; one signing each death certificate. The police in Gary are re-opening the cases based on her statement.

"Shirley's drugs led to a psychiatrist in New Hampshire, Dr. Norman, who has been treating Shirley for DID, Dissociative Identity Disorder and depression for several years. He did not know she was a nurse practitioner. She told him her illness allowed her to work only occasionally in retail. She was always reasonably controlled when he saw her which was monthly. He was not convinced at the time if she truly suffered from DID or that she was unable to handle the responsibilities of an adult. She was thoughtful but distant in her stories, but he never heard any conflicting statements. A few times she appeared untoward (his word) and left before her time was up. She'd call later and say she was hungry and her IBS was acting up. If she did have DID and knew about it or was overwhelmed by its symptoms, he could not relate an alter coming out, but could confirm the typical scenario of a repressed woman who was resistant to change or responsibility or a relationship with a man. He thought her a handsome woman, but so held back, she was not interesting. He thought she tried to be uninteresting; that her demeanor was deliberate. She did speak openly about a wonderful relationship with her father, grandfather, and grandmother in that order. She once inferred her mother caused the father's death.

Mason added, "What about chasing prescriptions that use her name, Captain? It would help to define the start of her seeking help. And, her not using her insurance to pay her therapy bills does show her trying to cover up her condition; that she knew it was a problem."

The Captain said, "ADA Miller will make the decision; we'll help if asked. What bothers me is she fooled two men into fancying her, but she doesn't want a relationship. The shrinks in this case will have a field day. There is still some required work left for the DA. Once her arrest is public, the public will contact us. It bothers me mostly that Shirley can pack away any guilt in a little suitcase and say she could not do what we know she did. I want alibis for Chad and Jesse for all seventeen murders. I want to search Shirley's home. It would be wonderful if she is a hoarder and saved some of the designer sweat suits. We should have been more certain she was the perp. The sweat suits were perfect and all different. Guys are too cheap to buy seventeen sweat suits and throw them away. They hoard a few and reuse them."

Bill answered, "Not Jesse, Captain, he has to look perfect. Probably would discard only those that had acquired a pulled thread."

Beauregard asked about the Uber and Taxi searches for someone whose destination was the parking lots where the cars were stolen. There was no record. He hit his head with his hand and said, "Check all the van drivers' schedules for taking any patient or caretaker to a hospital parking lot from the Ware hospital."

Mason responded, "On it, Captain. Why did I not think of it when the Uber use came back negatively?"

Bobby said, "Captain, I never saw the likes of this when I was in Traffic. This case and these murders have to be the most remarkable traffic related cases ever. The horror of this gal fooling us all is galling. Who, just who, would expect such perverted actions from this lady. My mother, if I brought her home, would love her. How do we know about people, Captain; just how can we know?"

The Captain answered, "We can't. We must be vigilant, but sociopaths can always fool us; at least for a while."

Bobby replied, "You can bet Dr. Teague and Chad Roswell will be vigilant now!

Acknowledgments

To my husband Joe for his unquestionable loyalty, kindness, and love.

To my children: The lights of my life.

To my grandchildren: Continue to Dream, Endure, and Prevail!

I am grateful for all technical assistance I received from my good friends:

Police Matters:

Retired Springfield, Massachusetts Chief of Police Paula Meara

Massachusetts State Police Officer John Ferrera

Retired Springfield Police Officer Michael Carney

Attorneys:

Charles E. Dolan

Joseph A. Pellegrino, Sr. (ret. Justice, Massachusetts Trial Courts)

Raipher D. Pellegrino

And to my editors: I thank you for your editing, support, and counsel.

To all above: All errors on implementation are solely mine.

Care to Review My Book?
(or "Honest Reviews Don't Kill")

Now that you've read the story to the end, I'd love to know what you think of it – and read your honest review about the book on Amazon, Goodreads or other major online book retailers where it is featured.

https://kbpellegrino.com/review-killing-the-venerable

Review some of my other books:

https://kbpellegrino.com/review-a-predatory-cabal

https://kbpellegrino.com/review-mary-lou

https://kbpellegrino.com/review-him-me-paulie

Thank you for your interest in my books!

Kathleen

More Books by K.B. Pellegrino

The Captain Beauregard Mystery Series

Evil Exists in West Side Trilogy:

–Sunnyside Road: Paradise Dissembling (Liferich Publishing) 2018

–Mary Lou: Oh! What Did She Do? (Liferich Publishing) 2018

–Brothers of Another Mother: All for One! Always? (Liferich Publishing) 2019

–Him, Me and Paulie: Drugs, Murder and Undercover (Livres-Ici Publishing) 2019

–A Predatory Cabal: Worm in the Apple (Livres-Ici Publishing) 2020

Coming Soon!

–Killing the Venerable: It's Their Time!   Winter 2020/2021

You can find K. B. Pellegrino's books on all major online Book Stores, such as Amazon, Barnes & Noble, kobo, and iBooks.

Bonuses, Giveaways, and Freebies

Free Chapters

"Sunnyside Road: Paradise Dissembling"

Download a free chapter of the first book in the Evil Exists in West Side Trilogy "Sunnyside Road: Paradise Dissembling" at www.kbpellegrino.com/sunnyside-road/FreeChapter

"Him, Me, and Paulie: Drugs, Murder and Undercover"

Download a free chapter of the Captain Beauregard Series book #4 "Him, Me, and Paulie: Drugs, Murder and Undercover" at www.kbpellegrino.com/him-me-paulie/FreeChapter

Join My Private Email List

To received updates about books, new releases, upcoming events, or to simply keep in touch with me join my private email list. We do not release your information to any other vendors.

www.kbpellegrino.com/join-list

To access more freebies, visit: www.kbpellegrino.com/bonus

Follow K. B. Pellegrino

On her website at www.kbpellegrino.com

On Facebook: https://www.facebook.com/kbpellegrino

On Instagram: https://www.instagram.com/kbpellegrino_author/

On Twitter: https://twitter.com/kbpellegrino

www.ingramcontent.com/pod-product-compliance
Lightning Source LLC
Chambersburg PA
CBHW070757190726
48292CB00002B/571